THE DRAGONSLAYER

BY JEFF SMITH

WITH COLOR BY STEVE HAMAKER

An Imprint of

SCHOLASTIC

New York   Toronto   London   Auckland   Sydney   Mexico City   New Delhi   Hong Kong   Buenos Aires

All rights reserved. Published by Graphix, an imprint of Scholastic Inc., *Publishers since 1920*. SCHOLASTIC, GRAPHIX, and associated logos are trademarks and/or registered trademarks of Scholastic Inc.

Library of Congress Catalog Card Number 95068403.
ISBN 0-439-70626-2 (hardcover) — ISBN 0-439-70637-8 (paperback)

ACKNOWLEDGMENTS
Harvestar Family Crest designed by Charles Vess
Map of *The Valley* by Mark Crilley
Color by Steve Hamaker

10 9 8 7 6 5 4 3 2 1   06 07 08 09
First Scholastic edition, August 2006
Book design by David Saylor
Printed in Singapore 46

This book is for Irene Kilty

for inspiring her grandson's imagination

CONTENTS

PROLOGUE

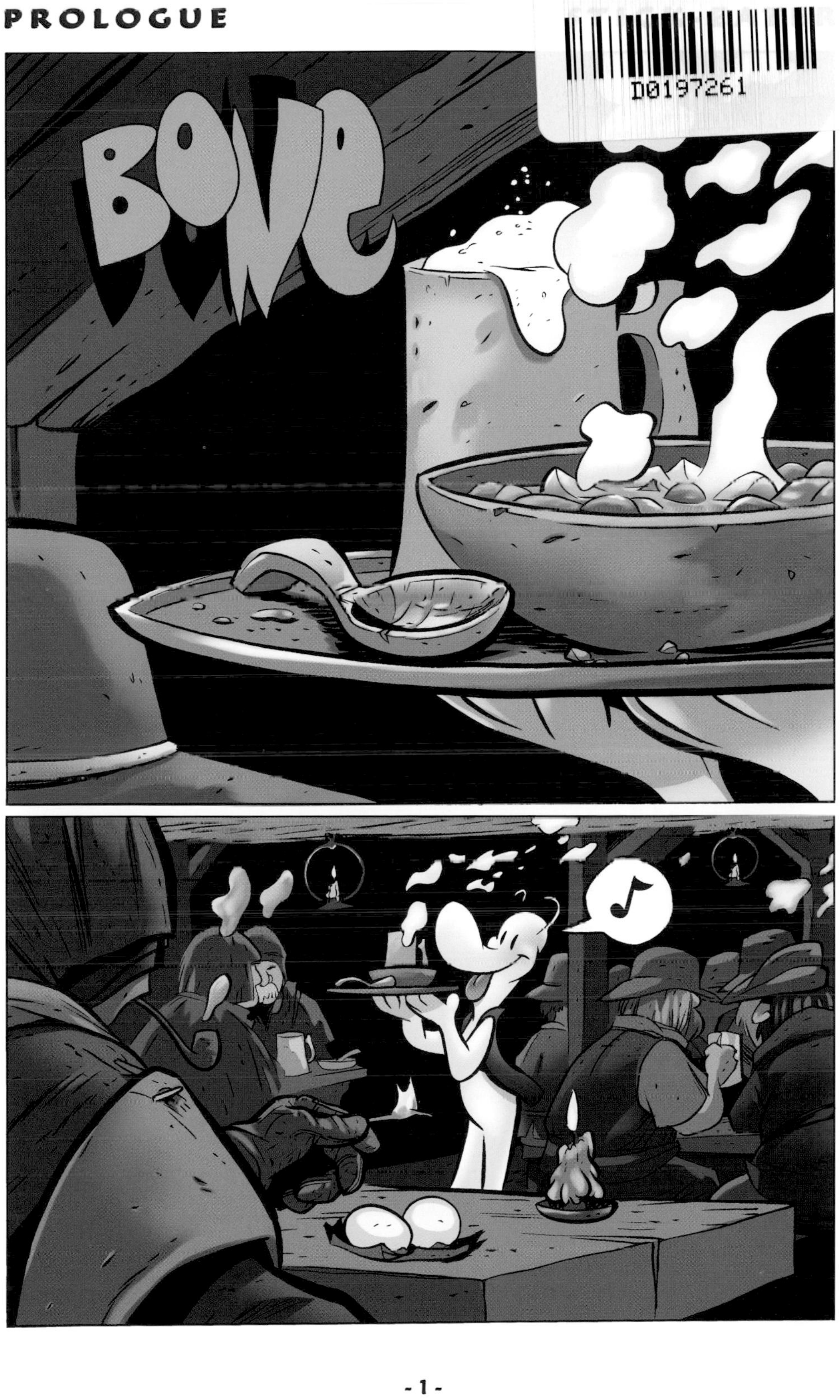
BONE

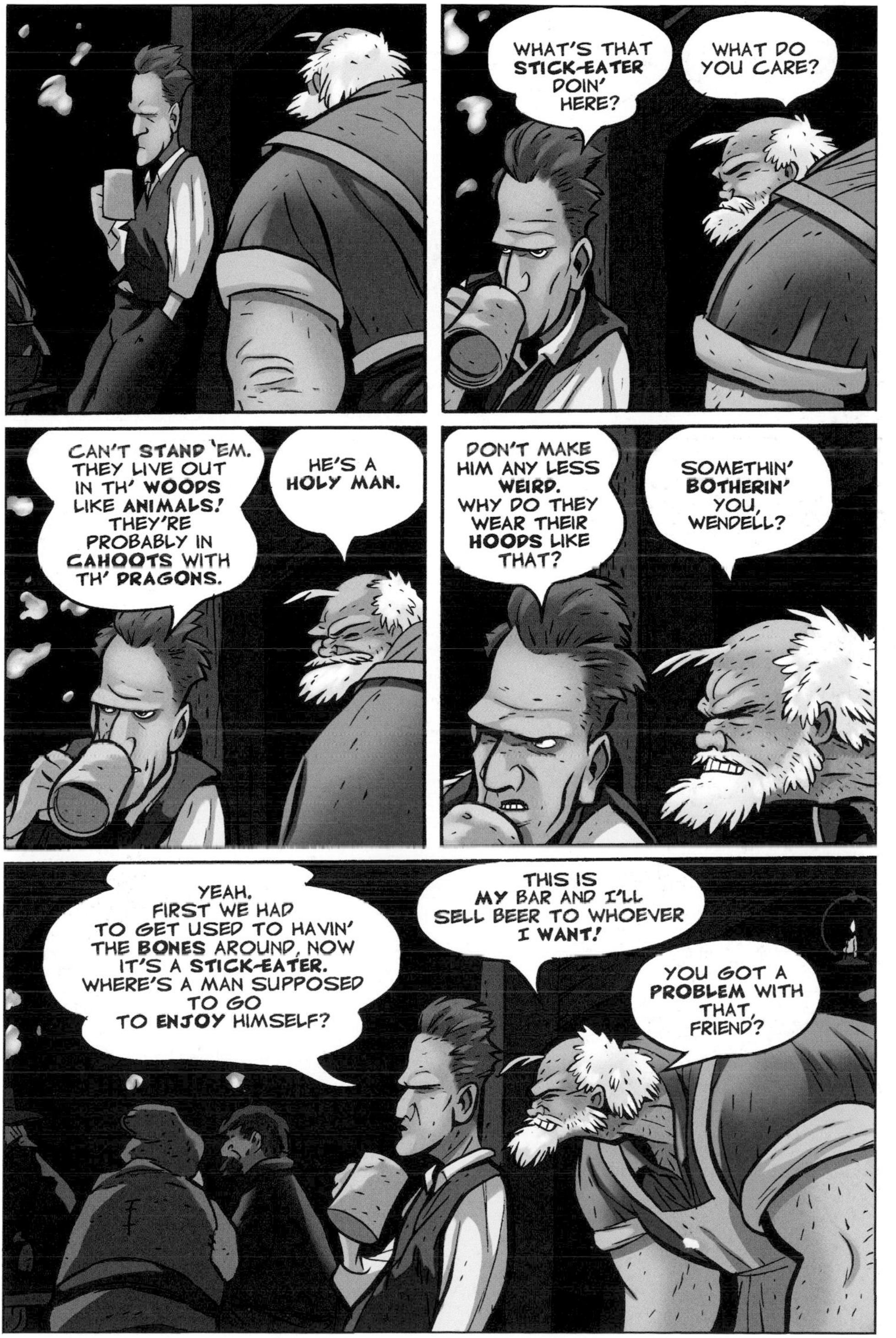
WHAT'S THAT STICK-EATER DOIN' HERE?
WHAT DO YOU CARE?
CAN'T STAND 'EM. THEY LIVE OUT IN TH' WOODS LIKE ANIMALS! THEY'RE PROBABLY IN CAHOOTS WITH TH' DRAGONS.
HE'S A HOLY MAN.
DON'T MAKE HIM ANY LESS WEIRD. WHY DO THEY WEAR THEIR HOODS LIKE THAT?
SOMETHIN' BOTHERIN' YOU, WENDELL?
YEAH. FIRST WE HAD TO GET USED TO HAVIN' THE BONES AROUND, NOW IT'S A STICK-EATER. WHERE'S A MAN SUPPOSED TO GO TO ENJOY HIMSELF?
THIS IS MY BAR AND I'LL SELL BEER TO WHOEVER I WANT!
YOU GOT A PROBLEM WITH THAT, FRIEND?

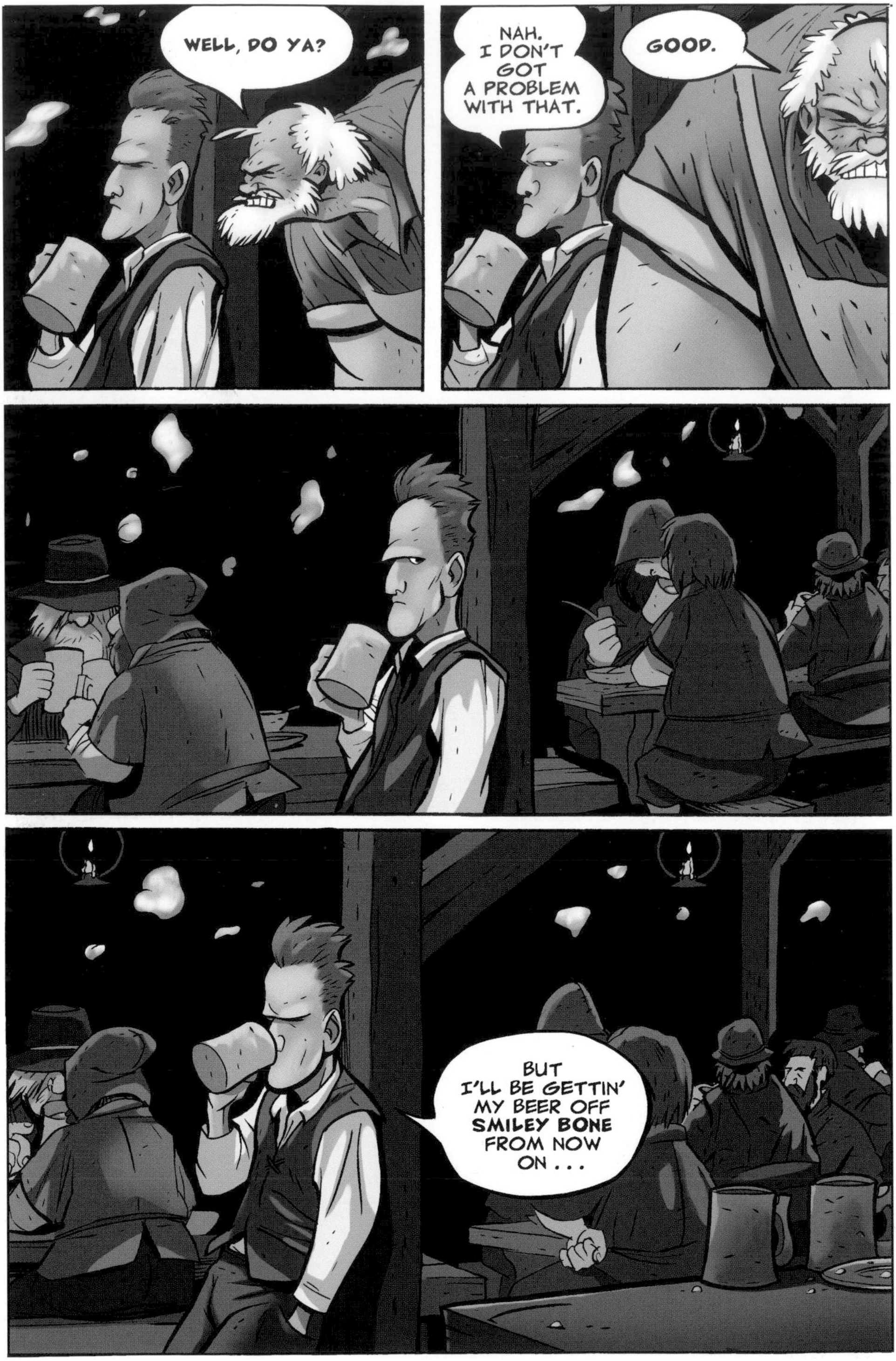
WELL, DO YA?
NAH. I DON'T GOT A PROBLEM WITH THAT.
GOOD.
BUT I'LL BE GETTIN' MY BEER OFF SMILEY BONE FROM NOW ON . . .

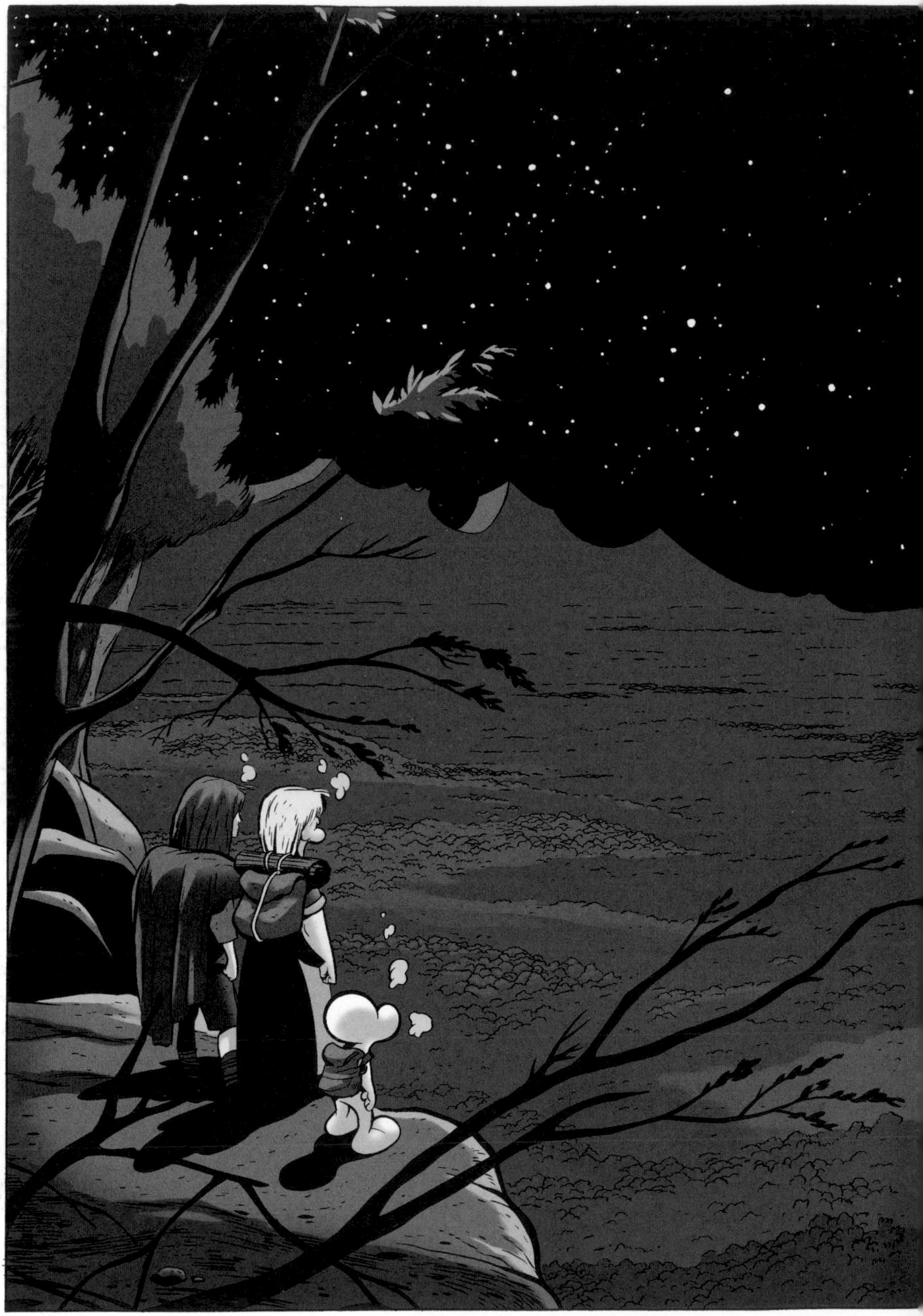

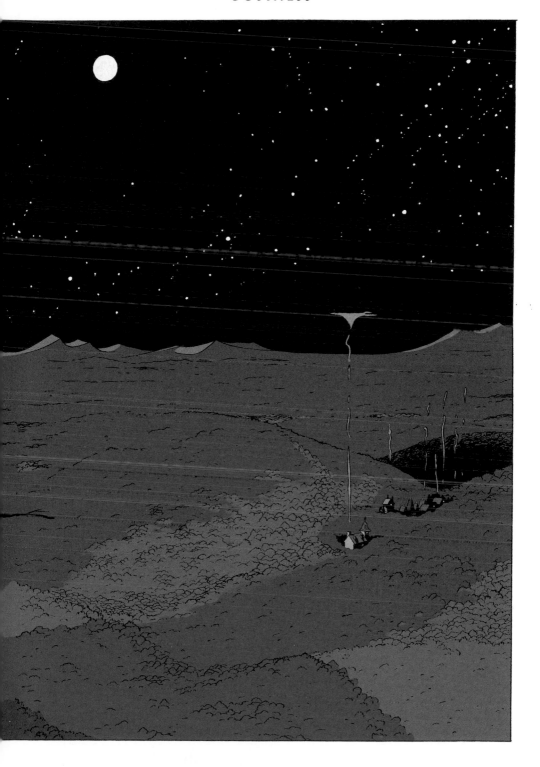

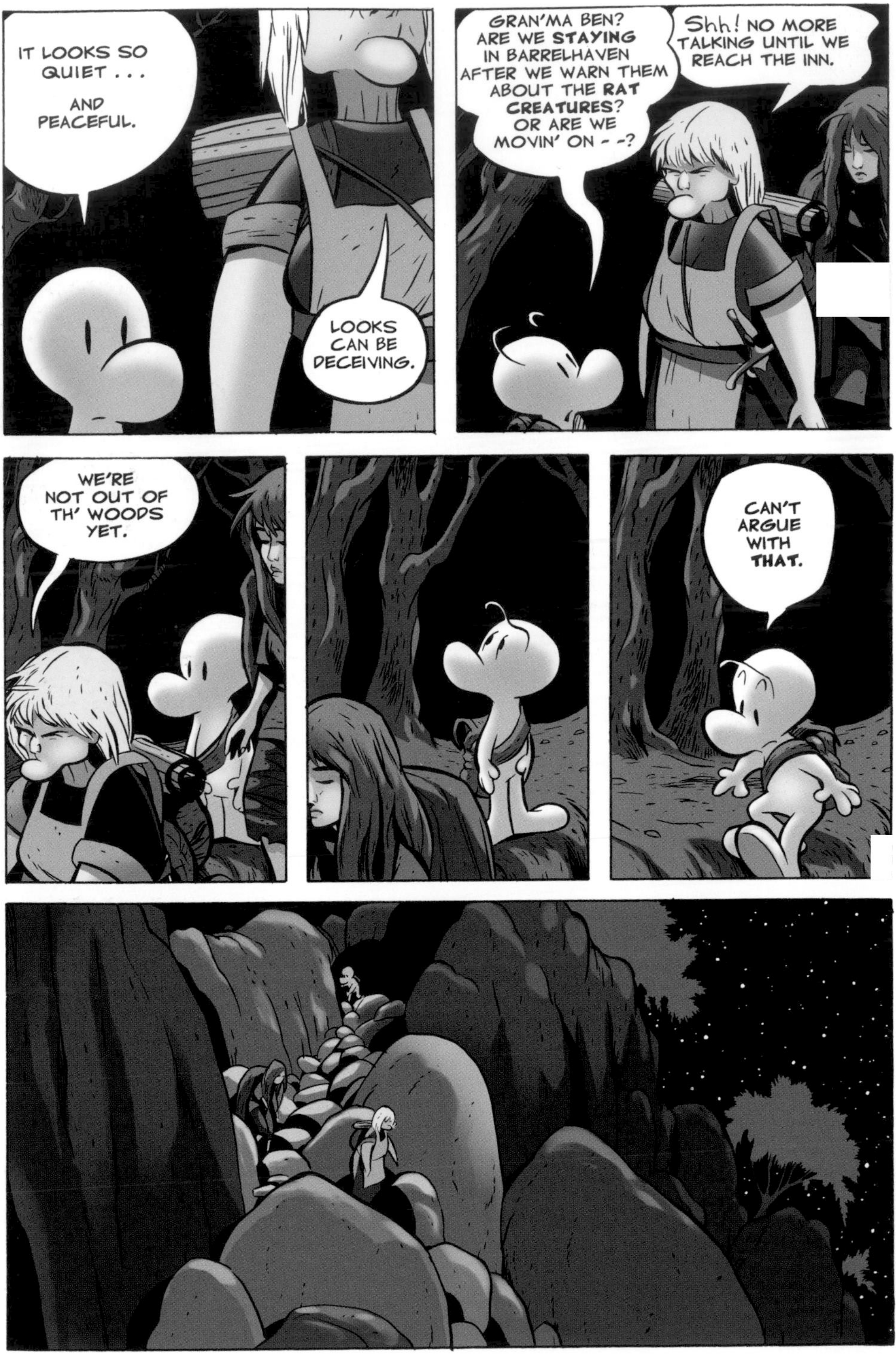
IT LOOKS SO QUIET . . .
AND PEACEFUL.
LOOKS CAN BE DECEIVING.
GRAN'MA BEN? ARE WE STAYING IN BARRELHAVEN AFTER WE WARN THEM ABOUT THE RAT CREATURES? OR ARE WE MOVIN' ON - -?
Shh! NO MORE TALKING UNTIL WE REACH THE INN.
WE'RE NOT OUT OF TH' WOODS YET.
CAN'T ARGUE WITH THAT.

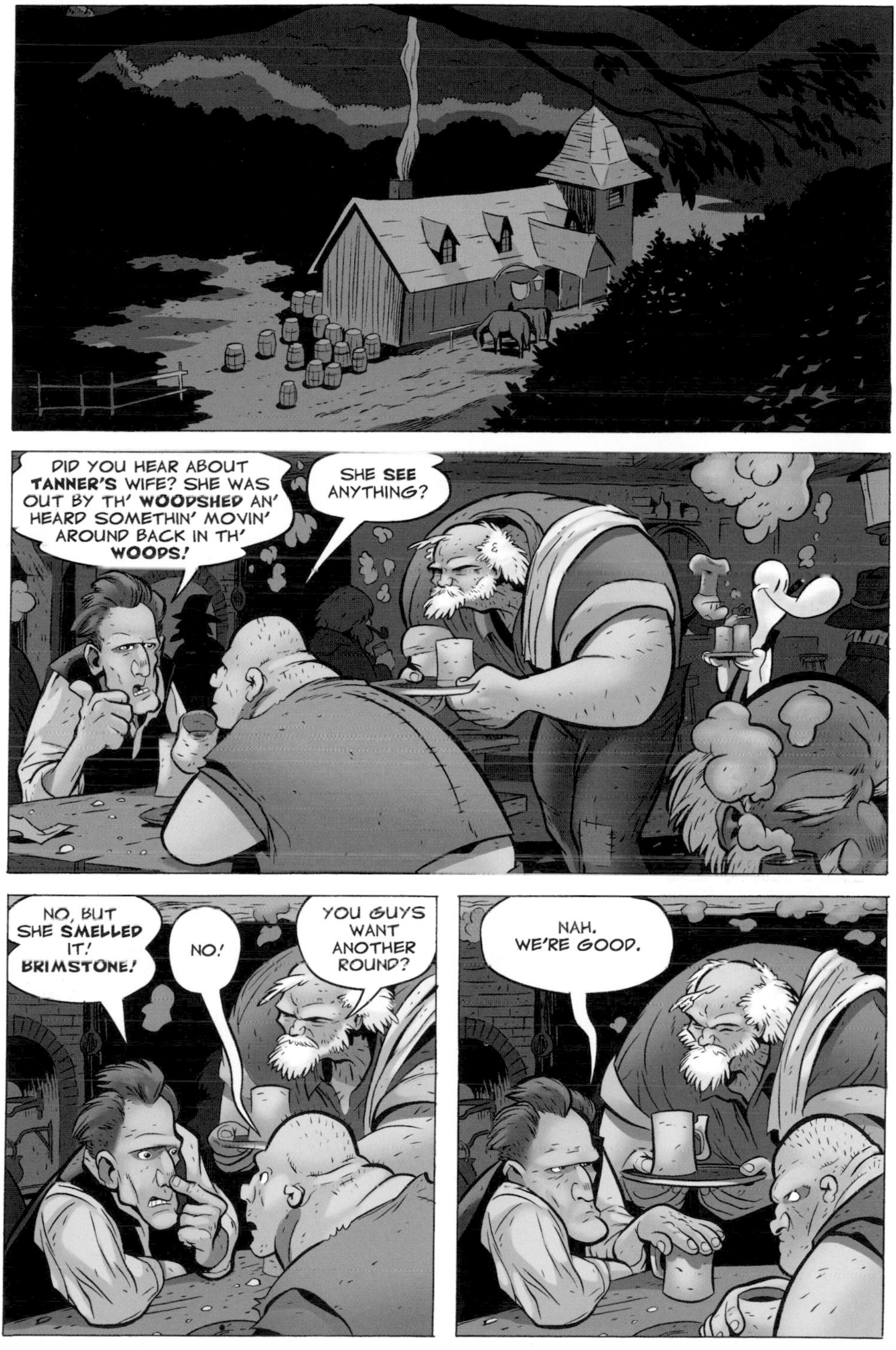
DID YOU HEAR ABOUT TANNER'S WIFE? SHE WAS OUT BY TH' WOODSHED AN' HEARD SOMETHIN' MOVIN' AROUND BACK IN TH' WOODS!
SHE SEE ANYTHING?
NO, BUT SHE SMELLED IT! BRIMSTONE!
NO!
YOU GUYS WANT ANOTHER ROUND?
NAH. WE'RE GOOD.

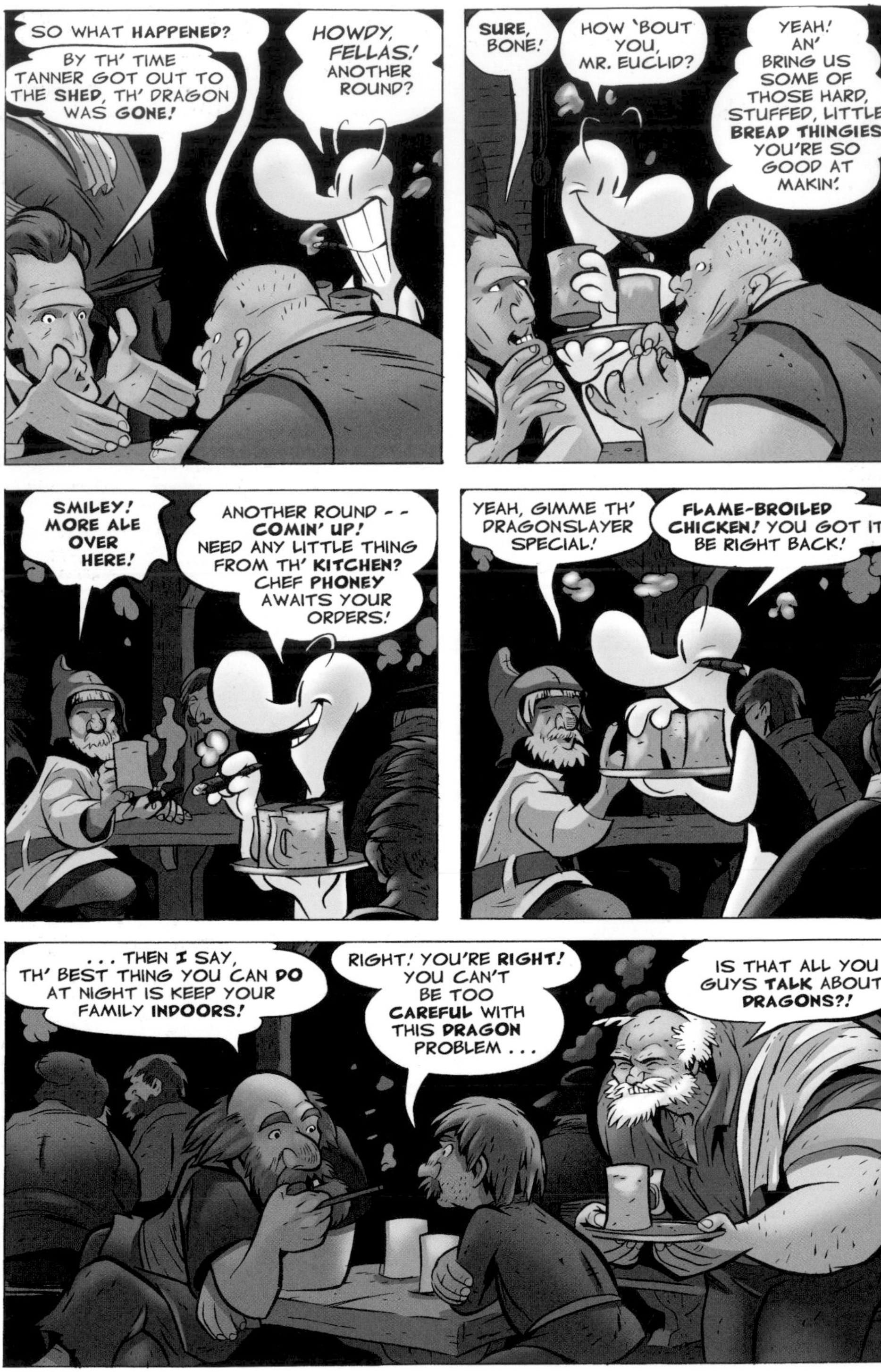
SO WHAT HAPPENED?
BY TH' TIME TANNER GOT OUT TO THE SHED, TH' DRAGON WAS GONE!
HOWDY, FELLAS! ANOTHER ROUND?
SURE, BONE!
HOW 'BOUT YOU, MR. EUCLID?
YEAH! AN' BRING US SOME OF THOSE HARD, STUFFED, LITTLE BREAD THINGIES YOU'RE SO GOOD AT MAKIN'.
SMILEY! MORE ALE OVER HERE!
ANOTHER ROUND - - COMIN' UP! NEED ANY LITTLE THING FROM TH' KITCHEN? CHEF PHONEY AWAITS YOUR ORDERS!
YEAH, GIMME TH' DRAGONSLAYER SPECIAL!
FLAME-BROILED CHICKEN! YOU GOT IT! BE RIGHT BACK!
. . . THEN I SAY, TH' BEST THING YOU CAN DO AT NIGHT IS KEEP YOUR FAMILY INDOORS!
RIGHT! YOU'RE RIGHT! YOU CAN'T BE TOO CAREFUL WITH THIS DRAGON PROBLEM . . .
IS THAT ALL YOU GUYS TALK ABOUT? DRAGONS?!

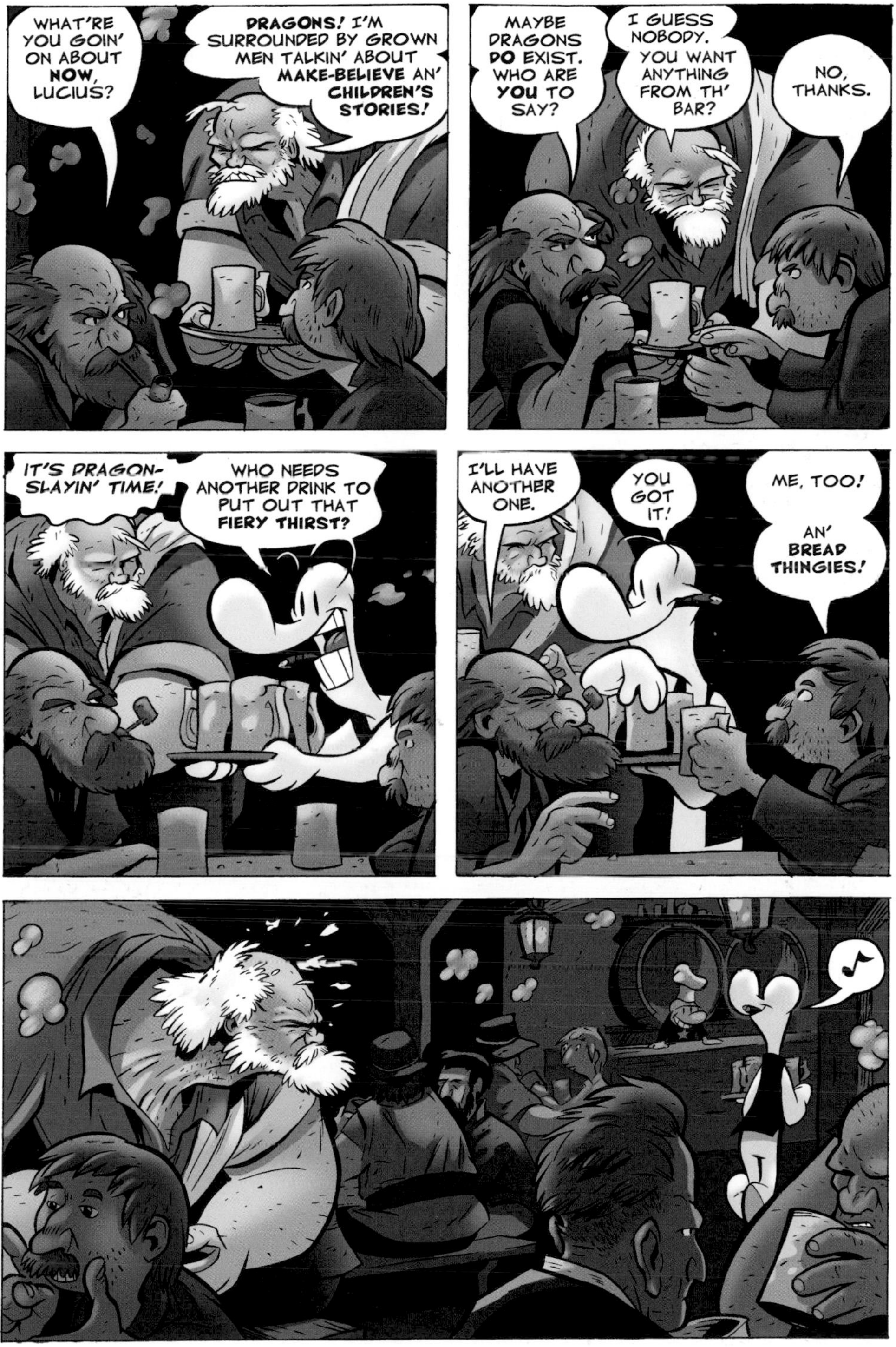
WHAT'RE YOU GOIN' ON ABOUT NOW, LUCIUS?
DRAGONS! I'M SURROUNDED BY GROWN MEN TALKIN' ABOUT MAKE-BELIEVE AN' CHILDREN'S STORIES!
MAYBE DRAGONS DO EXIST. WHO ARE YOU TO SAY?
I GUESS NOBODY. YOU WANT ANYTHING FROM TH' BAR?
NO, THANKS.
IT'S DRAGON-SLAYIN' TIME!
WHO NEEDS ANOTHER DRINK TO PUT OUT THAT FIERY THIRST?
I'LL HAVE ANOTHER ONE.
YOU GOT IT!
ME, TOO!
AN' BREAD THINGIES!

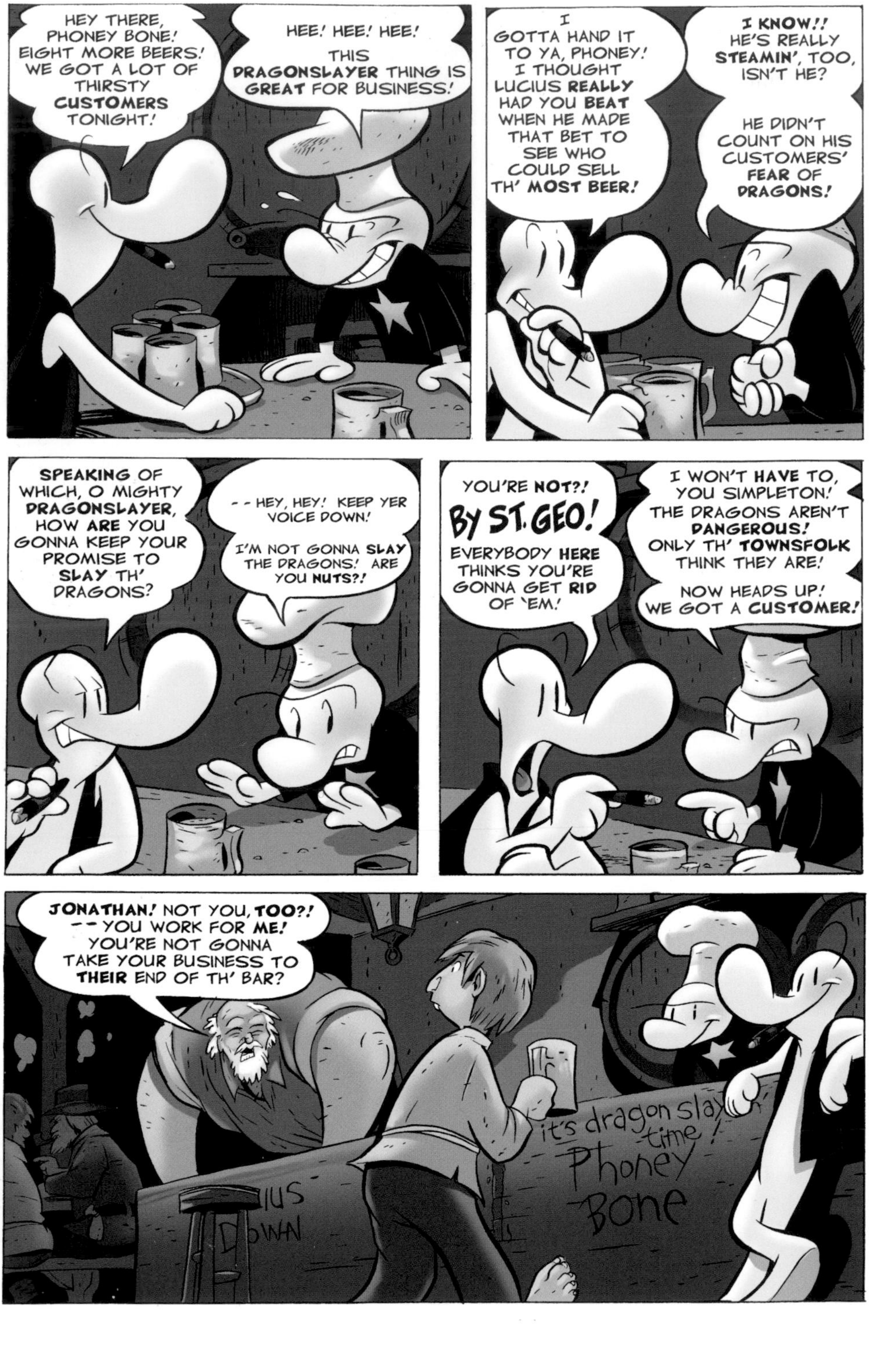
HEY THERE, PHONEY BONE! EIGHT MORE BEERS! WE GOT A LOT OF THIRSTY CUSTOMERS TONIGHT!
HEE! HEE! HEE! THIS DRAGONSLAYER THING IS GREAT FOR BUSINESS!
I GOTTA HAND IT TO YA, PHONEY! I THOUGHT LUCIUS REALLY HAD YOU BEAT WHEN HE MADE THAT BET TO SEE WHO COULD SELL TH' MOST BEER!
I KNOW!! HE'S REALLY STEAMIN', TOO, ISN'T HE?
HE DIDN'T COUNT ON HIS CUSTOMERS' FEAR OF DRAGONS!
SPEAKING OF WHICH, O MIGHTY DRAGONSLAYER, HOW ARE YOU GONNA KEEP YOUR PROMISE TO SLAY TH' DRAGONS?
-- HEY, HEY! KEEP YER VOICE DOWN!
I'M NOT GONNA SLAY THE DRAGONS! ARE YOU NUTS?!
YOU'RE NOT?! BY ST. GEO! EVERYBODY HERE THINKS YOU'RE GONNA GET RID OF 'EM!
I WON'T HAVE TO, YOU SIMPLETON! THE DRAGONS AREN'T DANGEROUS! ONLY TH' TOWNSFOLK THINK THEY ARE!
NOW HEADS UP! WE GOT A CUSTOMER!
JONATHAN! NOT YOU, TOO?! -- YOU WORK FOR ME! YOU'RE NOT GONNA TAKE YOUR BUSINESS TO THEIR END OF TH' BAR?
it's dragon slay time! Phoney Bone

OH, WELL, GEE, MR. DOWN... EVERYBODY **ELSE** IS, SO I JUST FIGURED --

DON'T YOU GET IT? ALL THIS TALK ABOUT **DRAGONS** IS JUST A **TRICK** TO GET YOU TO ORDER YOUR DRINKS FROM **HIM!**

HEY, JONATHAN! HOW WAS YOUR CROP LAST YEAR? GOOD HARVEST?

KINDA POOR. WASN'T MUCH RAIN.

YOU KNOW, SOME FOLKS CLAIM IT'S **DRAGONS** THAT CAUSE **DROUGHT.**

THEY **DO?!!** OOH! BUT Y'KNOW? THAT MAKES **SENSE** WHEN YA THINK ABOUT IT!

HOW ABOUT THAT BEER?

MM? OH! YEAH! RIGHT!

FILL 'ER UP!

MY PLEASURE, FRIEND!

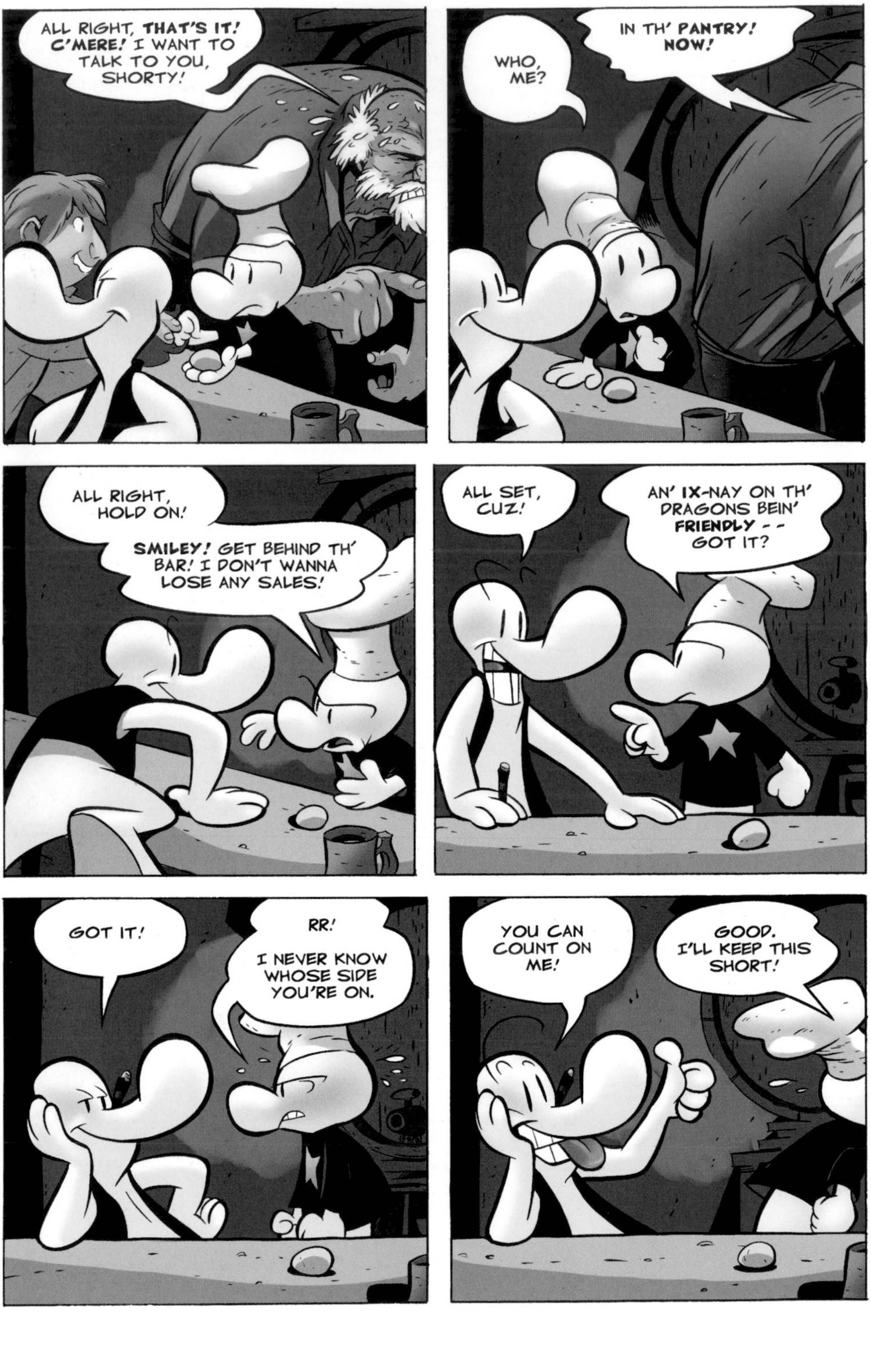
ALL RIGHT, THAT'S IT! C'MERE! I WANT TO TALK TO YOU, SHORTY!
WHO, ME?
IN TH' PANTRY! NOW!
ALL RIGHT, HOLD ON!
SMILEY! GET BEHIND TH' BAR! I DON'T WANNA LOSE ANY SALES!
ALL SET, CUZ!
AN' IX-NAY ON TH' DRAGONS BEIN' FRIENDLY -- GOT IT?
GOT IT!
RR!
I NEVER KNOW WHOSE SIDE YOU'RE ON.
YOU CAN COUNT ON ME!
GOOD. I'LL KEEP THIS SHORT!

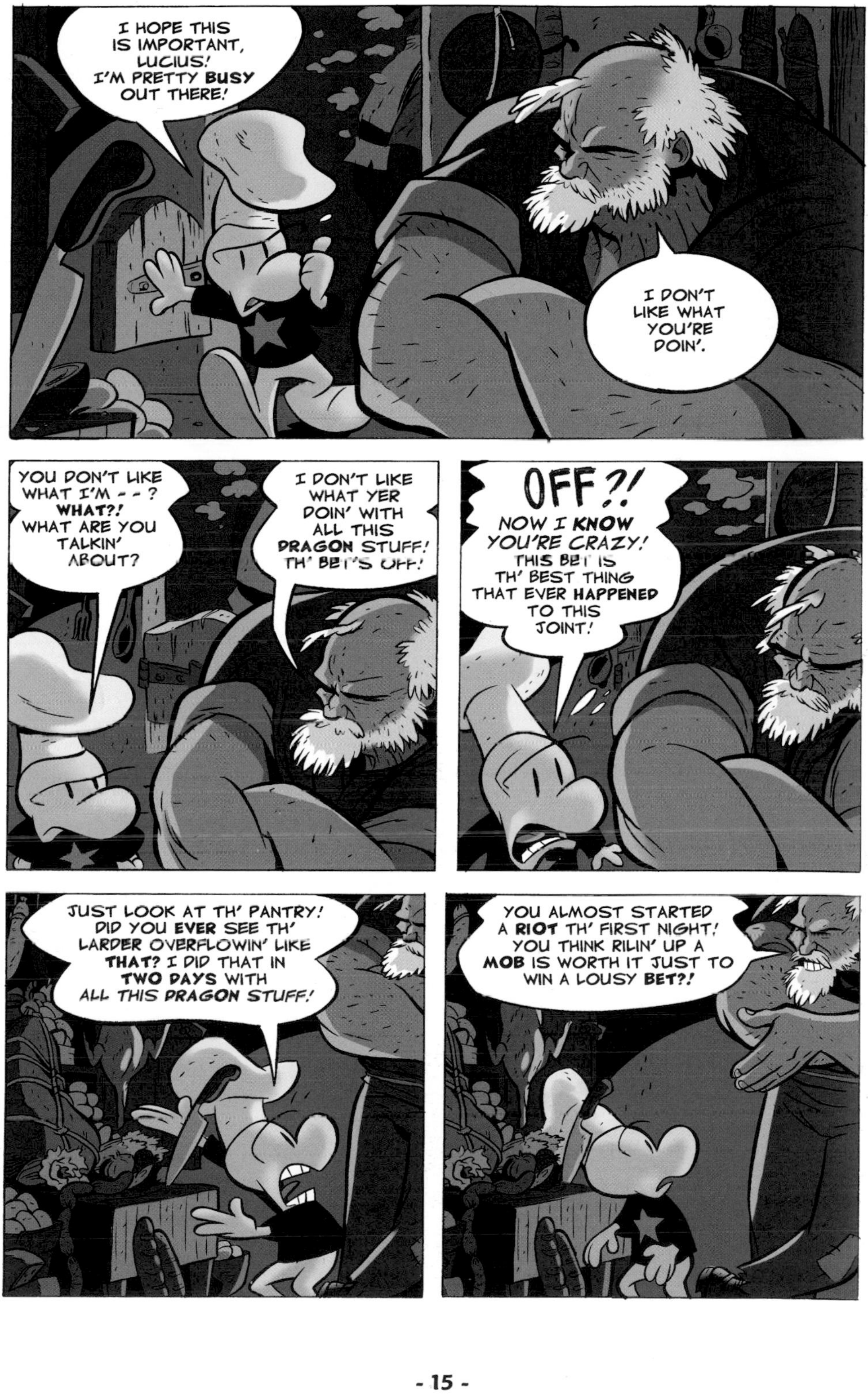
I HOPE THIS IS IMPORTANT, LUCIUS! I'M PRETTY BUSY OUT THERE!
I DON'T LIKE WHAT YOU'RE DOIN'.
YOU DON'T LIKE WHAT I'M - - ? WHAT?! WHAT ARE YOU TALKIN' ABOUT?
I DON'T LIKE WHAT YER DOIN' WITH ALL THIS DRAGON STUFF! TH' BET'S OFF!
OFF?! NOW I KNOW YOU'RE CRAZY! THIS BET IS TH' BEST THING THAT EVER HAPPENED TO THIS JOINT!
JUST LOOK AT TH' PANTRY! DID YOU EVER SEE TH' LARDER OVERFLOWIN' LIKE THAT? I DID THAT IN TWO DAYS WITH ALL THIS DRAGON STUFF!
YOU ALMOST STARTED A RIOT TH' FIRST NIGHT! YOU THINK RILIN' UP A MOB IS WORTH IT JUST TO WIN A LOUSY BET?!

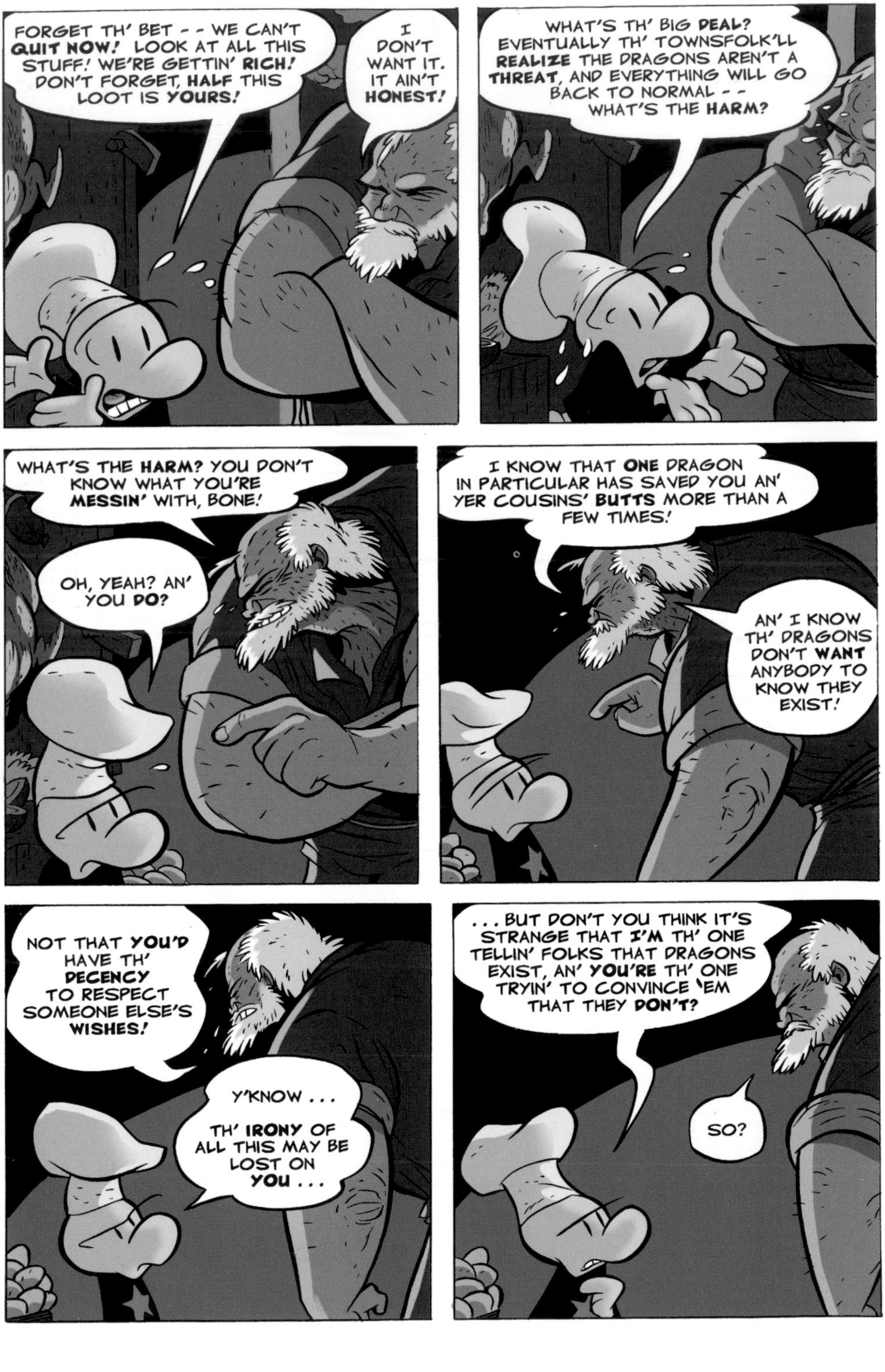
FORGET TH' BET - - WE CAN'T QUIT NOW! LOOK AT ALL THIS STUFF! WE'RE GETTIN' RICH! DON'T FORGET, HALF THIS LOOT IS YOURS!
I DON'T WANT IT. IT AIN'T HONEST!
WHAT'S TH' BIG DEAL? EVENTUALLY TH' TOWNSFOLK'LL REALIZE THE DRAGONS AREN'T A THREAT, AND EVERYTHING WILL GO BACK TO NORMAL - - WHAT'S THE HARM?
WHAT'S THE HARM? YOU DON'T KNOW WHAT YOU'RE MESSIN' WITH, BONE!
OH, YEAH? AN' YOU DO?
I KNOW THAT ONE DRAGON IN PARTICULAR HAS SAVED YOU AN' YER COUSINS' BUTTS MORE THAN A FEW TIMES!
AN' I KNOW TH' DRAGONS DON'T WANT ANYBODY TO KNOW THEY EXIST!
NOT THAT YOU'D HAVE TH' DECENCY TO RESPECT SOMEONE ELSE'S WISHES!
Y'KNOW . . .
TH' IRONY OF ALL THIS MAY BE LOST ON YOU . . .
. . . BUT DON'T YOU THINK IT'S STRANGE THAT I'M TH' ONE TELLIN' FOLKS THAT DRAGONS EXIST, AN' YOU'RE TH' ONE TRYIN' TO CONVINCE 'EM THAT THEY DON'T?
SO?

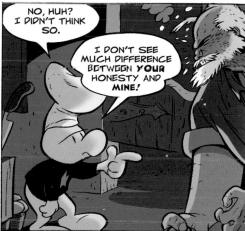

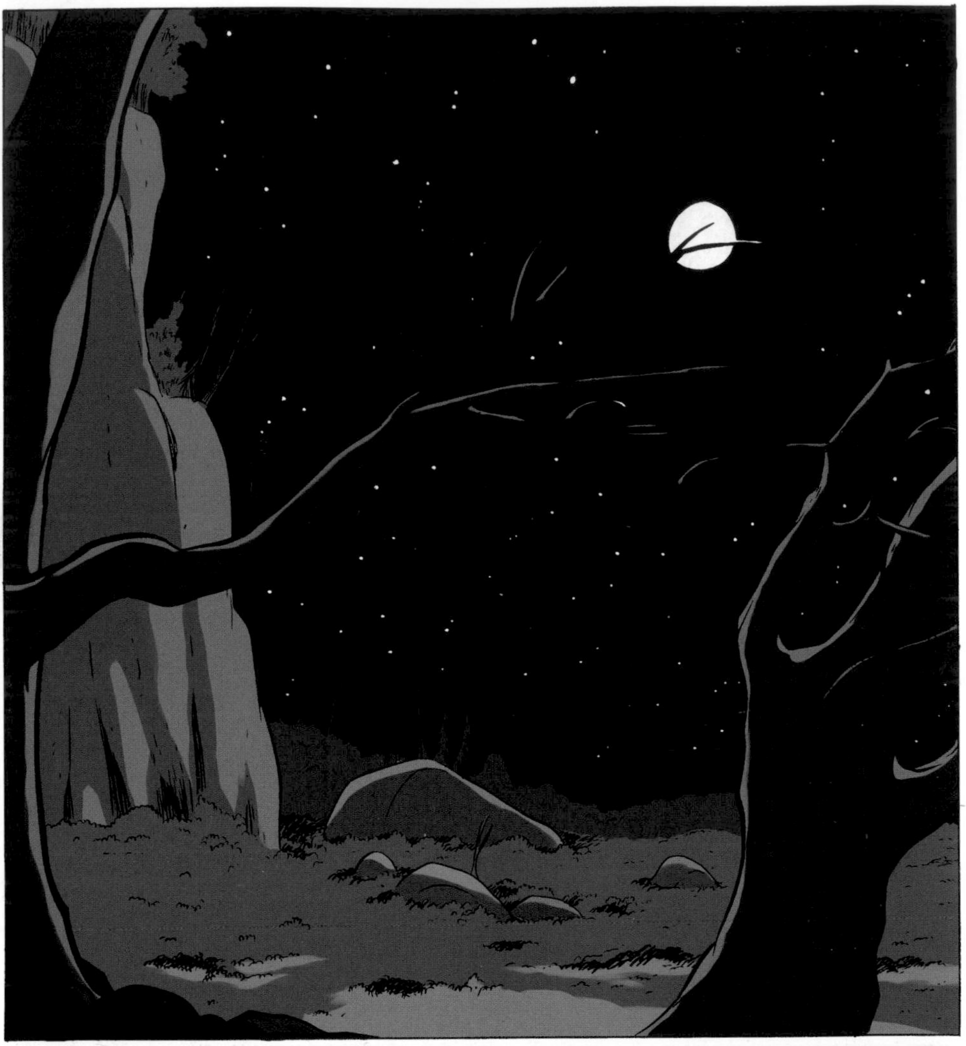

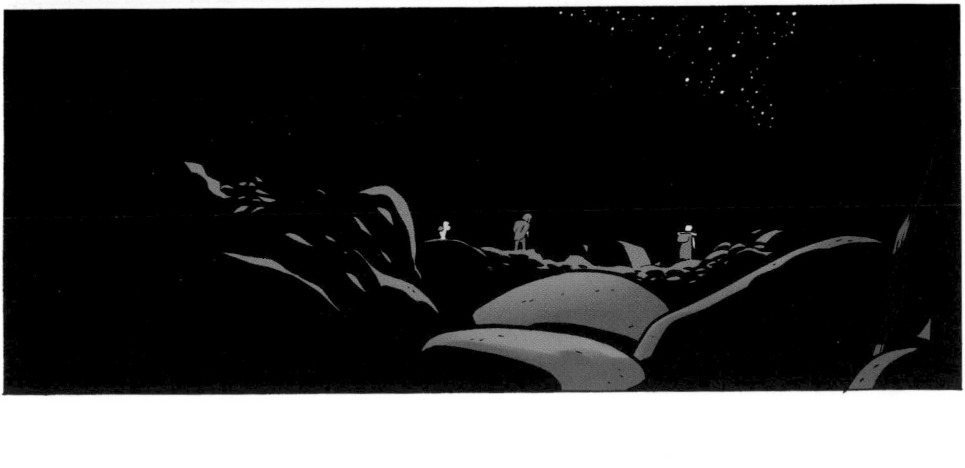

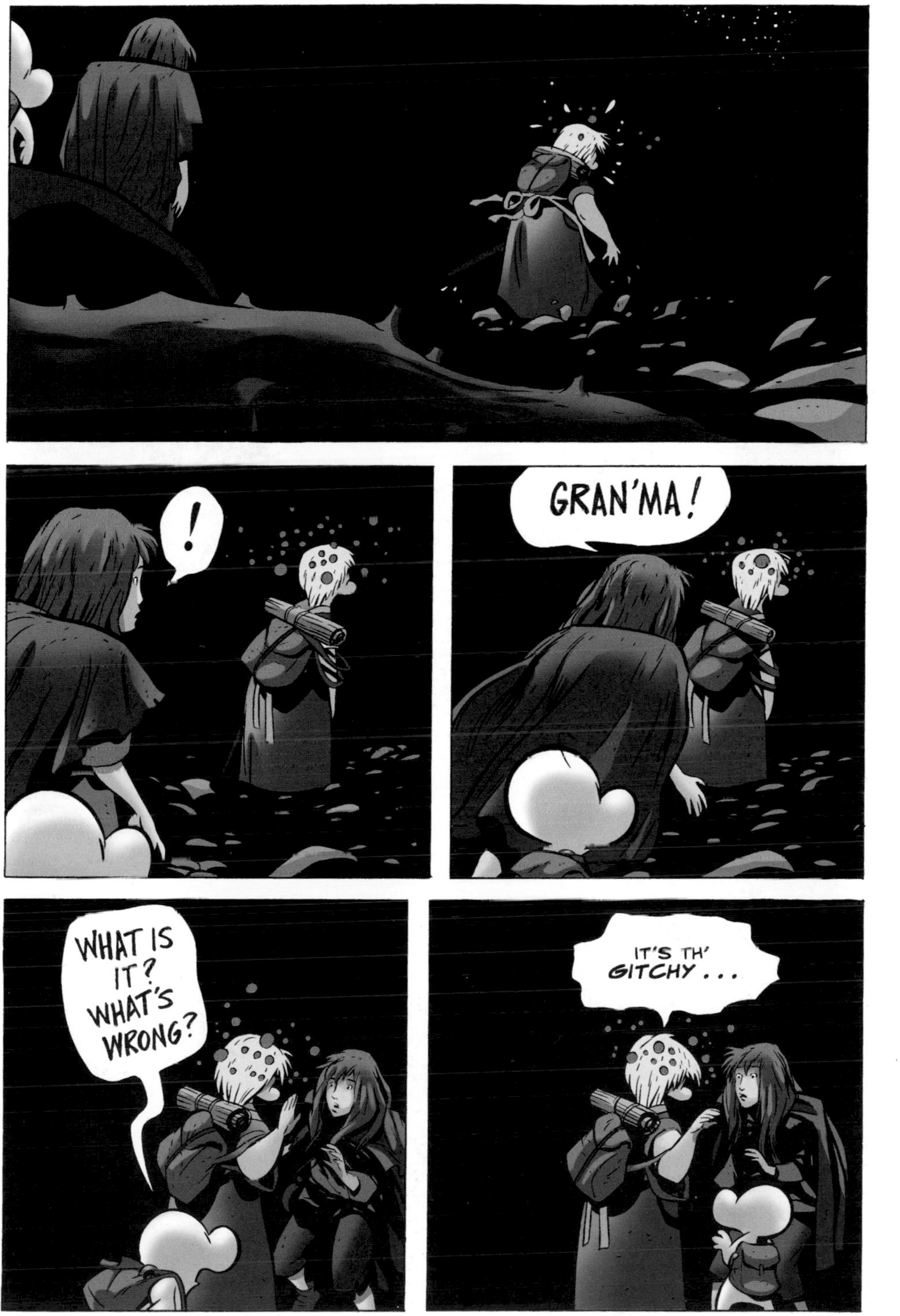
!
GRAN'MA!
WHAT IS IT? WHAT'S WRONG?
IT'S TH' GITCHY . . .

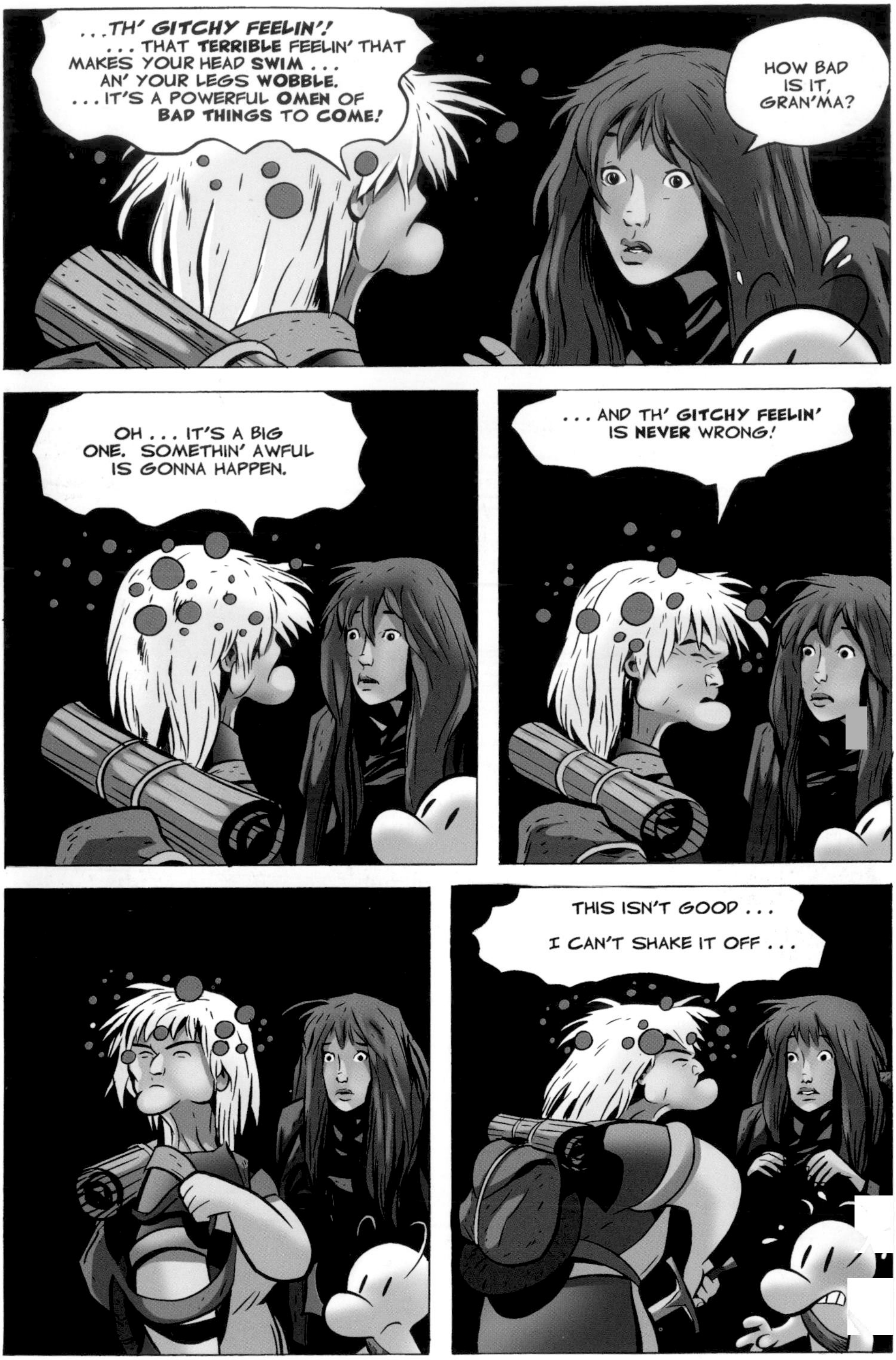
...TH' GITCHY FEELIN'! ... THAT TERRIBLE FEELIN' THAT MAKES YOUR HEAD SWIM ... AN' YOUR LEGS WOBBLE. ... IT'S A POWERFUL OMEN OF BAD THINGS TO COME!
HOW BAD IS IT, GRAN'MA?
OH ... IT'S A BIG ONE. SOMETHIN' AWFUL IS GONNA HAPPEN.
... AND TH' GITCHY FEELIN' IS NEVER WRONG!
THIS ISN'T GOOD ...
I CAN'T SHAKE IT OFF ...

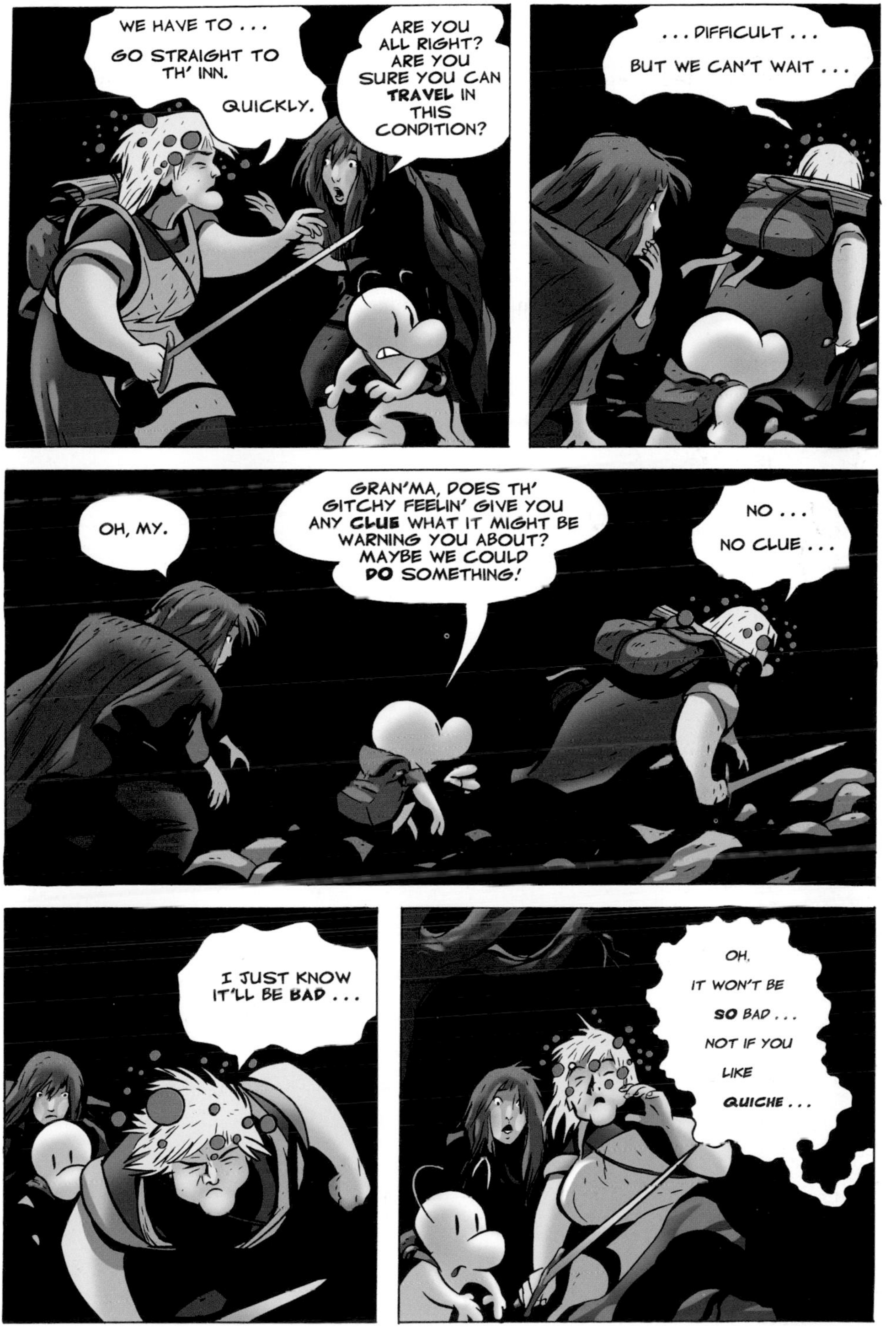
WE HAVE TO . . .
GO STRAIGHT TO TH' INN.
QUICKLY.
ARE YOU ALL RIGHT? ARE YOU SURE YOU CAN TRAVEL IN THIS CONDITION?
. . . DIFFICULT . . .
BUT WE CAN'T WAIT . . .
OH, MY.
GRAN'MA, DOES TH' GITCHY FEELIN' GIVE YOU ANY CLUE WHAT IT MIGHT BE WARNING YOU ABOUT? MAYBE WE COULD DO SOMETHING!
NO . . .
NO CLUE . . .
I JUST KNOW IT'LL BE BAD . . .
OH, IT WON'T BE SO BAD . . . NOT IF YOU LIKE QUICHE . . .

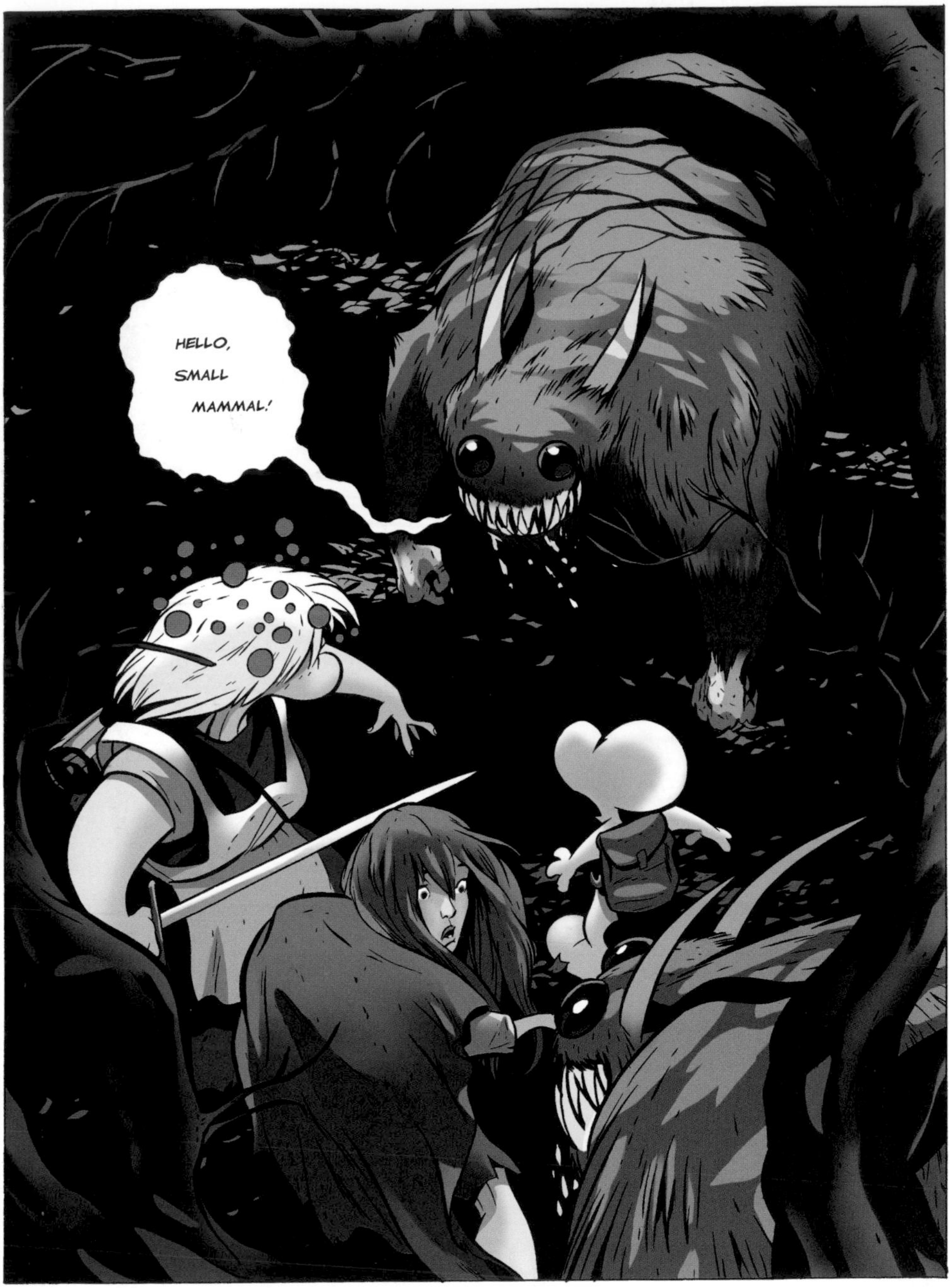
HELLO, SMALL MAMMAL!

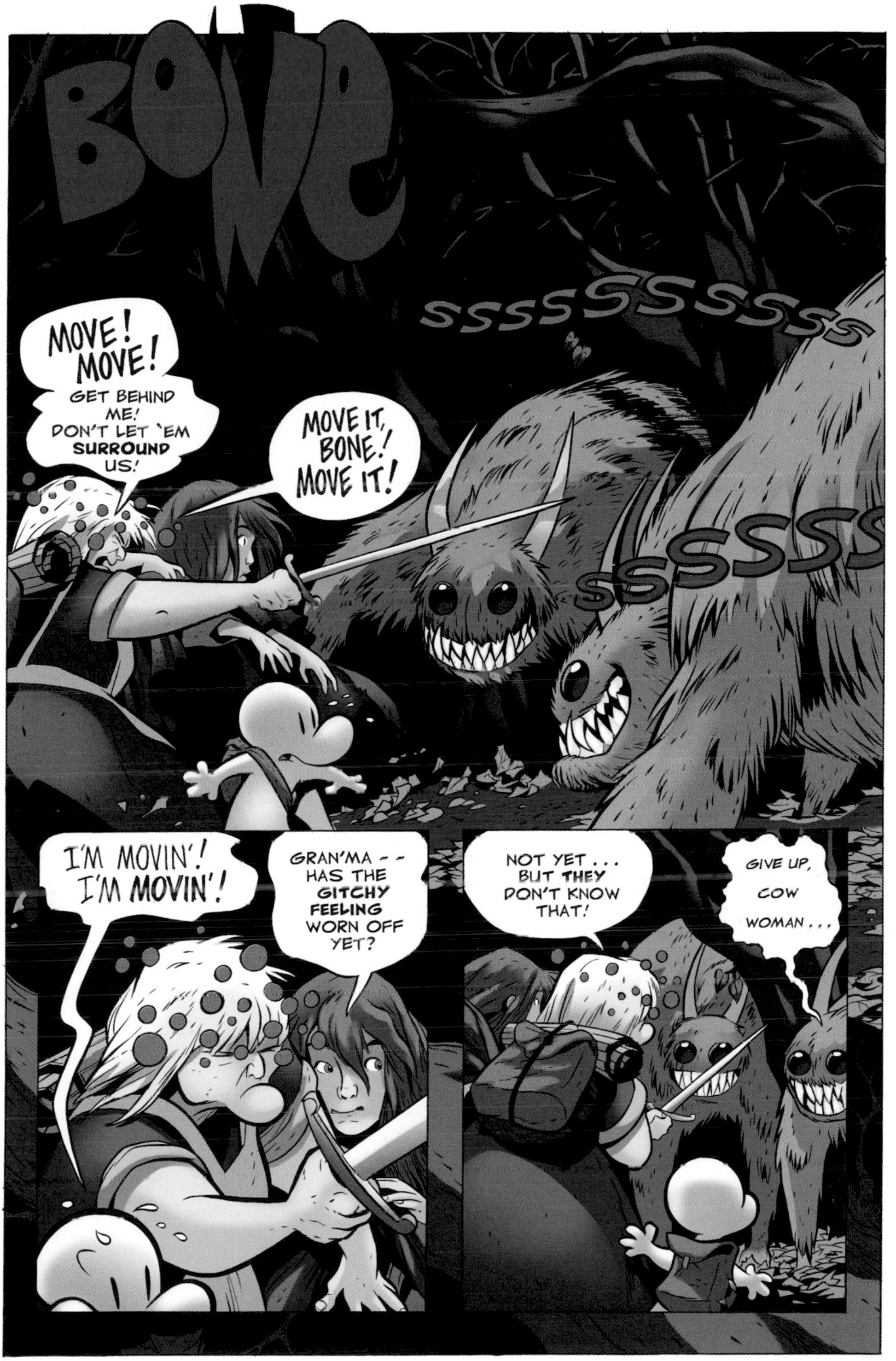
BONE
SSSSSSSSSSSSS
MOVE! MOVE! GET BEHIND ME! DON'T LET 'EM SURROUND US!
MOVE IT, BONE! MOVE IT!
SSSSSSSSS
I'M MOVIN'! I'M MOVIN'!
GRAN'MA - - HAS THE GITCHY FEELING WORN OFF YET?
NOT YET . . . BUT THEY DON'T KNOW THAT!
GIVE UP, COW WOMAN . . .

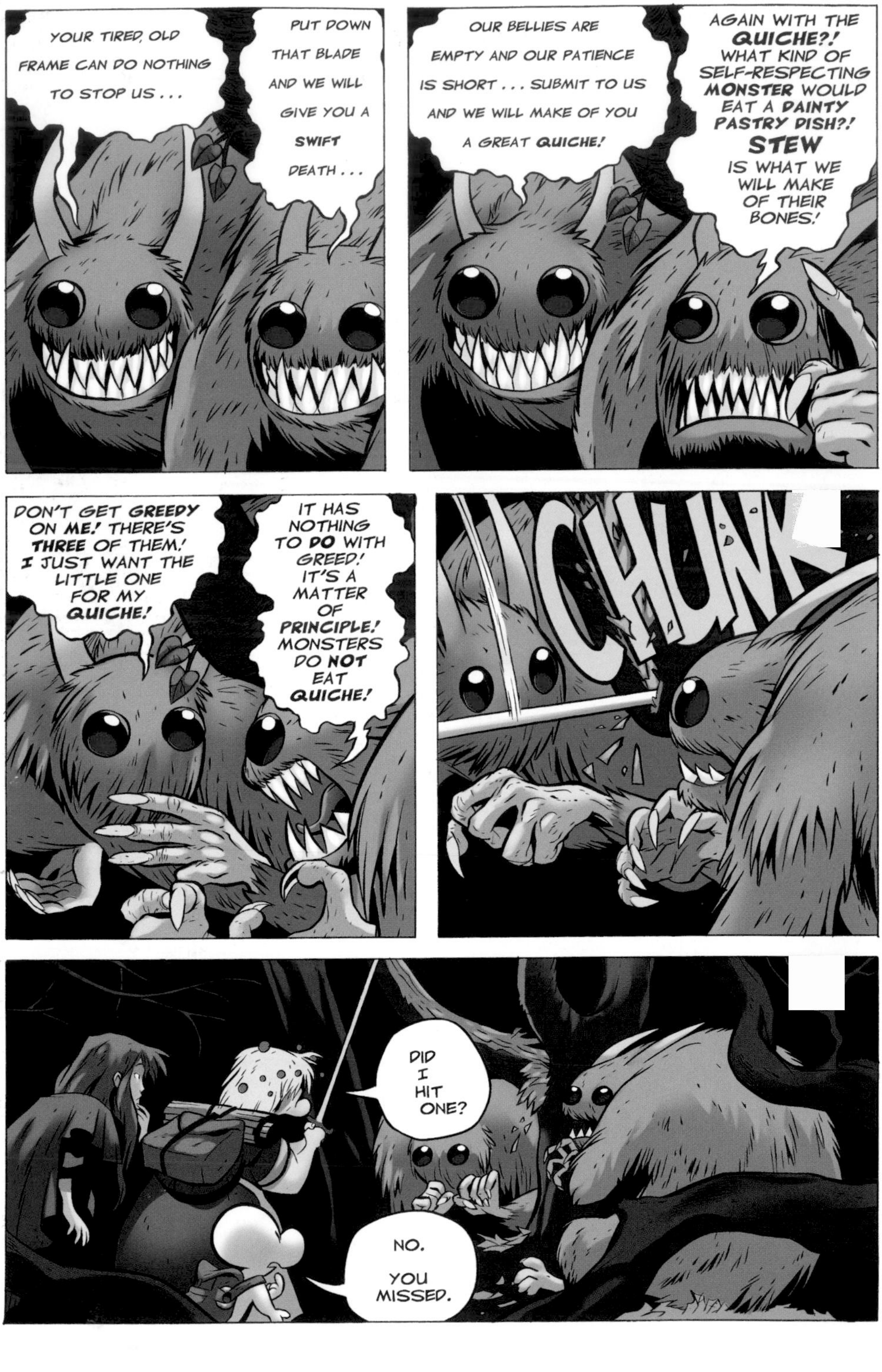
YOUR TIRED, OLD FRAME CAN DO NOTHING TO STOP US . . .
PUT DOWN THAT BLADE AND WE WILL GIVE YOU A SWIFT DEATH . . .
OUR BELLIES ARE EMPTY AND OUR PATIENCE IS SHORT . . . SUBMIT TO US AND WE WILL MAKE OF YOU A GREAT QUICHE!
AGAIN WITH THE QUICHE?! WHAT KIND OF SELF-RESPECTING MONSTER WOULD EAT A DAINTY PASTRY DISH?! STEW IS WHAT WE WILL MAKE OF THEIR BONES!
DON'T GET GREEDY ON ME! THERE'S THREE OF THEM! I JUST WANT THE LITTLE ONE FOR MY QUICHE!
IT HAS NOTHING TO DO WITH GREED! IT'S A MATTER OF PRINCIPLE! MONSTERS DO NOT EAT QUICHE!
CHUNK
DID I HIT ONE?
NO. YOU MISSED.

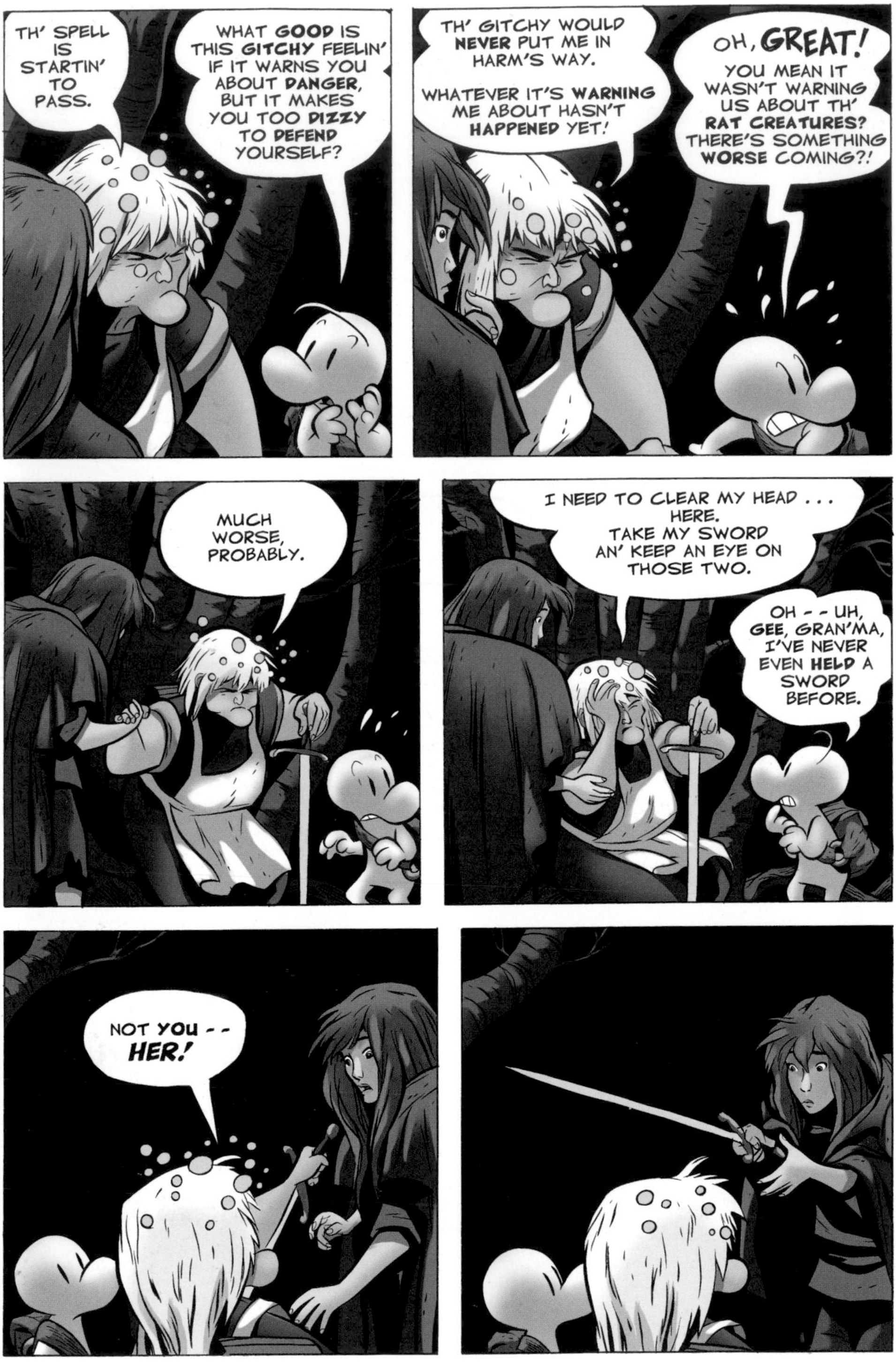
TH' SPELL IS STARTIN' TO PASS.
WHAT GOOD IS THIS GITCHY FEELIN' IF IT WARNS YOU ABOUT DANGER, BUT IT MAKES YOU TOO DIZZY TO DEFEND YOURSELF?
TH' GITCHY WOULD NEVER PUT ME IN HARM'S WAY.
WHATEVER IT'S WARNING ME ABOUT HASN'T HAPPENED YET!
OH, GREAT! YOU MEAN IT WASN'T WARNING US ABOUT TH' RAT CREATURES? THERE'S SOMETHING WORSE COMING?!
MUCH WORSE, PROBABLY.
I NEED TO CLEAR MY HEAD . . . HERE. TAKE MY SWORD AN' KEEP AN EYE ON THOSE TWO.
OH - - UH, GEE, GRAN'MA, I'VE NEVER EVEN HELD A SWORD BEFORE.
NOT YOU - - HER!

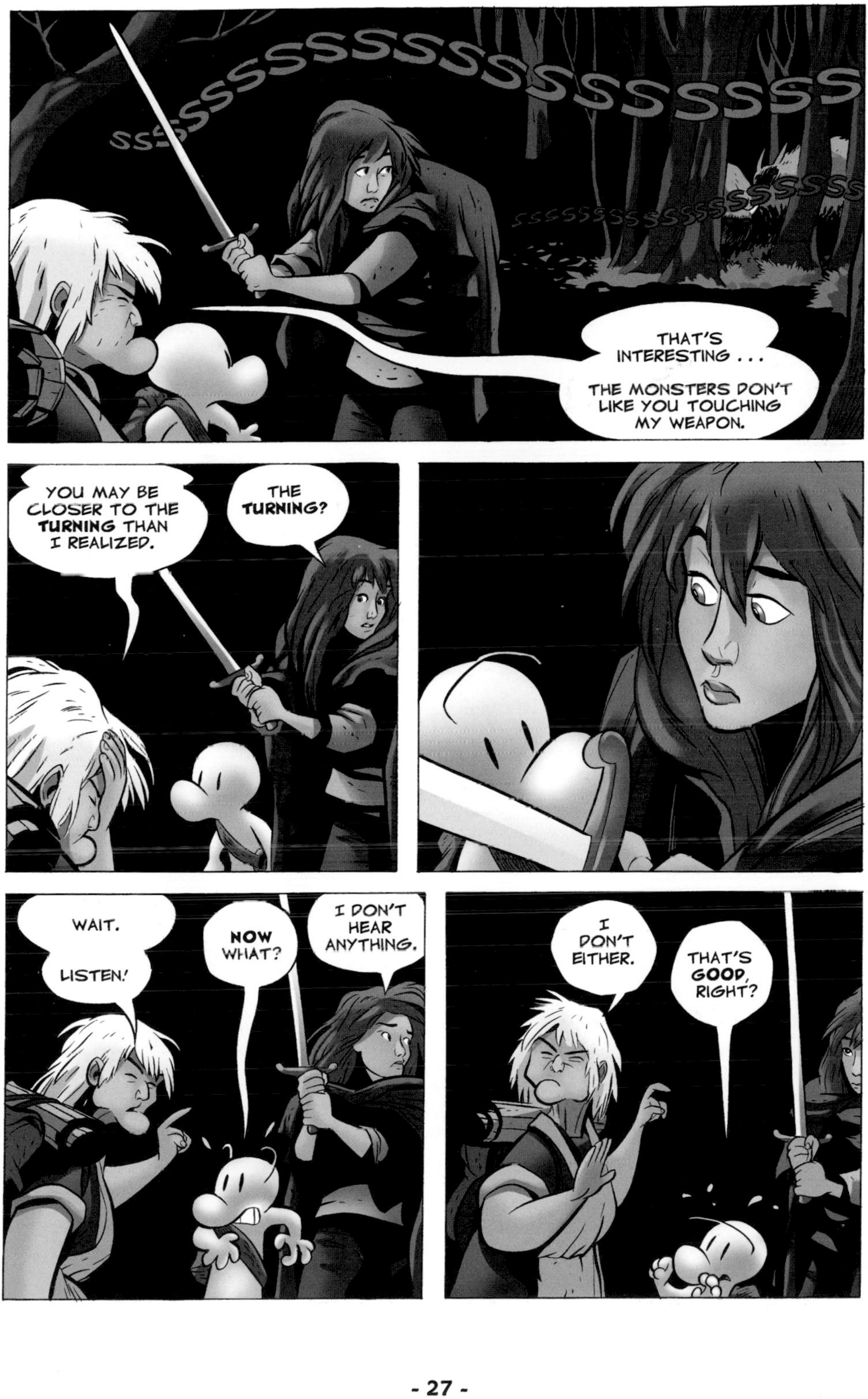
SSSSSSSSSSSSSSSSSSSSSSSSSSSS
THAT'S INTERESTING . . .
THE MONSTERS DON'T LIKE YOU TOUCHING MY WEAPON.
YOU MAY BE CLOSER TO THE **TURNING** THAN I REALIZED.
THE **TURNING?**
WAIT.
LISTEN!
NOW WHAT?
I DON'T HEAR ANYTHING.
I DON'T EITHER.
THAT'S **GOOD**, RIGHT?

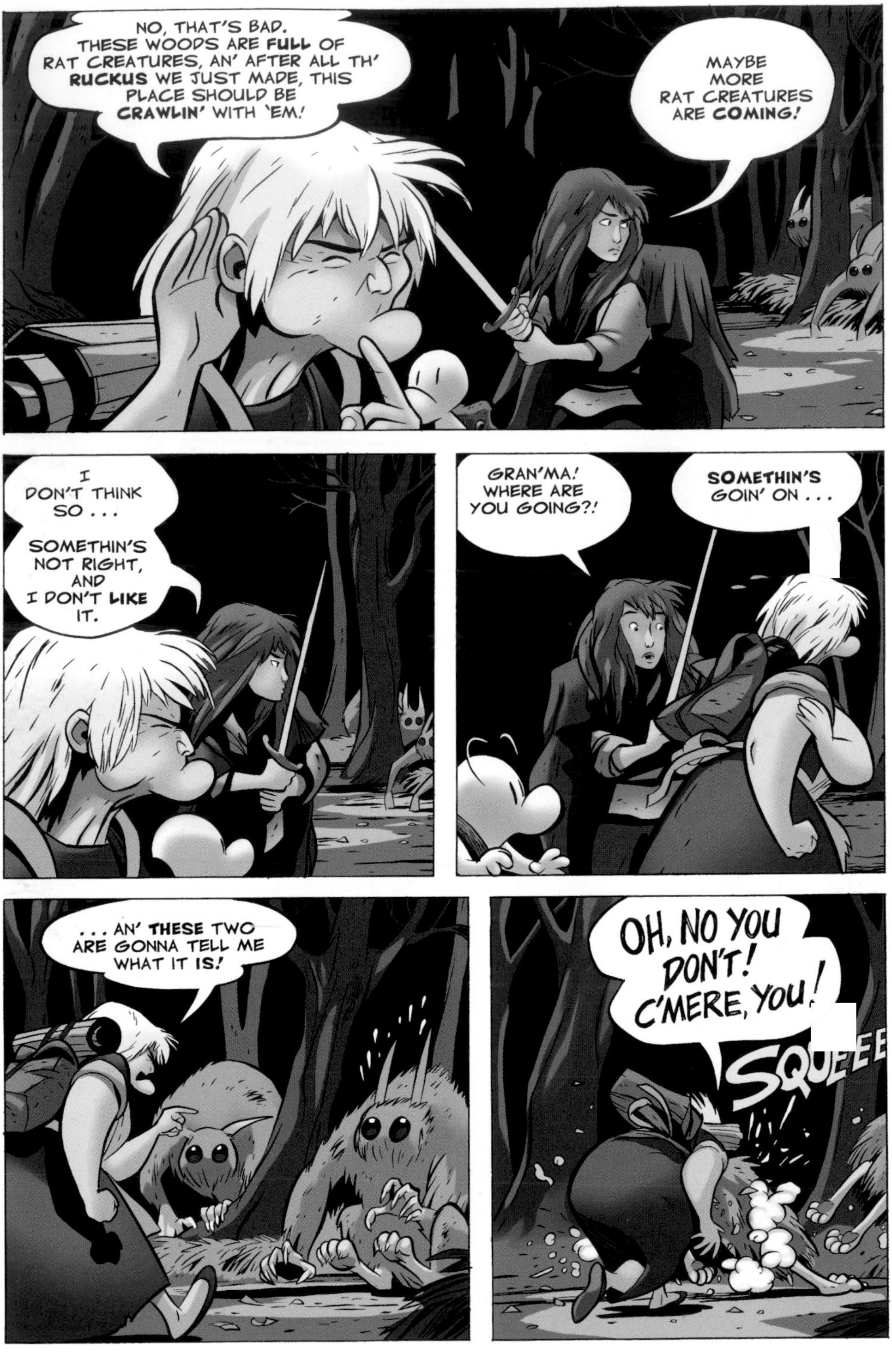
NO, THAT'S BAD. THESE WOODS ARE **FULL** OF RAT CREATURES, AN' AFTER ALL TH' **RUCKUS** WE JUST MADE, THIS PLACE SHOULD BE **CRAWLIN'** WITH 'EM!
MAYBE MORE RAT CREATURES ARE **COMING!**
I DON'T THINK SO . . .
SOMETHIN'S NOT RIGHT, AND I DON'T **LIKE** IT.
GRAN'MA! WHERE ARE YOU GOING?!
SOMETHIN'S GOIN' ON . . .
. . . AN' **THESE** TWO ARE GONNA TELL ME WHAT IT **IS!**
OH, NO YOU DON'T! C'MERE, YOU!
SQUEEE

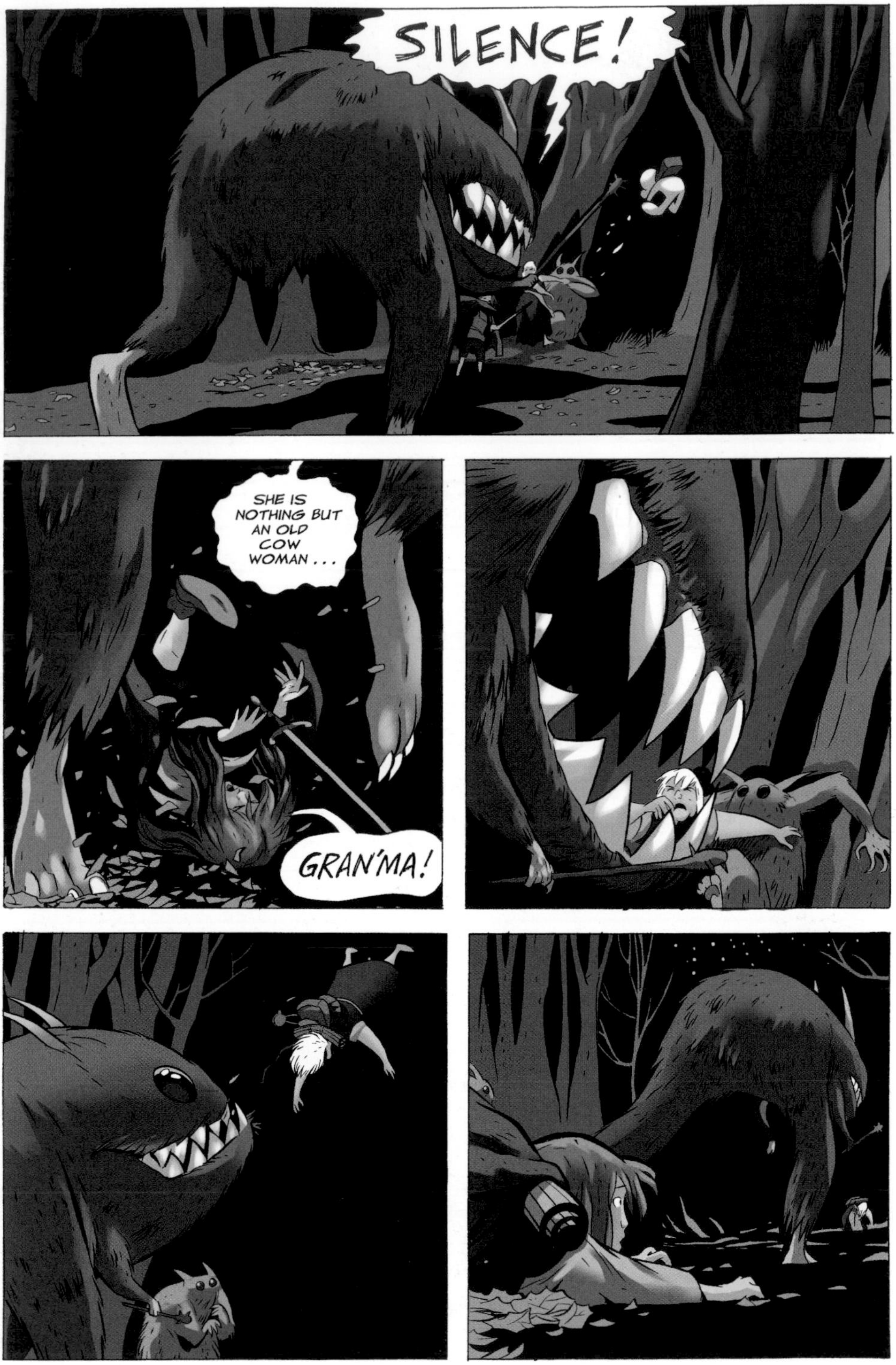
SILENCE!
SHE IS NOTHING BUT AN OLD COW WOMAN . . .
GRAN'MA!

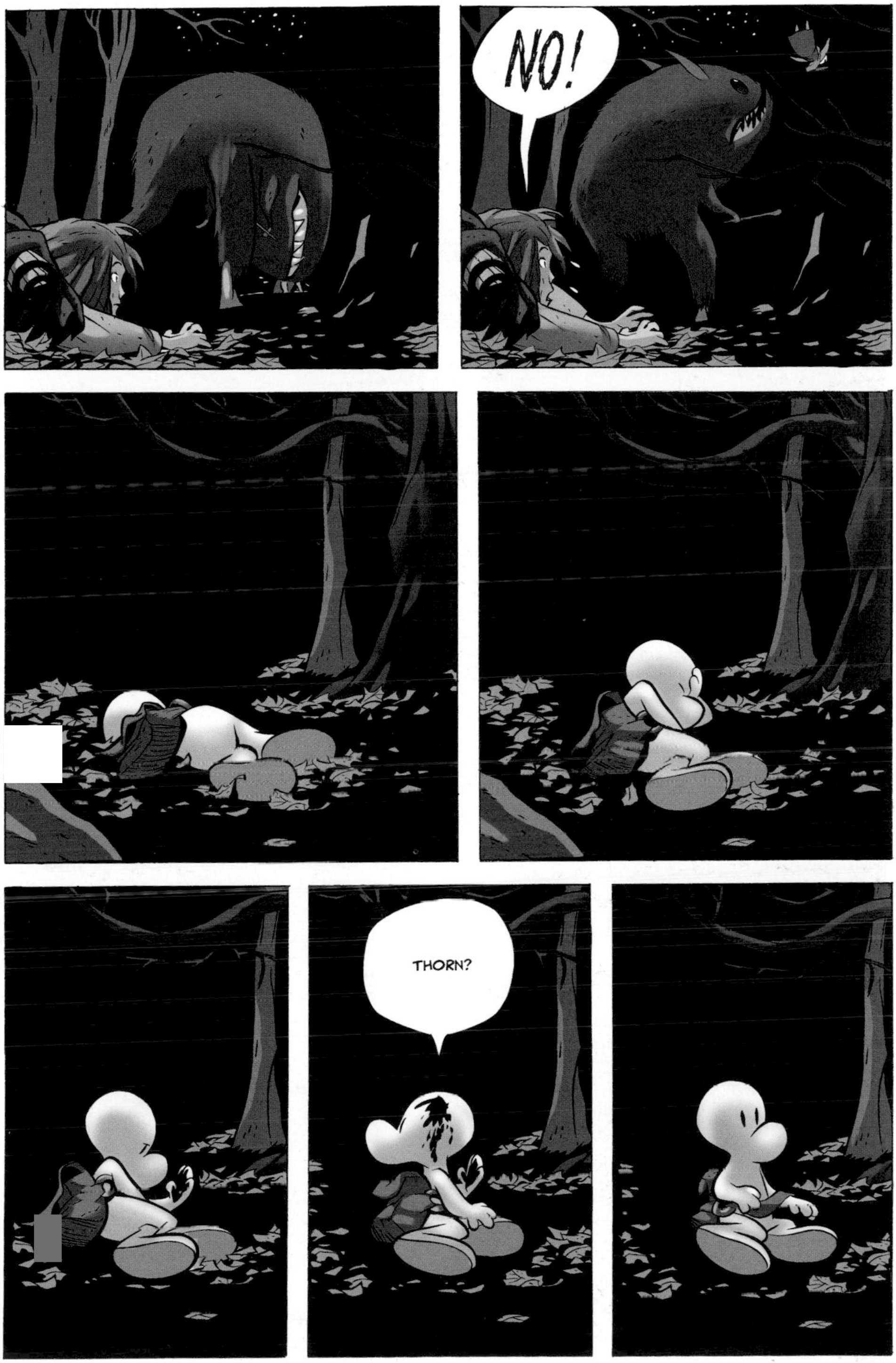
NO!
THORN?

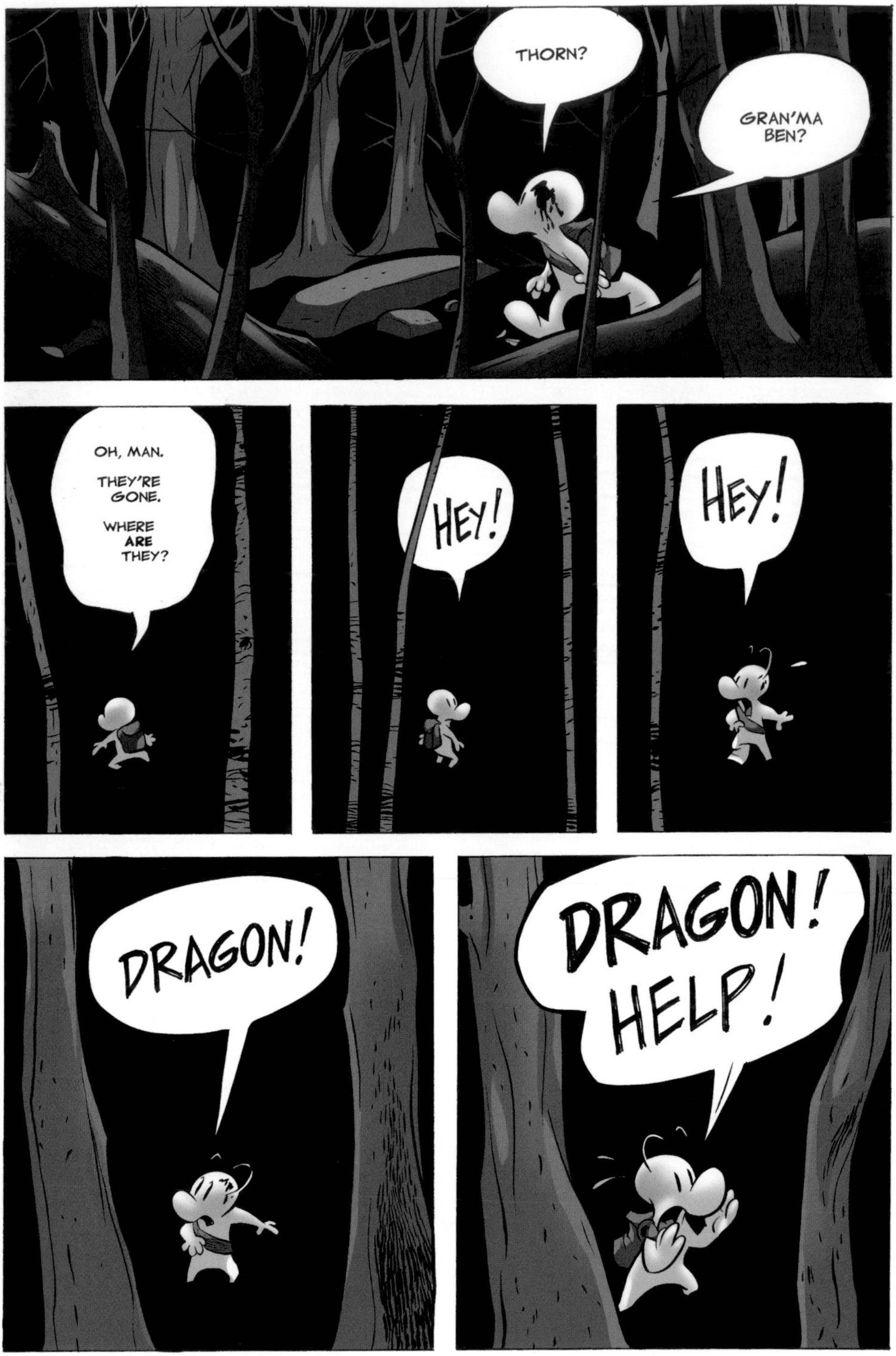
THORN?
GRAN'MA BEN?
OH, MAN.
THEY'RE GONE.
WHERE **ARE** THEY?
HEY!
HEY!
DRAGON!
DRAGON! HELP!

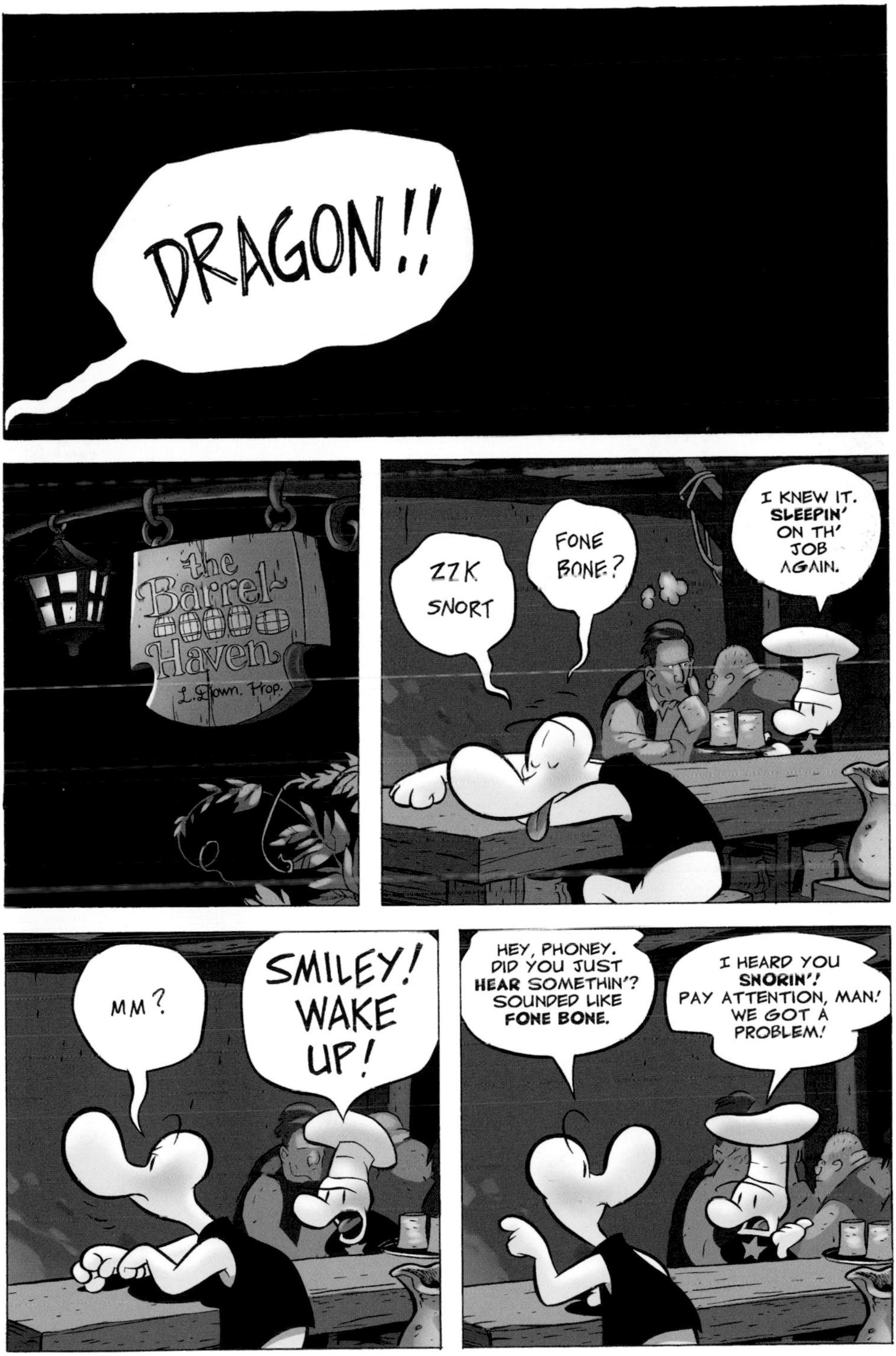
DRAGON!!
the Barrel Haven
L. Down. Prop.
ZZK SNORT
FONE BONE?
I KNEW IT. SLEEPIN' ON TH' JOB AGAIN.
MM?
SMILEY! WAKE UP!
HEY, PHONEY. DID YOU JUST HEAR SOMETHIN'? SOUNDED LIKE FONE BONE.
I HEARD YOU SNORIN'! PAY ATTENTION, MAN! WE GOT A PROBLEM!

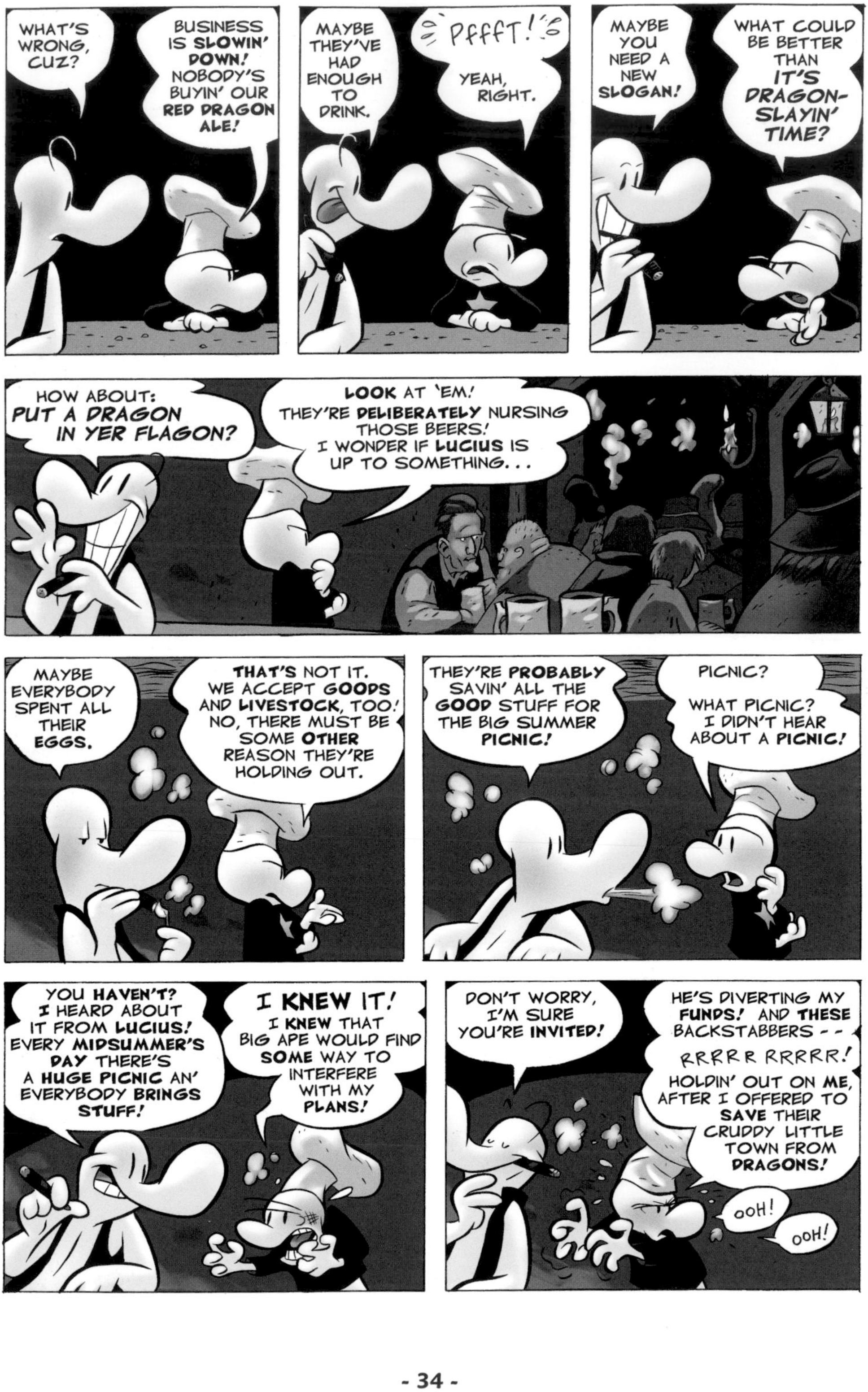
WHAT'S WRONG, CUZ?
BUSINESS IS SLOWIN' DOWN! NOBODY'S BUYIN' OUR RED DRAGON ALE!
MAYBE THEY'VE HAD ENOUGH TO DRINK.
PFFFT!
YEAH, RIGHT.
MAYBE YOU NEED A NEW SLOGAN!
WHAT COULD BE BETTER THAN IT'S DRAGON-SLAYIN' TIME?
HOW ABOUT: PUT A DRAGON IN YER FLAGON?
LOOK AT 'EM! THEY'RE DELIBERATELY NURSING THOSE BEERS! I WONDER IF LUCIUS IS UP TO SOMETHING...
MAYBE EVERYBODY SPENT ALL THEIR EGGS.
THAT'S NOT IT. WE ACCEPT GOODS AND LIVESTOCK, TOO! NO, THERE MUST BE SOME OTHER REASON THEY'RE HOLDING OUT.
THEY'RE PROBABLY SAVIN' ALL THE GOOD STUFF FOR THE BIG SUMMER PICNIC!
PICNIC?
WHAT PICNIC? I DIDN'T HEAR ABOUT A PICNIC!
YOU HAVEN'T? I HEARD ABOUT IT FROM LUCIUS! EVERY MIDSUMMER'S DAY THERE'S A HUGE PICNIC AN' EVERYBODY BRINGS STUFF!
I KNEW IT! I KNEW THAT BIG APE WOULD FIND SOME WAY TO INTERFERE WITH MY PLANS!
DON'T WORRY, I'M SURE YOU'RE INVITED!
HE'S DIVERTING MY FUNDS! AND THESE BACKSTABBERS --
RRRRR RRRRR!
HOLDIN' OUT ON ME, AFTER I OFFERED TO SAVE THEIR CRUDDY LITTLE TOWN FROM DRAGONS!
OOH!
OOH!

IT'S NOT LIKE YOU'RE ACTUALLY **DOIN'** ANYTHING ABOUT THE DRAGONS! MAYBE THEY'RE WAITIN' TO SEE IF YOU'RE REALLY GONNA **SLAY** ONE!

SLAY ONE?! DON'T BE RIDICULOUS! **YOU** KNOW THE ONLY DRAGON OUT THERE IS PEACEFUL!

HEY! THERE IT IS AGAIN! DID YOU HEAR THAT?

HUH?!

I DIDN'T HEAR ANYTHING!

IT'S FONE BONE! HE'S YELLIN' FOR **HELP!**

WHAT?

I HEARD IT, TOO!

HE'S YELLIN' SOMETHIN' ABOUT A **DRAGON!**

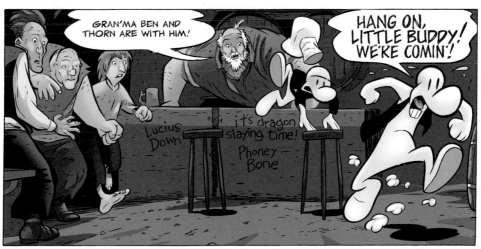

GRAN'MA BEN AND THORN ARE WITH HIM!

HANG ON, LITTLE BUDDY! WE'RE COMIN'!

Lucius Down

it's dragon slaying time!

Phoney Bone

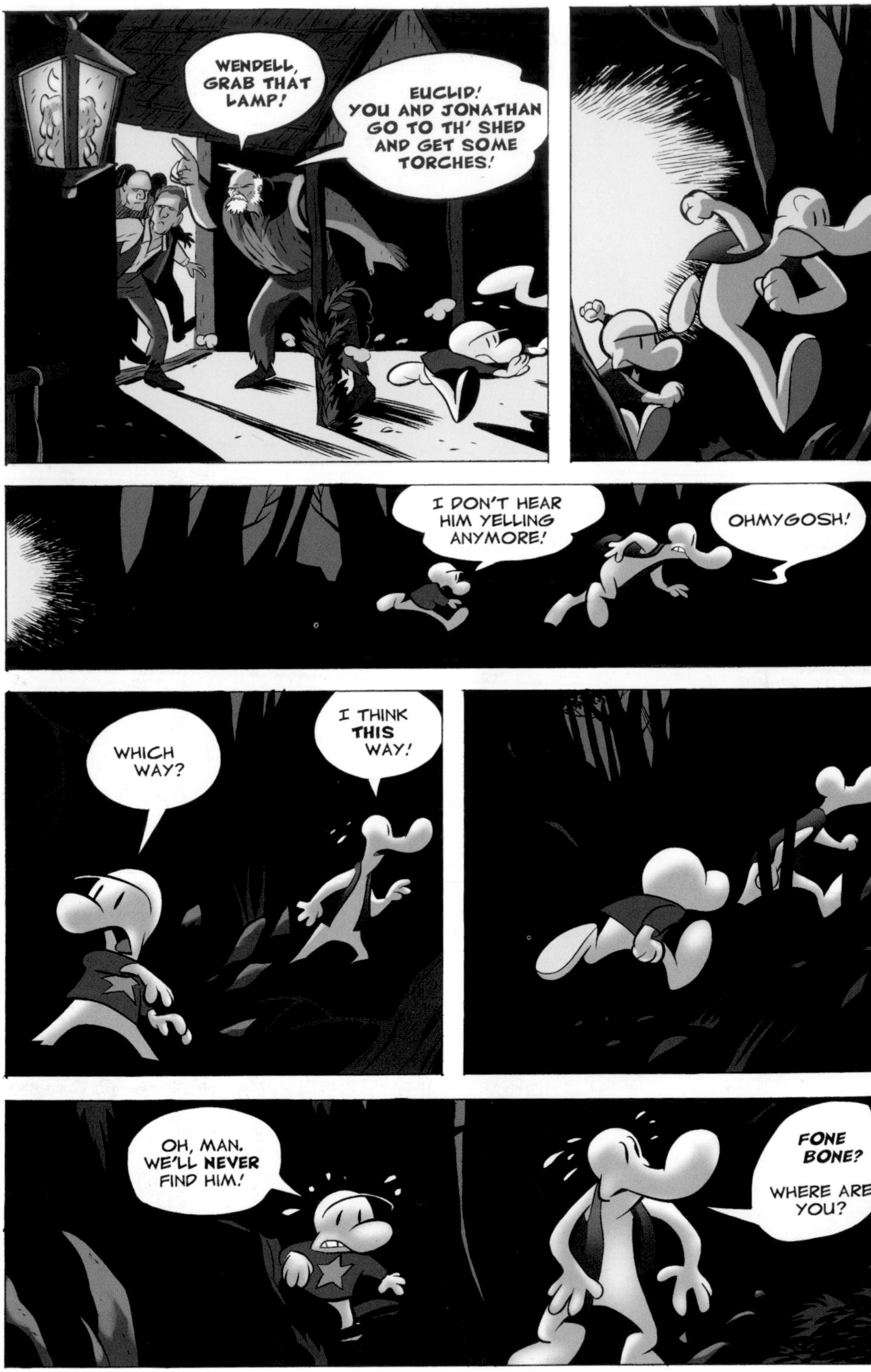
WENDELL, GRAB THAT LAMP!
EUCLID! YOU AND JONATHAN GO TO TH' SHED AND GET SOME TORCHES!
I DON'T HEAR HIM YELLING ANYMORE!
OHMYGOSH!
WHICH WAY?
I THINK THIS WAY!
OH, MAN. WE'LL NEVER FIND HIM!
FONE BONE?
WHERE ARE YOU?

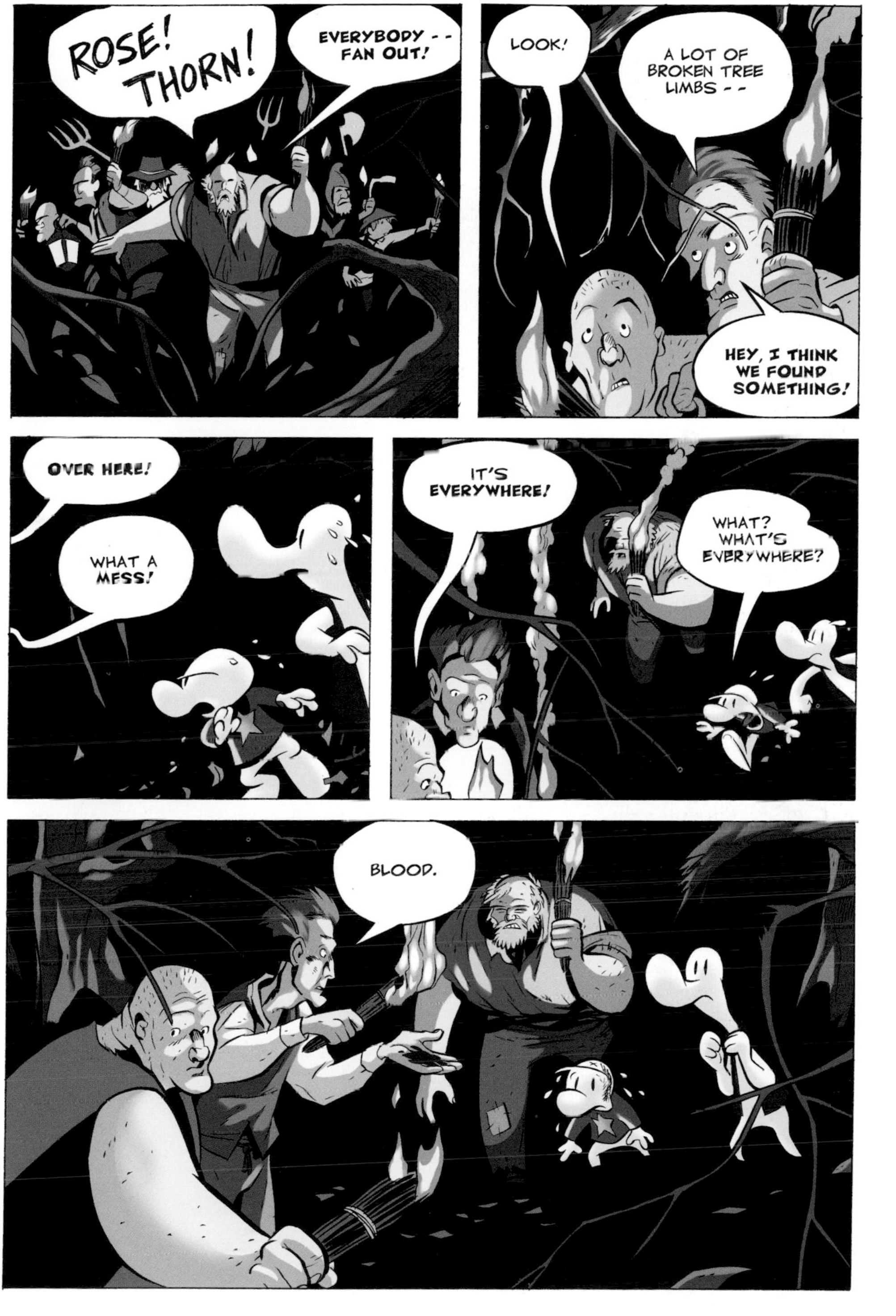
ROSE! THORN!
EVERYBODY -- FAN OUT!
LOOK!
A LOT OF BROKEN TREE LIMBS --
HEY, I THINK WE FOUND SOMETHING!
OVER HERE!
WHAT A MESS!
IT'S EVERYWHERE!
WHAT? WHAT'S EVERYWHERE?
BLOOD.

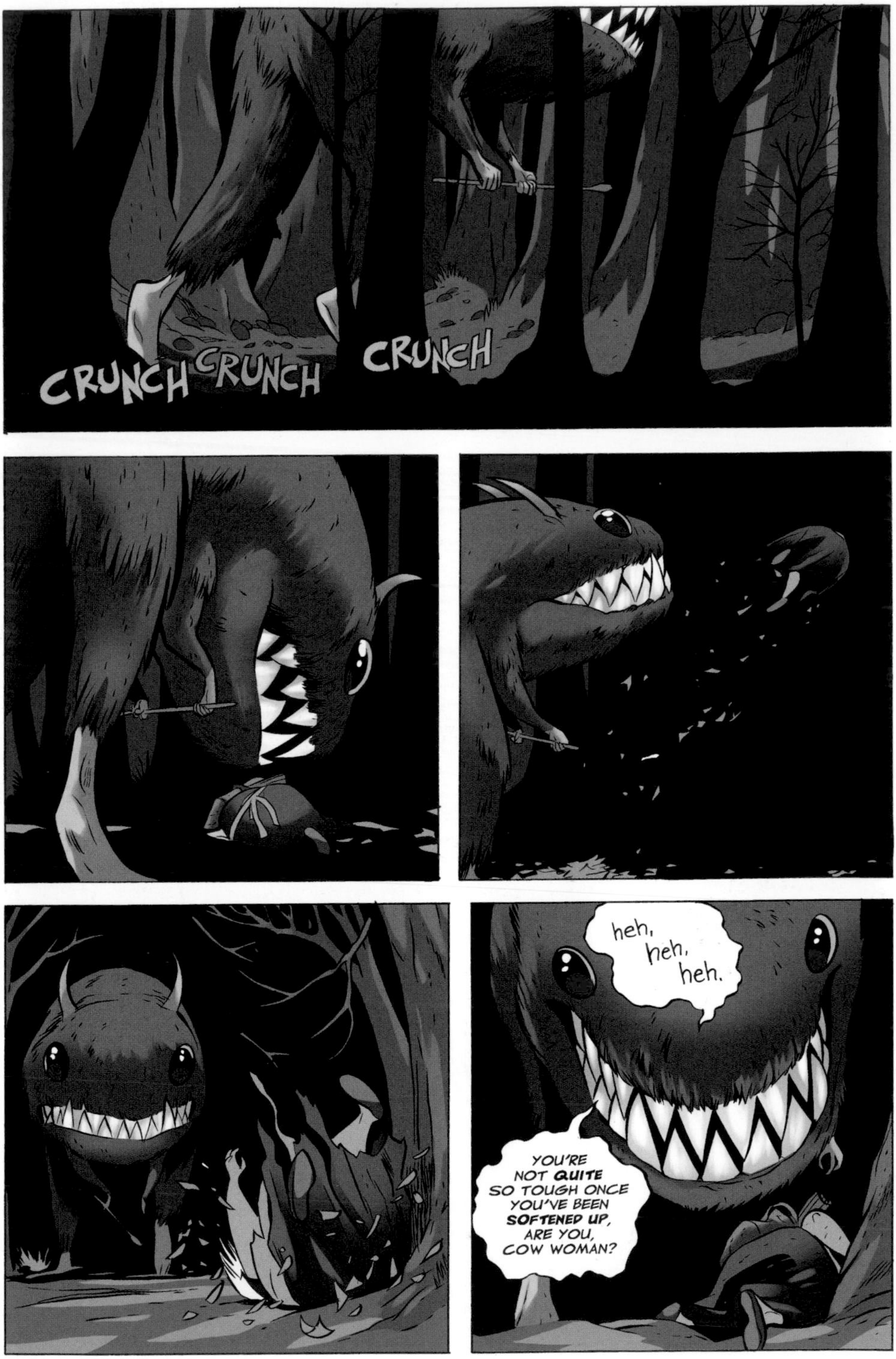
CRUNCH CRUNCH CRUNCH
heh, heh, heh.
YOU'RE NOT QUITE SO TOUGH ONCE YOU'VE BEEN SOFTENED UP, ARE YOU, COW WOMAN?

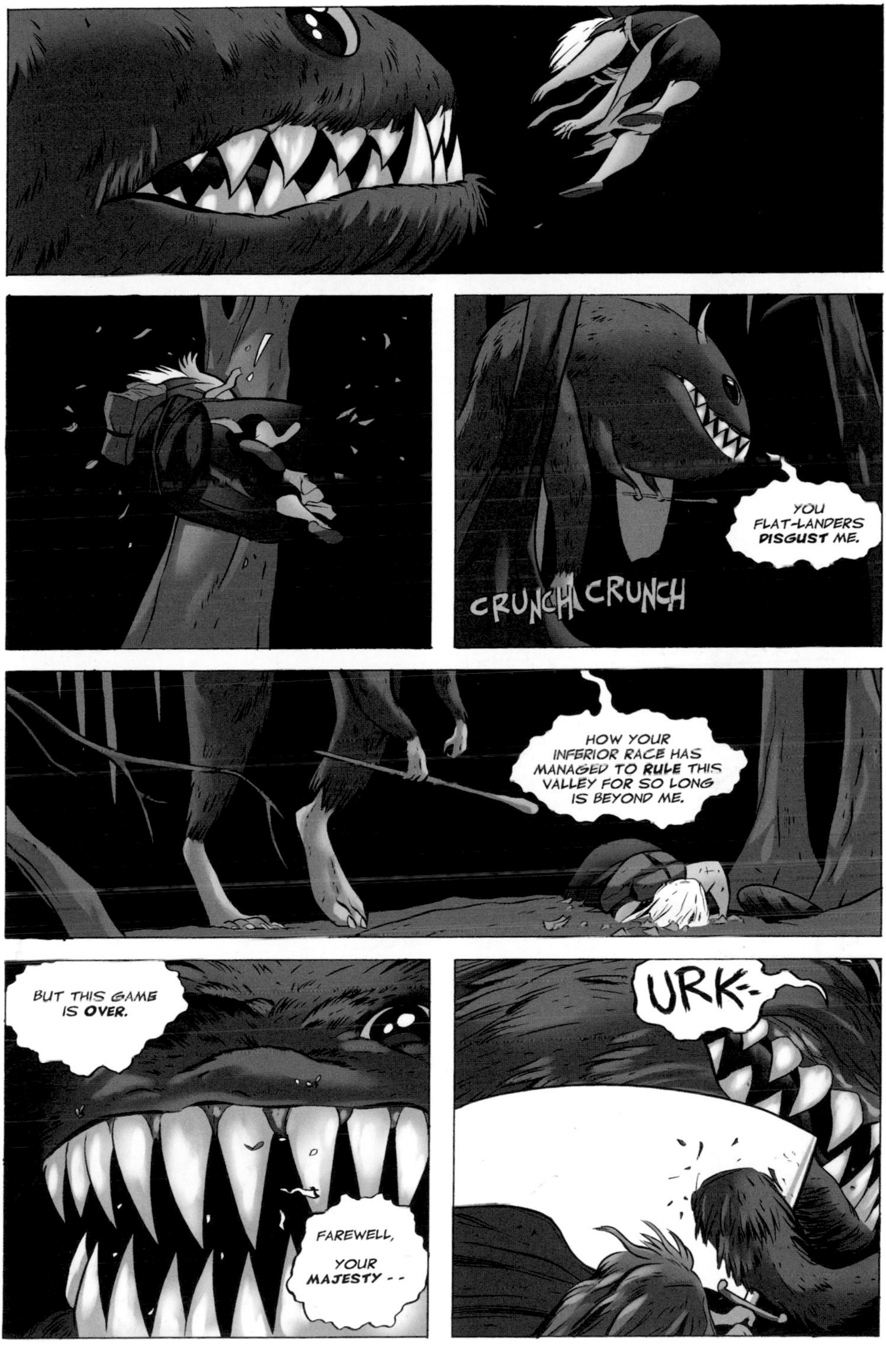
YOU FLAT-LANDERS DISGUST ME.
CRUNCH CRUNCH
HOW YOUR INFERIOR RACE HAS MANAGED TO RULE THIS VALLEY FOR SO LONG IS BEYOND ME.
BUT THIS GAME IS OVER.
FAREWELL, YOUR MAJESTY --
URK--

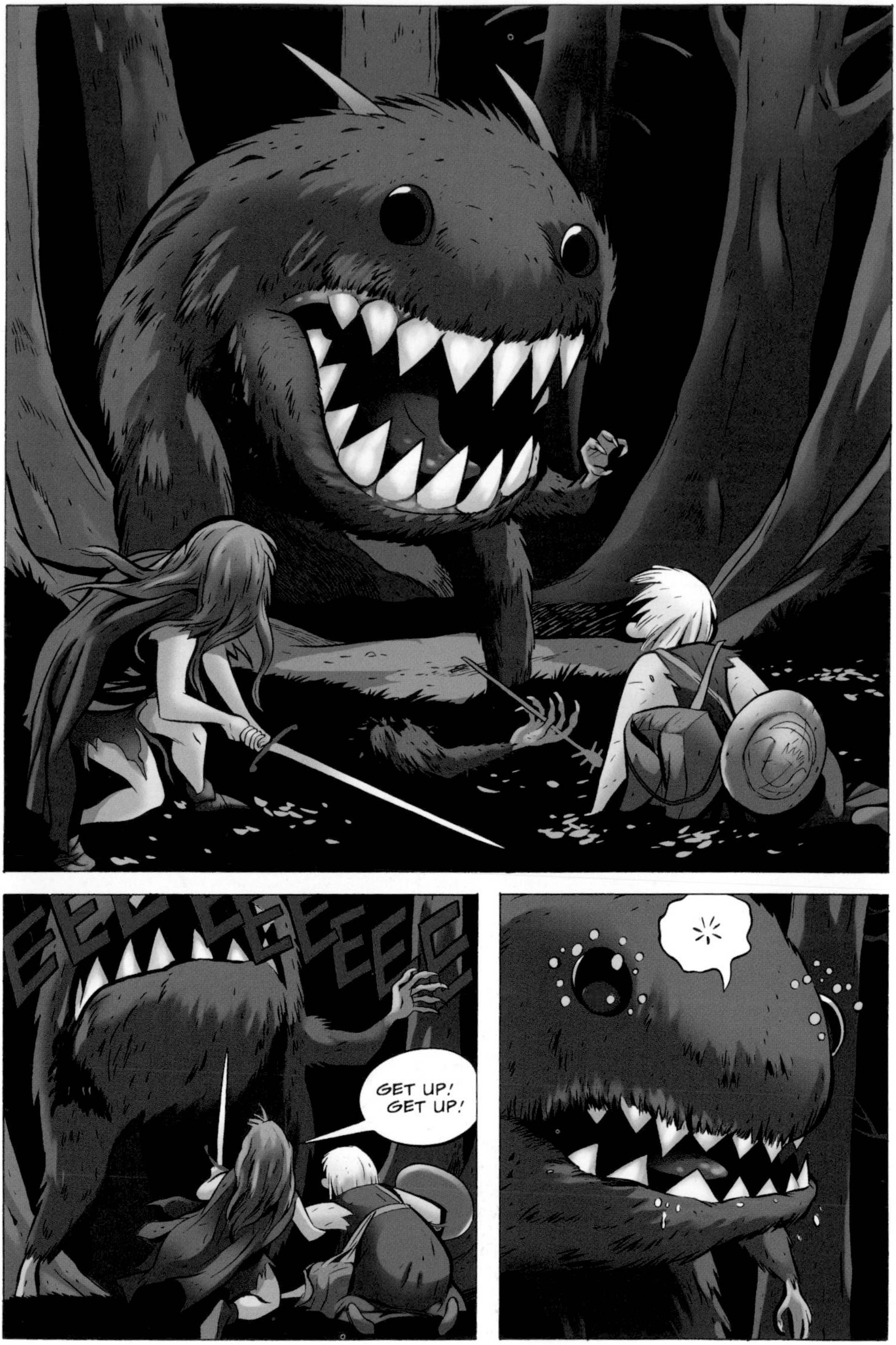
EEEEEEEEEEEE
GET UP! GET UP!
!

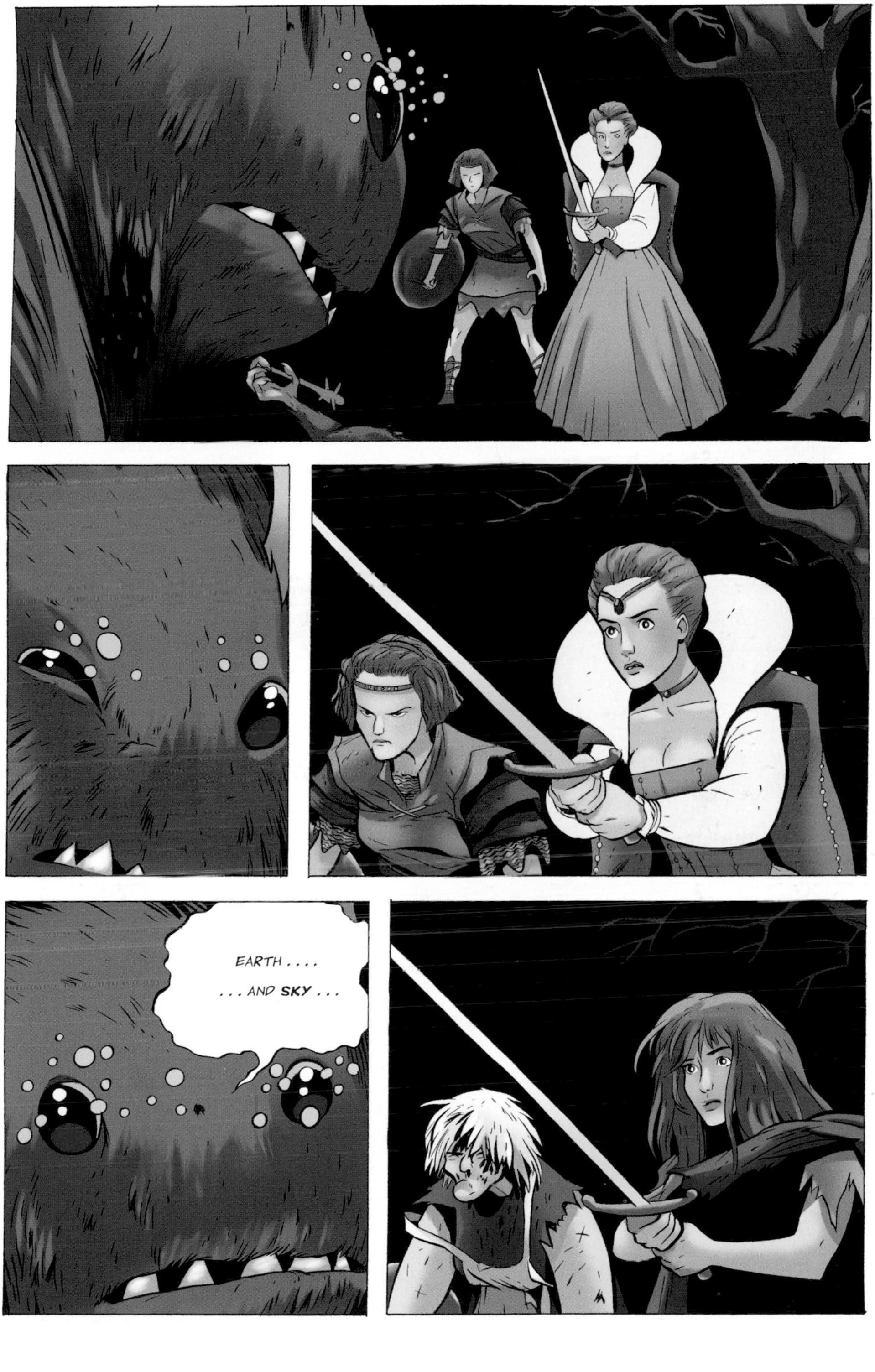
EARTH . . . .
. . . AND SKY . . .

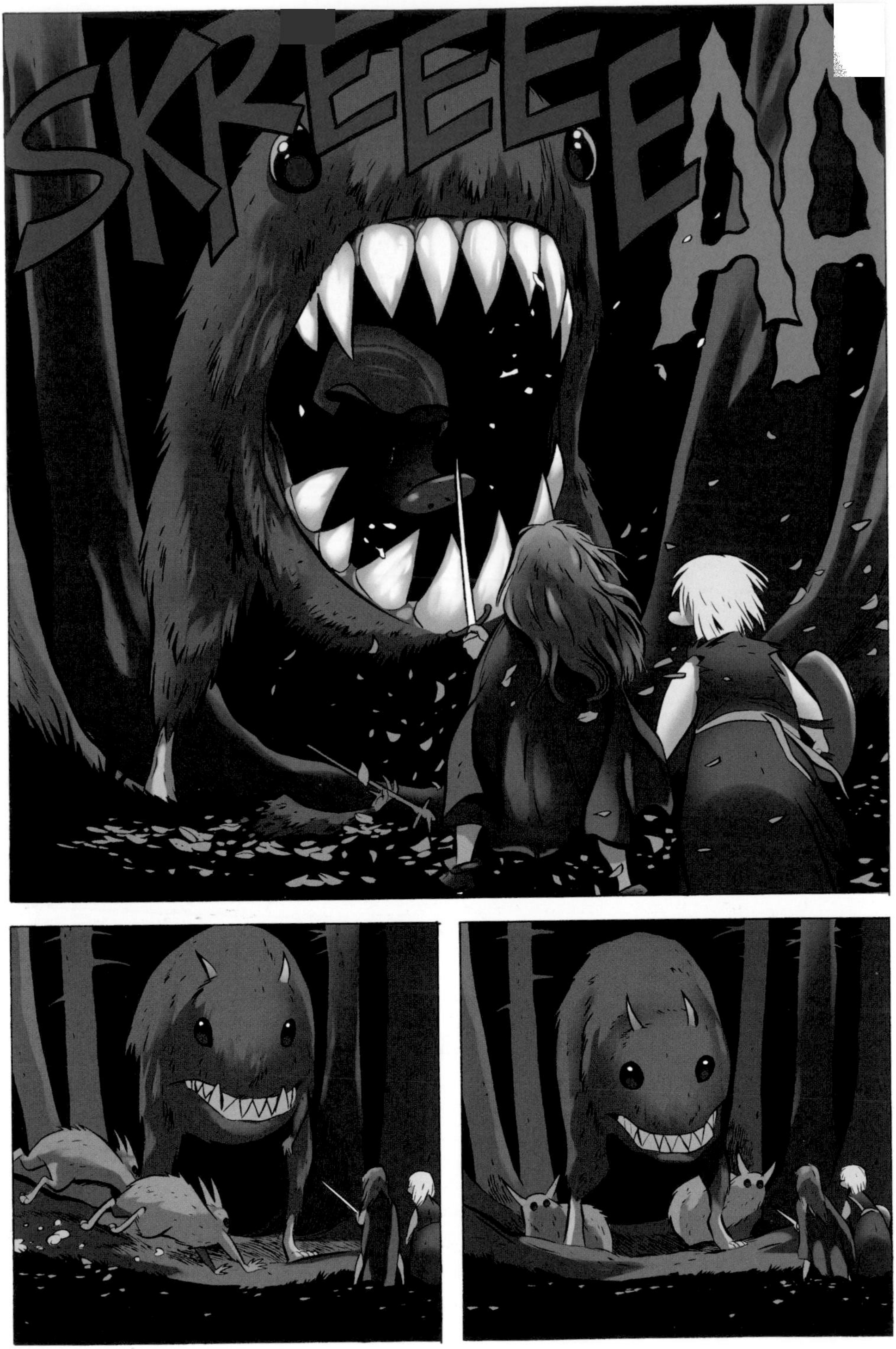
SKREEEEAH

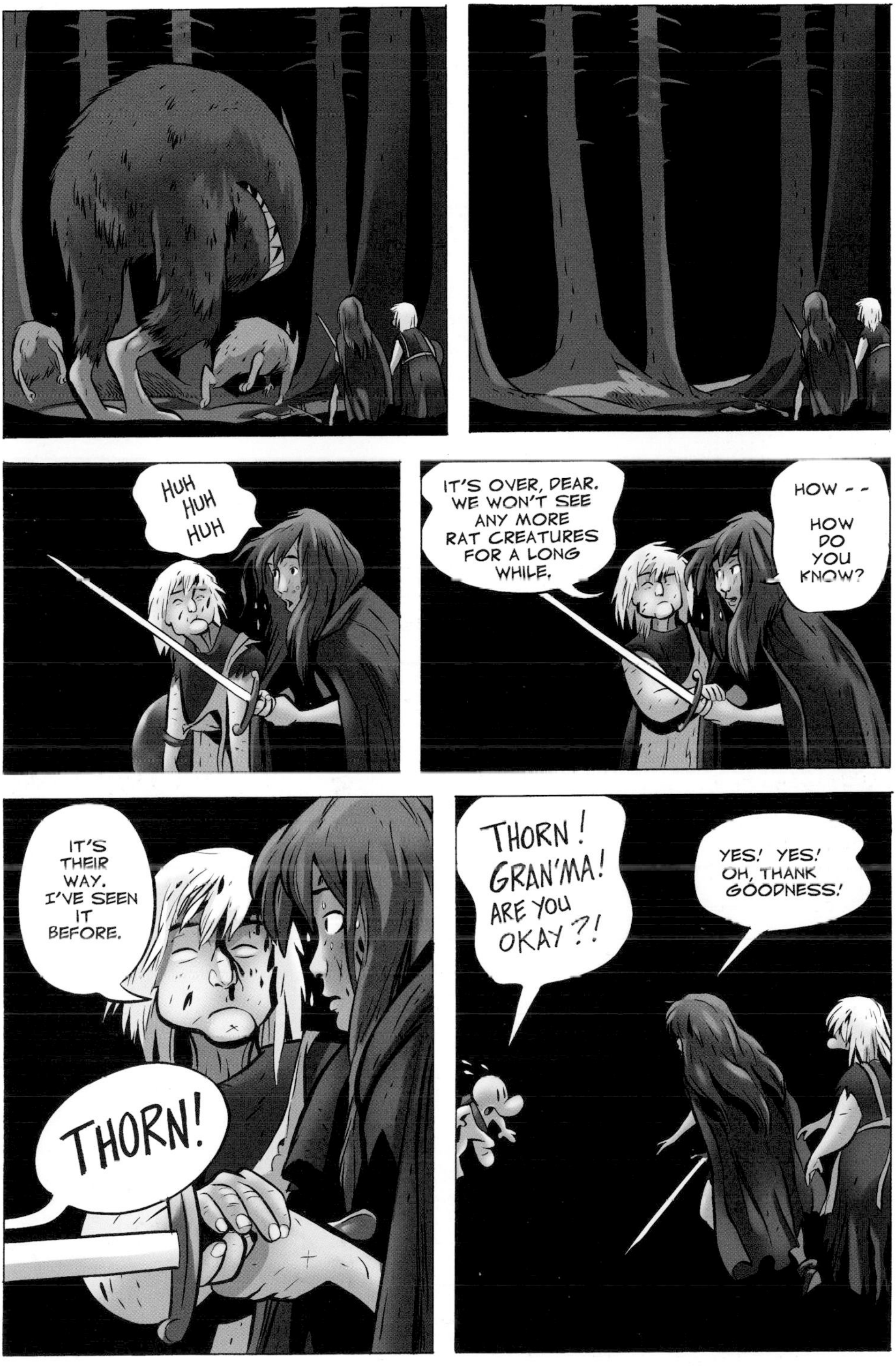
HUH
HUH
HUH
IT'S OVER, DEAR. WE WON'T SEE ANY MORE RAT CREATURES FOR A LONG WHILE.
HOW - -
HOW DO YOU KNOW?
IT'S THEIR WAY. I'VE SEEN IT BEFORE.
THORN!
THORN! GRAN'MA! ARE YOU OKAY?!
YES! YES! OH, THANK GOODNESS!

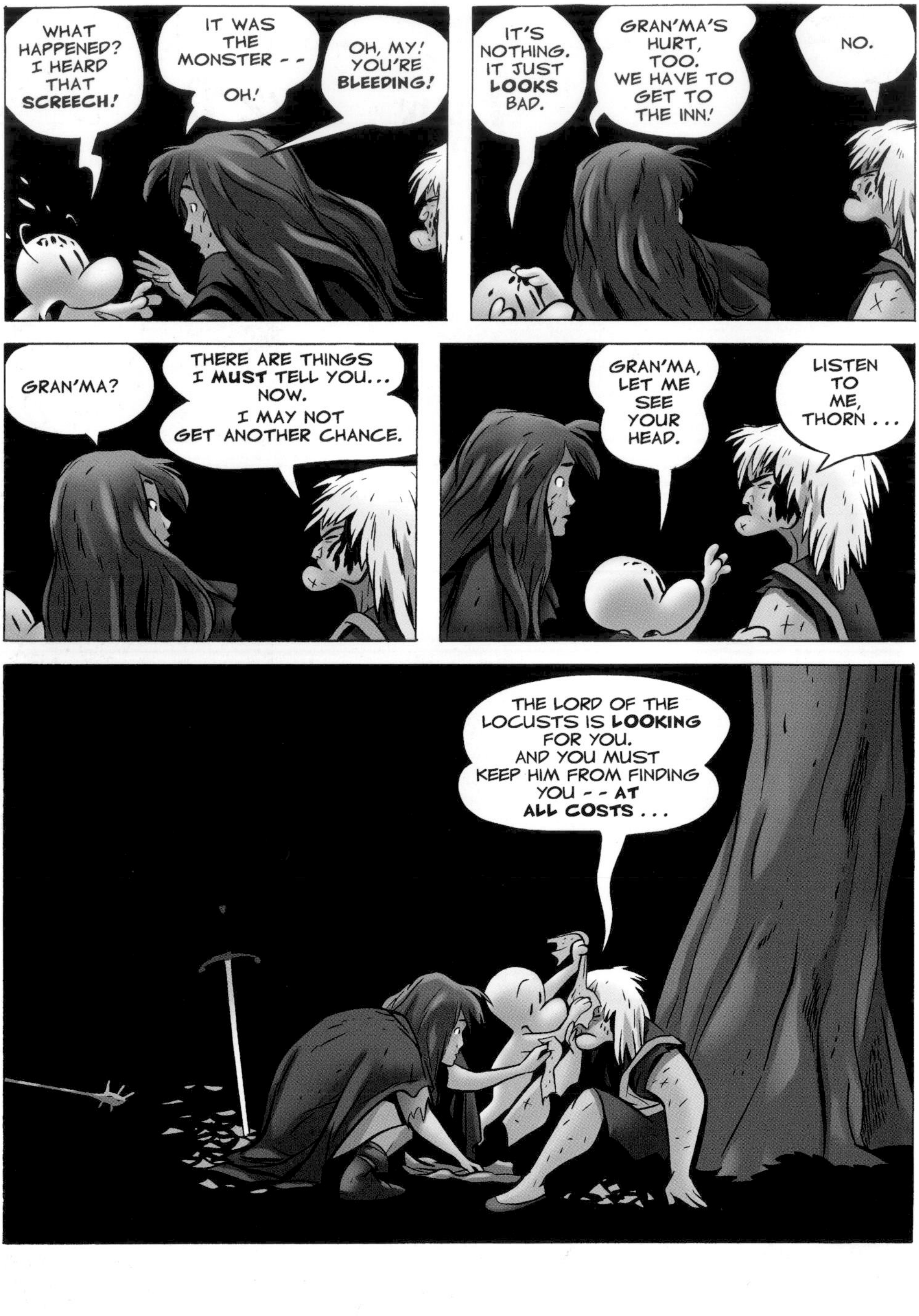
WHAT HAPPENED? I HEARD THAT SCREECH!
IT WAS THE MONSTER - - OH!
OH, MY! YOU'RE BLEEDING!
IT'S NOTHING. IT JUST LOOKS BAD.
GRAN'MA'S HURT, TOO. WE HAVE TO GET TO THE INN!
NO.
GRAN'MA?
THERE ARE THINGS I MUST TELL YOU... NOW. I MAY NOT GET ANOTHER CHANCE.
GRAN'MA, LET ME SEE YOUR HEAD.
LISTEN TO ME, THORN...
THE LORD OF THE LOCUSTS IS LOOKING FOR YOU. AND YOU MUST KEEP HIM FROM FINDING YOU - - AT ALL COSTS...

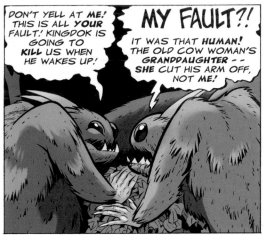

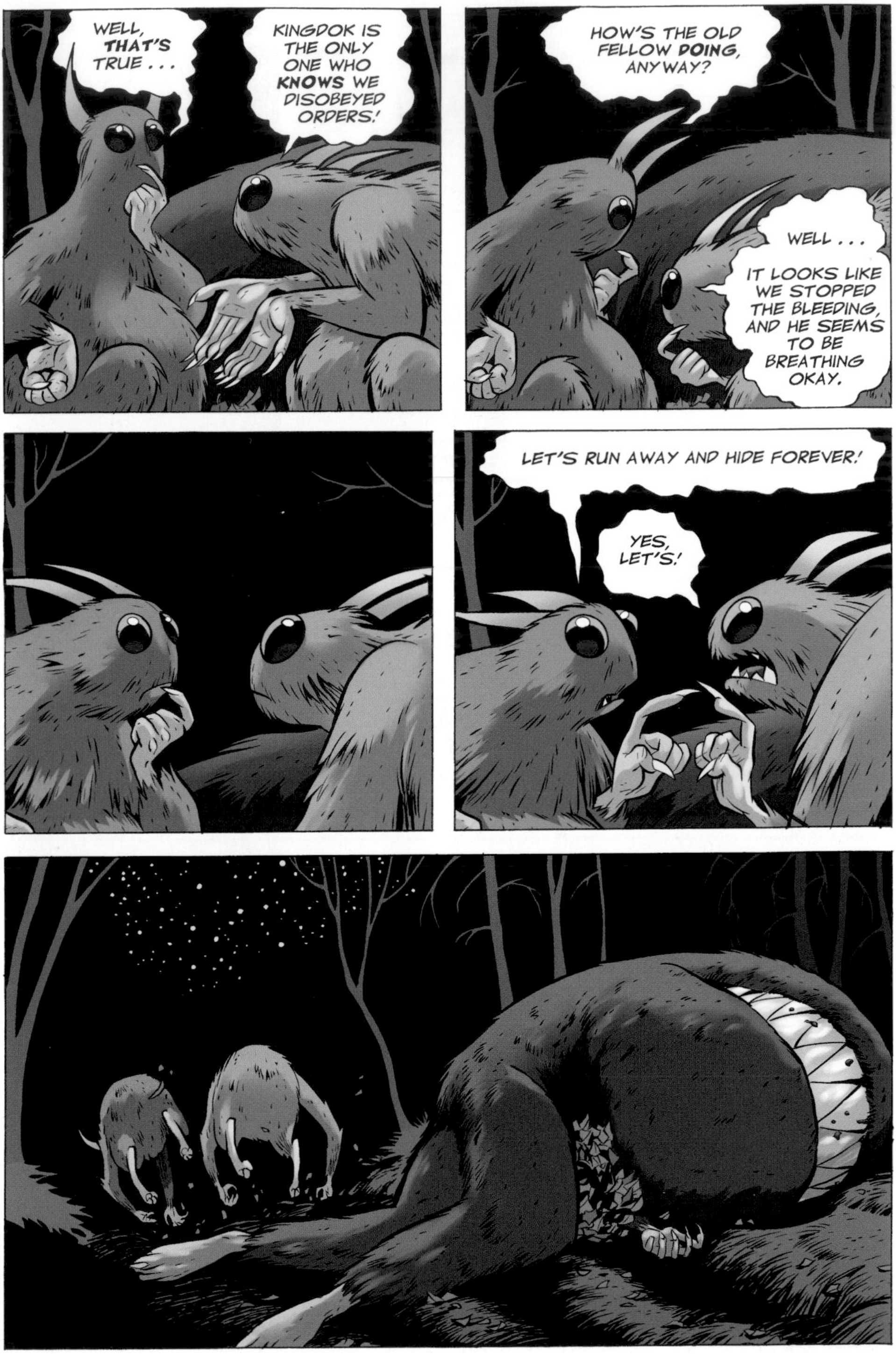
WELL, **THAT'S** TRUE . . .
KINGDOK IS THE ONLY ONE WHO **KNOWS** WE DISOBEYED ORDERS!
HOW'S THE OLD FELLOW **DOING**, ANYWAY?
WELL . . .
IT LOOKS LIKE WE STOPPED THE BLEEDING, AND HE SEEMS TO BE BREATHING OKAY.
LET'S RUN AWAY AND HIDE FOREVER!
YES, LET'S!

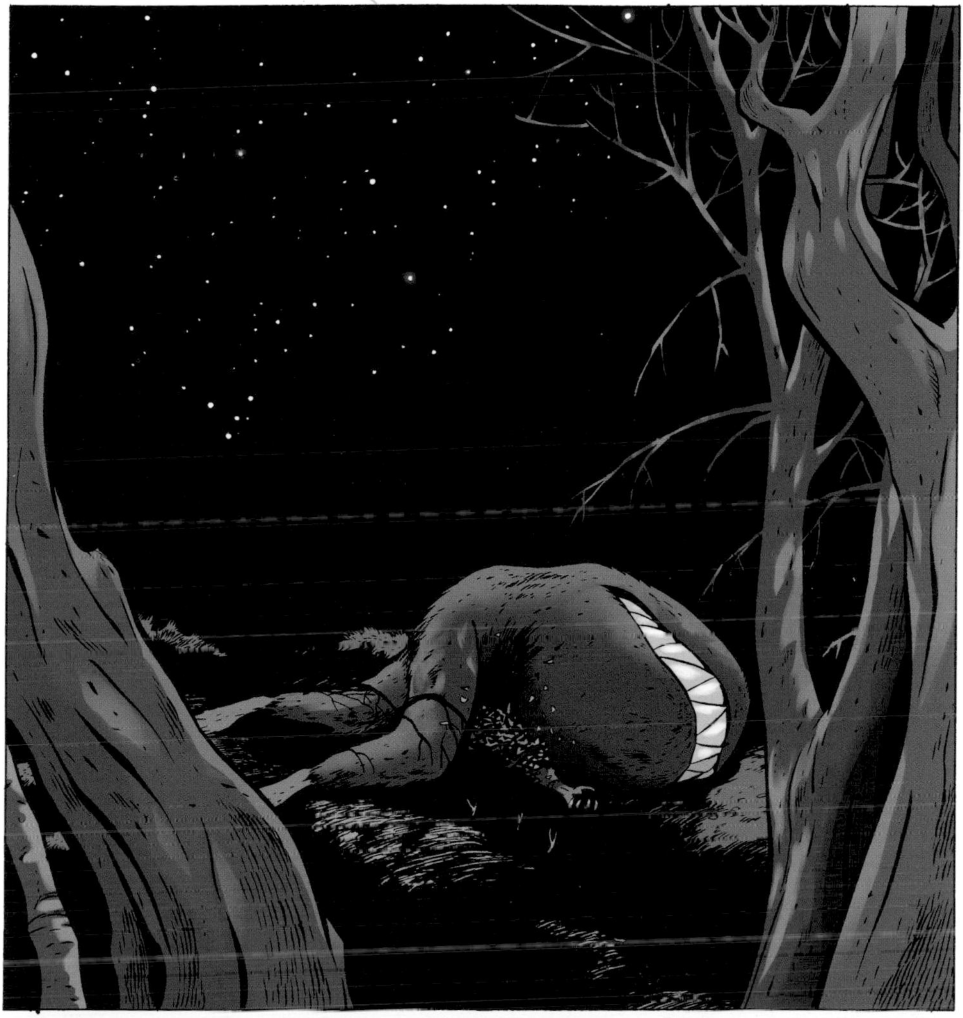

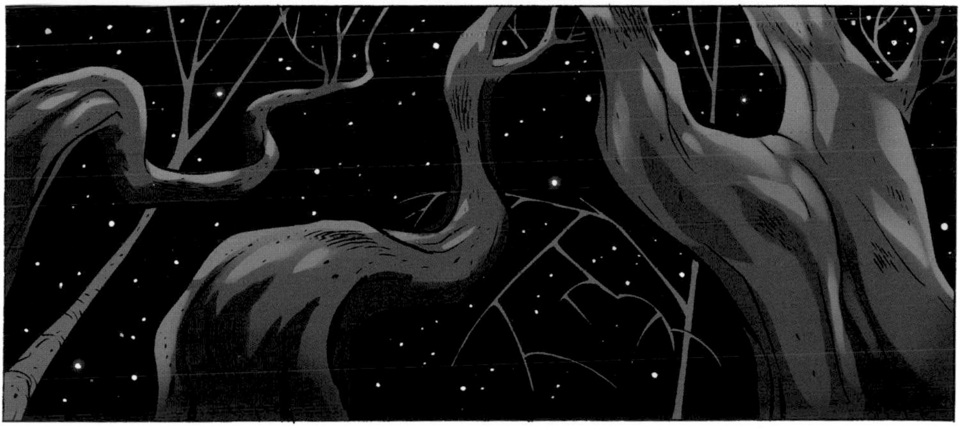

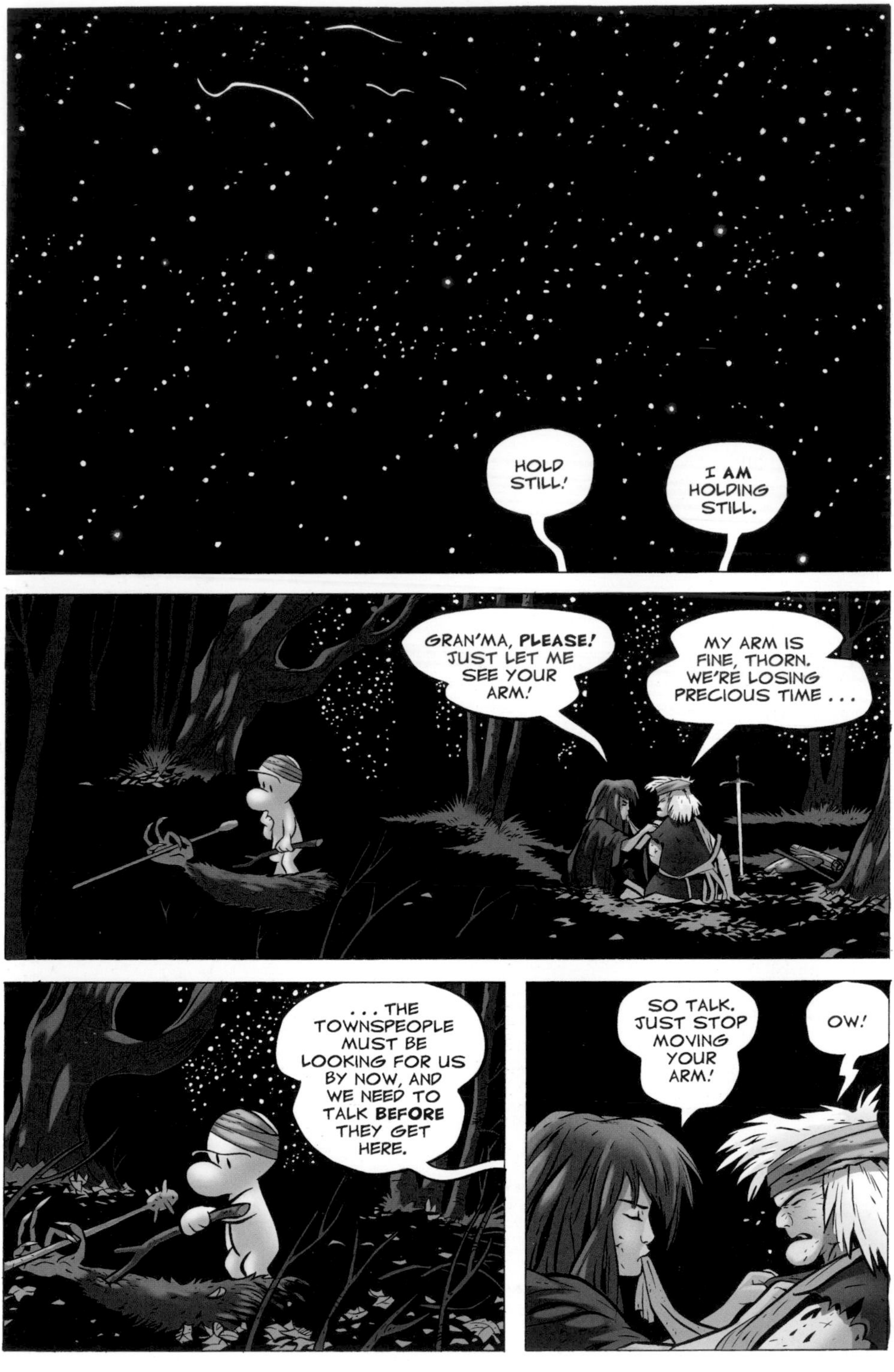
HOLD STILL!
I **AM** HOLDING STILL.
GRAN'MA, **PLEASE!** JUST LET ME SEE YOUR ARM!
MY ARM IS FINE, THORN. WE'RE LOSING PRECIOUS TIME . . .
. . . THE TOWNSPEOPLE MUST BE LOOKING FOR US BY NOW, AND WE NEED TO TALK **BEFORE** THEY GET HERE.
SO TALK. JUST STOP MOVING YOUR ARM!
OW!

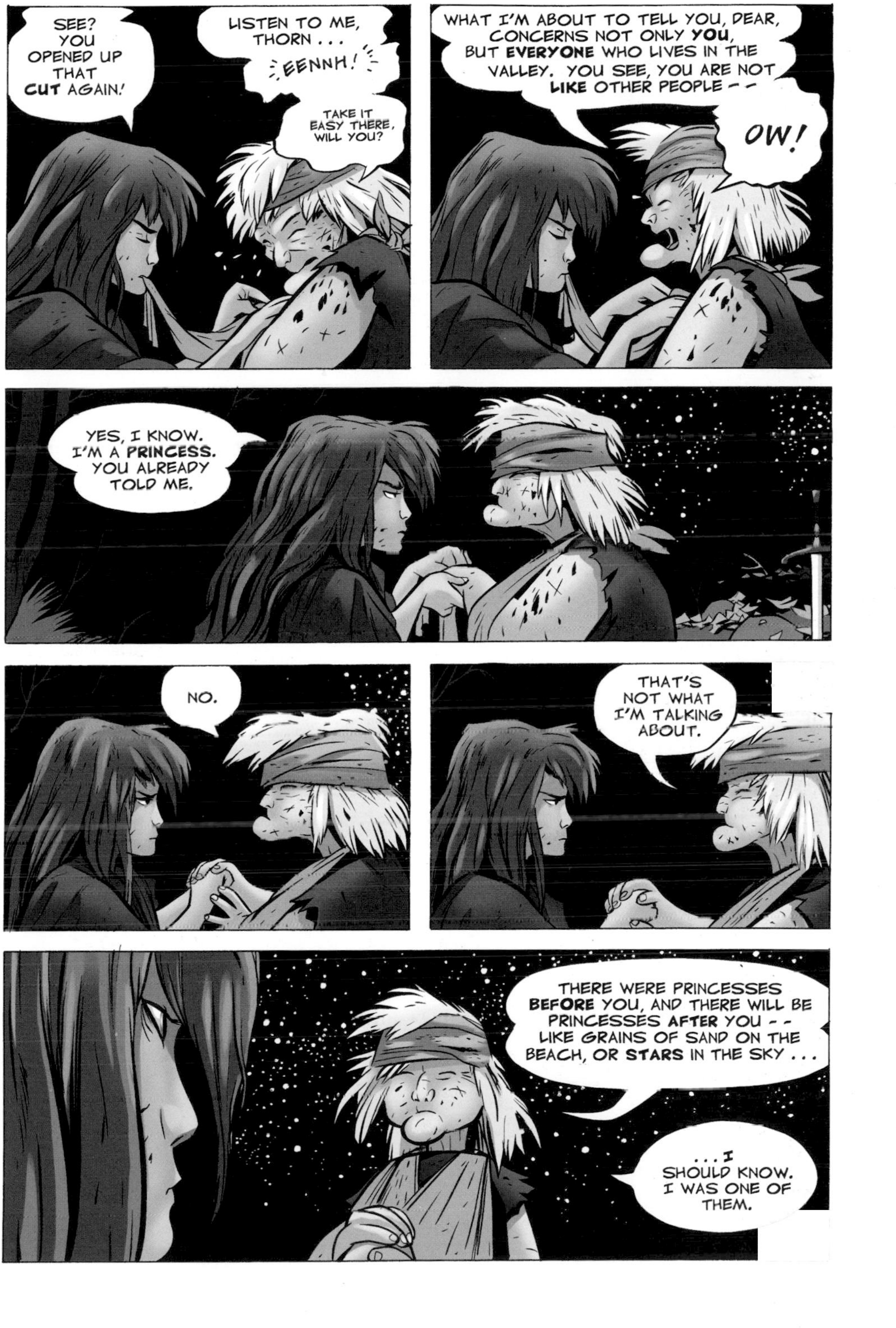
SEE? YOU OPENED UP THAT CUT AGAIN!
LISTEN TO ME, THORN . . .
EENNH!
TAKE IT EASY THERE, WILL YOU?
WHAT I'M ABOUT TO TELL YOU, DEAR, CONCERNS NOT ONLY YOU, BUT EVERYONE WHO LIVES IN THE VALLEY. YOU SEE, YOU ARE NOT LIKE OTHER PEOPLE - -
OW!
YES, I KNOW. I'M A PRINCESS. YOU ALREADY TOLD ME.
NO.
THAT'S NOT WHAT I'M TALKING ABOUT.
THERE WERE PRINCESSES BEFORE YOU, AND THERE WILL BE PRINCESSES AFTER YOU - - LIKE GRAINS OF SAND ON THE BEACH, OR STARS IN THE SKY . . .
. . . I SHOULD KNOW. I WAS ONE OF THEM.

BUT YOU WERE HIDDEN AS A CHILD BECAUSE YOU ARE A **VENI-YAN-CARI.** AN **AWAKENED ONE!** AND YOU HAVE A **TERRIBLE** PATH BEFORE YOU.

GRAN'MA?

AN AWAKENED ONE CAN WALK FREELY BETWEEN THE **WAKING WORLD** AND THE **DREAMING WORLD!** AGENTS OF THE **LOCUST** WILL BE SEARCHING FOR YOU.

WHOA! GRAN'MA! WHAT ARE YOU **TALKING** ABOUT?

THEY'LL HAVE TO GO THROUGH **ME** FIRST!

hmm.

I DON'T THINK THEY'LL EVEN NOTICE YOU, BONE . . . AGENTS OF THE LOCUST WILL STOP AT **NOTHING** TO FREE THEIR MASTER.

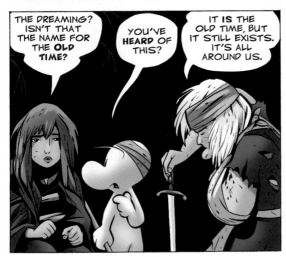

THE DREAMING? ISN'T THAT THE NAME FOR THE **OLD TIME?**

YOU'VE **HEARD** OF THIS?

IT **IS** THE OLD TIME, BUT IT STILL EXISTS. IT'S ALL AROUND US.

IT'S A FORGOTTEN **HUM** THAT ALL THE ANIMALS AND ALL THE TREES ARE STILL LISTENING TO. IT'S JUST **US** WHO CAN'T HEAR IT ANYMORE.

MOST OF US, ANYWAY.

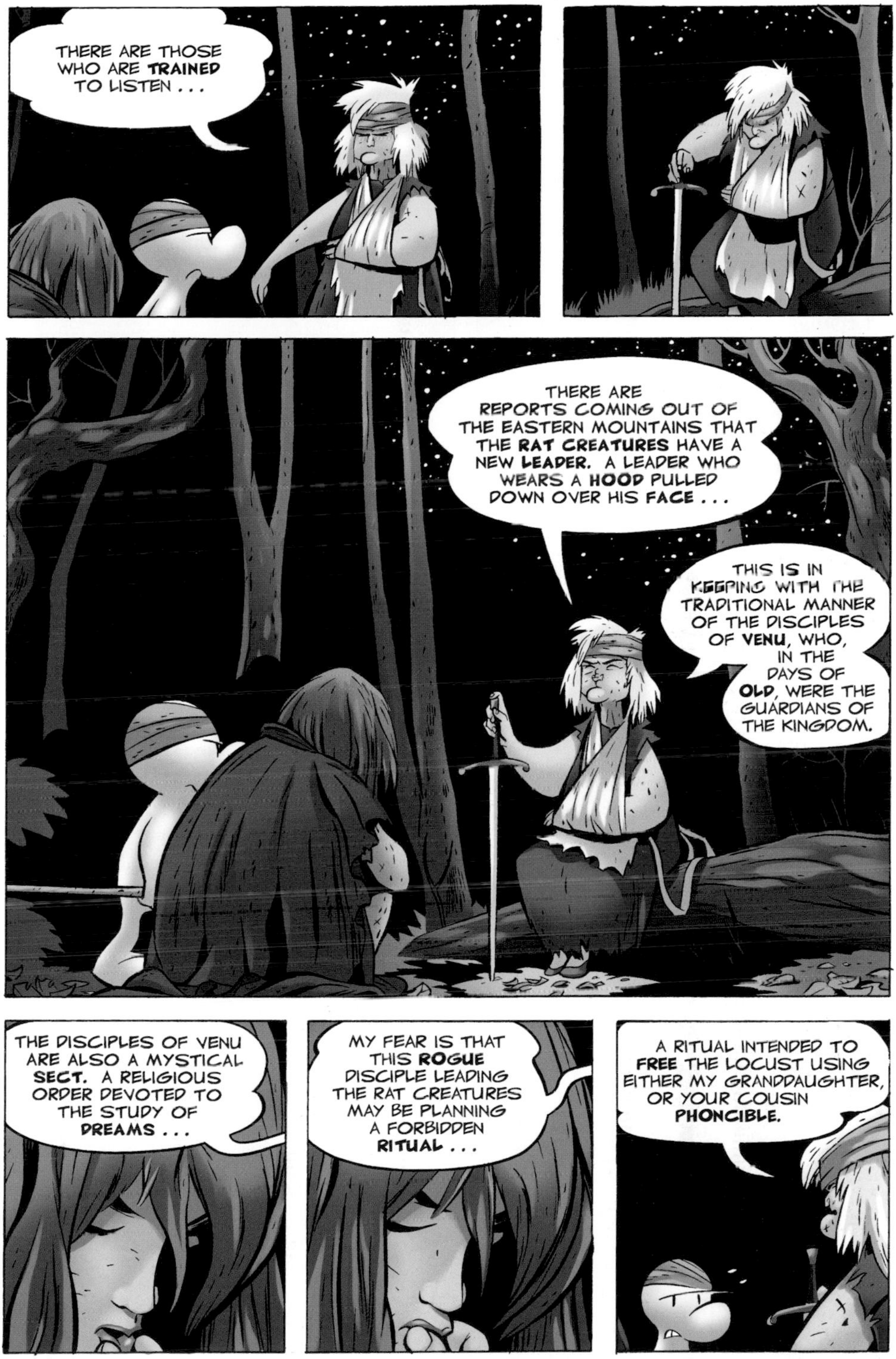
THERE ARE THOSE WHO ARE TRAINED TO LISTEN . . .
THERE ARE REPORTS COMING OUT OF THE EASTERN MOUNTAINS THAT THE RAT CREATURES HAVE A NEW LEADER. A LEADER WHO WEARS A HOOD PULLED DOWN OVER HIS FACE . . .
THIS IS IN KEEPING WITH THE TRADITIONAL MANNER OF THE DISCIPLES OF VENU, WHO, IN THE DAYS OF OLD, WERE THE GUARDIANS OF THE KINGDOM.
THE DISCIPLES OF VENU ARE ALSO A MYSTICAL SECT. A RELIGIOUS ORDER DEVOTED TO THE STUDY OF DREAMS . . .
MY FEAR IS THAT THIS ROGUE DISCIPLE LEADING THE RAT CREATURES MAY BE PLANNING A FORBIDDEN RITUAL . . .
A RITUAL INTENDED TO FREE THE LOCUST USING EITHER MY GRANDDAUGHTER, OR YOUR COUSIN PHONCIBLE.

THAT'S WHY WE'RE TAKING THORN TO THE ANCIENT CITY OF ATHEIA, WHERE SHE'LL BE **SAFE.**

I'M NOT GOING TO ATHEIA.

I'M NOT GOING **ANYWHERE** WITH **YOU.** YOU'RE CRAZY!

DEAR, YOU'RE **UPSET** -- LISTEN TO ME -

LISTEN TO YOU? **WHY?** EVERYTHING YOU EVER **TOLD** ME WAS A **LIE!**

NO, DEAR! **LISTEN!** WHAT I'M TELLING YOU IS **TRUE!**

THIS IS SUDDENLY THE **TRUTH?!** MY PARENTS ARE DEAD, AND I'M A **PRINCESS** WITH **MAGIC POWERS?!!**

WHAT DOES THAT MAKE ME?!

A FAIRY PRINCESS?

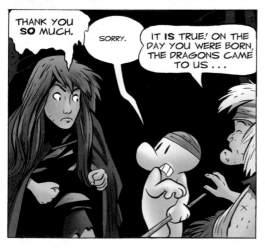

THANK YOU **SO** MUCH.

SORRY.

IT **IS** TRUE! ON THE DAY YOU WERE BORN, THE DRAGONS CAME TO US . . .

THEY TOLD US THEY COULD SEE YOUR DREAMS ON THE HORIZON LIKE A **PILLAR OF FIRE.**

LET GO!

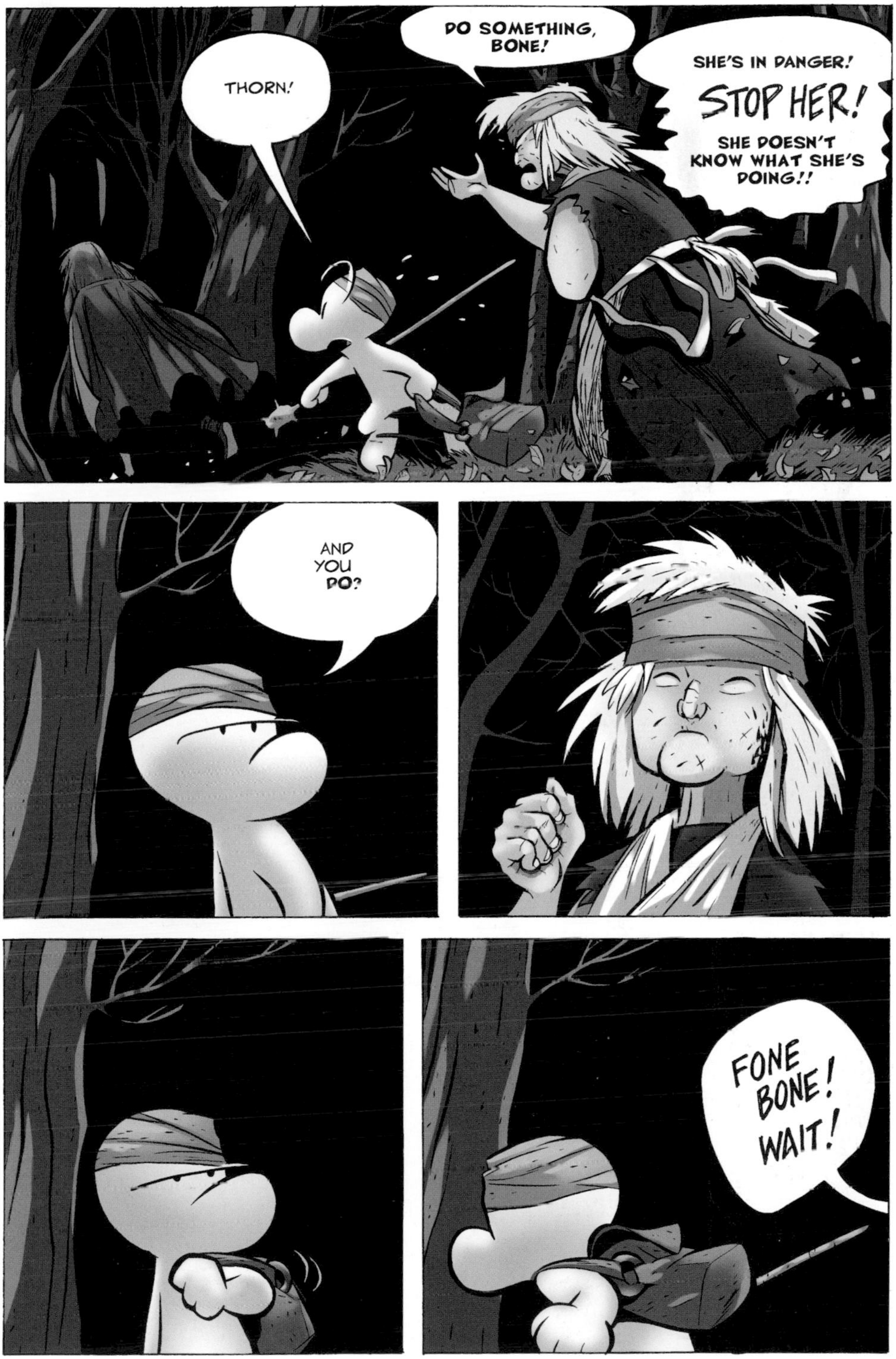
THORN!
DO SOMETHING, BONE!
SHE'S IN DANGER!
STOP HER!
SHE DOESN'T KNOW WHAT SHE'S DOING!!
AND YOU DO?
FONE BONE! WAIT!

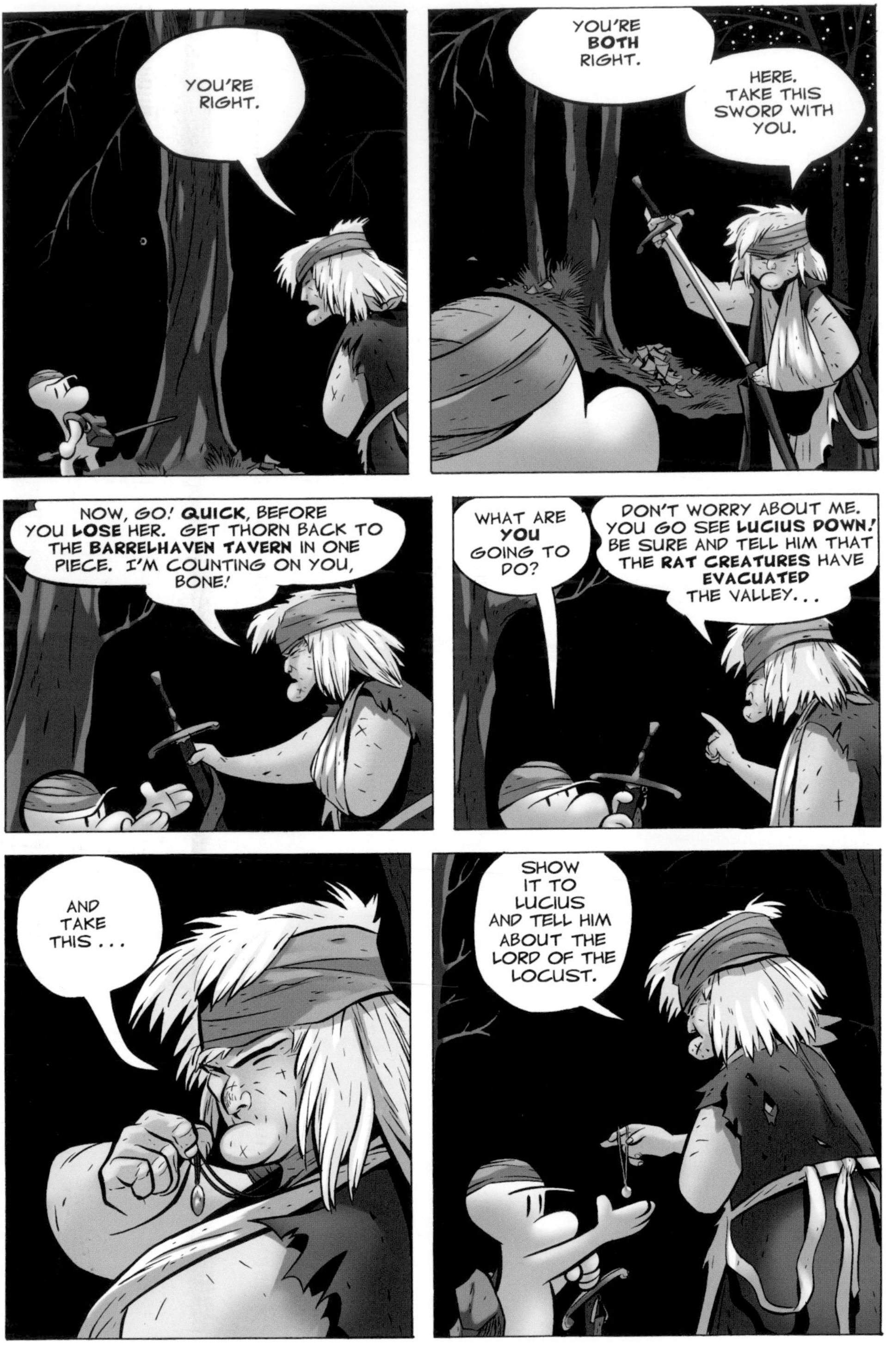
YOU'RE RIGHT.
YOU'RE BOTH RIGHT.
HERE. TAKE THIS SWORD WITH YOU.
NOW, GO! QUICK, BEFORE YOU LOSE HER. GET THORN BACK TO THE BARRELHAVEN TAVERN IN ONE PIECE. I'M COUNTING ON YOU, BONE!
WHAT ARE YOU GOING TO DO?
DON'T WORRY ABOUT ME. YOU GO SEE LUCIUS DOWN! BE SURE AND TELL HIM THAT THE RAT CREATURES HAVE EVACUATED THE VALLEY...
AND TAKE THIS...
SHOW IT TO LUCIUS AND TELL HIM ABOUT THE LORD OF THE LOCUST.

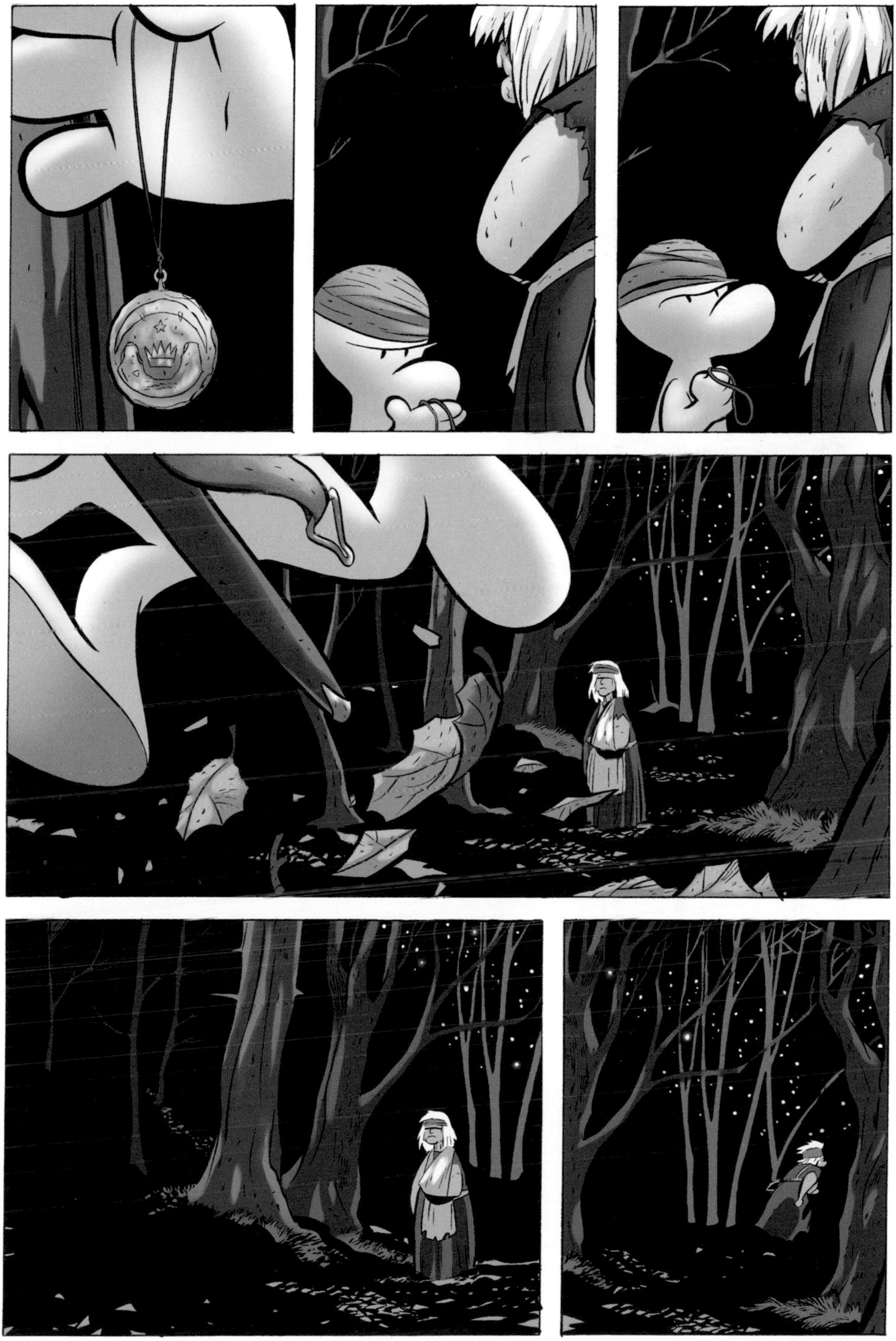

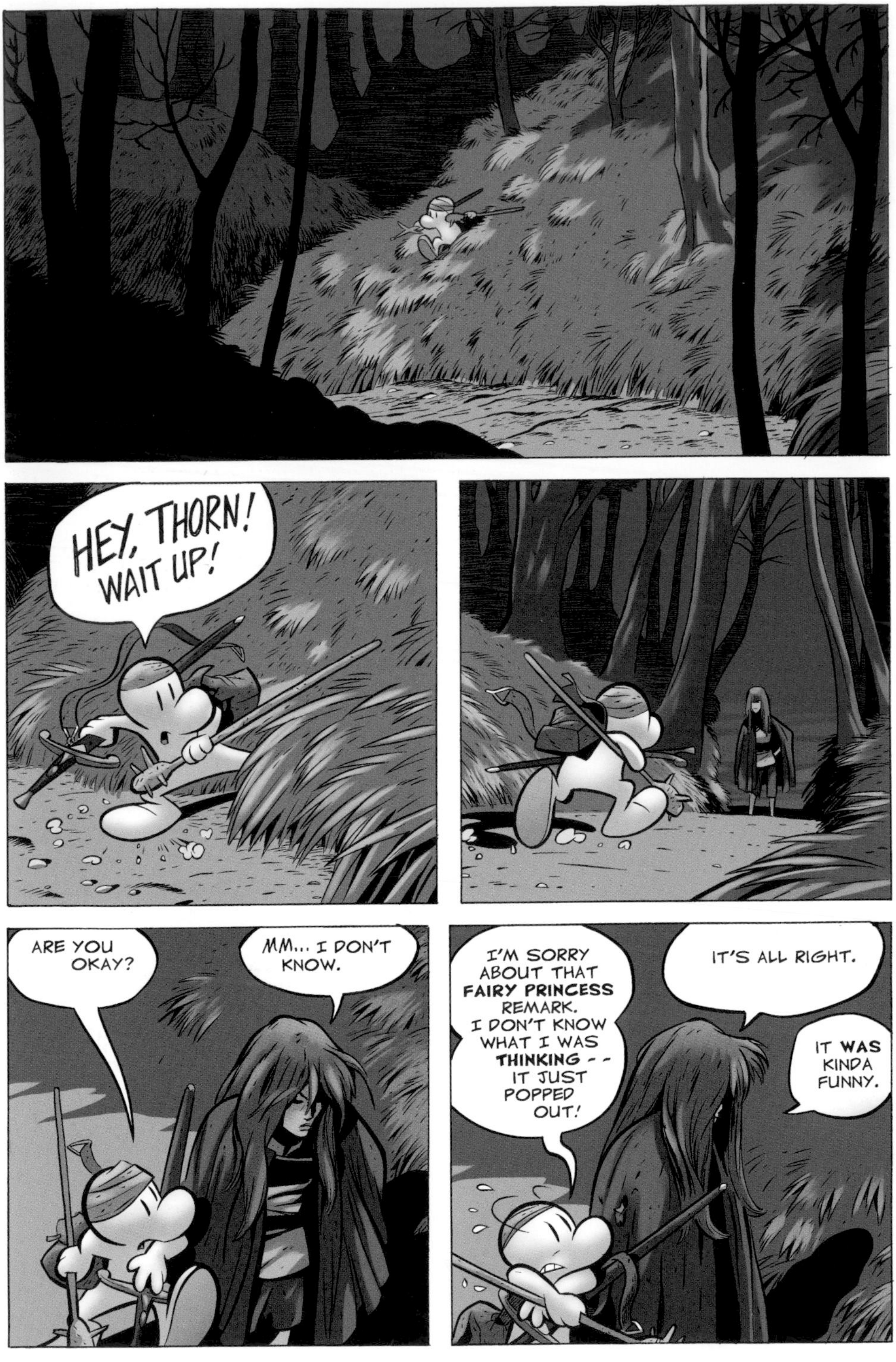
HEY, THORN! WAIT UP!
ARE YOU OKAY?
MM... I DON'T KNOW.
I'M SORRY ABOUT THAT FAIRY PRINCESS REMARK. I DON'T KNOW WHAT I WAS THINKING -- IT JUST POPPED OUT!
IT'S ALL RIGHT.
IT WAS KINDA FUNNY.

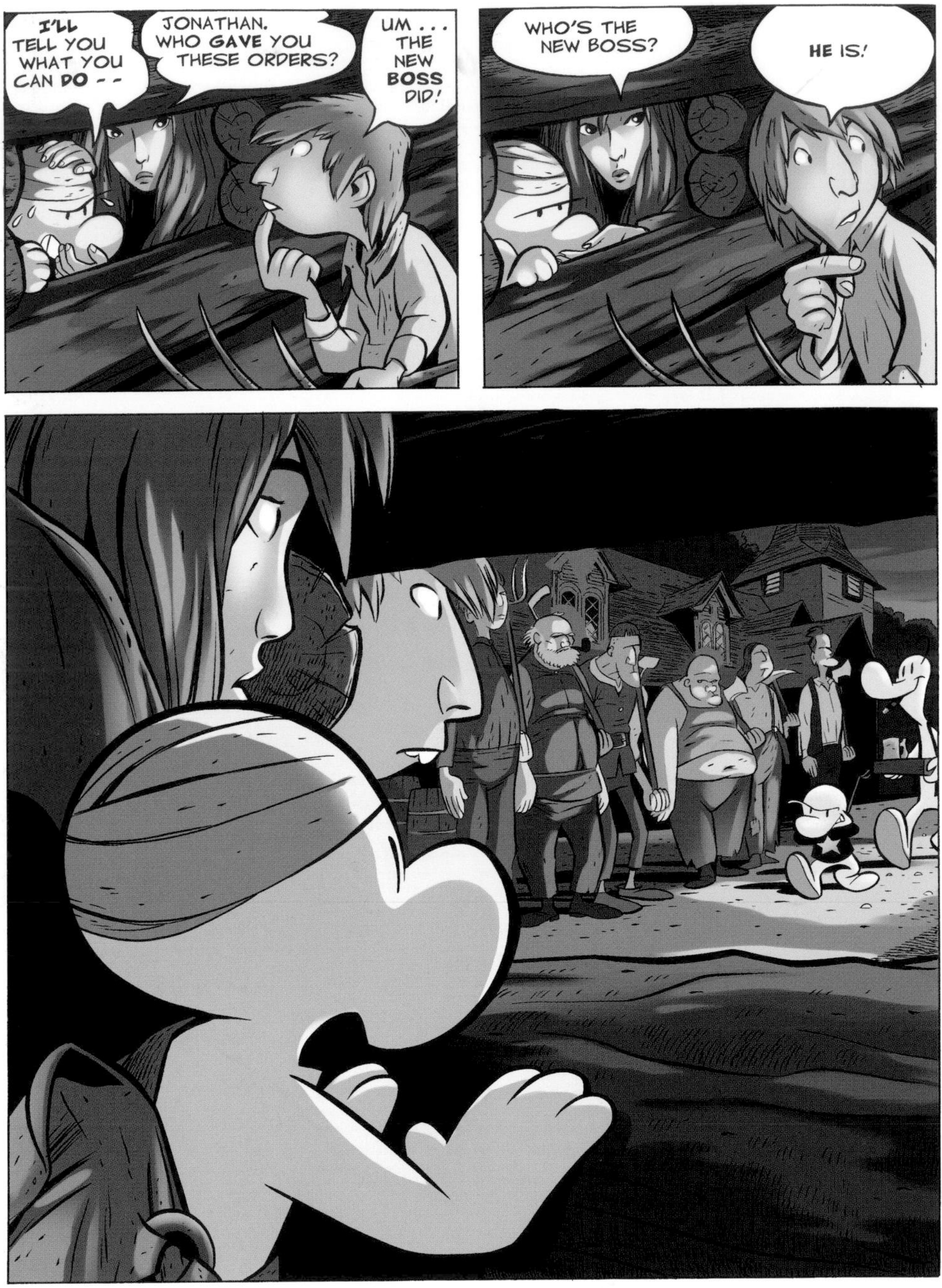
I'LL TELL YOU WHAT YOU CAN DO - -
JONATHAN. WHO GAVE YOU THESE ORDERS?
UM . . . THE NEW BOSS DID!
WHO'S THE NEW BOSS?
HE IS!

CHAPTER FOUR THE STRAGGLER

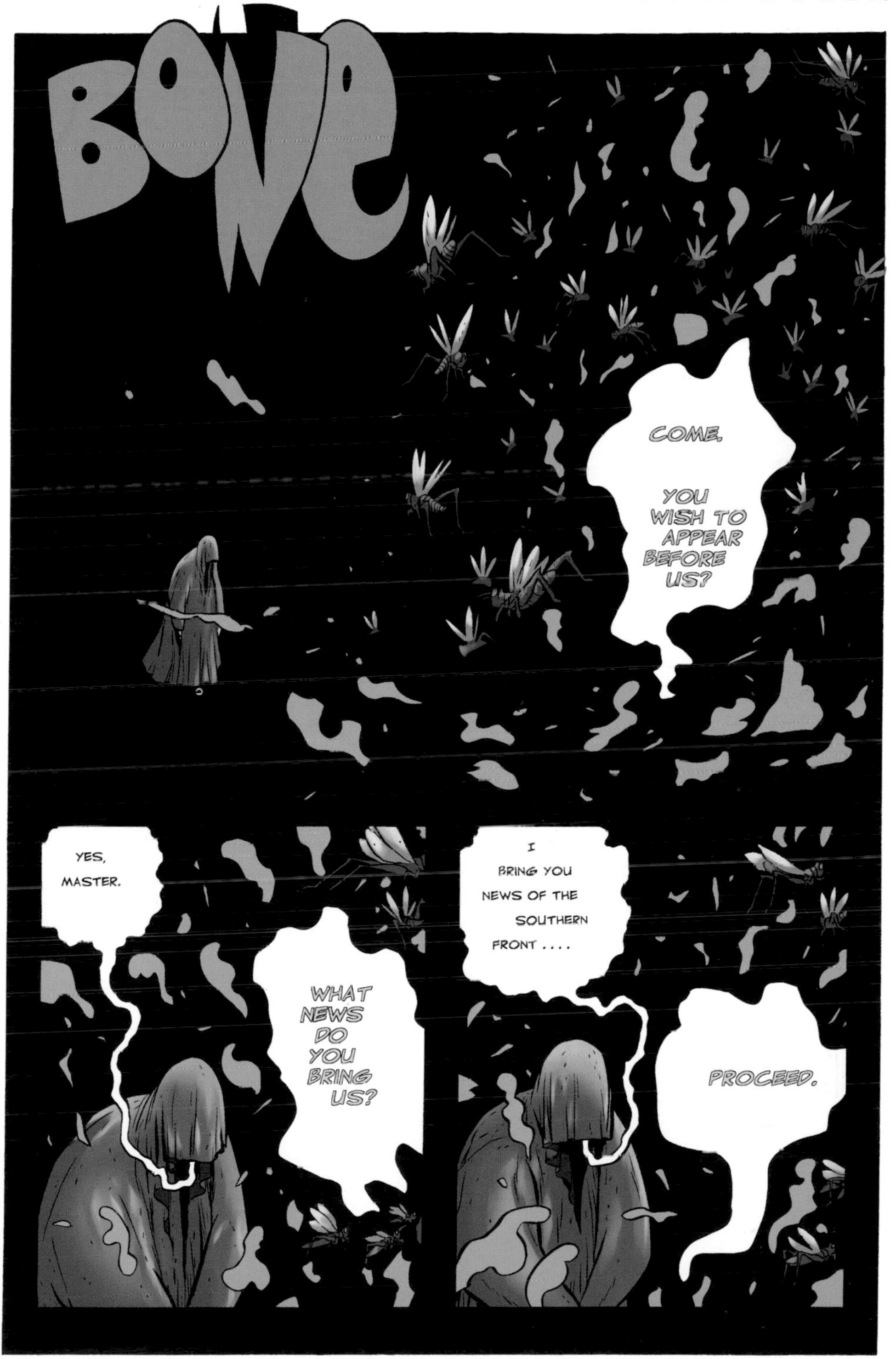
BONE
COME.
YOU WISH TO APPEAR BEFORE US?
YES, MASTER.
WHAT NEWS DO YOU BRING US?
I BRING YOU NEWS OF THE SOUTHERN FRONT . . . .
PROCEED.

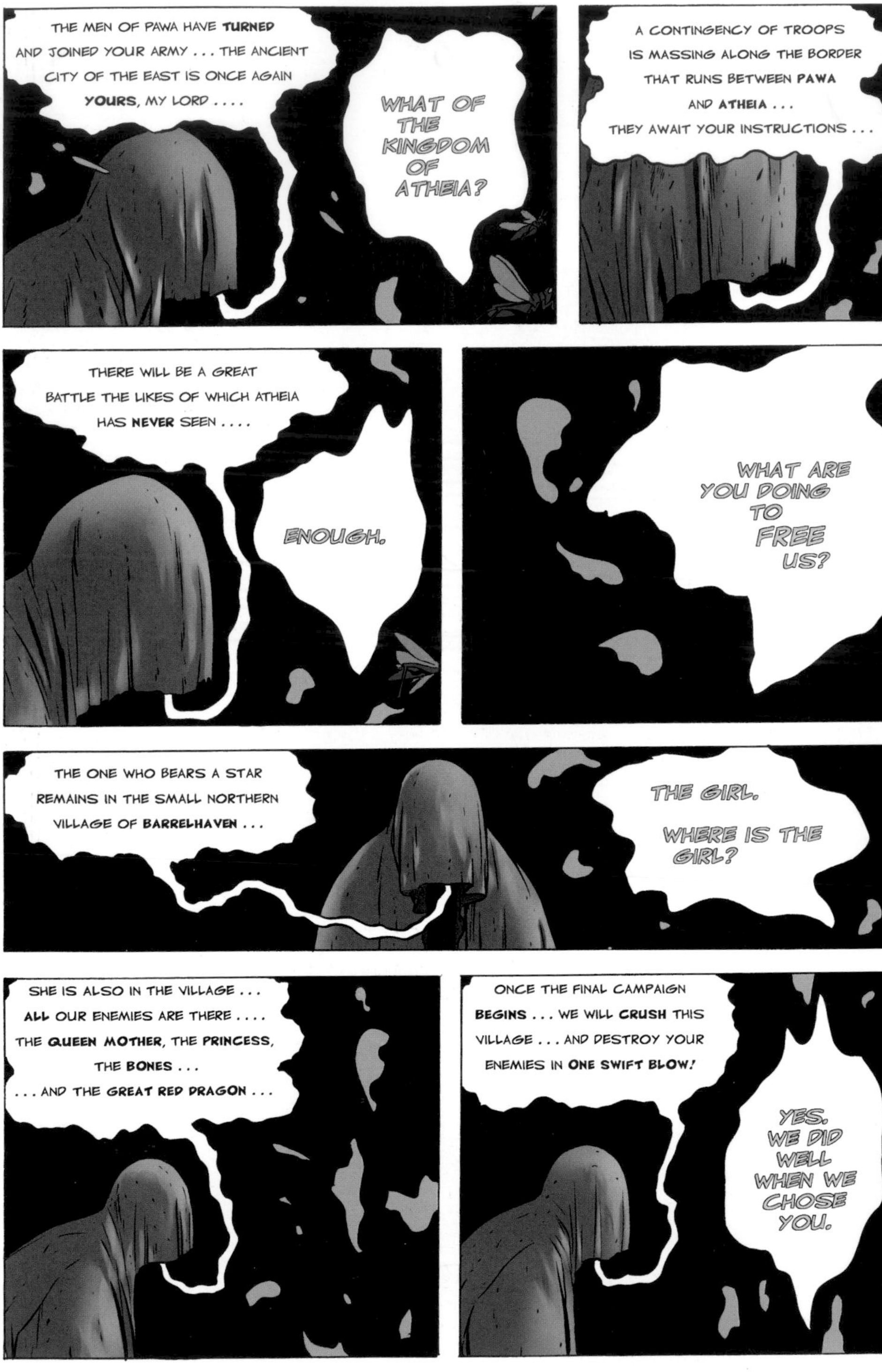
THE MEN OF PAWA HAVE TURNED AND JOINED YOUR ARMY . . . THE ANCIENT CITY OF THE EAST IS ONCE AGAIN YOURS, MY LORD . . . .
WHAT OF THE KINGDOM OF ATHEIA?
A CONTINGENCY OF TROOPS IS MASSING ALONG THE BORDER THAT RUNS BETWEEN PAWA AND ATHEIA . . . THEY AWAIT YOUR INSTRUCTIONS . . .
THERE WILL BE A GREAT BATTLE THE LIKES OF WHICH ATHEIA HAS NEVER SEEN . . . .
ENOUGH.
WHAT ARE YOU DOING TO FREE US?
THE ONE WHO BEARS A STAR REMAINS IN THE SMALL NORTHERN VILLAGE OF BARRELHAVEN . . .
THE GIRL.
WHERE IS THE GIRL?
SHE IS ALSO IN THE VILLAGE . . . ALL OUR ENEMIES ARE THERE . . . . THE QUEEN MOTHER, THE PRINCESS, THE BONES . . . . . . AND THE GREAT RED DRAGON . . .
ONCE THE FINAL CAMPAIGN BEGINS . . . WE WILL CRUSH THIS VILLAGE . . . AND DESTROY YOUR ENEMIES IN ONE SWIFT BLOW!
YES. WE DID WELL WHEN WE CHOSE YOU.

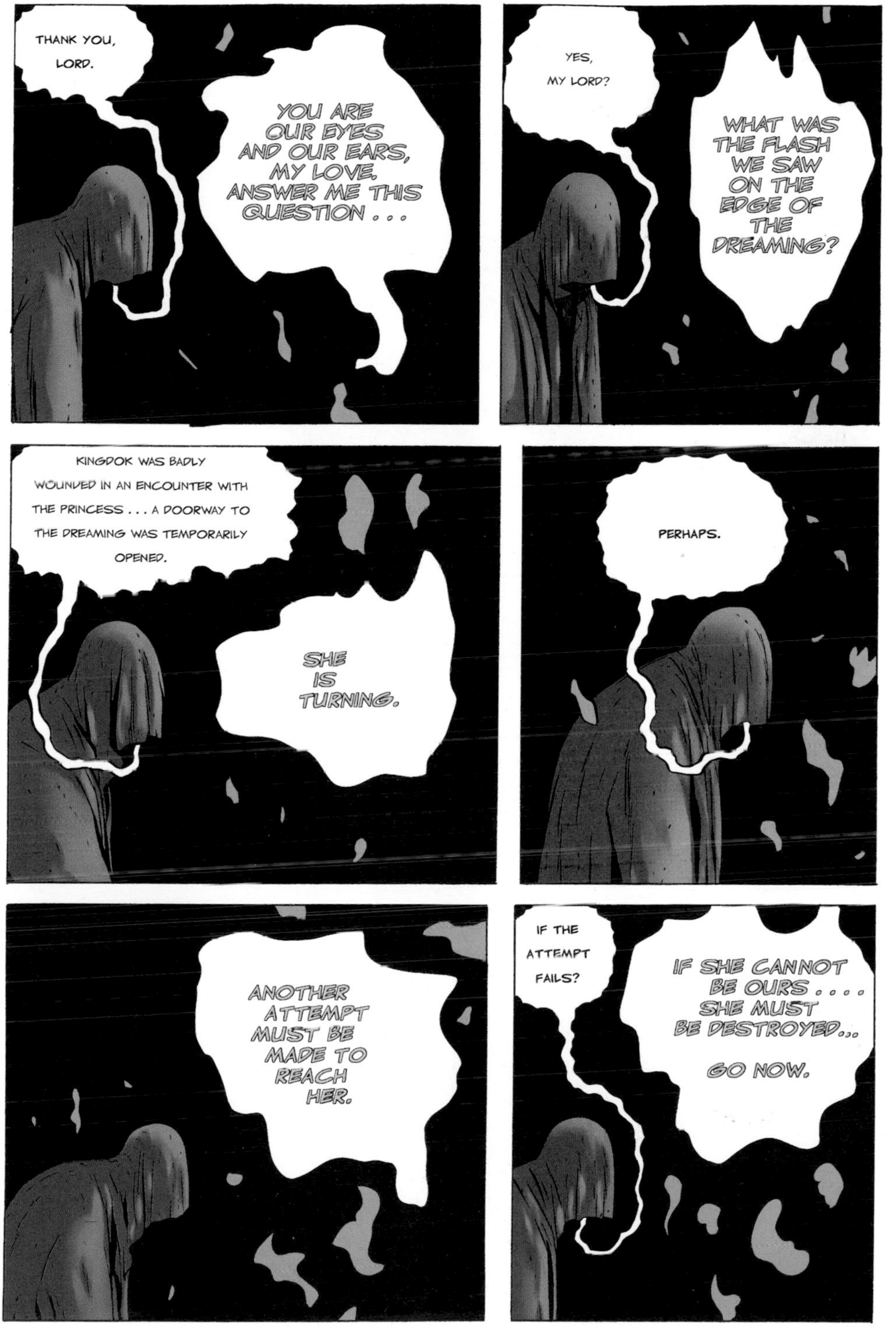
THANK YOU, LORD.
YOU ARE OUR EYES AND OUR EARS, MY LOVE. ANSWER ME THIS QUESTION . . .
YES, MY LORD?
WHAT WAS THE FLASH WE SAW ON THE EDGE OF THE DREAMING?
KINGDOK WAS BADLY WOUNDED IN AN ENCOUNTER WITH THE PRINCESS . . . A DOORWAY TO THE DREAMING WAS TEMPORARILY OPENED.
SHE IS TURNING.
PERHAPS.
ANOTHER ATTEMPT MUST BE MADE TO REACH HER.
IF THE ATTEMPT FAILS?
IF SHE CANNOT BE OURS . . . . SHE MUST BE DESTROYED. . .
GO NOW.

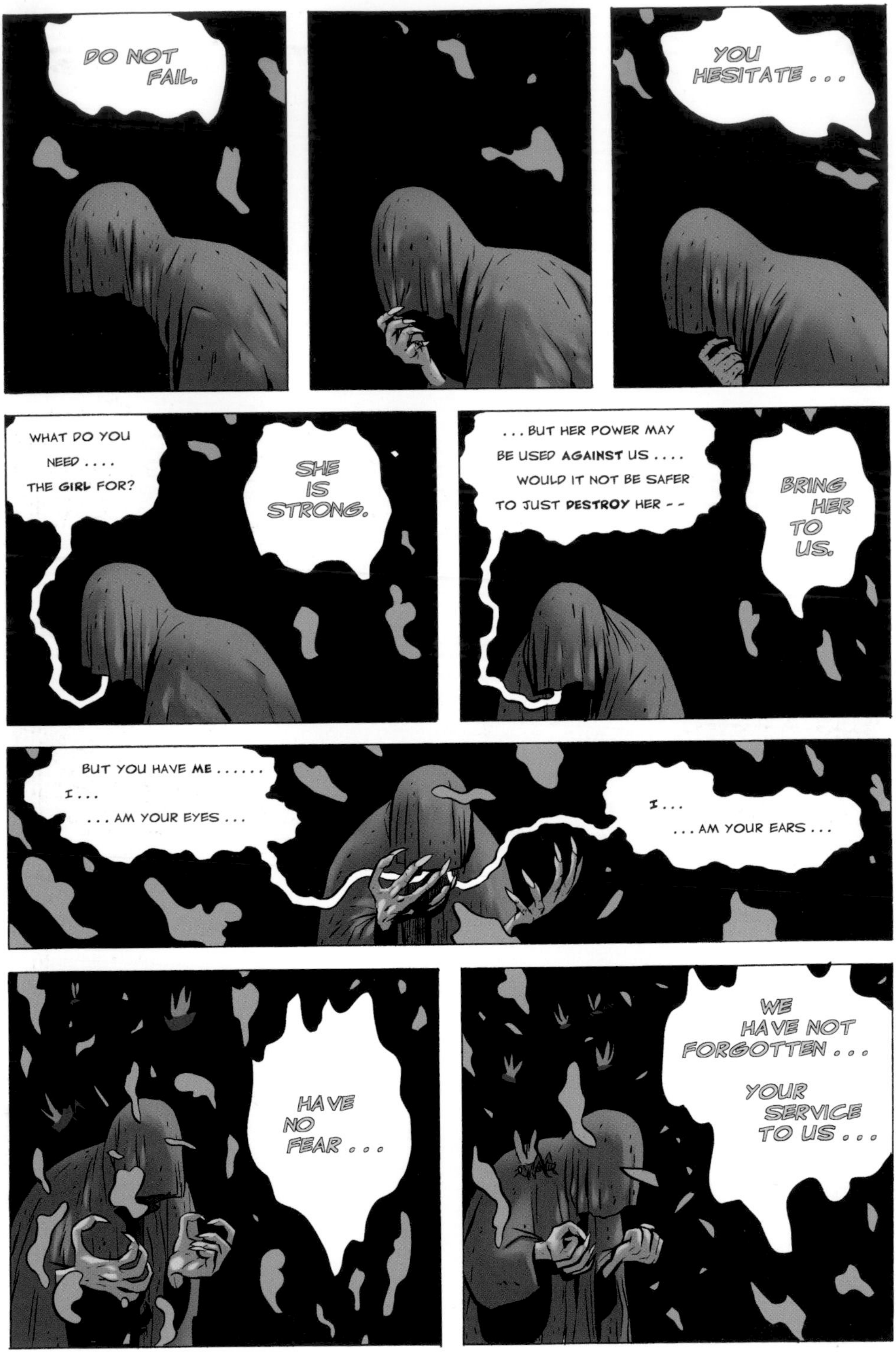

DO NOT FAIL.
YOU HESITATE . . .
WHAT DO YOU NEED . . . . THE GIRL FOR?
SHE IS STRONG.
. . . BUT HER POWER MAY BE USED AGAINST US . . . . WOULD IT NOT BE SAFER TO JUST DESTROY HER - -
BRING HER TO US.
BUT YOU HAVE ME . . . . . .
I . . .
. . . AM YOUR EYES . . .
I . . .
. . . AM YOUR EARS . . .
HAVE NO FEAR . . .
WE HAVE NOT FORGOTTEN . . .
YOUR SERVICE TO US . . .

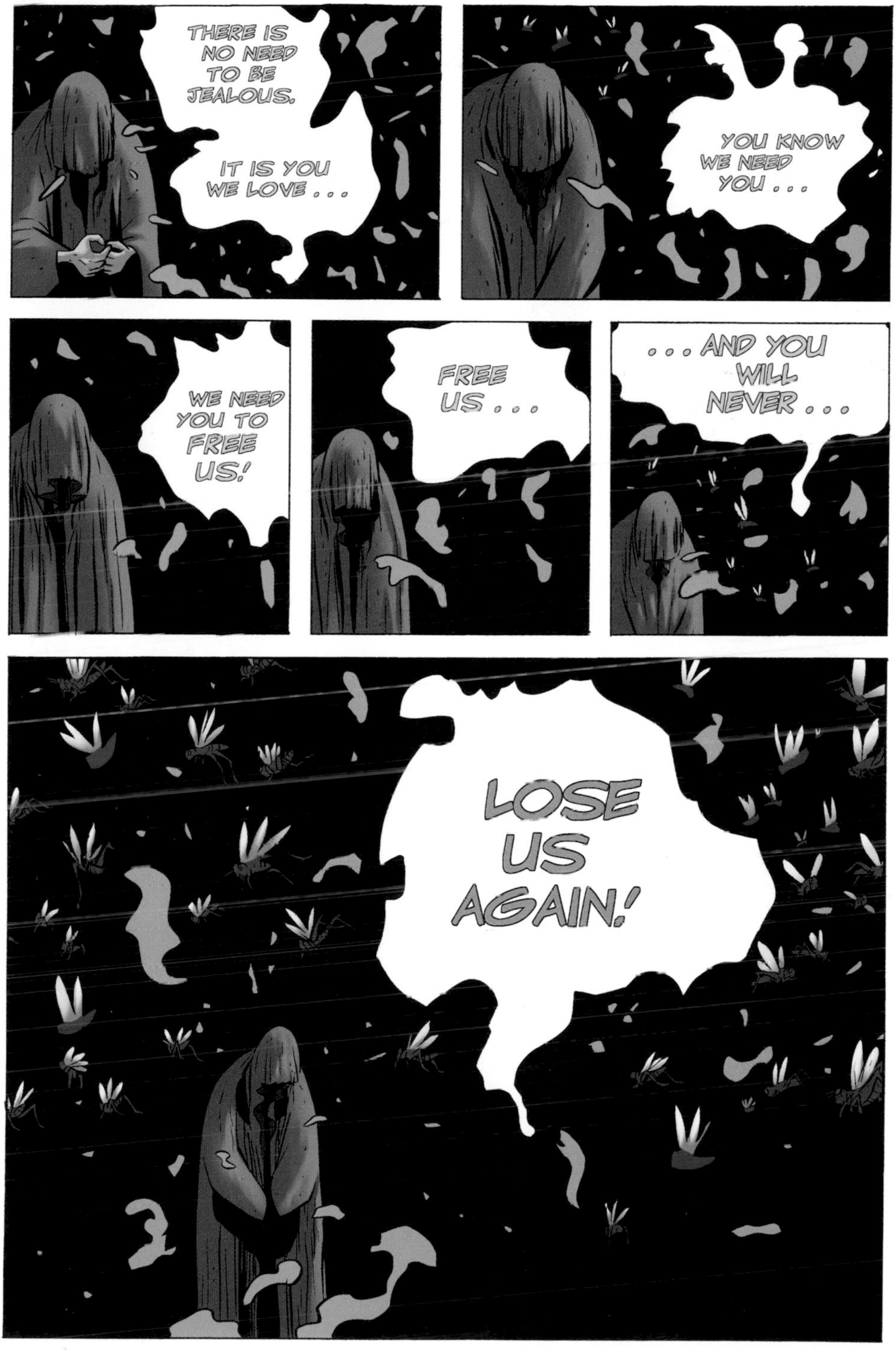
THERE IS NO NEED TO BE JEALOUS.
IT IS YOU WE LOVE . . .
YOU KNOW WE NEED YOU . . .
WE NEED YOU TO FREE US!
FREE US . . .
. . . AND YOU WILL NEVER . . .
LOSE US AGAIN!

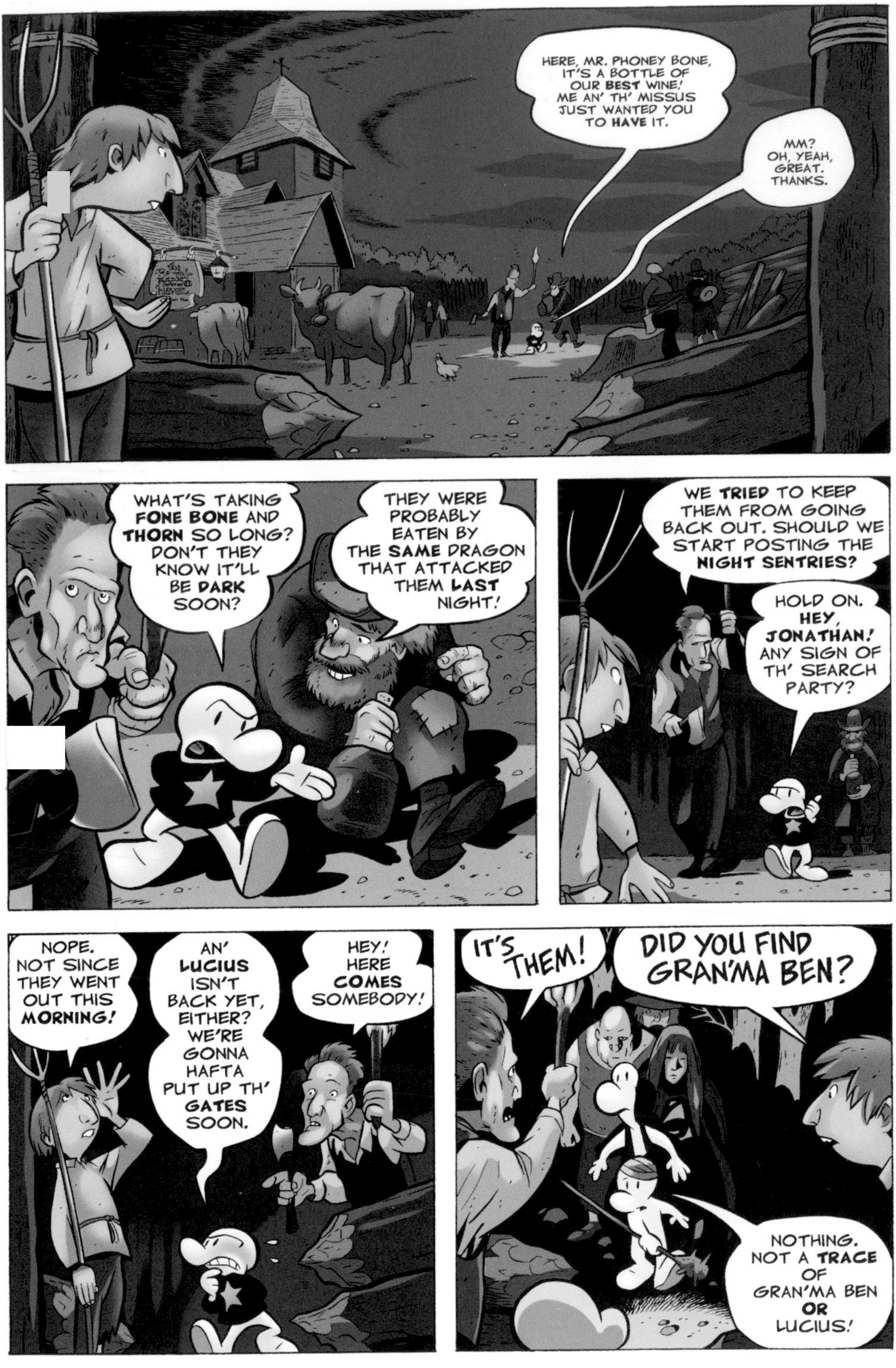
HERE, MR. PHONEY BONE, IT'S A BOTTLE OF OUR BEST WINE! ME AN' TH' MISSUS JUST WANTED YOU TO HAVE IT.
MM? OH, YEAH, GREAT. THANKS.
WHAT'S TAKING FONE BONE AND THORN SO LONG? DON'T THEY KNOW IT'LL BE DARK SOON?
THEY WERE PROBABLY EATEN BY THE SAME DRAGON THAT ATTACKED THEM LAST NIGHT!
WE TRIED TO KEEP THEM FROM GOING BACK OUT. SHOULD WE START POSTING THE NIGHT SENTRIES?
HOLD ON. HEY, JONATHAN! ANY SIGN OF TH' SEARCH PARTY?
NOPE. NOT SINCE THEY WENT OUT THIS MORNING!
AN' LUCIUS ISN'T BACK YET, EITHER? WE'RE GONNA HAFTA PUT UP TH' GATES SOON.
HEY! HERE COMES SOMEBODY!
IT'S THEM!
DID YOU FIND GRAN'MA BEN?
NOTHING. NOT A TRACE OF GRAN'MA BEN OR LUCIUS!

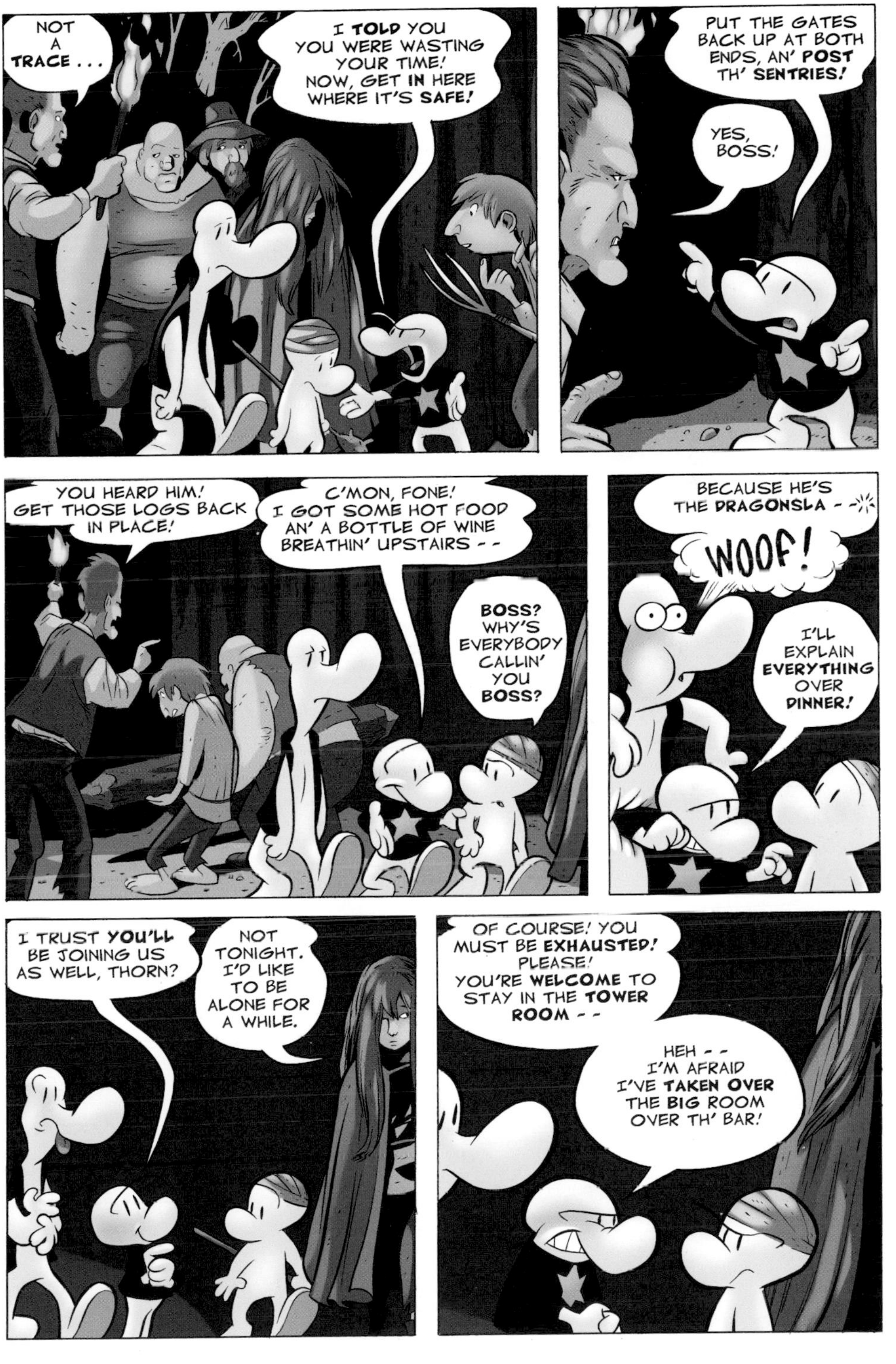
NOT A TRACE . . .
I TOLD YOU YOU WERE WASTING YOUR TIME! NOW, GET IN HERE WHERE IT'S SAFE!
PUT THE GATES BACK UP AT BOTH ENDS, AN' POST TH' SENTRIES!
YES, BOSS!
YOU HEARD HIM! GET THOSE LOGS BACK IN PLACE!
C'MON, FONE! I GOT SOME HOT FOOD AN' A BOTTLE OF WINE BREATHIN' UPSTAIRS - -
BOSS? WHY'S EVERYBODY CALLIN' YOU BOSS?
BECAUSE HE'S THE DRAGONSLA - -
WOOF!
I'LL EXPLAIN EVERYTHING OVER DINNER!
I TRUST YOU'LL BE JOINING US AS WELL, THORN?
NOT TONIGHT. I'D LIKE TO BE ALONE FOR A WHILE.
OF COURSE! YOU MUST BE EXHAUSTED! PLEASE! YOU'RE WELCOME TO STAY IN THE TOWER ROOM - -
HEH - - I'M AFRAID I'VE TAKEN OVER THE BIG ROOM OVER TH' BAR!

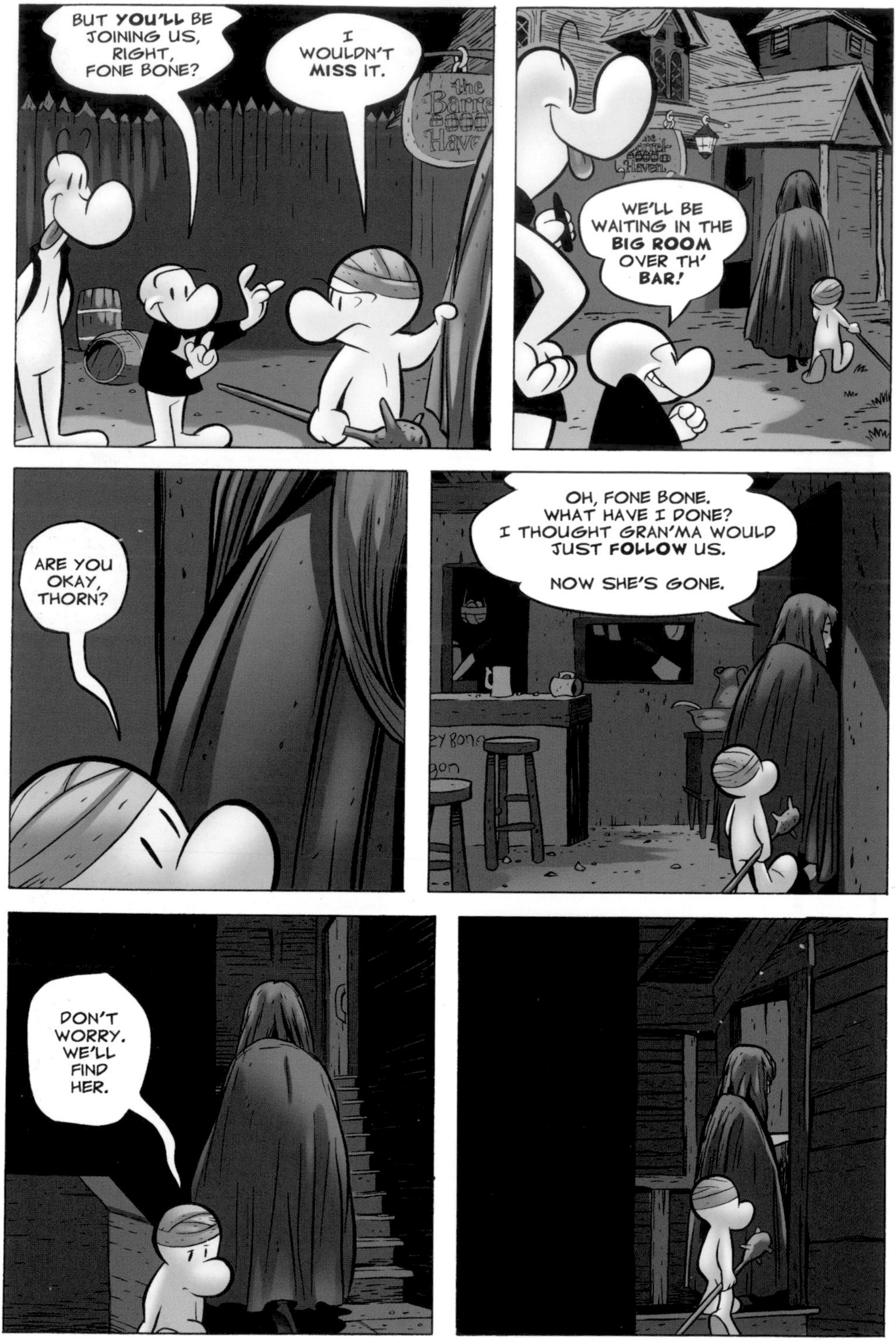
BUT YOU'LL BE JOINING US, RIGHT, FONE BONE?
I WOULDN'T MISS IT.
the Barrel Haven
WE'LL BE WAITING IN THE BIG ROOM OVER TH' BAR!
ARE YOU OKAY, THORN?
OH, FONE BONE. WHAT HAVE I DONE? I THOUGHT GRAN'MA WOULD JUST FOLLOW US.
NOW SHE'S GONE.
DON'T WORRY. WE'LL FIND HER.

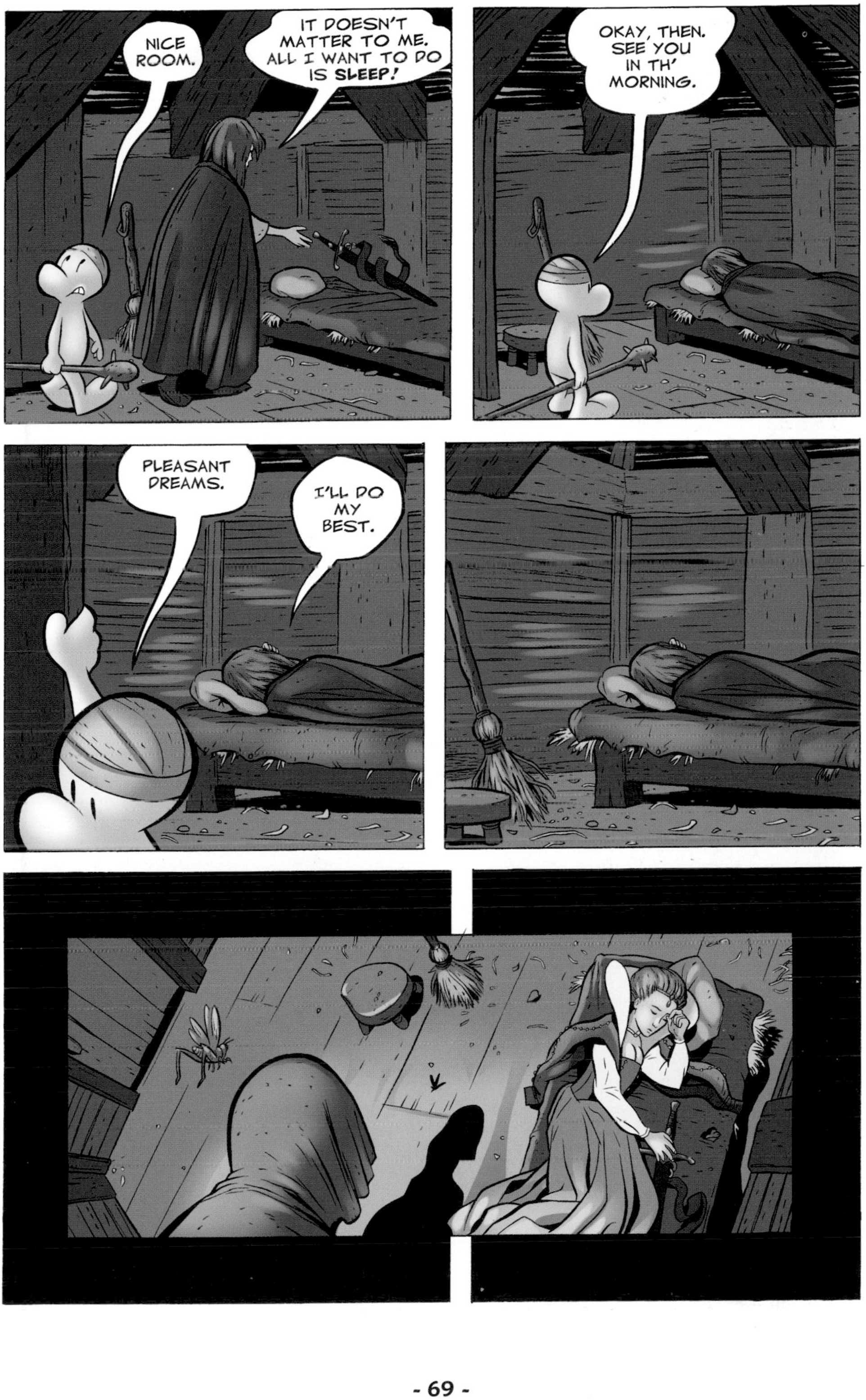
NICE ROOM.
IT DOESN'T MATTER TO ME. ALL I WANT TO DO IS **SLEEP!**
OKAY, THEN. SEE YOU IN TH' MORNING.
PLEASANT DREAMS.
I'LL DO MY BEST.

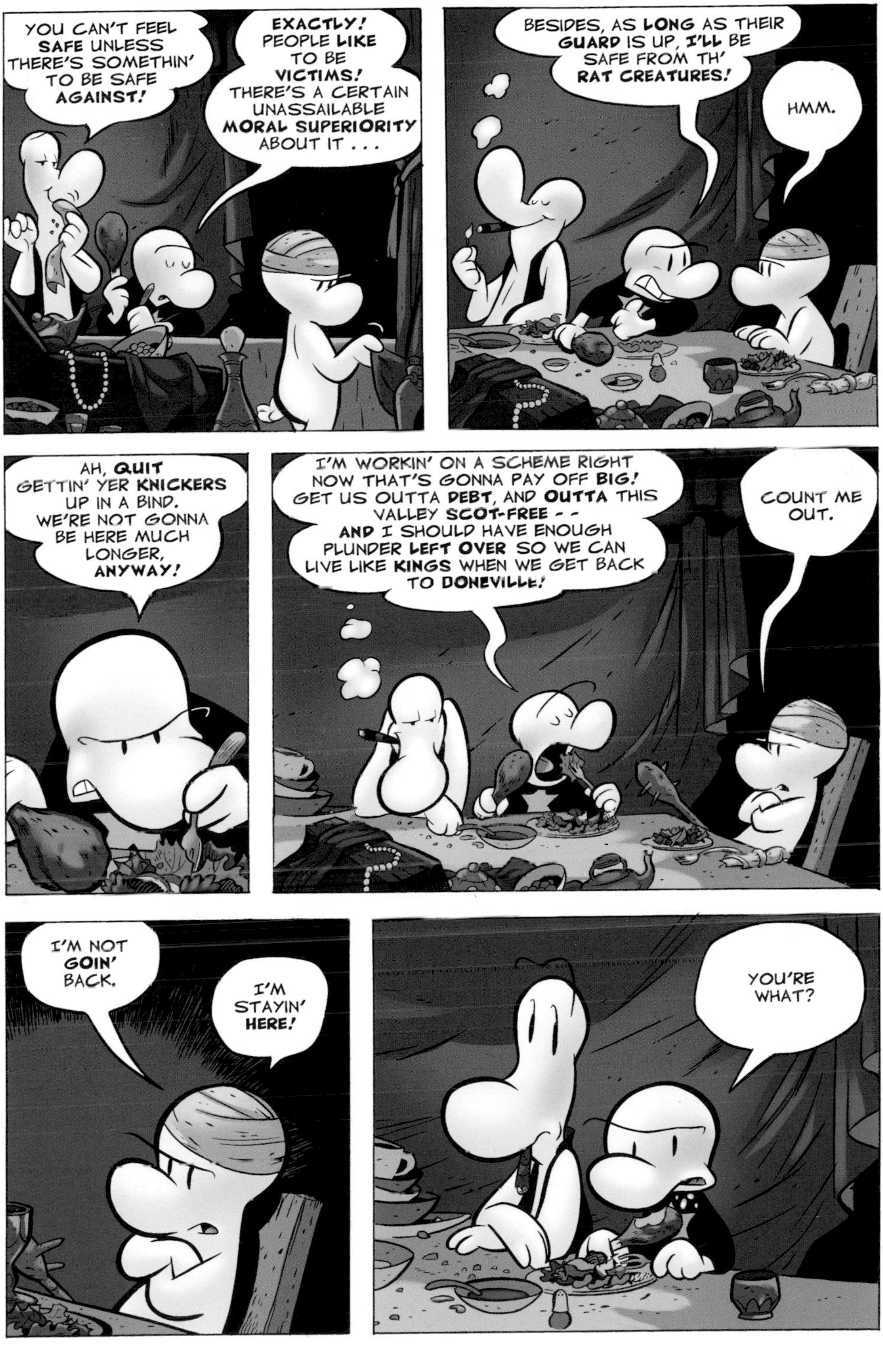
YOU CAN'T FEEL SAFE UNLESS THERE'S SOMETHIN' TO BE SAFE AGAINST!
EXACTLY! PEOPLE LIKE TO BE VICTIMS! THERE'S A CERTAIN UNASSAILABLE MORAL SUPERIORITY ABOUT IT . . .
BESIDES, AS LONG AS THEIR GUARD IS UP, I'LL BE SAFE FROM TH' RAT CREATURES!
HMM.
AH, QUIT GETTIN' YER KNICKERS UP IN A BIND. WE'RE NOT GONNA BE HERE MUCH LONGER, ANYWAY!
I'M WORKIN' ON A SCHEME RIGHT NOW THAT'S GONNA PAY OFF BIG! GET US OUTTA DEBT, AND OUTTA THIS VALLEY SCOT-FREE - - AND I SHOULD HAVE ENOUGH PLUNDER LEFT OVER SO WE CAN LIVE LIKE KINGS WHEN WE GET BACK TO DONEVILLE!
COUNT ME OUT.
I'M NOT GOIN' BACK.
I'M STAYIN' HERE!
YOU'RE WHAT?

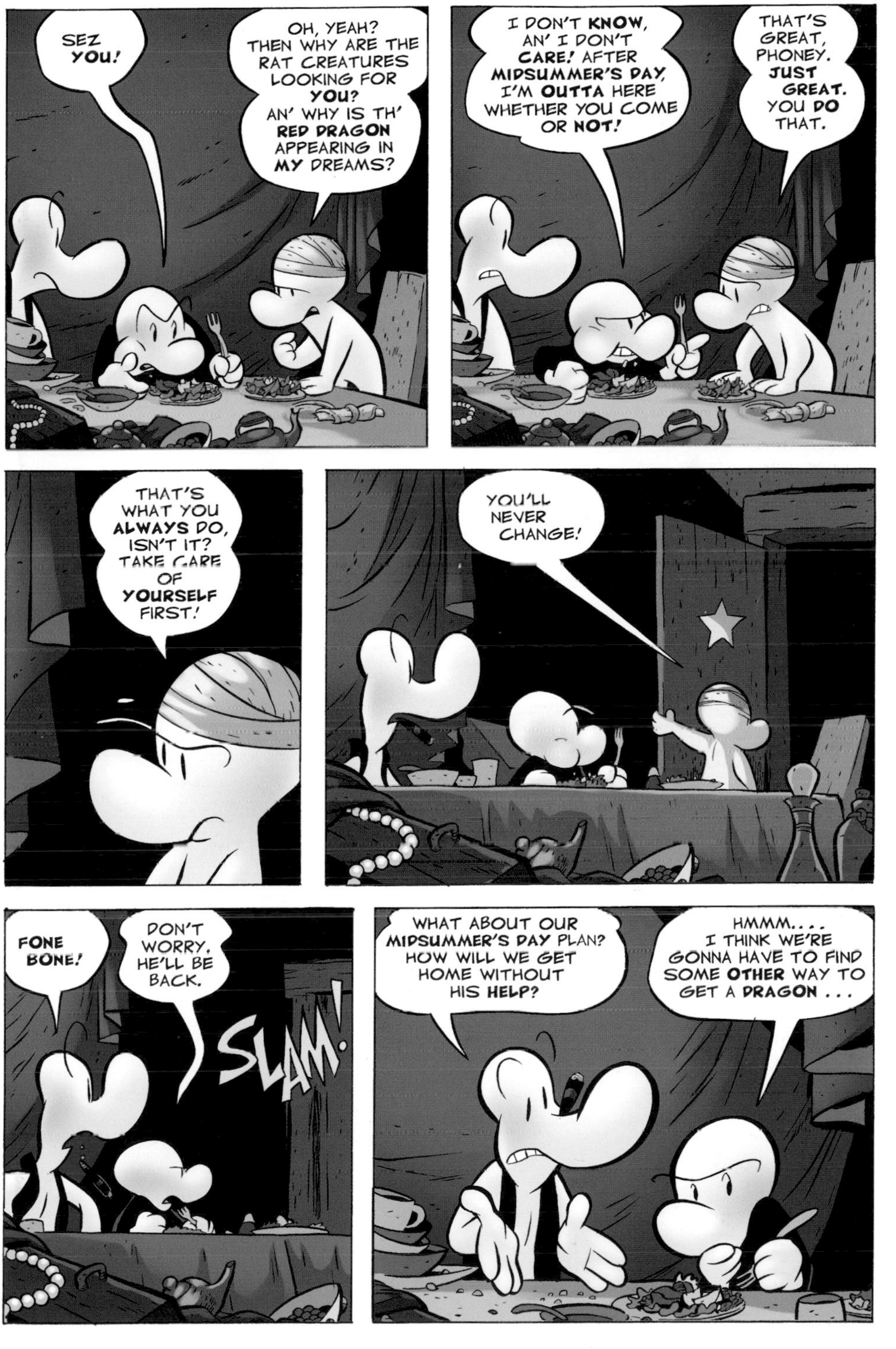
SEZ YOU!
OH, YEAH? THEN WHY ARE THE RAT CREATURES LOOKING FOR YOU? AN' WHY IS TH' RED DRAGON APPEARING IN MY DREAMS?
I DON'T KNOW, AN' I DON'T CARE! AFTER MIDSUMMER'S DAY, I'M OUTTA HERE WHETHER YOU COME OR NOT!
THAT'S GREAT, PHONEY. JUST GREAT. YOU DO THAT.
THAT'S WHAT YOU ALWAYS DO, ISN'T IT? TAKE CARE OF YOURSELF FIRST!
YOU'LL NEVER CHANGE!
FONE BONE!
DON'T WORRY. HE'LL BE BACK.
SLAM!
WHAT ABOUT OUR MIDSUMMER'S DAY PLAN? HOW WILL WE GET HOME WITHOUT HIS HELP?
HMMM. . . . I THINK WE'RE GONNA HAVE TO FIND SOME OTHER WAY TO GET A DRAGON . . .

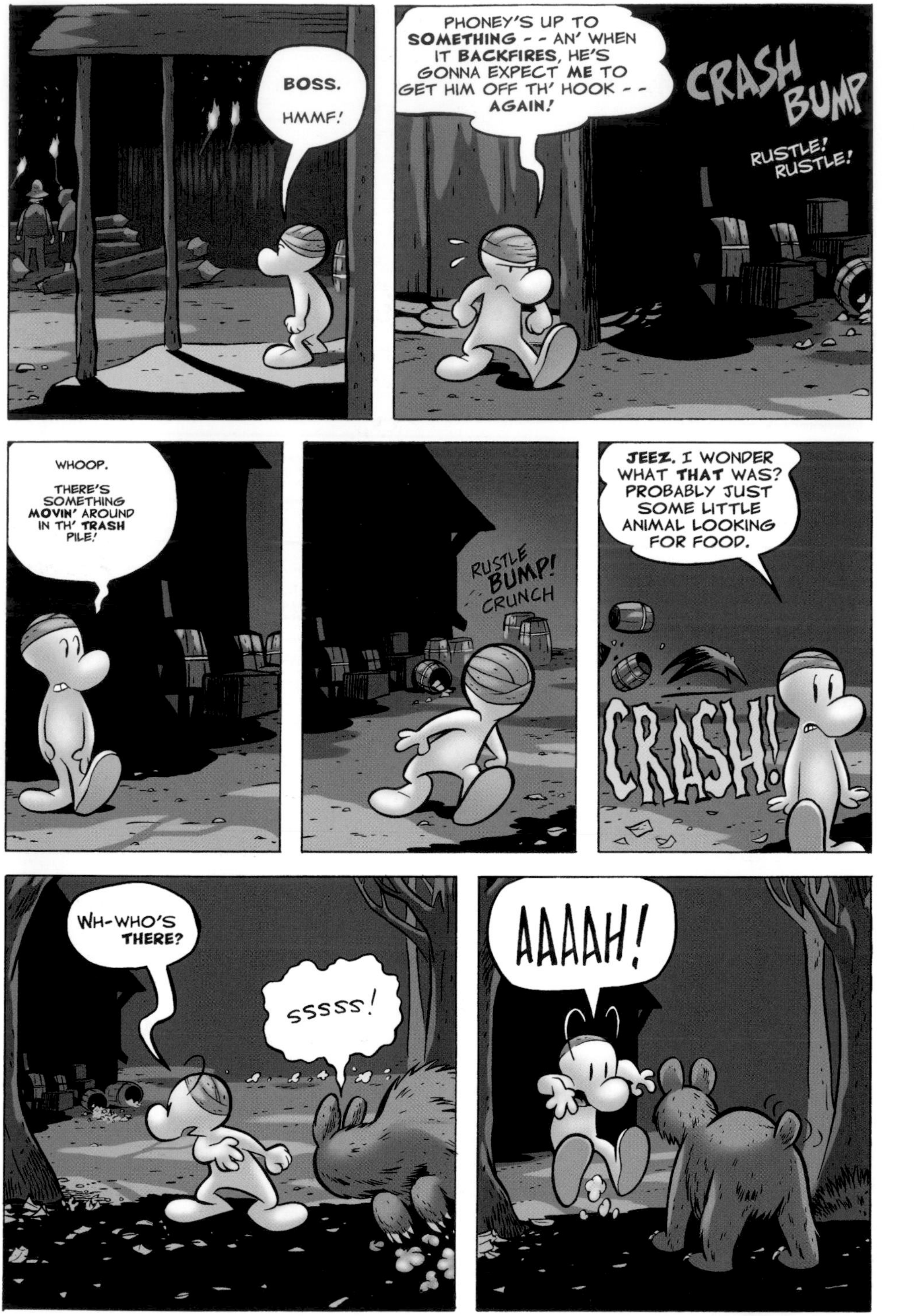
BOSS.
HMMF!
PHONEY'S UP TO SOMETHING - - AN' WHEN IT BACKFIRES, HE'S GONNA EXPECT ME TO GET HIM OFF TH' HOOK - - AGAIN!
CRASH BUMP
RUSTLE! RUSTLE!
WHOOP.
THERE'S SOMETHING MOVIN' AROUND IN TH' TRASH PILE!
RUSTLE BUMP! CRUNCH
JEEZ. I WONDER WHAT THAT WAS? PROBABLY JUST SOME LITTLE ANIMAL LOOKING FOR FOOD.
CRASH!
WH-WHO'S THERE?
SSSSS!
AAAAH!

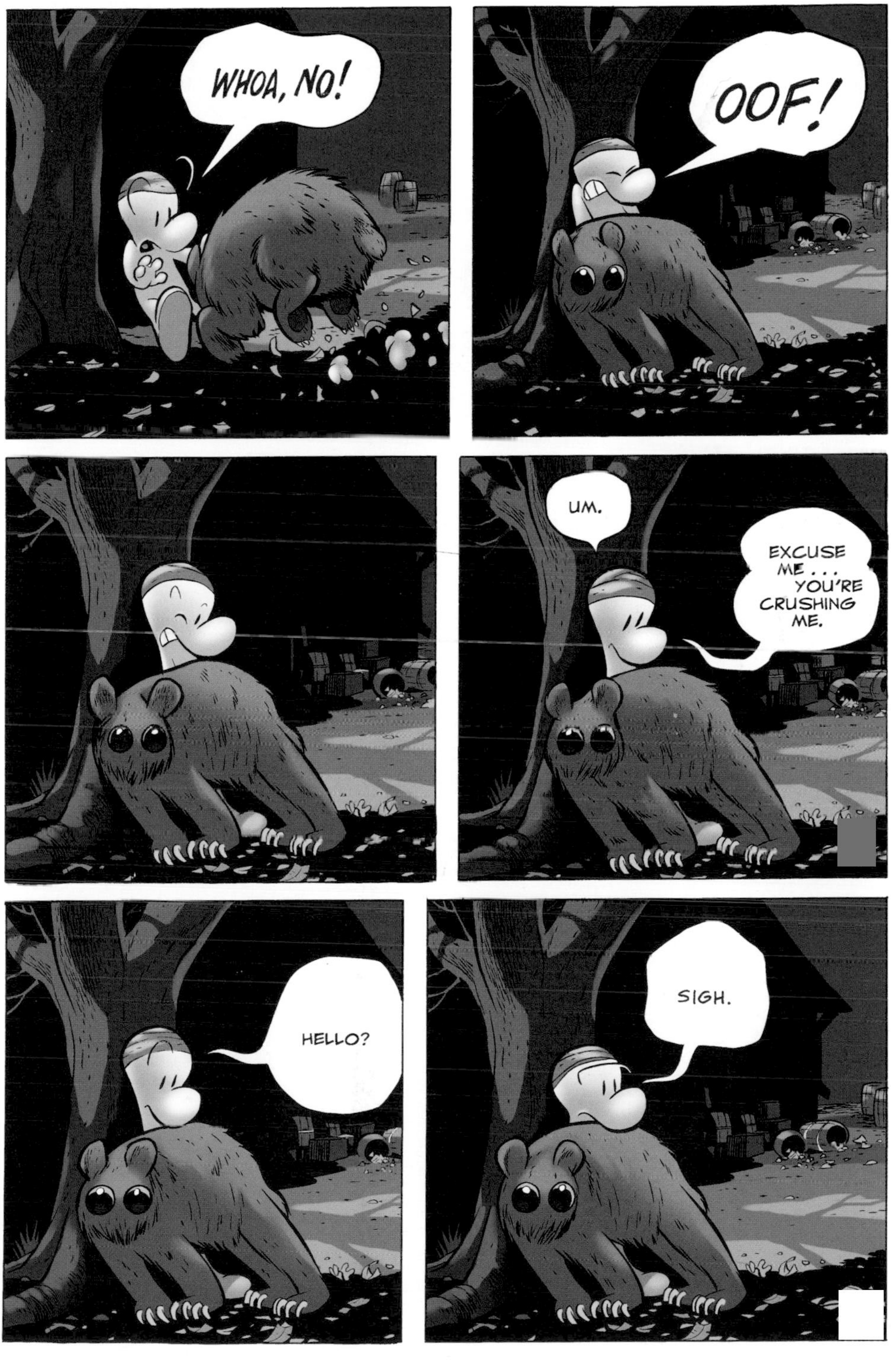
WHOA, NO!
OOF!
UM.
EXCUSE ME . . . YOU'RE CRUSHING ME.
HELLO?
SIGH.

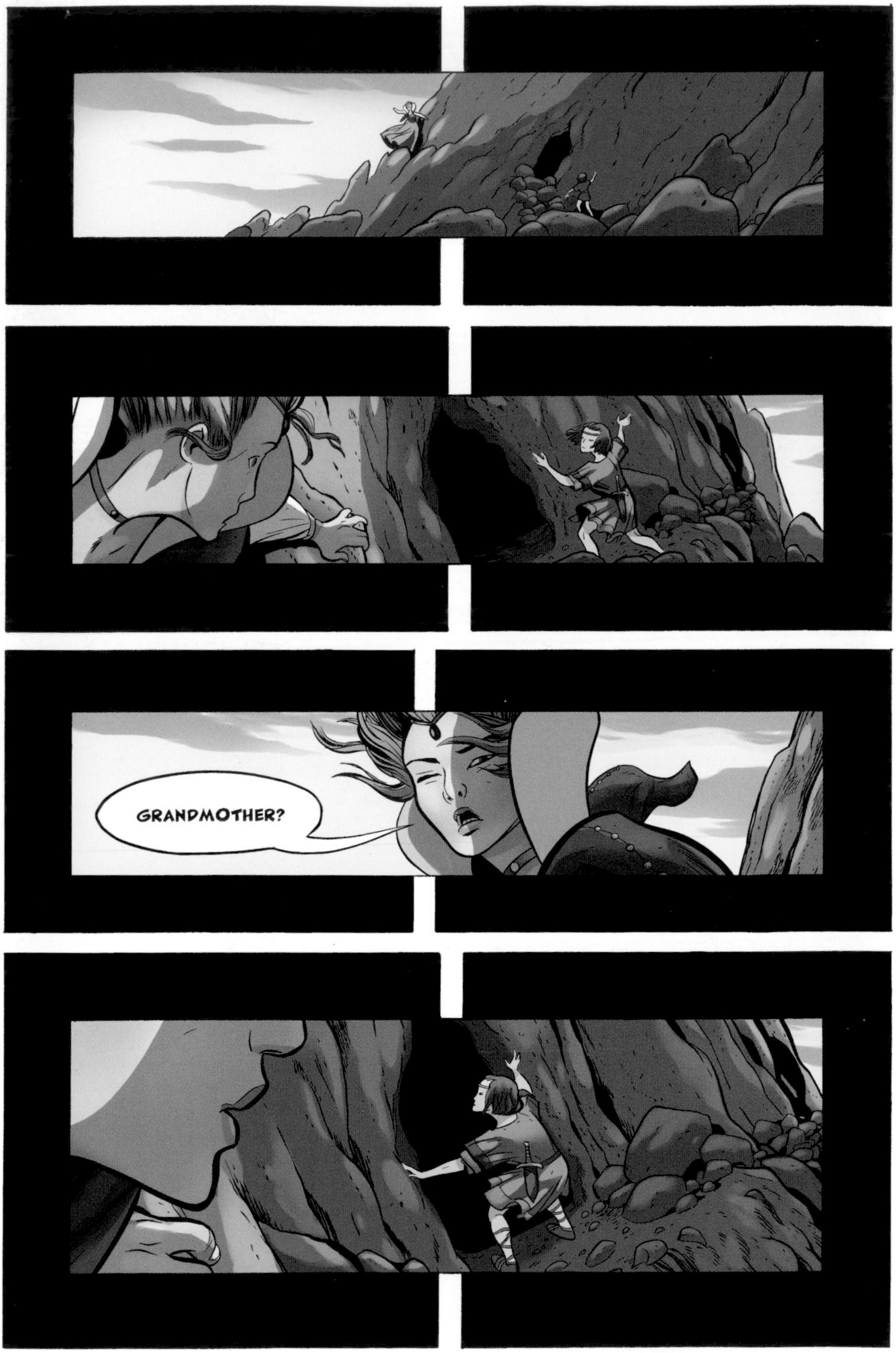
GRANDMOTHER?

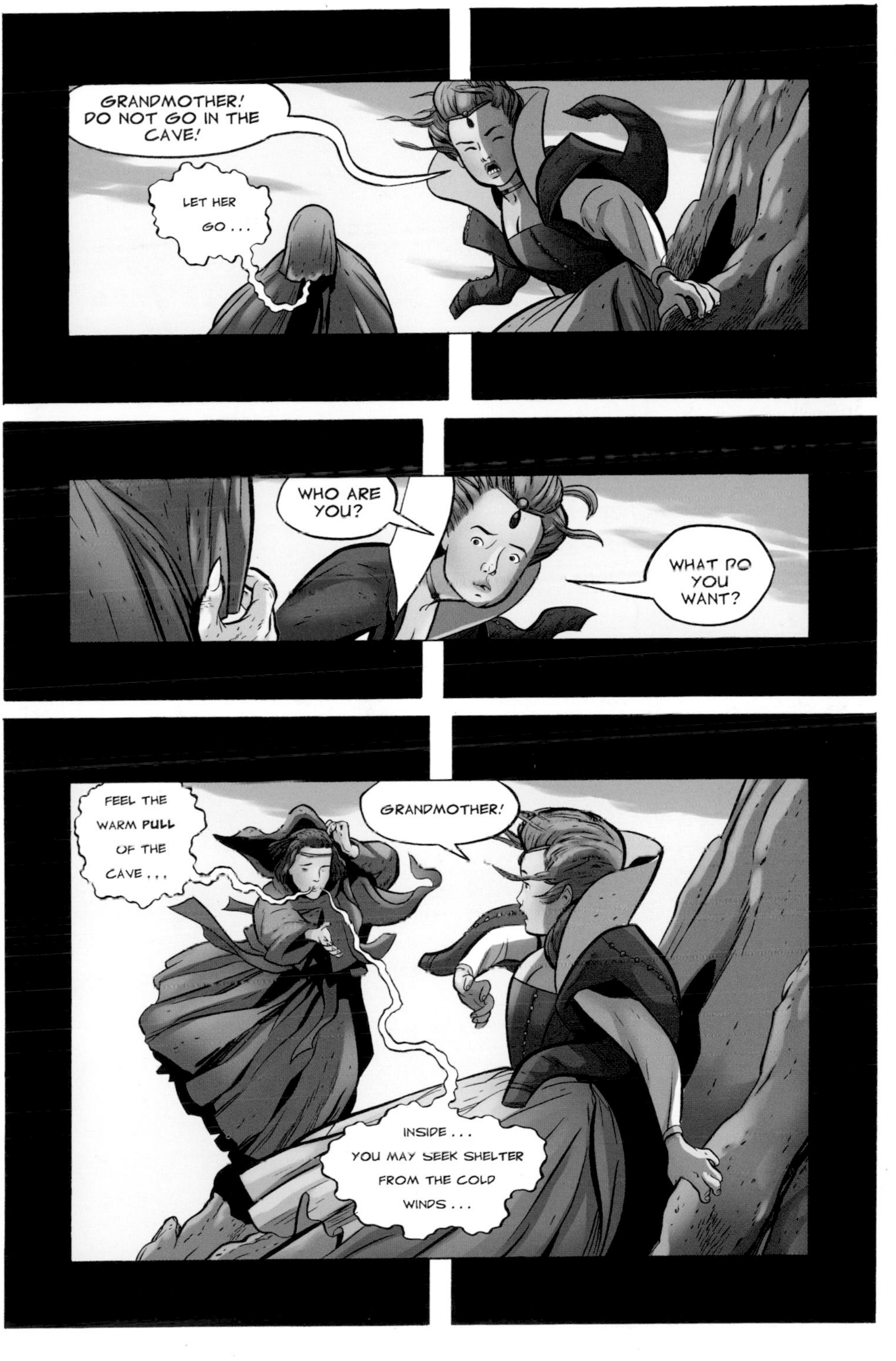
GRANDMOTHER! DO NOT GO IN THE CAVE!
LET HER GO . . .
WHO ARE YOU?
WHAT DO YOU WANT?
FEEL THE WARM PULL OF THE CAVE . . .
GRANDMOTHER!
INSIDE . . .
YOU MAY SEEK SHELTER FROM THE COLD WINDS . . .

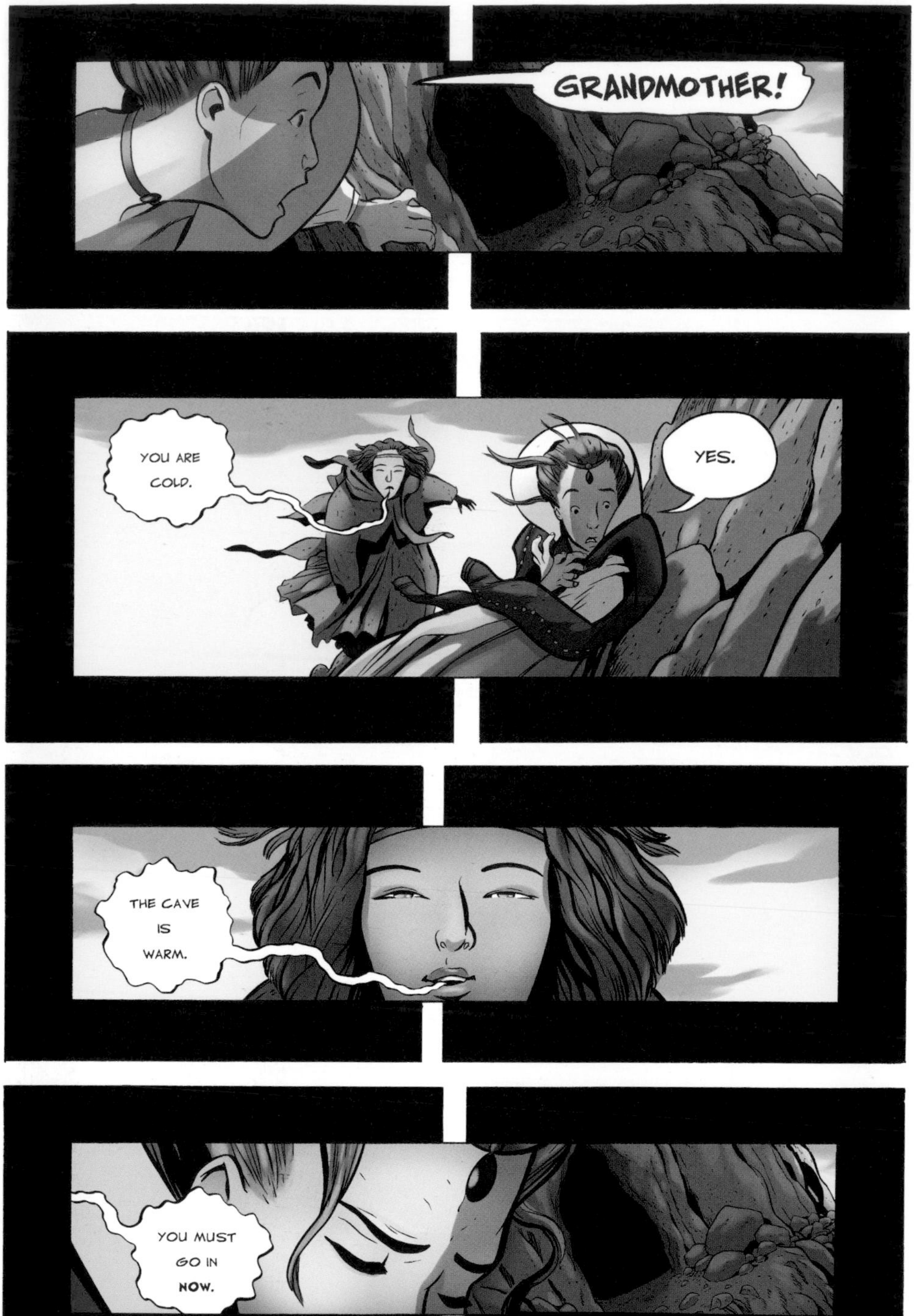
GRANDMOTHER!
YOU ARE COLD.
YES.
THE CAVE IS WARM.
YOU MUST GO IN NOW.

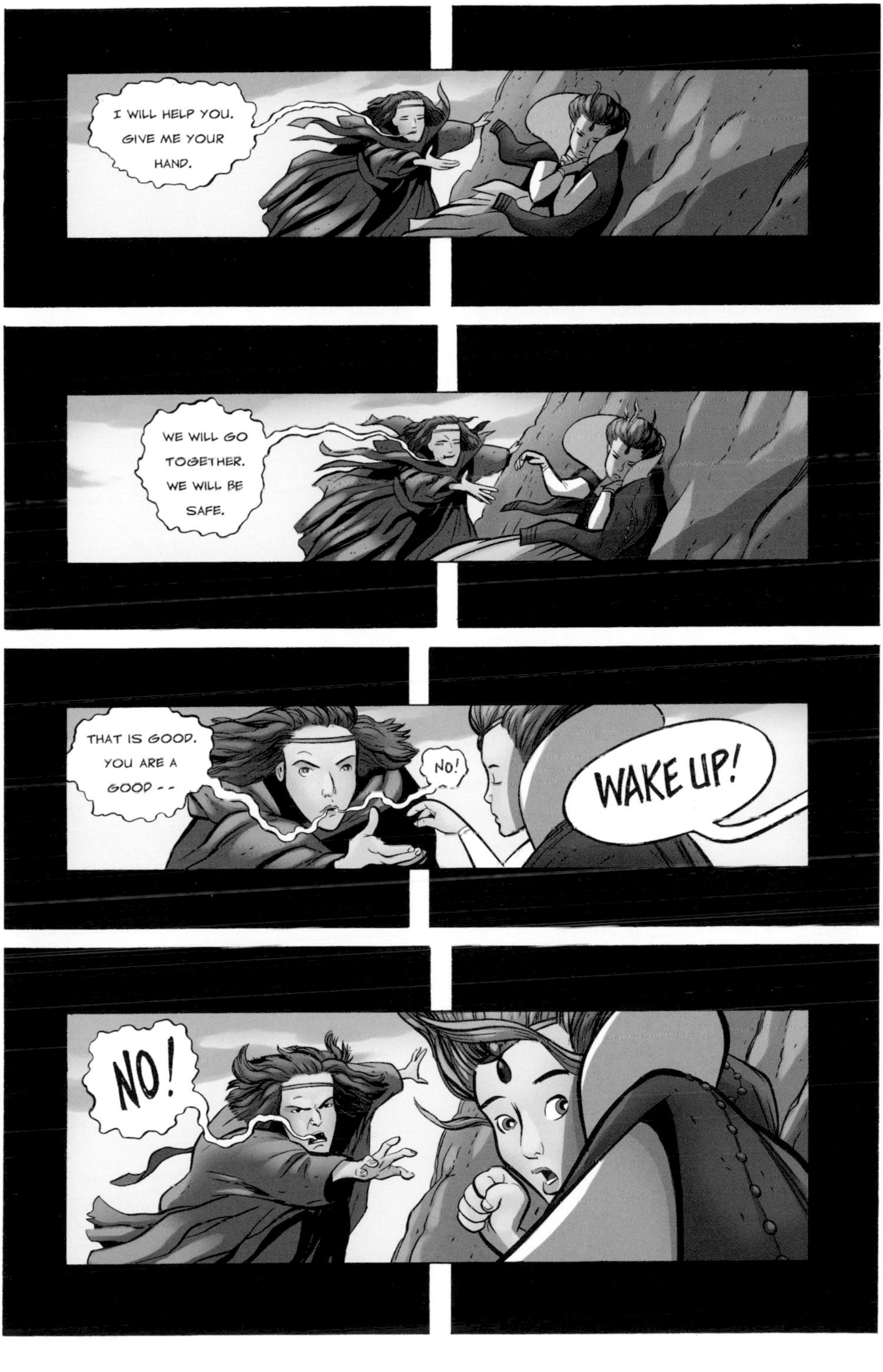
I WILL HELP YOU. GIVE ME YOUR HAND.
WE WILL GO TOGETHER. WE WILL BE SAFE.
THAT IS GOOD. YOU ARE A GOOD - -
NO!
WAKE UP!
NO!

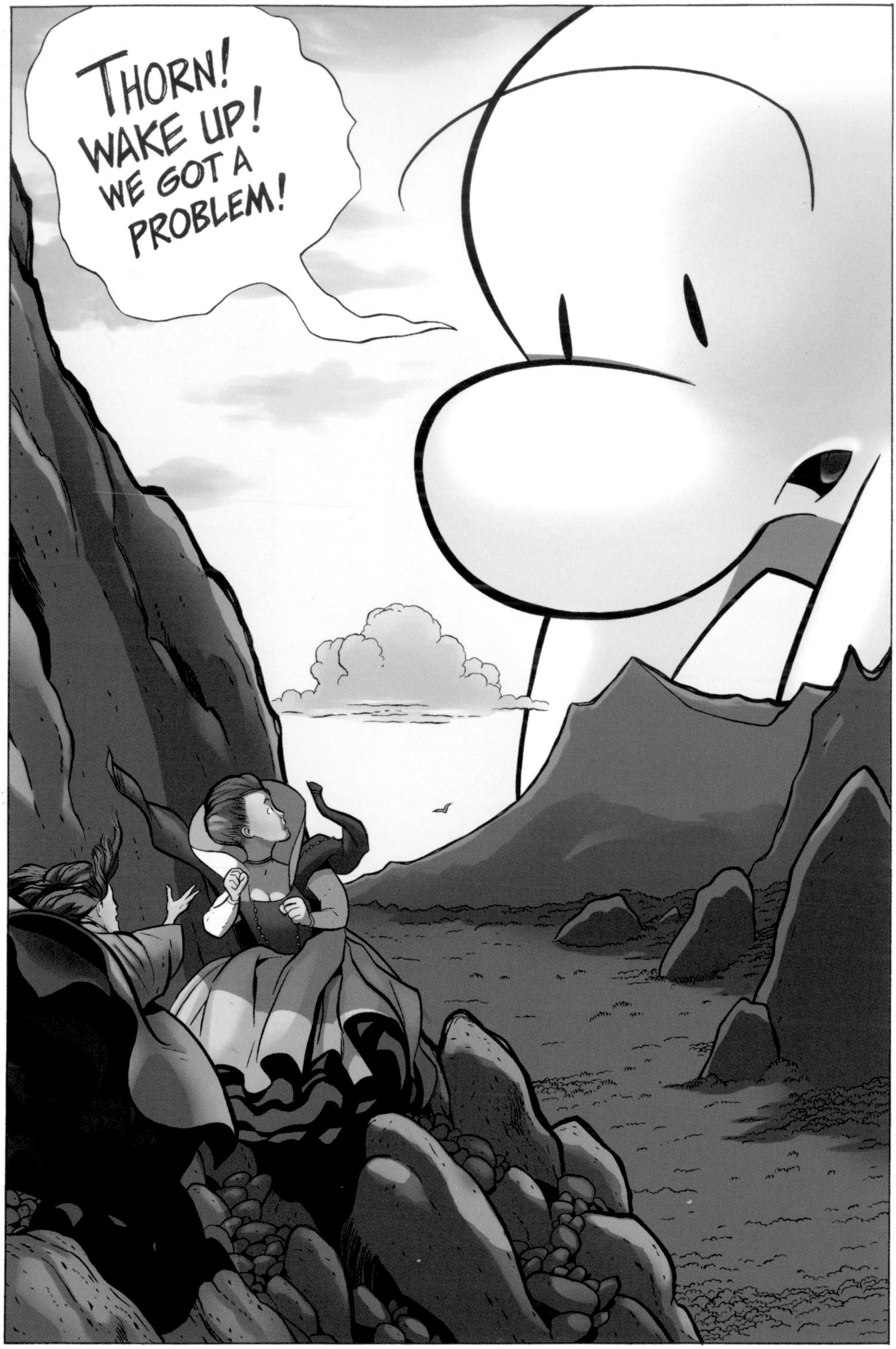
THORN! WAKE UP! WE GOT A PROBLEM!

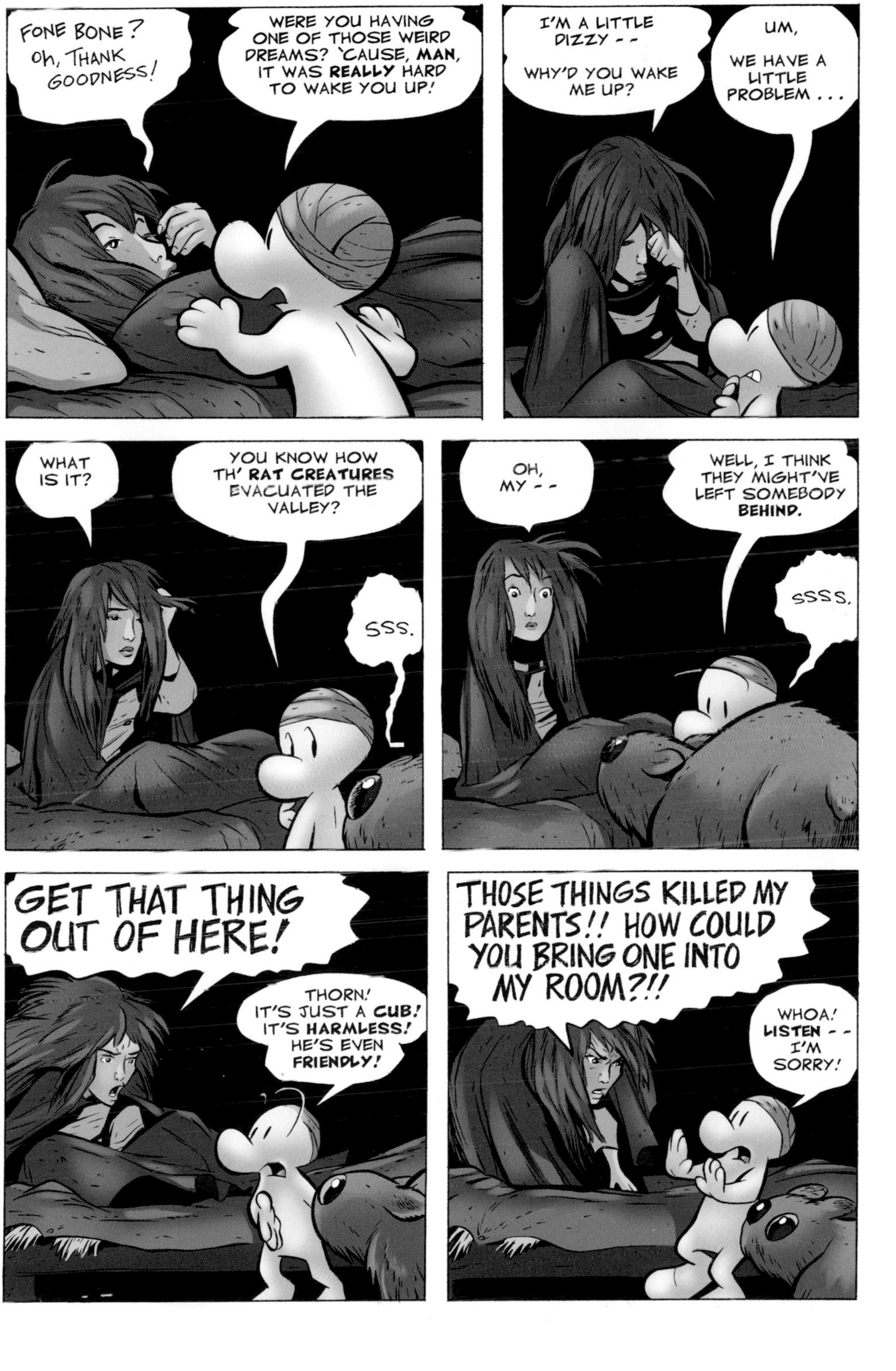
FONE BONE? Oh, THANK GOODNESS!
WERE YOU HAVING ONE OF THOSE WEIRD DREAMS? 'CAUSE, MAN, IT WAS REALLY HARD TO WAKE YOU UP!
I'M A LITTLE DIZZY - - WHY'D YOU WAKE ME UP?
UM, WE HAVE A LITTLE PROBLEM . . .
WHAT IS IT?
YOU KNOW HOW TH' RAT CREATURES EVACUATED THE VALLEY?
SSS.
OH, MY - -
WELL, I THINK THEY MIGHT'VE LEFT SOMEBODY BEHIND.
SSSS.
GET THAT THING OUT OF HERE!
THORN! IT'S JUST A CUB! IT'S HARMLESS! HE'S EVEN FRIENDLY!
THOSE THINGS KILLED MY PARENTS!! HOW COULD YOU BRING ONE INTO MY ROOM?!!
WHOA! LISTEN - - I'M SORRY!

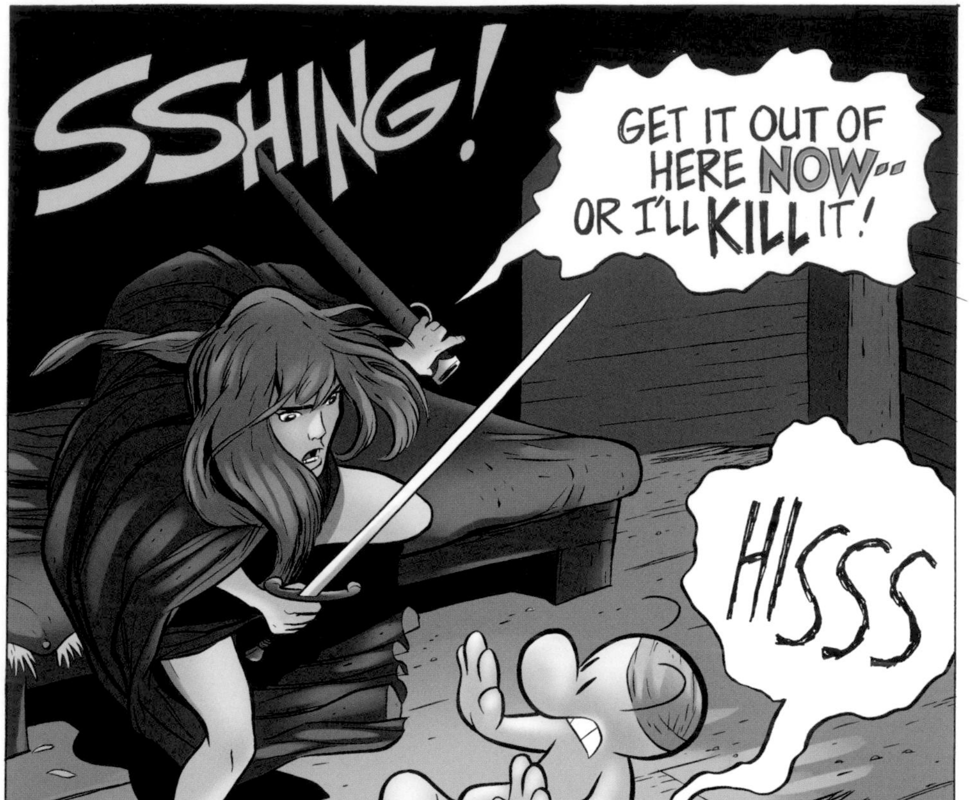
SSHING!
GET IT OUT OF HERE NOW-- OR I'LL KILL IT!
HISSS

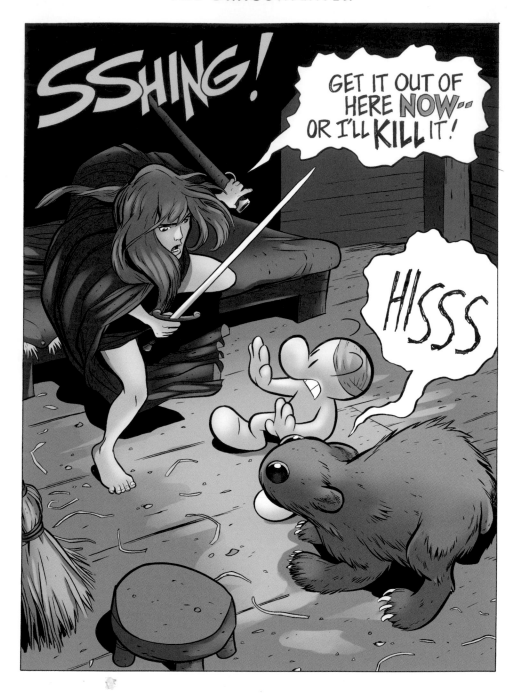

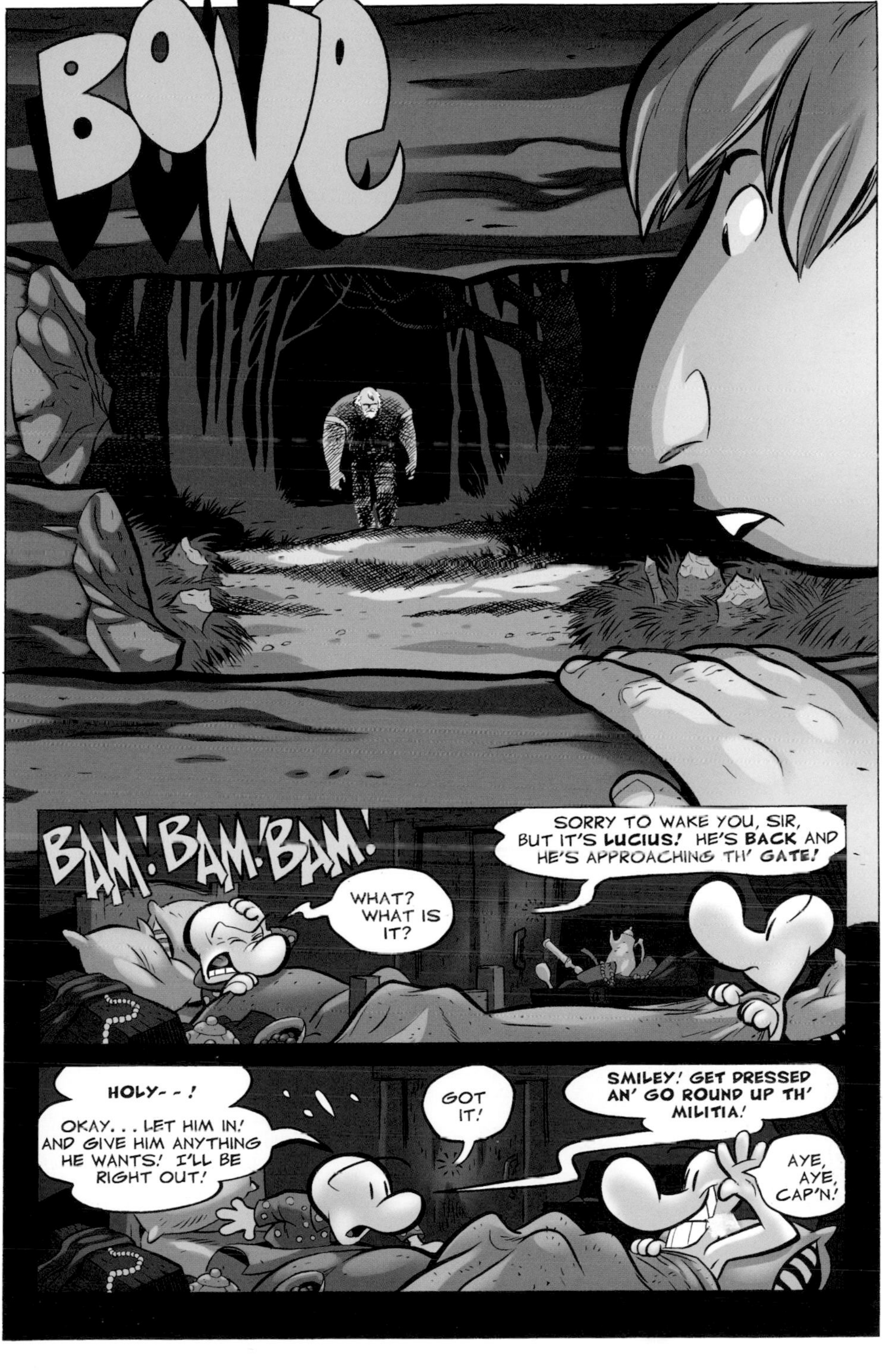
BONE
BAM! BAM! BAM!
WHAT? WHAT IS IT?
SORRY TO WAKE YOU, SIR, BUT IT'S LUCIUS! HE'S BACK AND HE'S APPROACHING TH' GATE!
HOLY--!
OKAY... LET HIM IN! AND GIVE HIM ANYTHING HE WANTS! I'LL BE RIGHT OUT!
GOT IT!
SMILEY! GET DRESSED AN' GO ROUND UP TH' MILITIA!
AYE, AYE, CAP'N!

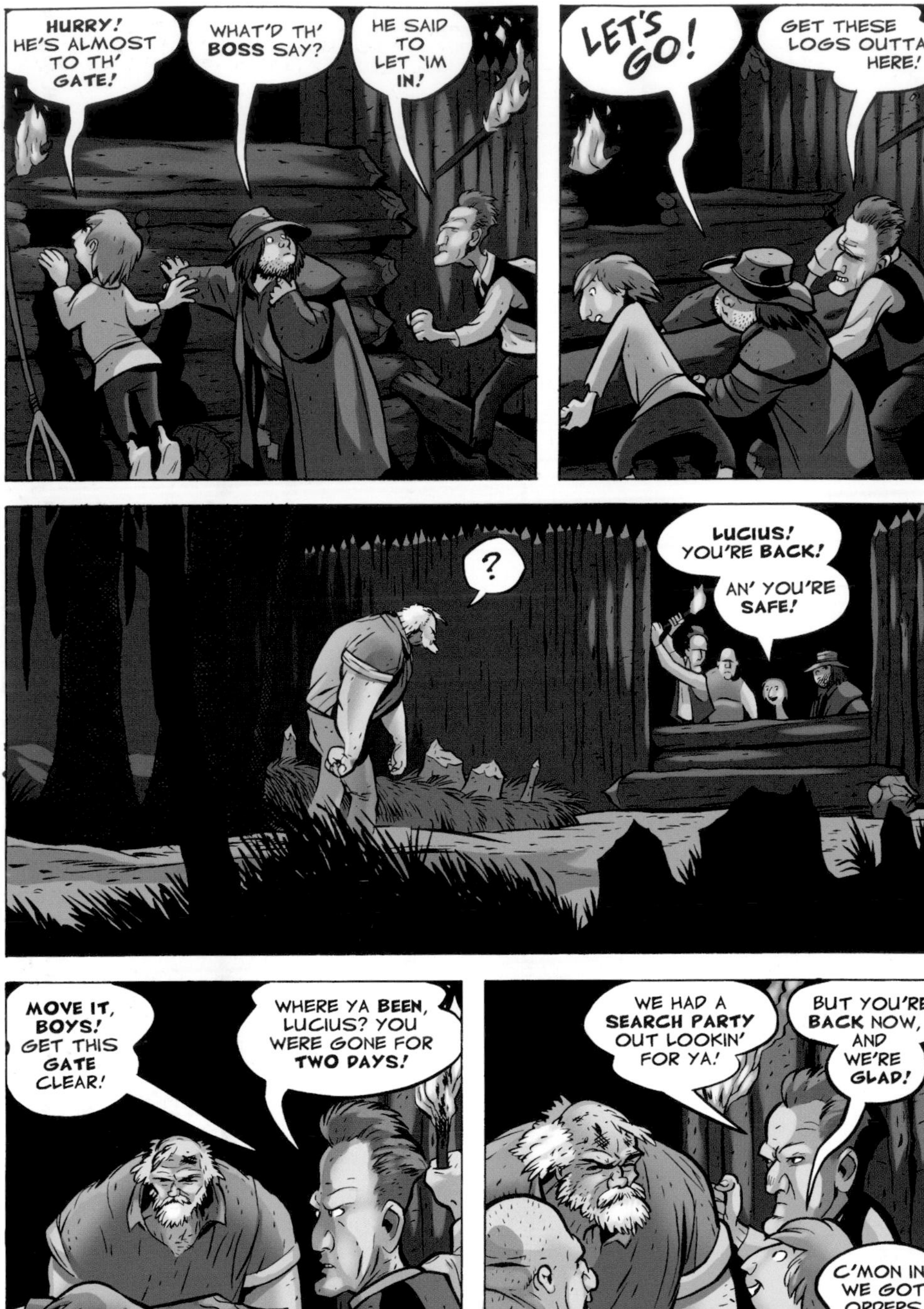
HURRY! HE'S ALMOST TO TH' GATE!
WHAT'D TH' BOSS SAY?
HE SAID TO LET 'IM IN!
LET'S GO!
GET THESE LOGS OUTTA HERE!
?
LUCIUS! YOU'RE BACK!
AN' YOU'RE SAFE!
MOVE IT, BOYS! GET THIS GATE CLEAR!
WHERE YA BEEN, LUCIUS? YOU WERE GONE FOR TWO DAYS!
WE HAD A SEARCH PARTY OUT LOOKIN' FOR YA!
BUT YOU'RE BACK NOW, AND WE'RE GLAD!
C'MON IN! WE GOT ORDERS TO LET YOU IN TH' GATE!

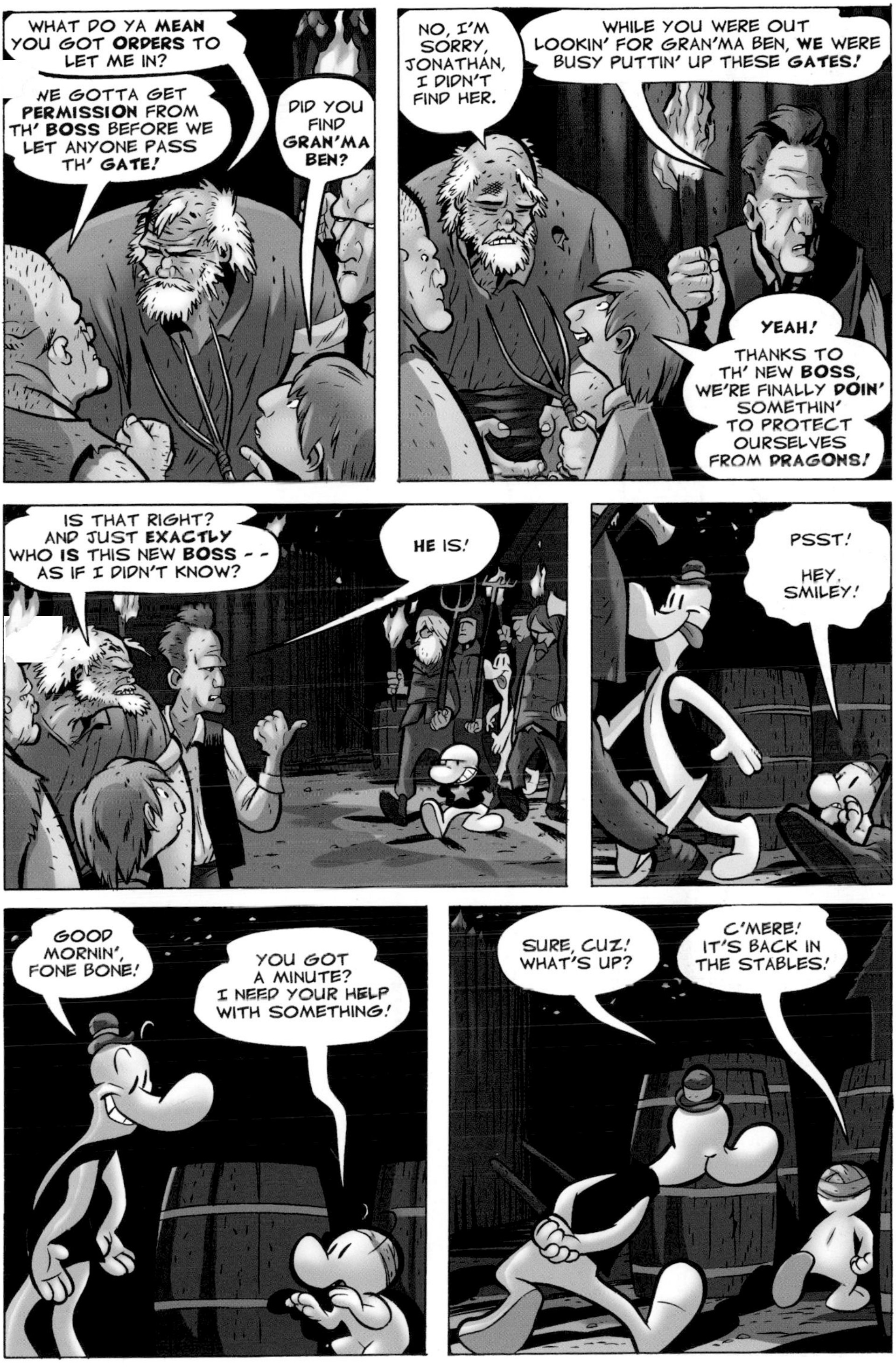
WHAT DO YA MEAN YOU GOT ORDERS TO LET ME IN?
WE GOTTA GET PERMISSION FROM TH' BOSS BEFORE WE LET ANYONE PASS TH' GATE!
DID YOU FIND GRAN'MA BEN?
NO, I'M SORRY, JONATHAN, I DIDN'T FIND HER.
WHILE YOU WERE OUT LOOKIN' FOR GRAN'MA BEN, WE WERE BUSY PUTTIN' UP THESE GATES!
YEAH! THANKS TO TH' NEW BOSS, WE'RE FINALLY DOIN' SOMETHIN' TO PROTECT OURSELVES FROM DRAGONS!
IS THAT RIGHT? AND JUST EXACTLY WHO IS THIS NEW BOSS - - AS IF I DIDN'T KNOW?
HE IS!
PSST! HEY, SMILEY!
GOOD MORNIN', FONE BONE!
YOU GOT A MINUTE? I NEED YOUR HELP WITH SOMETHING!
SURE, CUZ! WHAT'S UP?
C'MERE! IT'S BACK IN THE STABLES!

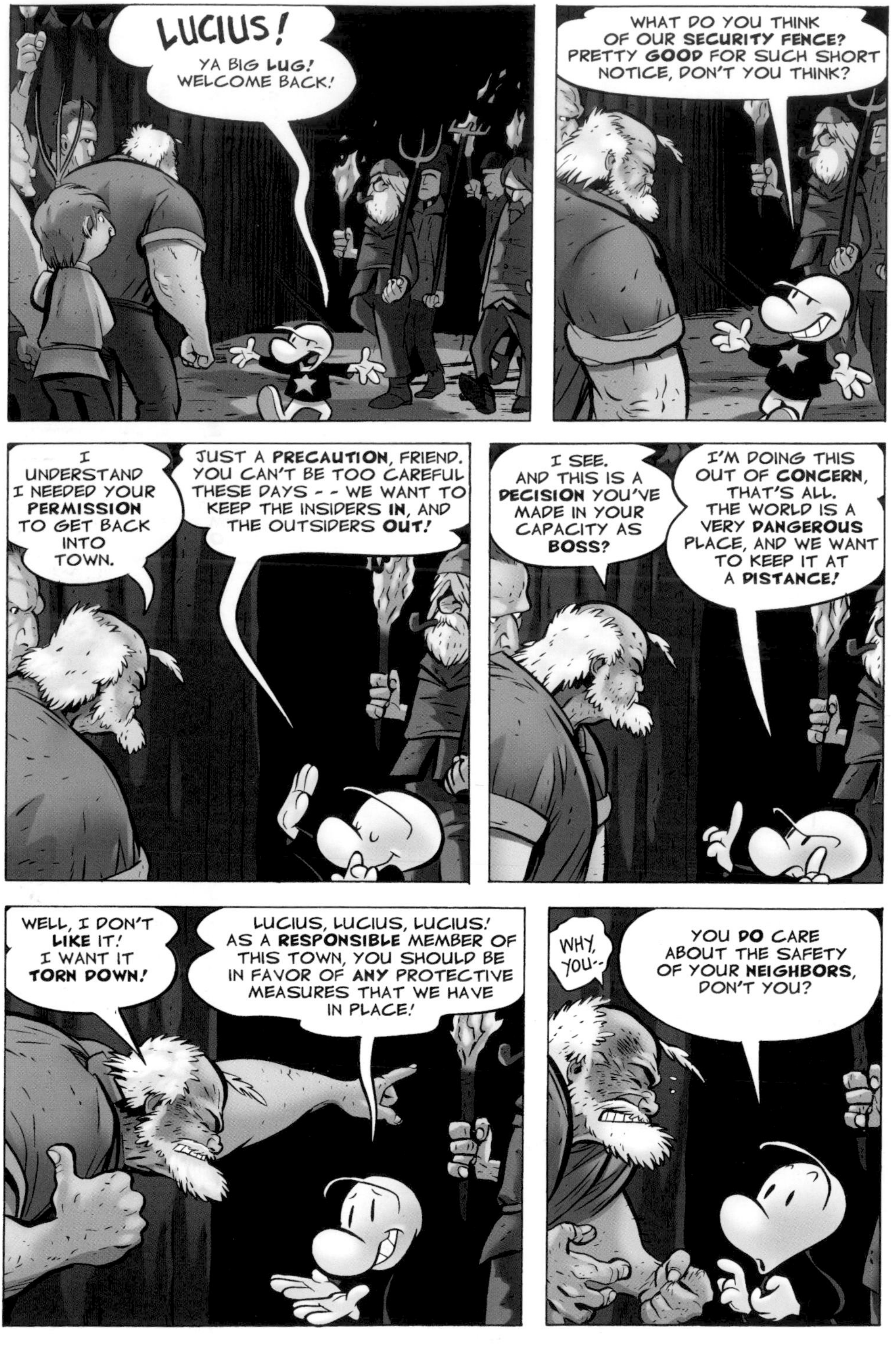
LUCIUS!
YA BIG LUG! WELCOME BACK!
WHAT DO YOU THINK OF OUR SECURITY FENCE? PRETTY GOOD FOR SUCH SHORT NOTICE, DON'T YOU THINK?
I UNDERSTAND I NEEDED YOUR PERMISSION TO GET BACK INTO TOWN.
JUST A PRECAUTION, FRIEND. YOU CAN'T BE TOO CAREFUL THESE DAYS - - WE WANT TO KEEP THE INSIDERS IN, AND THE OUTSIDERS OUT!
I SEE. AND THIS IS A DECISION YOU'VE MADE IN YOUR CAPACITY AS BOSS?
I'M DOING THIS OUT OF CONCERN, THAT'S ALL. THE WORLD IS A VERY DANGEROUS PLACE, AND WE WANT TO KEEP IT AT A DISTANCE!
WELL, I DON'T LIKE IT! I WANT IT TORN DOWN!
LUCIUS, LUCIUS, LUCIUS! AS A RESPONSIBLE MEMBER OF THIS TOWN, YOU SHOULD BE IN FAVOR OF ANY PROTECTIVE MEASURES THAT WE HAVE IN PLACE!
WHY, YOU--
YOU DO CARE ABOUT THE SAFETY OF YOUR NEIGHBORS, DON'T YOU?

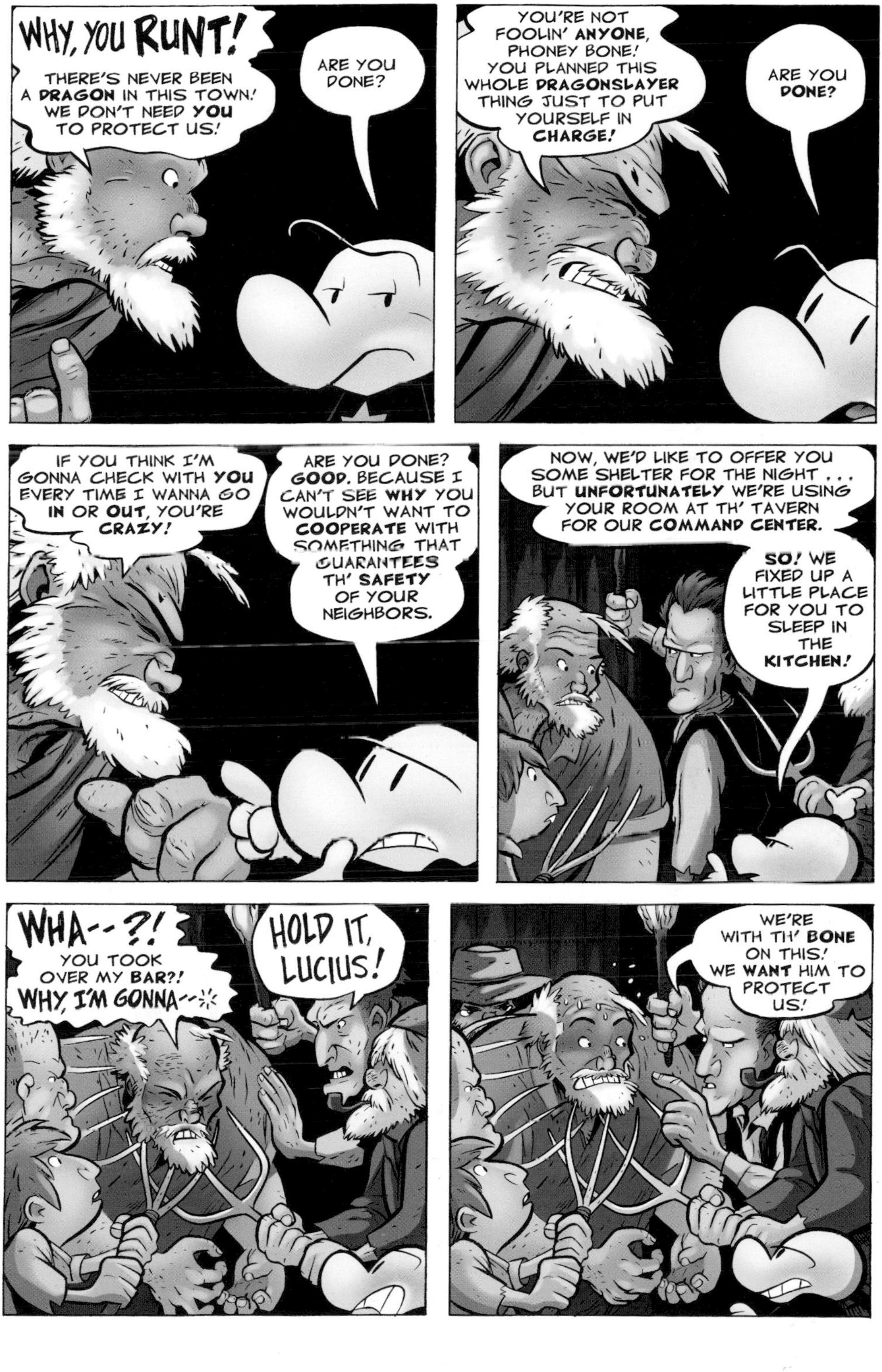
WHY, YOU RUNT!
THERE'S NEVER BEEN A DRAGON IN THIS TOWN! WE DON'T NEED YOU TO PROTECT US!
ARE YOU DONE?
YOU'RE NOT FOOLIN' ANYONE, PHONEY BONE! YOU PLANNED THIS WHOLE DRAGONSLAYER THING JUST TO PUT YOURSELF IN CHARGE!
ARE YOU DONE?
IF YOU THINK I'M GONNA CHECK WITH YOU EVERY TIME I WANNA GO IN OR OUT, YOU'RE CRAZY!
ARE YOU DONE? GOOD. BECAUSE I CAN'T SEE WHY YOU WOULDN'T WANT TO COOPERATE WITH SOMETHING THAT GUARANTEES TH' SAFETY OF YOUR NEIGHBORS.
NOW, WE'D LIKE TO OFFER YOU SOME SHELTER FOR THE NIGHT . . . BUT UNFORTUNATELY WE'RE USING YOUR ROOM AT TH' TAVERN FOR OUR COMMAND CENTER.
SO! WE FIXED UP A LITTLE PLACE FOR YOU TO SLEEP IN THE KITCHEN!
WHA--?! YOU TOOK OVER MY BAR?! WHY, I'M GONNA--
HOLD IT, LUCIUS!
WE'RE WITH TH' BONE ON THIS! WE WANT HIM TO PROTECT US!

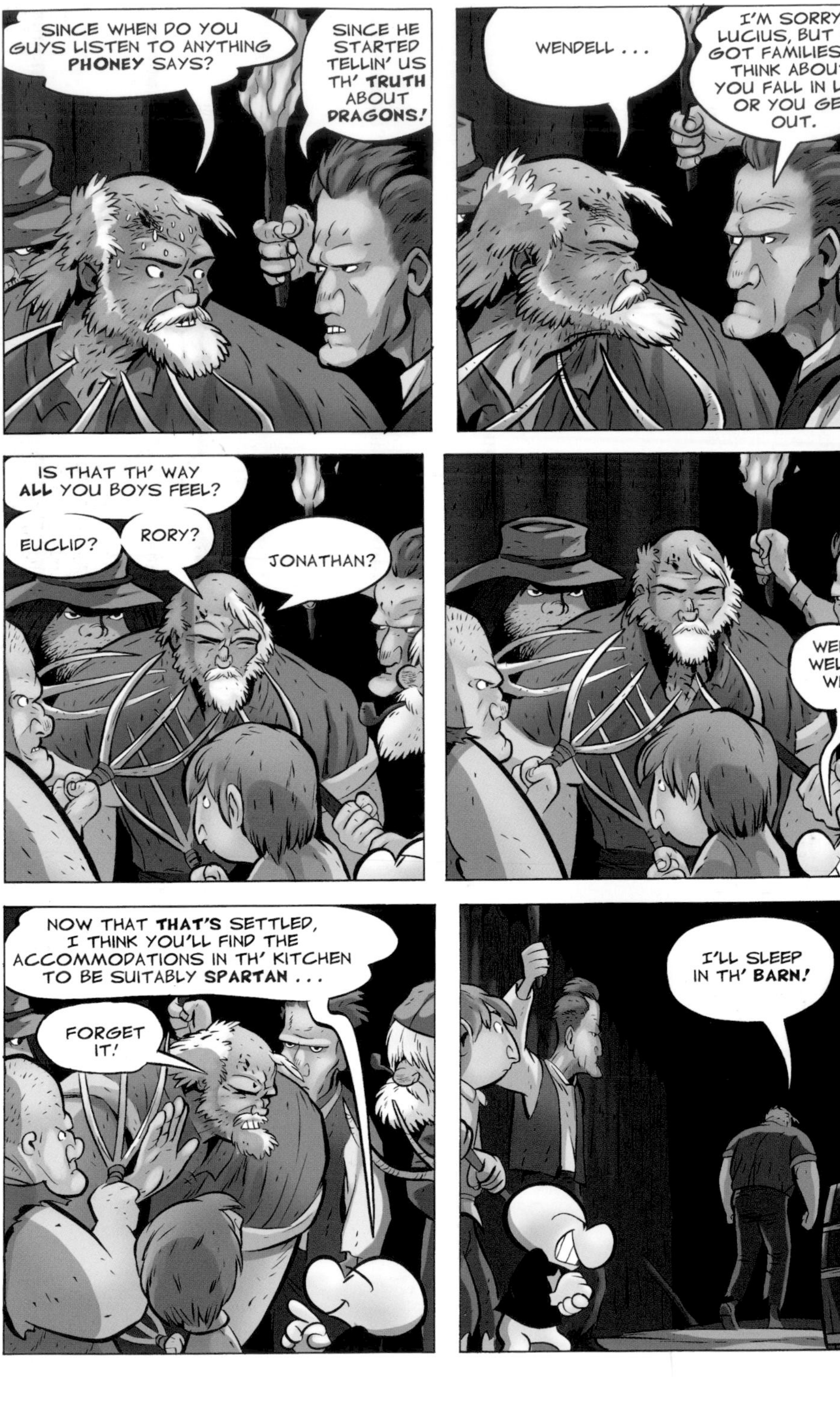
SINCE WHEN DO YOU GUYS LISTEN TO ANYTHING **PHONEY** SAYS?
SINCE HE STARTED TELLIN' US TH' **TRUTH** ABOUT **DRAGONS!**
WENDELL . . .
I'M SORRY, LUCIUS, BUT WE GOT FAMILIES TO THINK ABOUT. YOU FALL IN LINE, OR YOU GET OUT.
IS THAT TH' WAY **ALL** YOU BOYS FEEL?
EUCLID?
RORY?
JONATHAN?
WELL, WELL, WELL.
NOW THAT **THAT'S** SETTLED, I THINK YOU'LL FIND THE ACCOMMODATIONS IN TH' KITCHEN TO BE SUITABLY **SPARTAN** . . .
FORGET IT!
I'LL SLEEP IN TH' **BARN!**

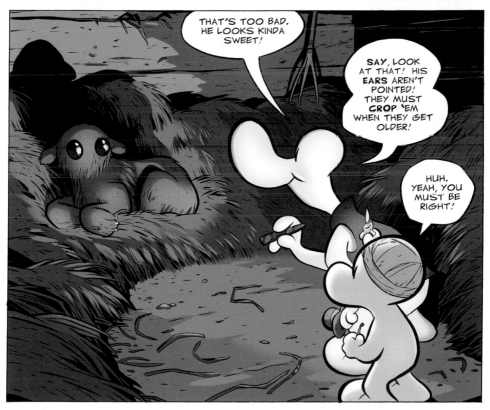

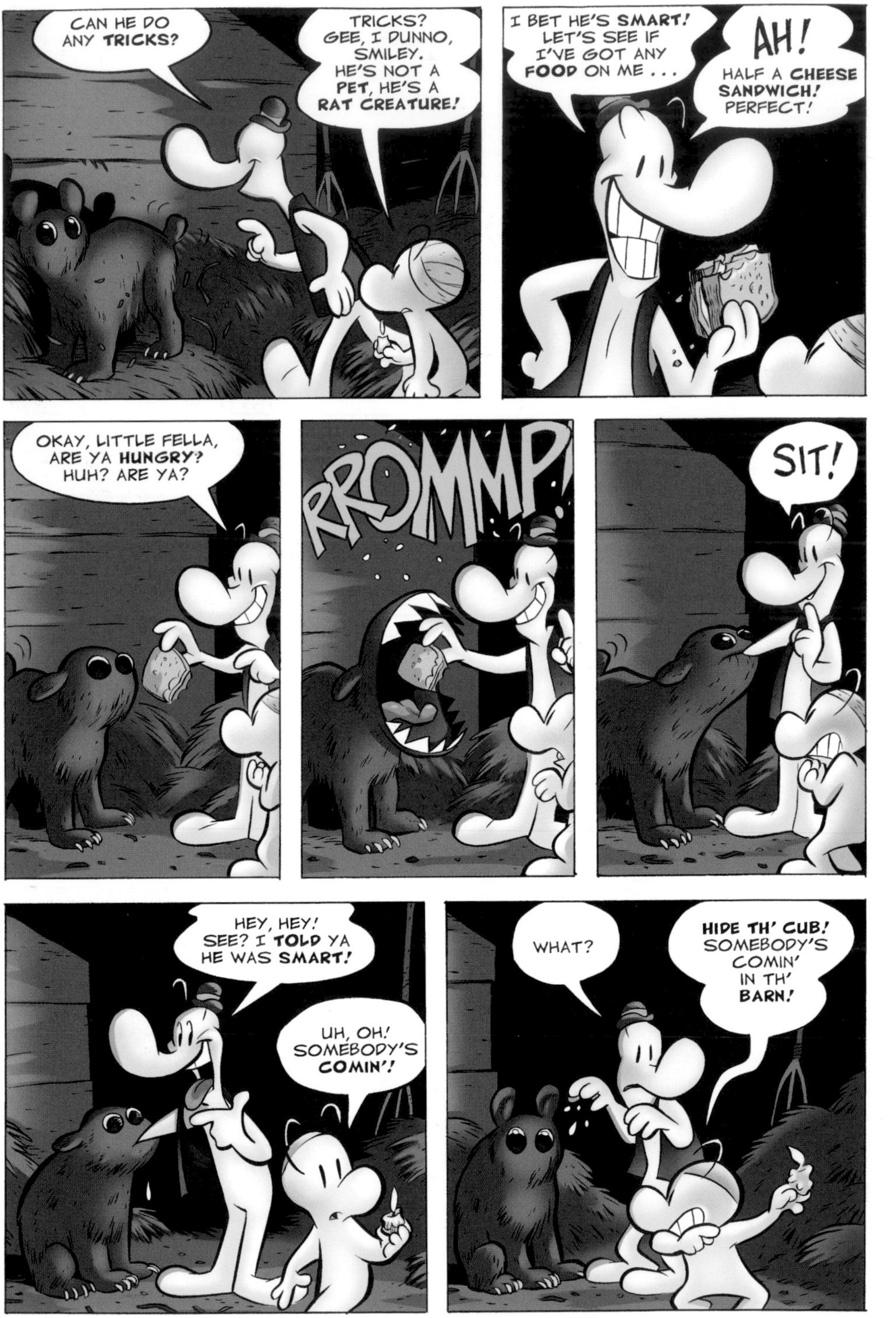
CAN HE DO ANY TRICKS?
TRICKS? GEE, I DUNNO, SMILEY. HE'S NOT A PET, HE'S A RAT CREATURE!
I BET HE'S SMART! LET'S SEE IF I'VE GOT ANY FOOD ON ME . . .
AH!
HALF A CHEESE SANDWICH! PERFECT!
OKAY, LITTLE FELLA, ARE YA HUNGRY? HUH? ARE YA?
RROMMP!
SIT!
HEY, HEY! SEE? I TOLD YA HE WAS SMART!
UH, OH! SOMEBODY'S COMIN'!
WHAT?
HIDE TH' CUB! SOMEBODY'S COMIN' IN TH' BARN!

CREEEEK

WHO'S IN THERE?

SPEAK UP! WHO'S THERE?

IT'S US, MR. DOWN! FONE BONE AND SMILEY BONE!

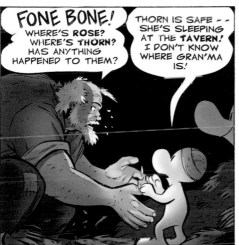

FONE BONE! WHERE'S ROSE? WHERE'S THORN? HAS ANYTHING HAPPENED TO THEM?

THORN IS SAFE -- SHE'S SLEEPING AT THE TAVERN! I DON'T KNOW WHERE GRAN'MA IS!

WHEN DID YOU SEE HER LAST? WAS SHE ALL RIGHT?

YES! YES! SHE AND THORN HAD A FIGHT! THORN RAN OFF, AN' GRAN'MA WANTED ME TO FOLLOW HER! WHEN I LEFT GRAN'MA BEN, SHE WAS STANDING OUT IN THE WOODS!

BUT BEFORE I WENT SHE HANDED ME THIS!

YOU GOT THIS FROM GRAN'MA BEN?

YES. SHE WANTED ME TO TELL YOU THAT THE RAT CREATURES HAVE EVACUATED TH' VALLEY!

MMMM...
EVACUATED THE VALLEY...
IT'S THE **NIGHTS OF LIGHTNING** ALL OVER AGAIN...

THE NIGHTS OF LIGHTNING!

WHAT'S A NIGHT OF LIGHTNING?

IT'S A **VICIOUS ATTACK** BY THE **RAT CREATURES!!**

ROSE MUST THINK THE RAT CREATURES ARE GOING TO BREAK TH' **TREATY.**

GULP!

WILL THEY COME HERE?

THIS IS TH' TREATY ZONE.

DID ROSE TELL YOU ANYTHING ELSE? DID SHE SAY WHERE SHE WAS GOING?

NO...

BUT SHE **DID** TELL US THE TRUTH ABOUT HER BEING THE **QUEEN OF ATHEIA,** AN' THAT **THORN** IS THE **HEIR TO THE THRONE!**

HEL-LO!

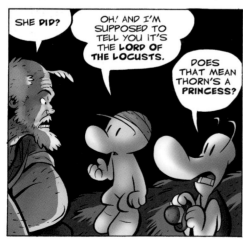

SHE **DID?**

OH! AND I'M SUPPOSED TO TELL YOU IT'S THE **LORD OF THE LOCUSTS.**

DOES THAT MEAN THORN'S A **PRINCESS?**

THAT'S ODD. THE LORD OF THE LOCUSTS WAS AN ANCIENT ENEMY OF THE **DRAGONS!** I THOUGHT HE GOT TURNED INTO **STONE** OR SOMETHING BACK WHEN THE **DRAGONS** STILL RULED THE EARTH.

GRAN'MA WAS PRETTY **UPSET** ABOUT IT --

SACRÉ BLEU!

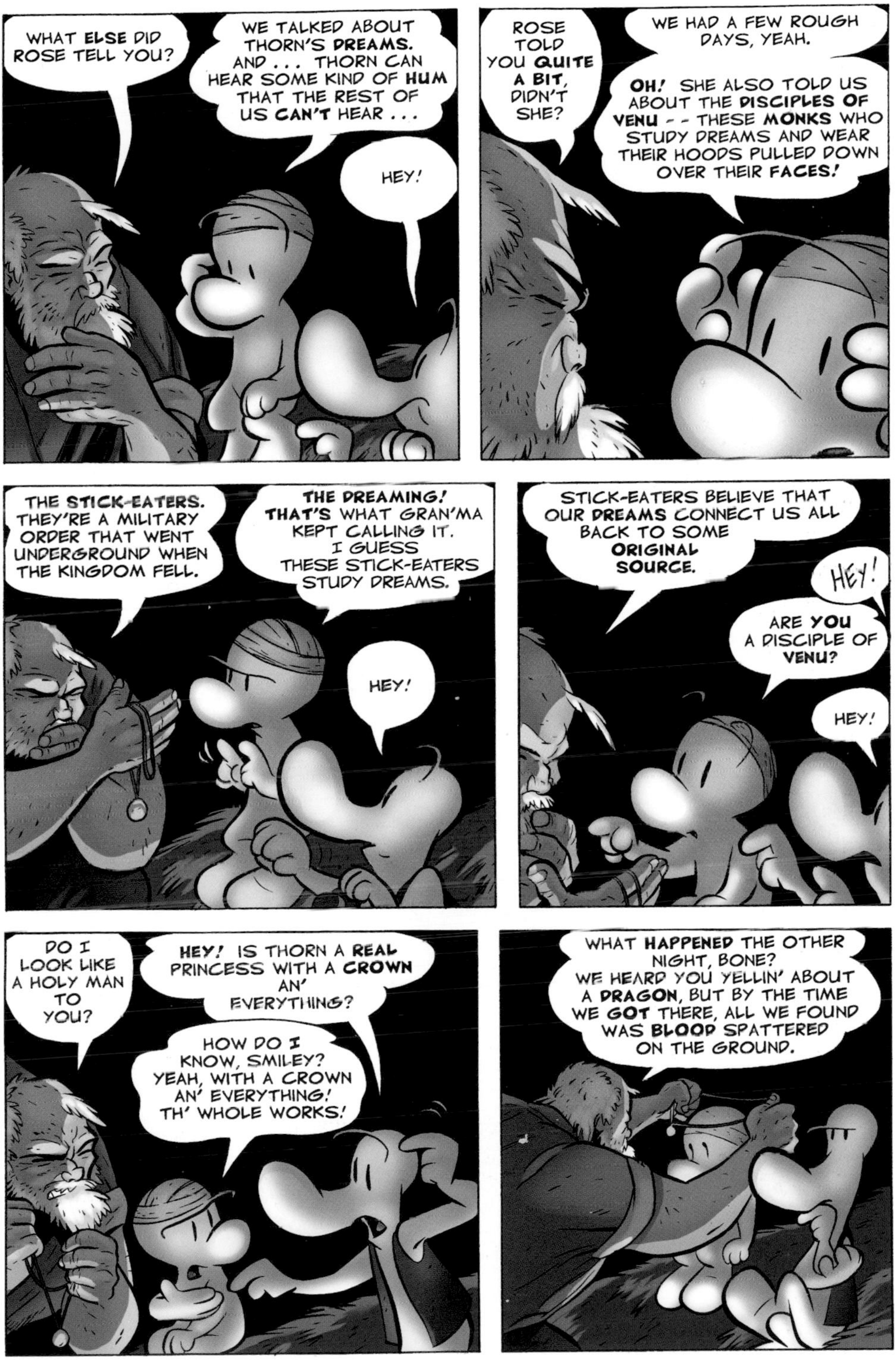
WHAT ELSE DID ROSE TELL YOU?
WE TALKED ABOUT THORN'S DREAMS. AND . . . THORN CAN HEAR SOME KIND OF HUM THAT THE REST OF US CAN'T HEAR . . .
HEY!
ROSE TOLD YOU QUITE A BIT, DIDN'T SHE?
WE HAD A FEW ROUGH DAYS, YEAH.
OH! SHE ALSO TOLD US ABOUT THE DISCIPLES OF VENU - - THESE MONKS WHO STUDY DREAMS AND WEAR THEIR HOODS PULLED DOWN OVER THEIR FACES!
THE STICK-EATERS. THEY'RE A MILITARY ORDER THAT WENT UNDERGROUND WHEN THE KINGDOM FELL.
THE DREAMING! THAT'S WHAT GRAN'MA KEPT CALLING IT. I GUESS THESE STICK-EATERS STUDY DREAMS.
HEY!
STICK-EATERS BELIEVE THAT OUR DREAMS CONNECT US ALL BACK TO SOME ORIGINAL SOURCE.
HEY!
ARE YOU A DISCIPLE OF VENU?
HEY!
DO I LOOK LIKE A HOLY MAN TO YOU?
HEY! IS THORN A REAL PRINCESS WITH A CROWN AN' EVERYTHING?
HOW DO I KNOW, SMILEY? YEAH, WITH A CROWN AN' EVERYTHING! TH' WHOLE WORKS!
WHAT HAPPENED THE OTHER NIGHT, BONE? WE HEARD YOU YELLIN' ABOUT A DRAGON, BUT BY THE TIME WE GOT THERE, ALL WE FOUND WAS BLOOD SPATTERED ON THE GROUND.

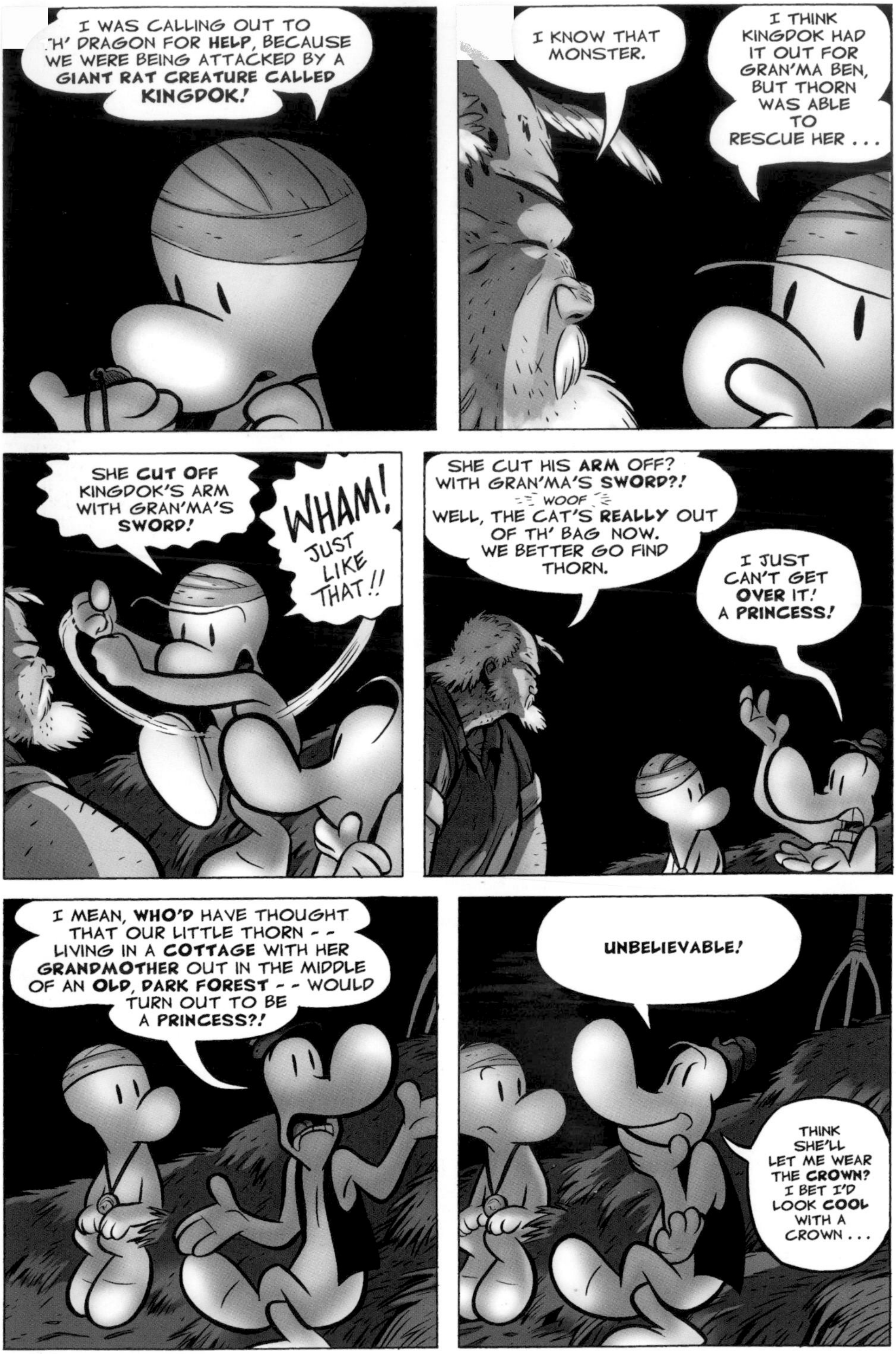
I WAS CALLING OUT TO TH' DRAGON FOR HELP, BECAUSE WE WERE BEING ATTACKED BY A GIANT RAT CREATURE CALLED KINGDOK!
I KNOW THAT MONSTER.
I THINK KINGDOK HAD IT OUT FOR GRAN'MA BEN, BUT THORN WAS ABLE TO RESCUE HER . . .
SHE CUT OFF KINGDOK'S ARM WITH GRAN'MA'S SWORD!
WHAM! JUST LIKE THAT!!
SHE CUT HIS ARM OFF? WITH GRAN'MA'S SWORD?! WOOF WELL, THE CAT'S REALLY OUT OF TH' BAG NOW. WE BETTER GO FIND THORN.
I JUST CAN'T GET OVER IT! A PRINCESS!
I MEAN, WHO'D HAVE THOUGHT THAT OUR LITTLE THORN - - LIVING IN A COTTAGE WITH HER GRANDMOTHER OUT IN THE MIDDLE OF AN OLD, DARK FOREST - - WOULD TURN OUT TO BE A PRINCESS?!
UNBELIEVABLE!
THINK SHE'LL LET ME WEAR THE CROWN? I BET I'D LOOK COOL WITH A CROWN . . .

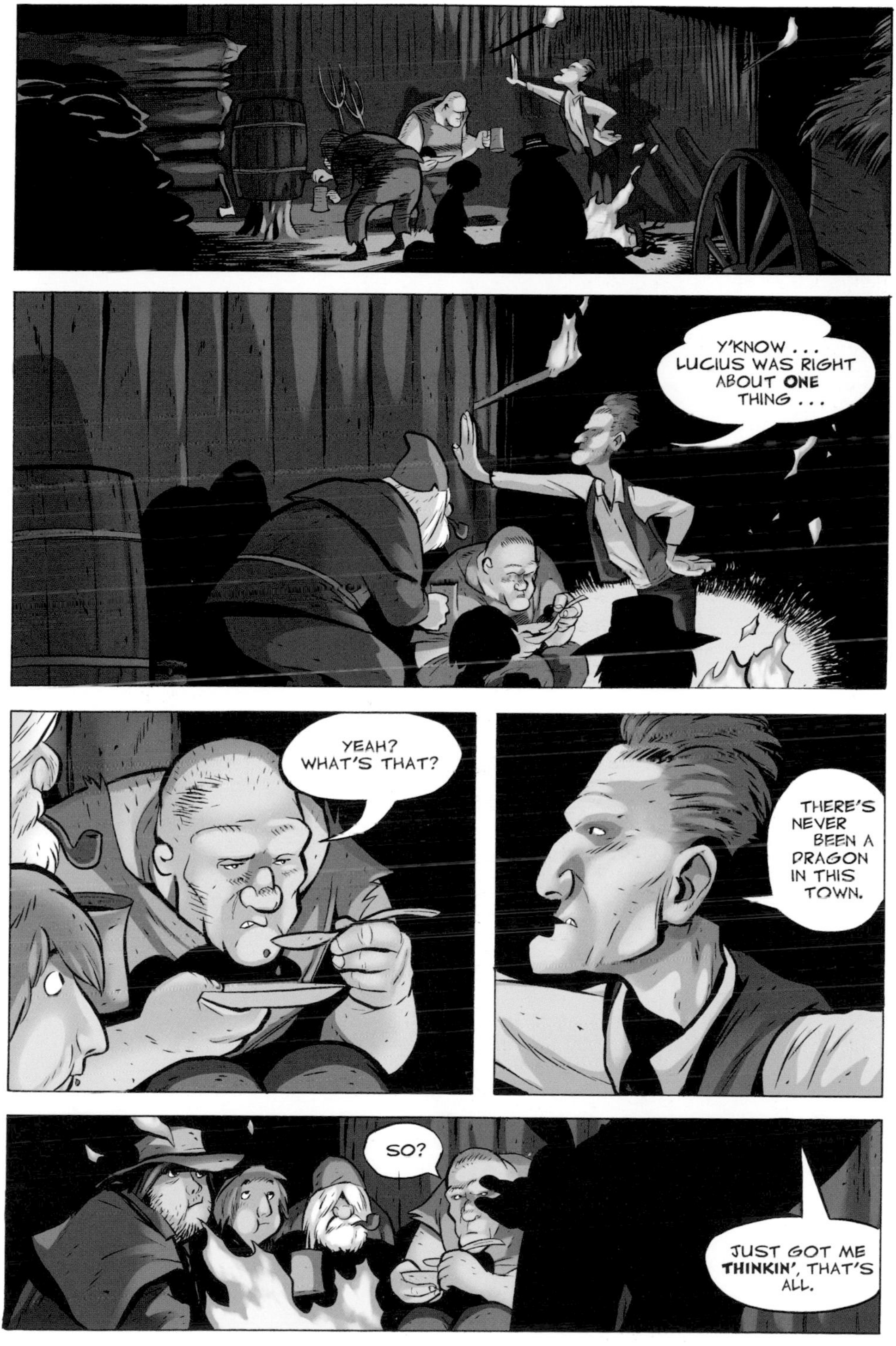
Y'KNOW . . . LUCIUS WAS RIGHT ABOUT ONE THING . . .
YEAH? WHAT'S THAT?
THERE'S NEVER BEEN A DRAGON IN THIS TOWN.
SO?
JUST GOT ME THINKIN', THAT'S ALL.

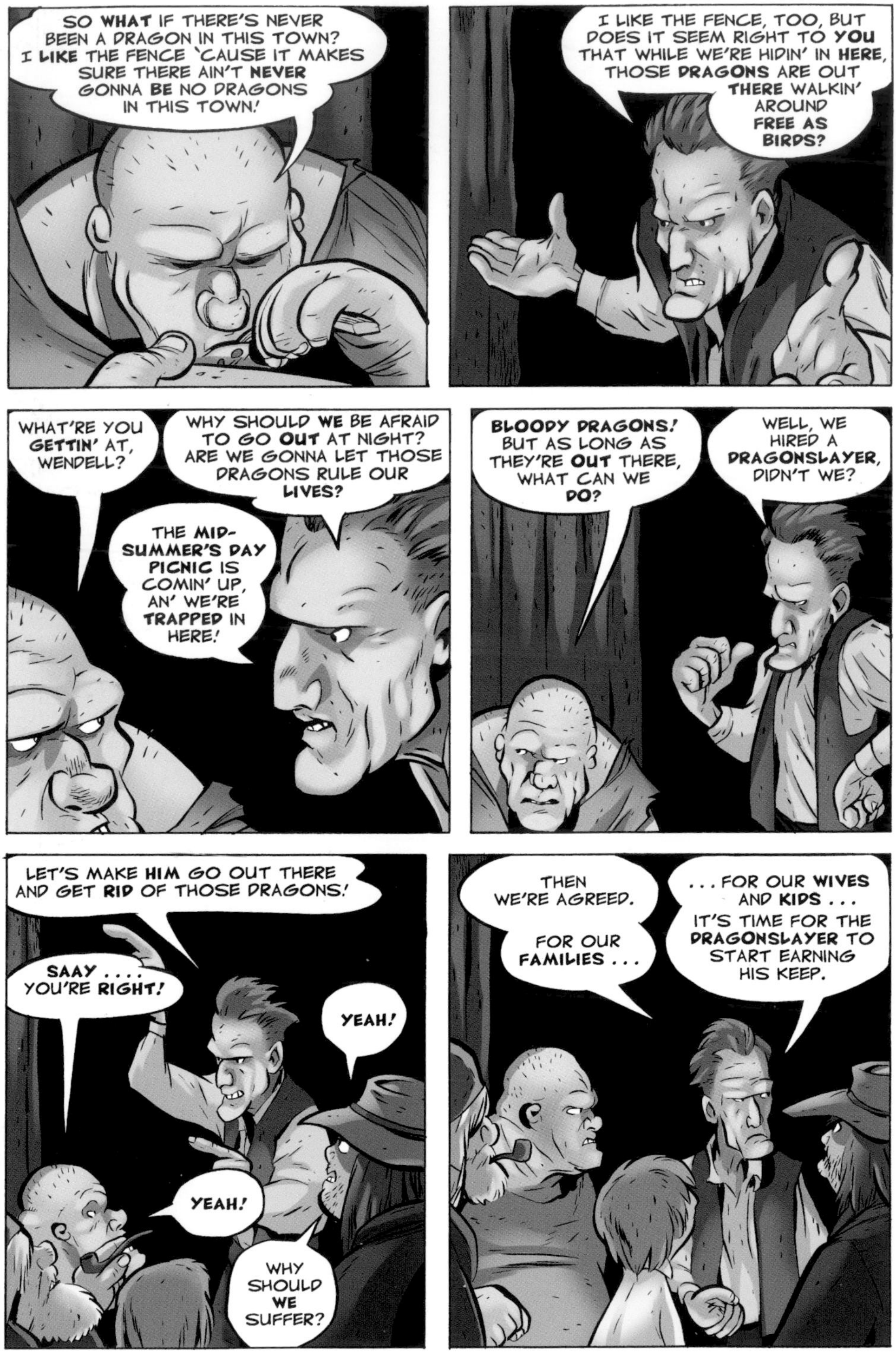
SO WHAT IF THERE'S NEVER BEEN A DRAGON IN THIS TOWN? I LIKE THE FENCE 'CAUSE IT MAKES SURE THERE AIN'T NEVER GONNA BE NO DRAGONS IN THIS TOWN!
I LIKE THE FENCE, TOO, BUT DOES IT SEEM RIGHT TO YOU THAT WHILE WE'RE HIDIN' IN HERE, THOSE DRAGONS ARE OUT THERE WALKIN' AROUND FREE AS BIRDS?
WHAT'RE YOU GETTIN' AT, WENDELL?
WHY SHOULD WE BE AFRAID TO GO OUT AT NIGHT? ARE WE GONNA LET THOSE DRAGONS RULE OUR LIVES?
THE MID-SUMMER'S DAY PICNIC IS COMIN' UP, AN' WE'RE TRAPPED IN HERE!
BLOODY DRAGONS! BUT AS LONG AS THEY'RE OUT THERE, WHAT CAN WE DO?
WELL, WE HIRED A DRAGONSLAYER, DIDN'T WE?
LET'S MAKE HIM GO OUT THERE AND GET RID OF THOSE DRAGONS!
SAAY . . . . YOU'RE RIGHT!
YEAH!
YEAH!
WHY SHOULD WE SUFFER?
THEN WE'RE AGREED.
FOR OUR FAMILIES . . .
. . . FOR OUR WIVES AND KIDS . . .
IT'S TIME FOR THE DRAGONSLAYER TO START EARNING HIS KEEP.

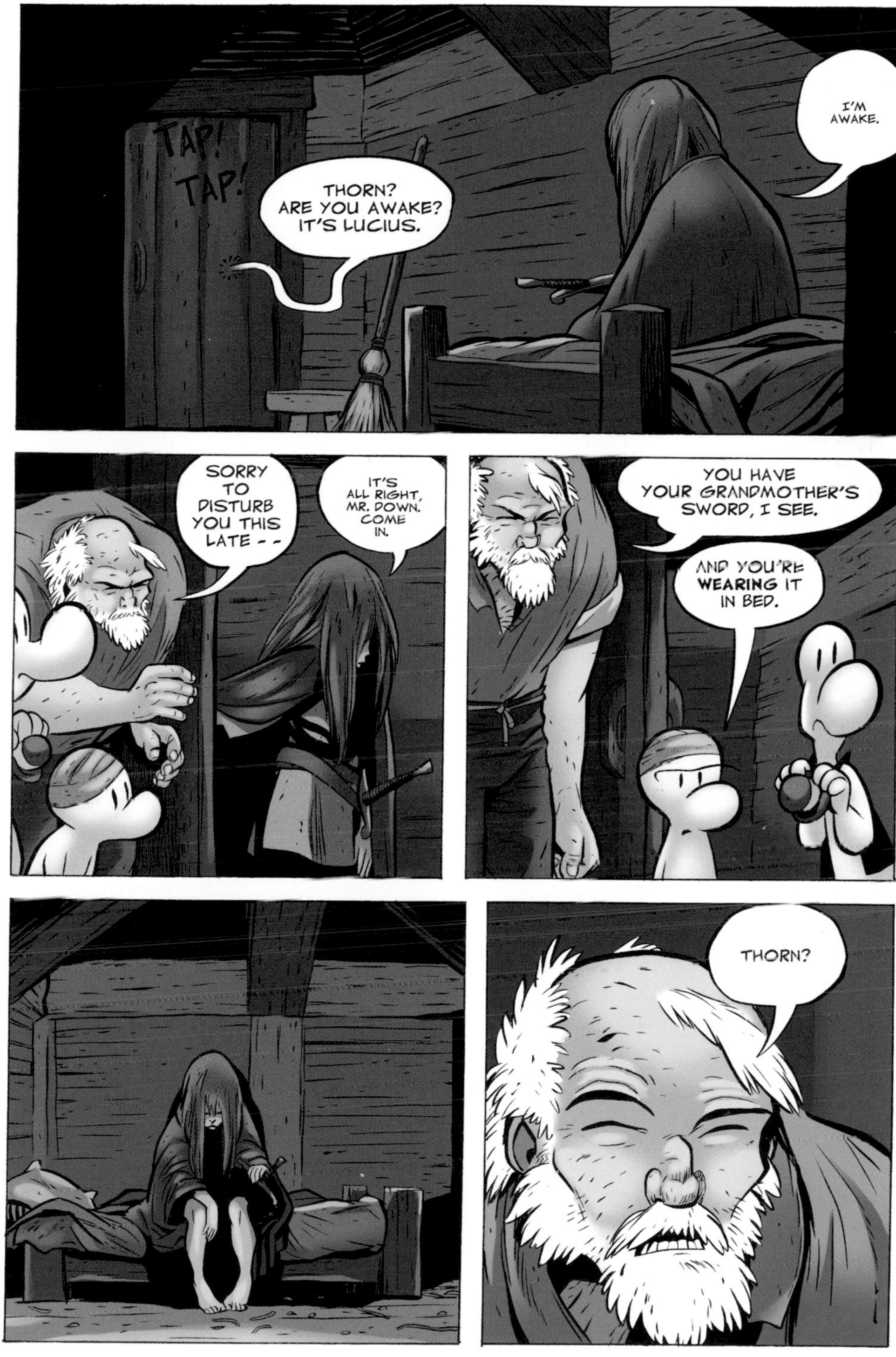
TAP! TAP!
THORN? ARE YOU AWAKE? IT'S LUCIUS.
I'M AWAKE.
SORRY TO DISTURB YOU THIS LATE - -
IT'S ALL RIGHT, MR. DOWN. COME IN.
YOU HAVE YOUR GRANDMOTHER'S SWORD, I SEE.
AND YOU'RE **WEARING** IT IN BED.
THORN?

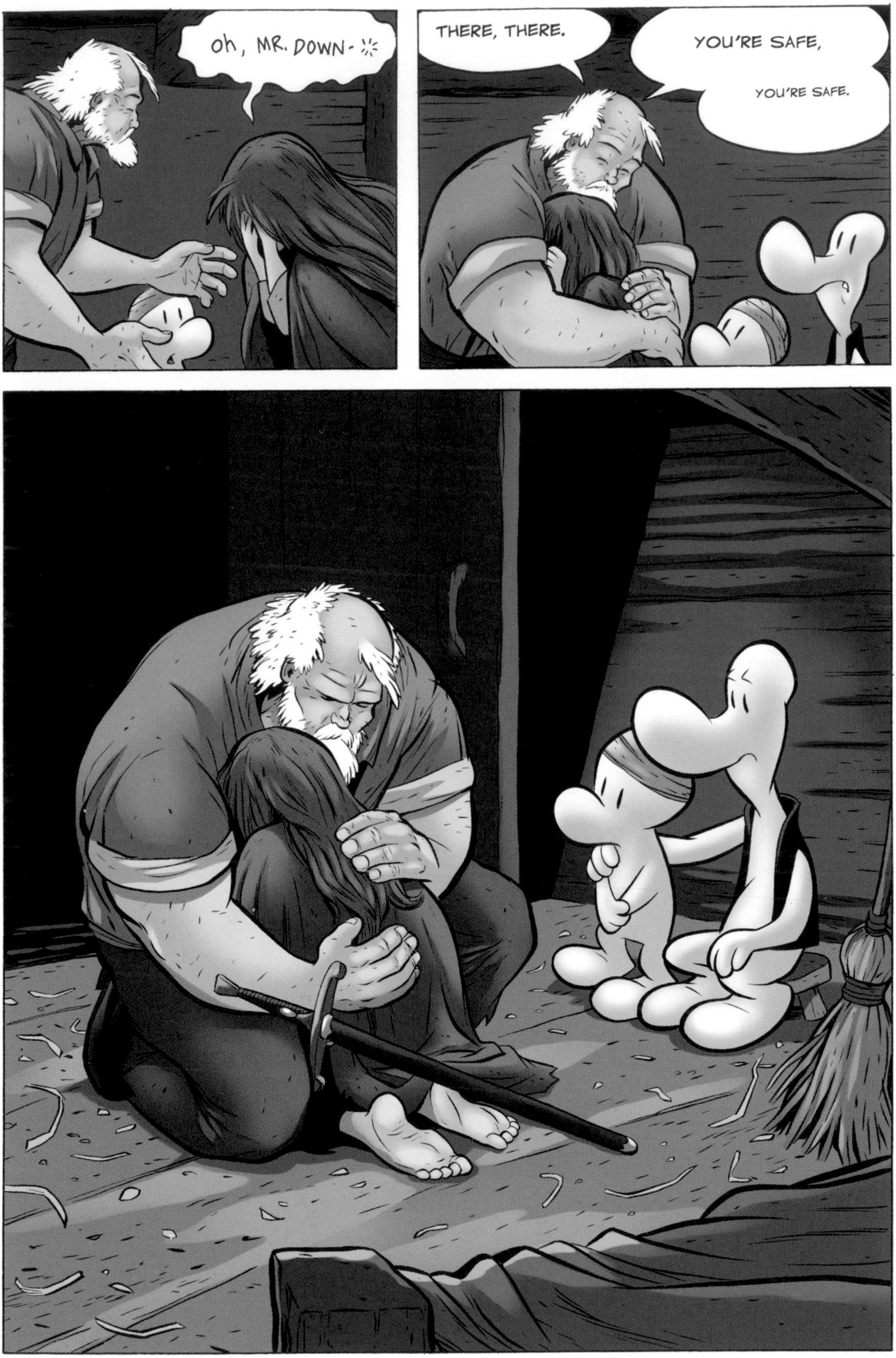
Oh, MR. DOWN-
THERE, THERE.
YOU'RE SAFE,
YOU'RE SAFE.

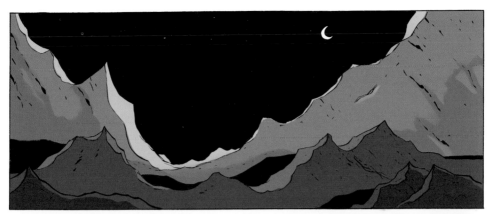

. . . TONIGHT . . .

. . . . WE BEGIN ANEW . . . .

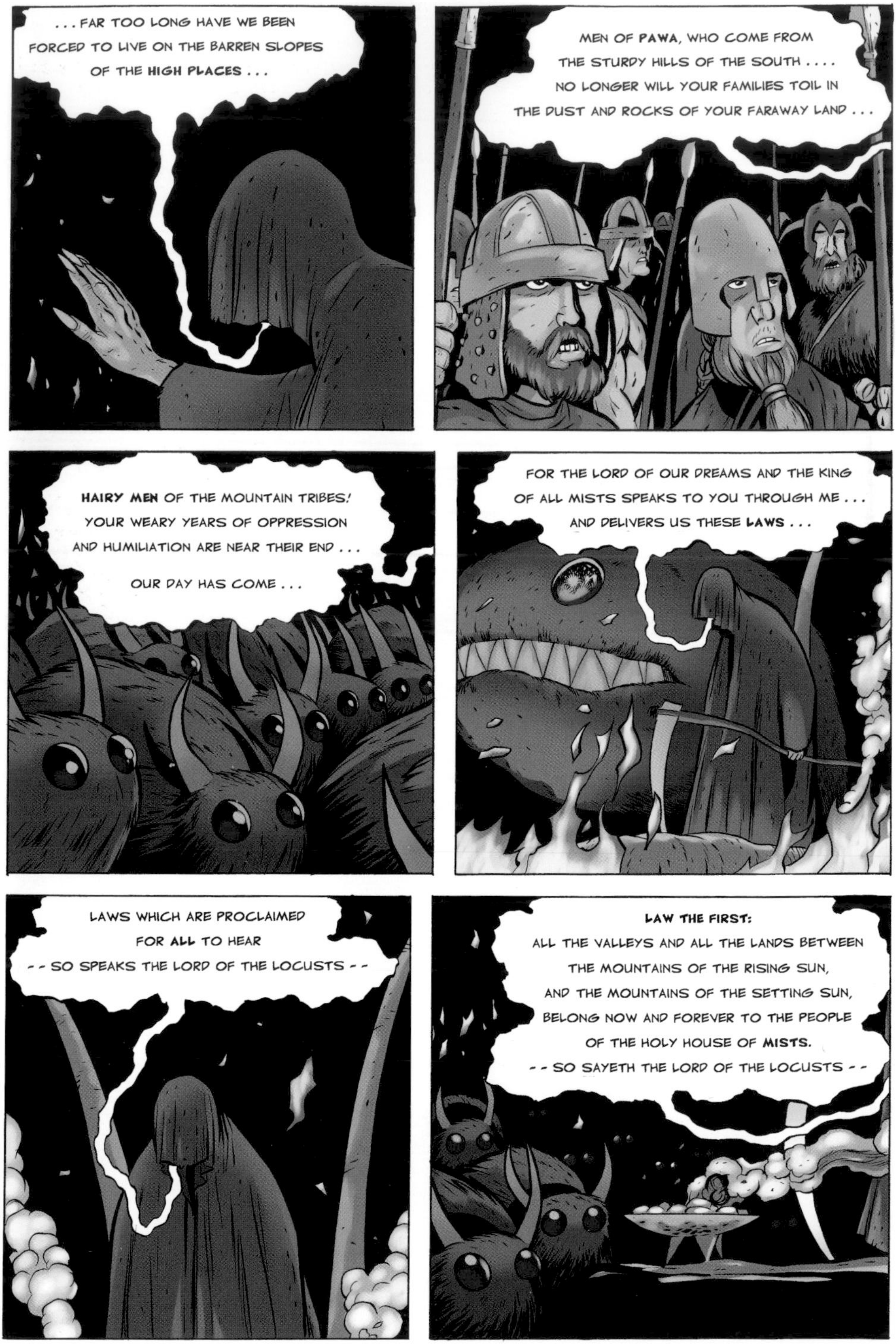
. . . FAR TOO LONG HAVE WE BEEN FORCED TO LIVE ON THE BARREN SLOPES OF THE HIGH PLACES . . .
MEN OF PAWA, WHO COME FROM THE STURDY HILLS OF THE SOUTH . . . . NO LONGER WILL YOUR FAMILIES TOIL IN THE DUST AND ROCKS OF YOUR FARAWAY LAND . . .
HAIRY MEN OF THE MOUNTAIN TRIBES! YOUR WEARY YEARS OF OPPRESSION AND HUMILIATION ARE NEAR THEIR END . . . OUR DAY HAS COME . . .
FOR THE LORD OF OUR DREAMS AND THE KING OF ALL MISTS SPEAKS TO YOU THROUGH ME . . . AND DELIVERS US THESE LAWS . . .
LAWS WHICH ARE PROCLAIMED FOR ALL TO HEAR - - SO SPEAKS THE LORD OF THE LOCUSTS - -
LAW THE FIRST: ALL THE VALLEYS AND ALL THE LANDS BETWEEN THE MOUNTAINS OF THE RISING SUN, AND THE MOUNTAINS OF THE SETTING SUN, BELONG NOW AND FOREVER TO THE PEOPLE OF THE HOLY HOUSE OF MISTS. - - SO SAYETH THE LORD OF THE LOCUSTS - -

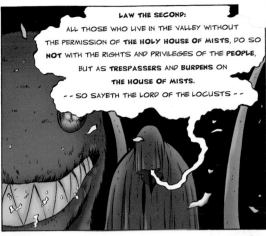

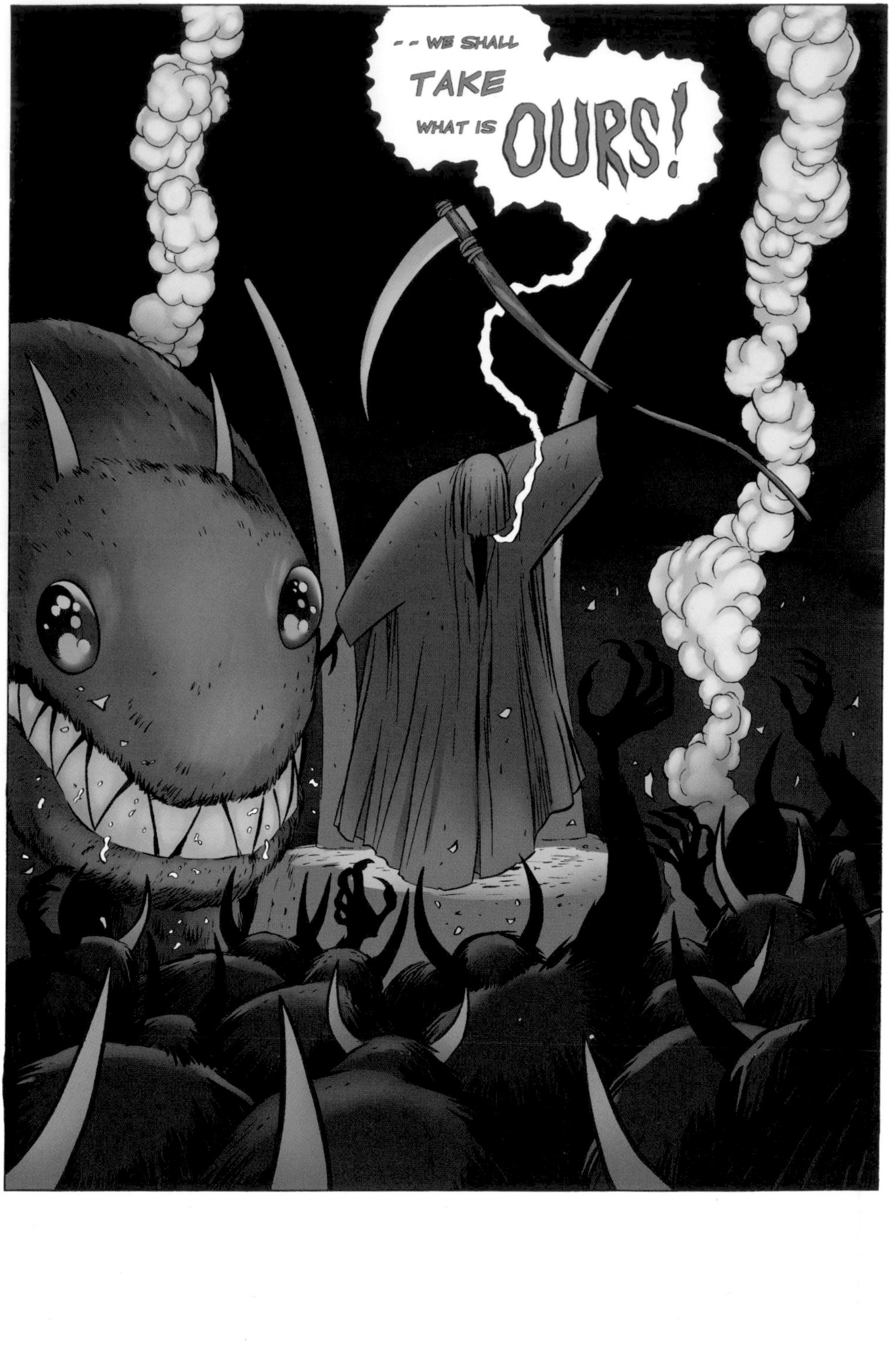

- - WE SHALL TAKE WHAT IS OURS!

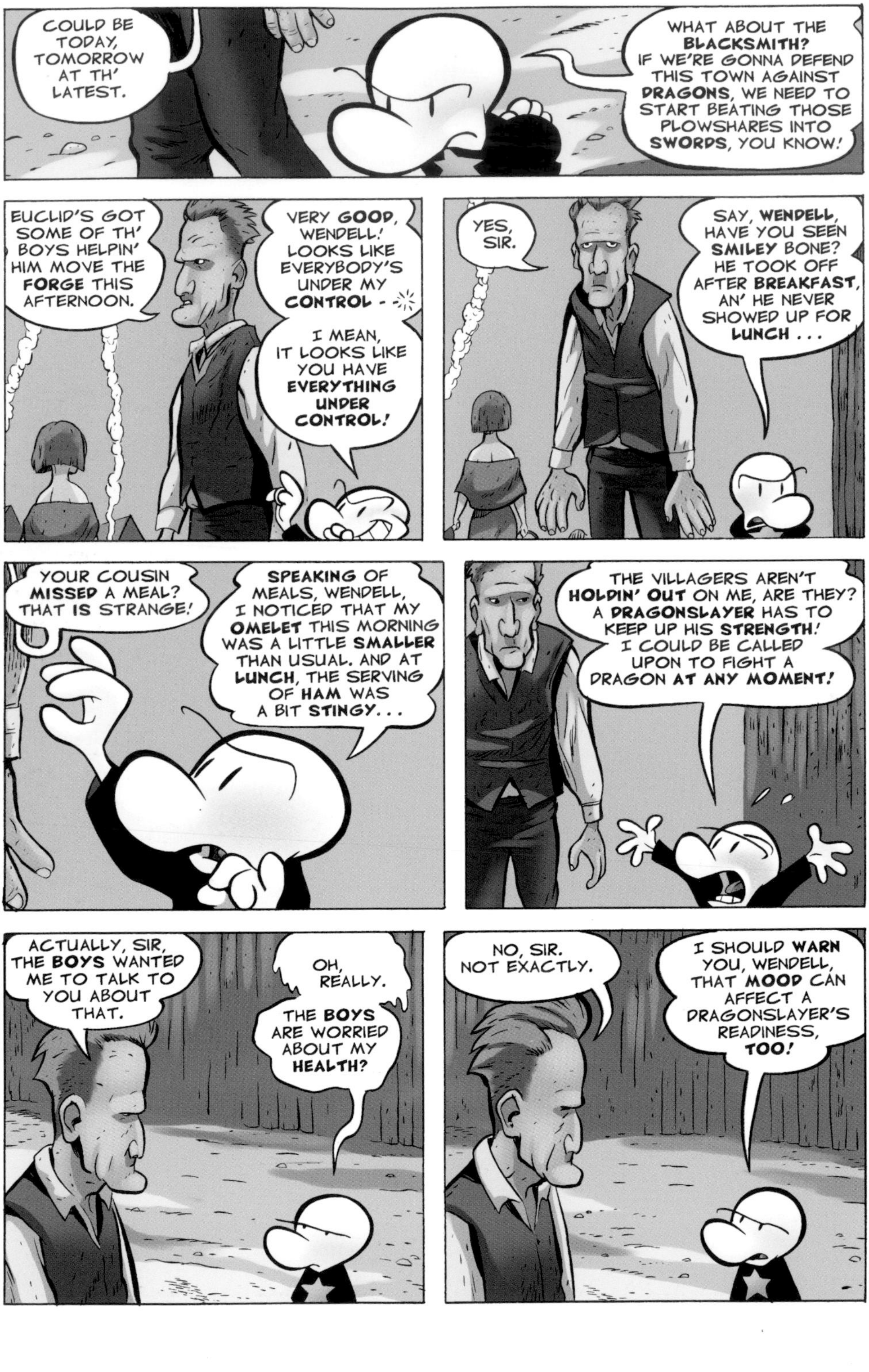
COULD BE TODAY, TOMORROW AT TH' LATEST.
WHAT ABOUT THE BLACKSMITH? IF WE'RE GONNA DEFEND THIS TOWN AGAINST DRAGONS, WE NEED TO START BEATING THOSE PLOWSHARES INTO SWORDS, YOU KNOW!
EUCLID'S GOT SOME OF TH' BOYS HELPIN' HIM MOVE THE FORGE THIS AFTERNOON.
VERY GOOD, WENDELL! LOOKS LIKE EVERYBODY'S UNDER MY CONTROL -
I MEAN, IT LOOKS LIKE YOU HAVE EVERYTHING UNDER CONTROL!
YES, SIR.
SAY, WENDELL, HAVE YOU SEEN SMILEY BONE? HE TOOK OFF AFTER BREAKFAST, AN' HE NEVER SHOWED UP FOR LUNCH . . .
YOUR COUSIN MISSED A MEAL? THAT IS STRANGE!
SPEAKING OF MEALS, WENDELL, I NOTICED THAT MY OMELET THIS MORNING WAS A LITTLE SMALLER THAN USUAL. AND AT LUNCH, THE SERVING OF HAM WAS A BIT STINGY. . .
THE VILLAGERS AREN'T HOLDIN' OUT ON ME, ARE THEY? A DRAGONSLAYER HAS TO KEEP UP HIS STRENGTH! I COULD BE CALLED UPON TO FIGHT A DRAGON AT ANY MOMENT!
ACTUALLY, SIR, THE BOYS WANTED ME TO TALK TO YOU ABOUT THAT.
OH, REALLY.
THE BOYS ARE WORRIED ABOUT MY HEALTH?
NO, SIR. NOT EXACTLY.
I SHOULD WARN YOU, WENDELL, THAT MOOD CAN AFFECT A DRAGONSLAYER'S READINESS, TOO!

IT'S JUST THAT TH' BOYS THOUGHT THAT A LOT OF **TIME** AN' **EFFORT** COULD BE SAVED IF YOU ACTUALLY WENT OUT AND **SLAYED** A **DRAGON!**

SO **THAT'S** HOW IT'S GONNA BE, HUH? **HOLDIN' OUT** ON ME, HUH?!

NO, IT'S JUST THAT WE'VE BEEN **FEEDIN'** YOU AN' YOUR COUSINS FOR OVER A **WEEK**, AN' YOU HAVEN'T GONE OUT TO KILL DRAGONS EVEN **ONCE!**

DON'T GET **CHEAP** ON ME, WENDELL! IF YOU CAN'T AFFORD TO HAVE A **DRAGONSLAYER** AROUND, JUST SAY SO, BUT DON'T GO **HOLDIN' OUT** ON ME!

WE'RE **NOT** HOLDIN' OUT ON YOU! WE PAID YOU TO BE A **DRAGONSLAYER**, AN' WE WANT YOU TO **SLAY** A DRAGON!!

FOR **SHAME!** YOU THINK I DON'T **KNOW** YER **HOLDIN' OUT** ON ME? YOU THINK I DON'T **KNOW** ABOUT THE **MIDSUMMER'S DAY PICNIC?**

GASP! YOU KNOW ABOUT TH' PICNIC?!

OF **COURSE** I DO! I KNOW THAT YOU AND THE VILLAGERS ARE **HOARDING** YOUR BEST GOODS AN' **LIVESTOCK** FOR IT! IS THAT ANY WAY TO TREAT YOUR **PROTECTOR?!**

B-BUT THE PICNIC IS A **TRADITION!** IT MEANS SO MUCH TO THE **CHILDREN!**

HOARDER!

THIS IS A STATE OF EMERGENCY, MISTER! WE **DON'T** HAVE TIME FOR FRIVOLOUS CELEBRATIONS!

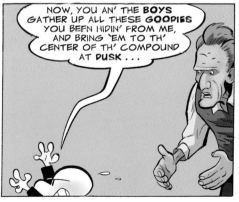

NOW, YOU AN' THE **BOYS** GATHER UP ALL THESE **GOODIES** YOU BEEN HIDIN' FROM ME, AND BRING 'EM TO TH' CENTER OF TH' COMPOUND AT **DUSK** . . .

. . . AND BRING TH' **VILLAGERS!** IT'S TIME YOU ALL LEARNED ABOUT **MY** PLANS FOR **MIDSUMMER'S DAY!**

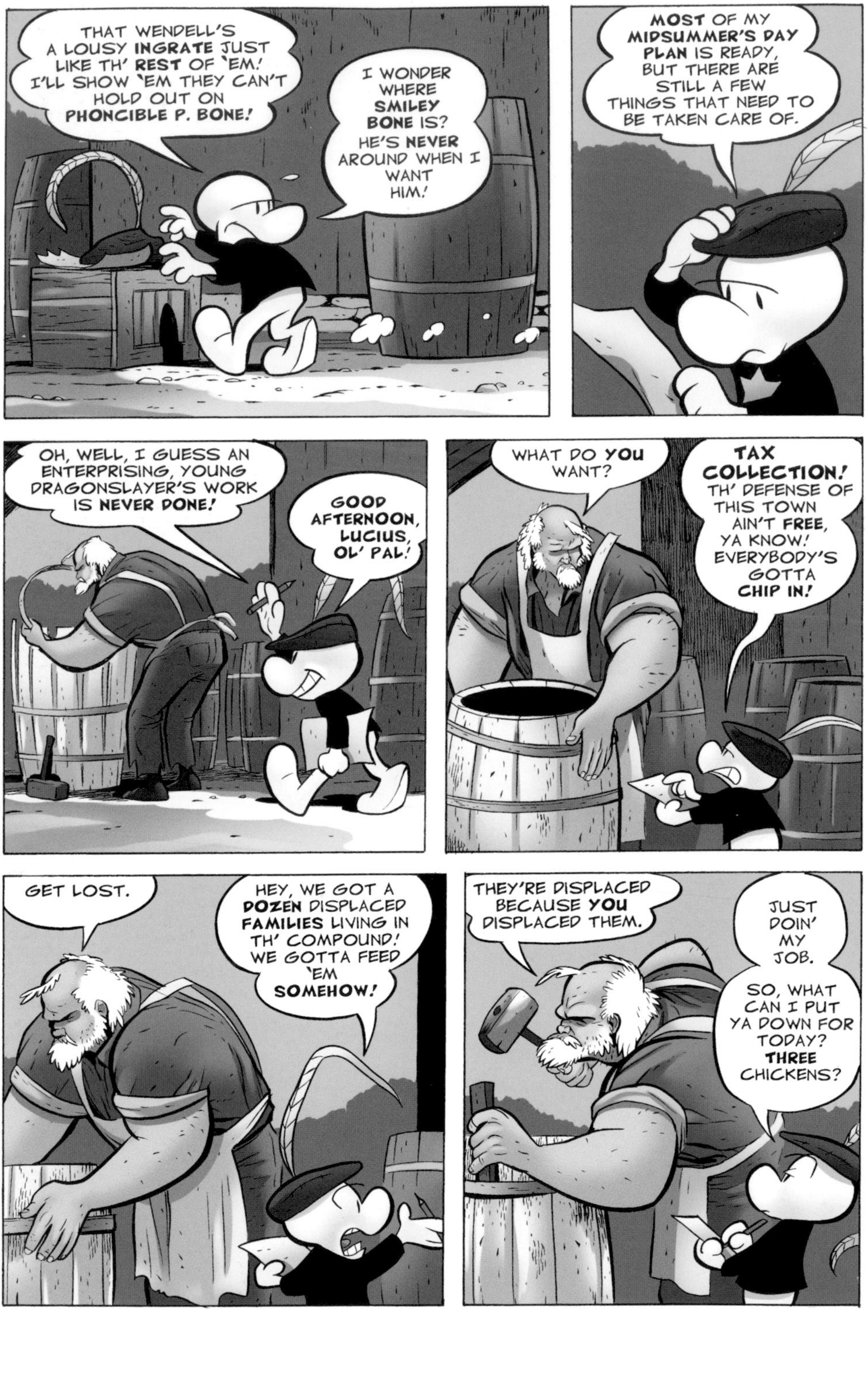
THAT WENDELL'S A LOUSY INGRATE JUST LIKE TH' REST OF 'EM! I'LL SHOW 'EM THEY CAN'T HOLD OUT ON PHONCIBLE P. BONE!
I WONDER WHERE SMILEY BONE IS? HE'S NEVER AROUND WHEN I WANT HIM!
MOST OF MY MIDSUMMER'S DAY PLAN IS READY, BUT THERE ARE STILL A FEW THINGS THAT NEED TO BE TAKEN CARE OF.
OH, WELL, I GUESS AN ENTERPRISING, YOUNG DRAGONSLAYER'S WORK IS NEVER DONE!
GOOD AFTERNOON, LUCIUS, OL' PAL!
WHAT DO YOU WANT?
TAX COLLECTION! TH' DEFENSE OF THIS TOWN AIN'T FREE, YA KNOW! EVERYBODY'S GOTTA CHIP IN!
GET LOST.
HEY, WE GOT A DOZEN DISPLACED FAMILIES LIVING IN TH' COMPOUND! WE GOTTA FEED 'EM SOMEHOW!
THEY'RE DISPLACED BECAUSE YOU DISPLACED THEM.
JUST DOIN' MY JOB.
SO, WHAT CAN I PUT YA DOWN FOR TODAY? THREE CHICKENS?

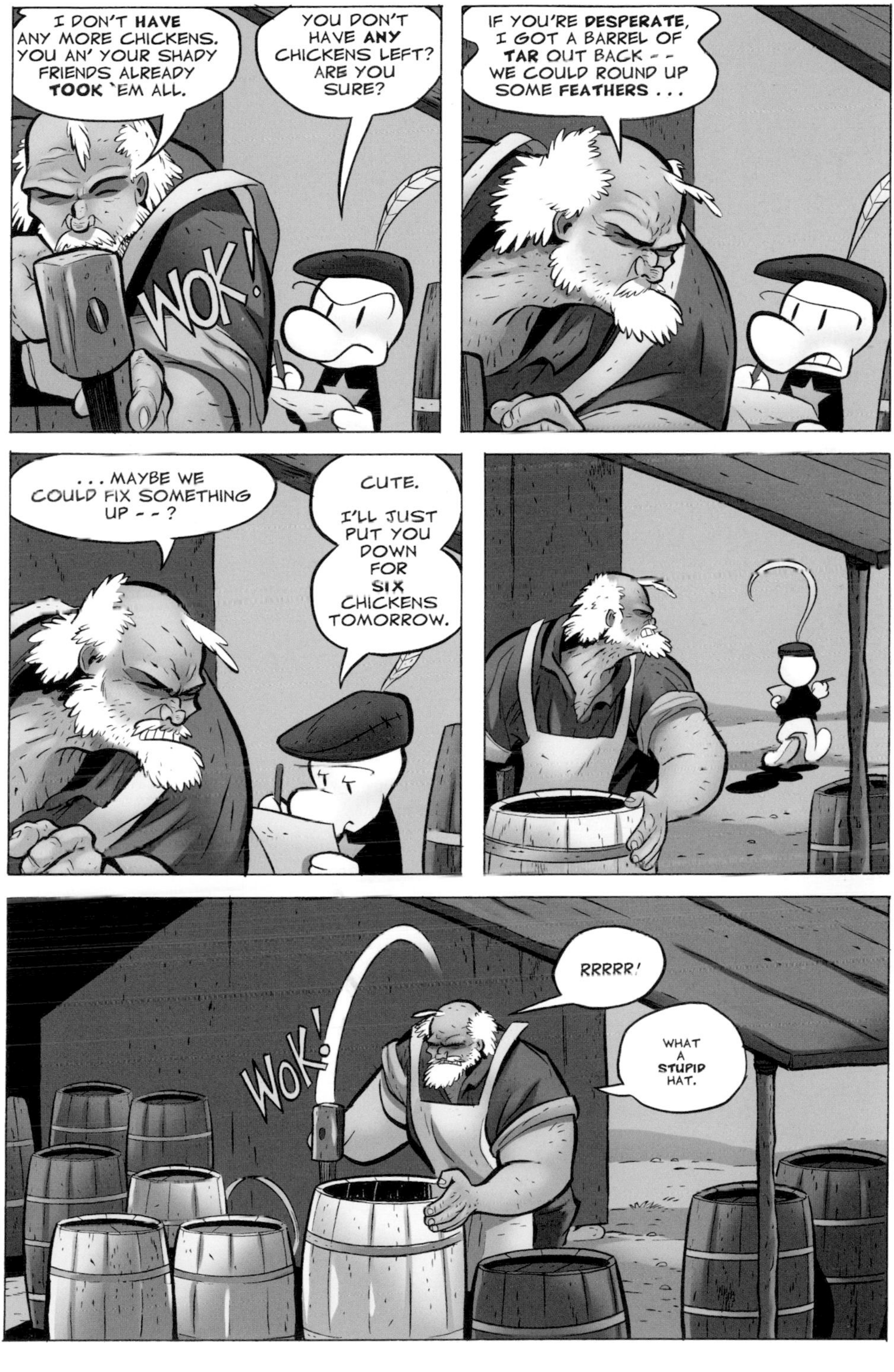
I DON'T **HAVE** ANY MORE CHICKENS. YOU AN' YOUR SHADY FRIENDS ALREADY **TOOK** 'EM ALL.
WOK!
YOU DON'T HAVE **ANY** CHICKENS LEFT? ARE YOU SURE?
IF YOU'RE **DESPERATE**, I GOT A BARREL OF **TAR** OUT BACK - - WE COULD ROUND UP SOME **FEATHERS** . . .
. . . MAYBE WE COULD FIX SOMETHING UP - - ?
CUTE.
I'LL JUST PUT YOU DOWN FOR **SIX** CHICKENS TOMORROW.
RRRRR!
WOK!
WHAT A **STUPID** HAT.

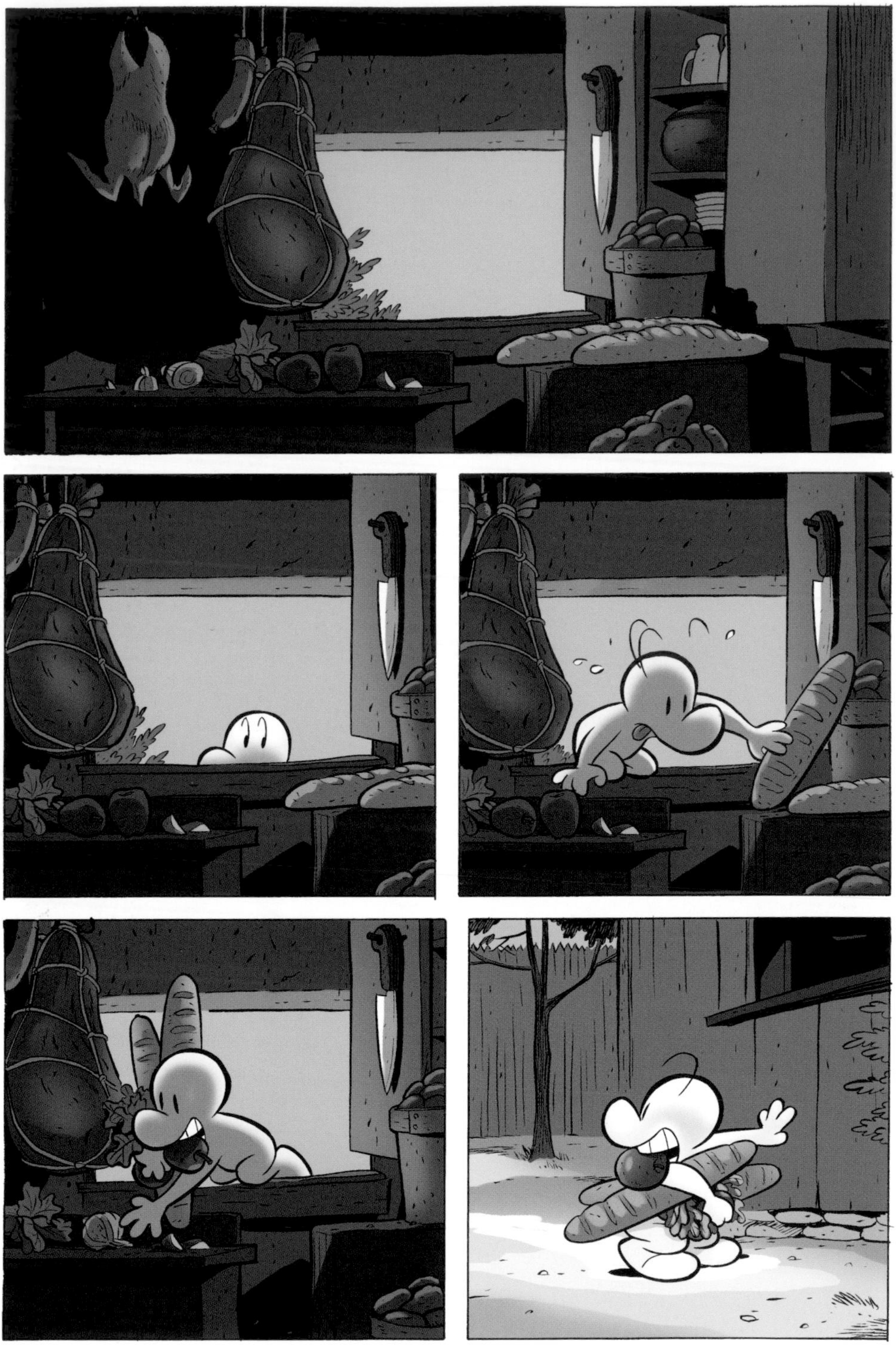

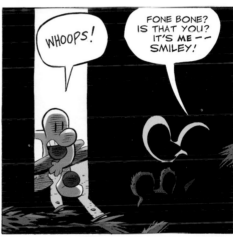

WHOOPS!

FONE BONE? IS THAT YOU? IT'S ME -- SMILEY!

SMILEY BONE? WHAT ARE **YOU** DOING HERE?

I'VE BEEN HERE ALL DAY SMUGGLIN' IN **FOOD** FOR TH' BABY **RAT CREATURE!**

OH! WELL, I GUESS I DIDN'T NEED TO BRING ALL **THIS**, THEN.

DON'T WORRY, IT WON'T GO TO WASTE --

SAY, YOU DIDN'T HAPPEN TO BRING ANY **SALT**, DIDJA?

SNIFF SNIFF

THE DRAGONSLAYER

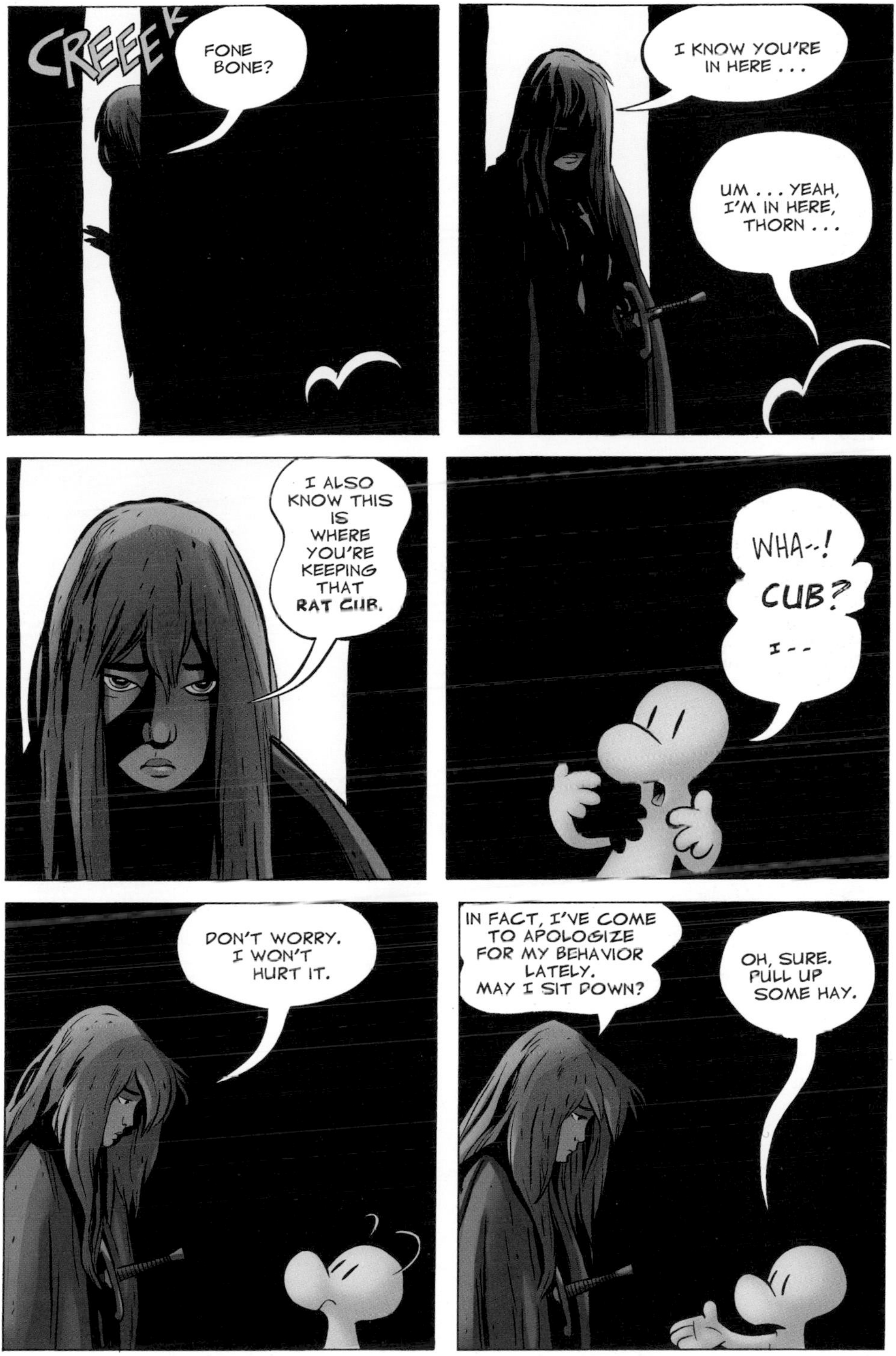
CREEEK
FONE BONE?
I KNOW YOU'RE IN HERE . . .
UM . . . YEAH, I'M IN HERE, THORN . . .
I ALSO KNOW THIS IS WHERE YOU'RE KEEPING THAT RAT CUB.
WHA--! CUB? I--
DON'T WORRY. I WON'T HURT IT.
IN FACT, I'VE COME TO APOLOGIZE FOR MY BEHAVIOR LATELY. MAY I SIT DOWN?
OH, SURE. PULL UP SOME HAY.

THANK YOU.

I DON'T REALLY KNOW HOW TO BEGIN . . .

THORN, YOU DON'T HAVE TO - -

THE DREAMS ARE GETTING WORSE.

WHAT? THEY ARE?

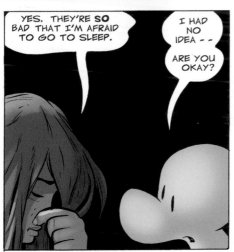

YES. THEY'RE **SO** BAD THAT I'M AFRAID TO GO TO SLEEP.

I HAD NO IDEA - -

ARE YOU OKAY?

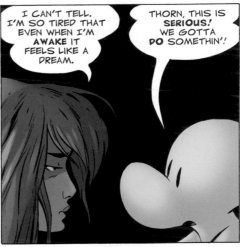

I CAN'T TELL. I'M SO TIRED THAT EVEN WHEN I'M **AWAKE** IT FEELS LIKE A DREAM.

THORN, THIS IS **SERIOUS!** WE GOTTA **DO** SOMETHIN'!

WHAT'S **HAPPENING,** FONE BONE? WHY IS EVERYTHING **CHANGING?!** WHY CAN'T WE GO BACK TO THE WAY IT WAS **BEFORE?**

UM . . .

I WANT TO GO HOME.

HOME? WHAT ARE YOU TALKIN' ABOUT?

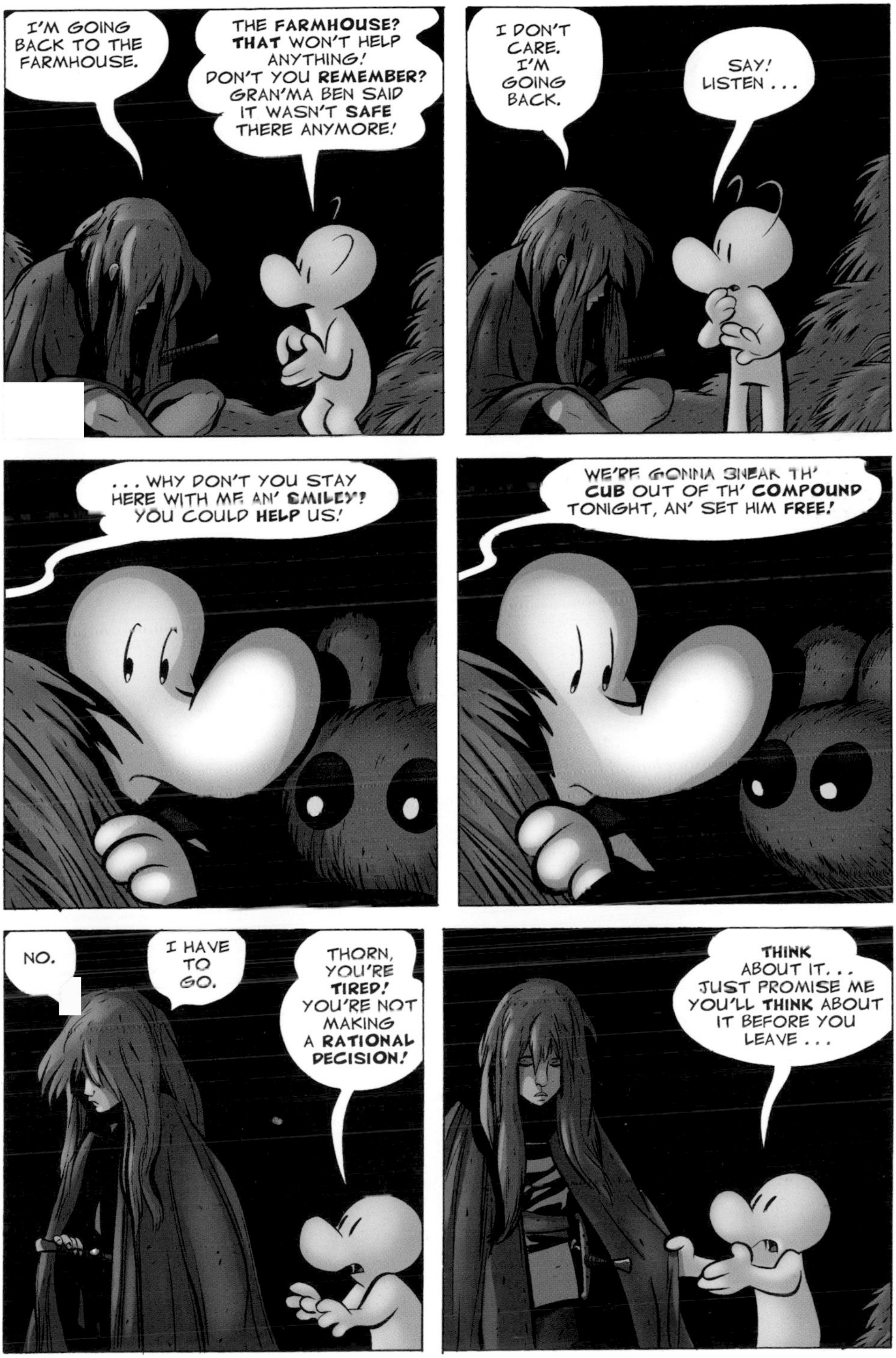
I'M GOING BACK TO THE FARMHOUSE.
THE FARMHOUSE? THAT WON'T HELP ANYTHING! DON'T YOU REMEMBER? GRAN'MA BEN SAID IT WASN'T SAFE THERE ANYMORE!
I DON'T CARE. I'M GOING BACK.
SAY! LISTEN . . .
. . . WHY DON'T YOU STAY HERE WITH ME AN' SMILEY? YOU COULD HELP US!
WE'RE GONNA SNEAK TH' CUB OUT OF TH' COMPOUND TONIGHT, AN' SET HIM FREE!
NO.
I HAVE TO GO.
THORN, YOU'RE TIRED! YOU'RE NOT MAKING A RATIONAL DECISION!
THINK ABOUT IT. . . JUST PROMISE ME YOU'LL THINK ABOUT IT BEFORE YOU LEAVE . . .

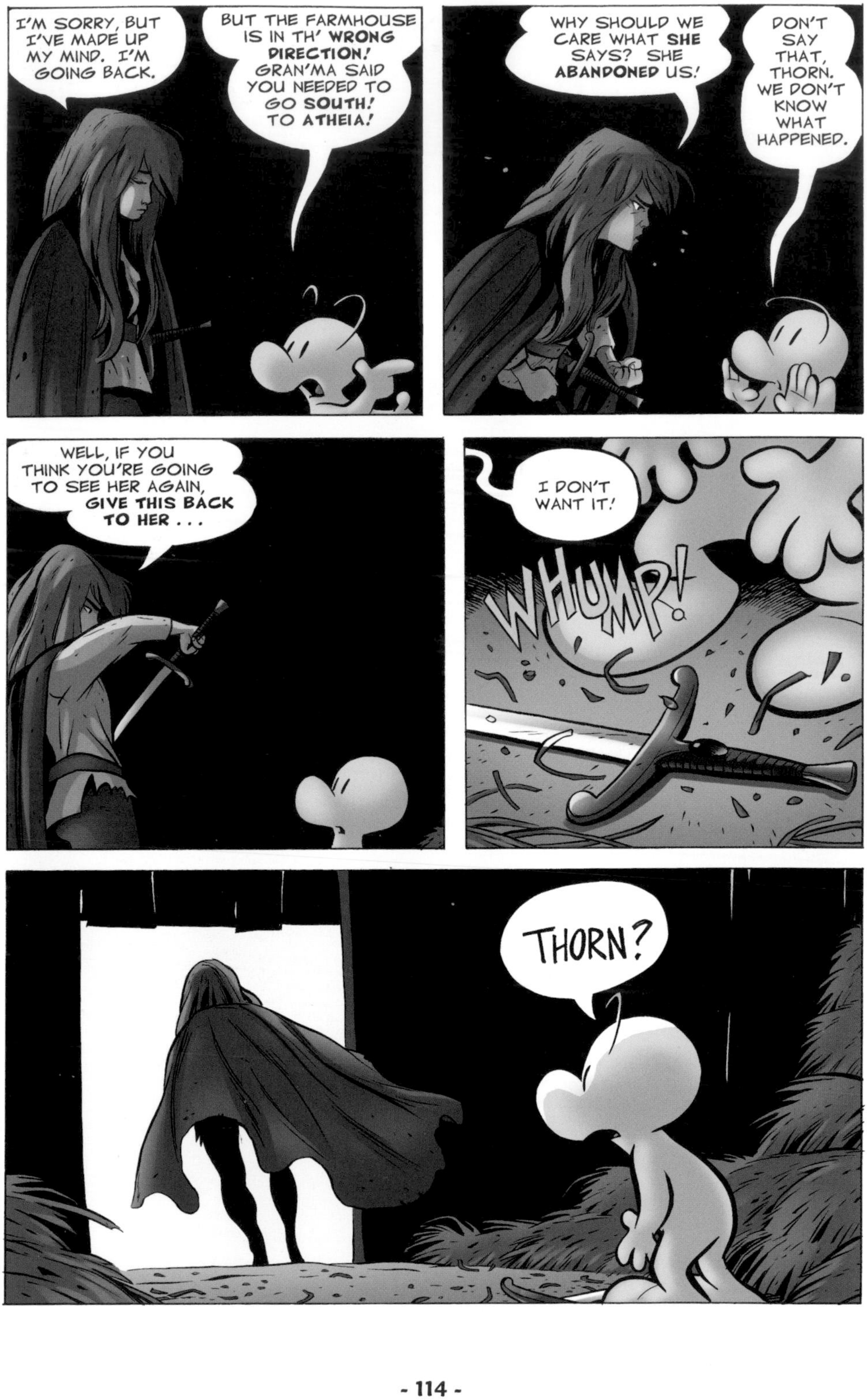
I'M SORRY, BUT I'VE MADE UP MY MIND. I'M GOING BACK.
BUT THE FARMHOUSE IS IN TH' WRONG DIRECTION! GRAN'MA SAID YOU NEEDED TO GO SOUTH! TO ATHEIA!
WHY SHOULD WE CARE WHAT SHE SAYS? SHE ABANDONED US!
DON'T SAY THAT, THORN. WE DON'T KNOW WHAT HAPPENED.
WELL, IF YOU THINK YOU'RE GOING TO SEE HER AGAIN, GIVE THIS BACK TO HER . . .
I DON'T WANT IT!
WHUMP!
THORN?

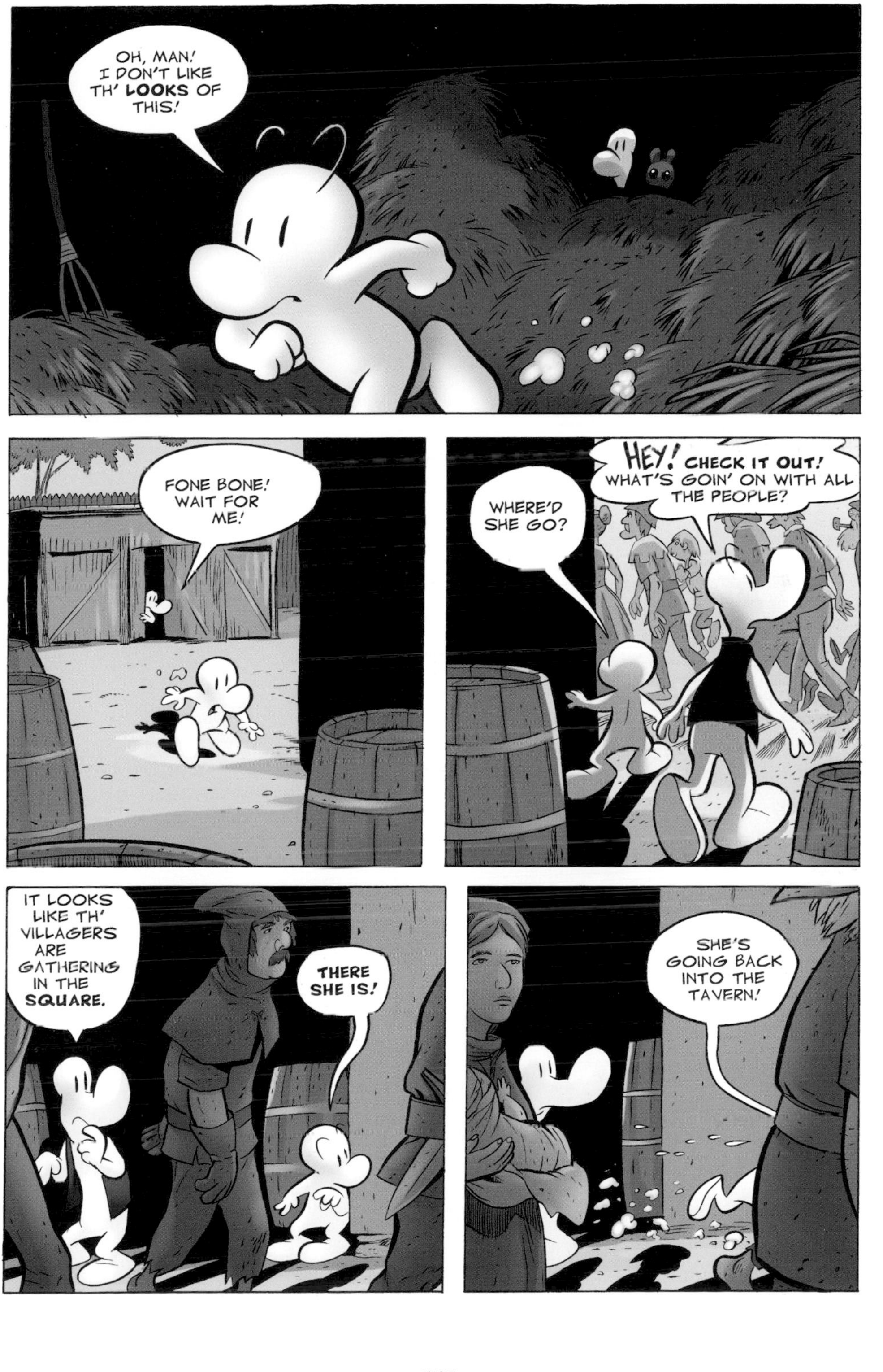
OH, MAN! I DON'T LIKE TH' LOOKS OF THIS!
FONE BONE! WAIT FOR ME!
WHERE'D SHE GO?
HEY! CHECK IT OUT! WHAT'S GOIN' ON WITH ALL THE PEOPLE?
IT LOOKS LIKE TH' VILLAGERS ARE GATHERING IN THE SQUARE.
THERE SHE IS!
SHE'S GOING BACK INTO THE TAVERN!

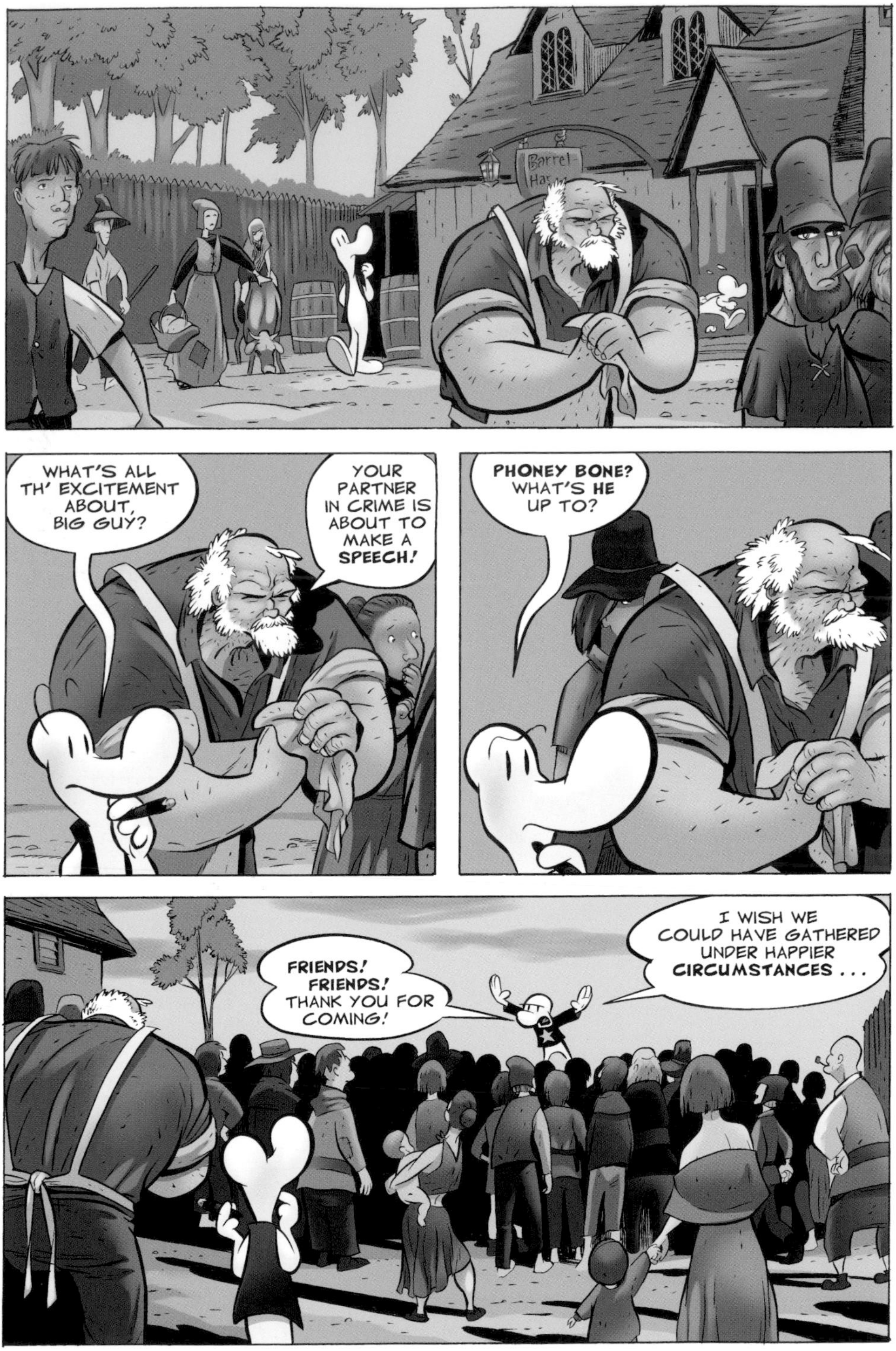
WHAT'S ALL TH' EXCITEMENT ABOUT, BIG GUY?
YOUR PARTNER IN CRIME IS ABOUT TO MAKE A **SPEECH!**
PHONEY BONE? WHAT'S **HE** UP TO?
FRIENDS! FRIENDS! THANK YOU FOR COMING!
I WISH WE COULD HAVE GATHERED UNDER HAPPIER **CIRCUMSTANCES . . .**

BUT IT HAS COME TO MY ATTENTION THAT THE **TREMENDOUS** PILE OF **WEALTH** THAT I'M STANDING ON WAS **SECRETLY** STOCKPILED AWAY FOR THE **MIDSUMMER'S DAY PICNIC!**

I'M **VERY** DISAPPOINTED.

TSK! TSK!

NOT **ONLY** WERE YOU HIDING IT FROM **ME** ... WHICH IS BAD **ENOUGH** ... BUT **LOOK** WHAT YOU'VE DONE TO **YOURSELVES!**

ALL THIS **HOARDING!** ALL THIS **DECEIT!**

THIS IS THE SORT OF THING THAT **ATTRACTS** DRAGONS AND OTHER HOUSEHOLD PESTS IN THE **FIRST PLACE!**

PEOPLE! PEOPLE! DON'T YOU **SEE?!** YOU **BROUGHT** THIS PLAGUE OF DRAGONS ON **YOURSELVES** WITH **ILLICIT** BEHAVIOR!

OH, FER TH' LOVE OF ...

WE MUST **ROOT OUT** THIS MORAL DECAY IN OUR MIDST BEFORE IT'S **TOO LATE!** GO TO YOUR HOMES AND GET EVERY SINGLE THING OF VALUE THAT YOU OWN, AND **BRING IT HERE IMMEDIATELY!**

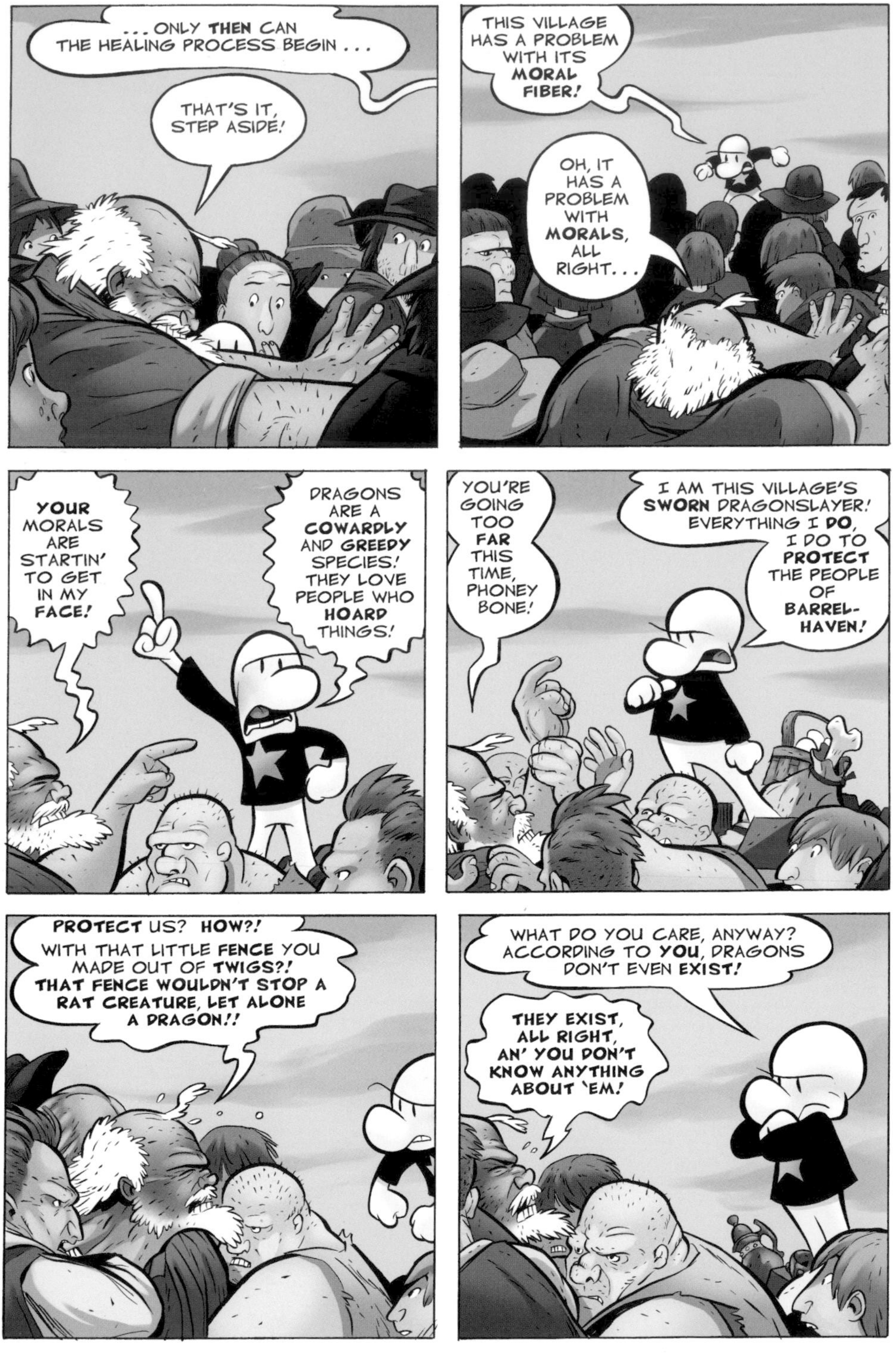
...ONLY THEN CAN THE HEALING PROCESS BEGIN...
THAT'S IT, STEP ASIDE!
THIS VILLAGE HAS A PROBLEM WITH ITS MORAL FIBER!
OH, IT HAS A PROBLEM WITH MORALS, ALL RIGHT...
DRAGONS ARE A COWARDLY AND GREEDY SPECIES! THEY LOVE PEOPLE WHO HOARD THINGS!
YOUR MORALS ARE STARTIN' TO GET IN MY FACE!
I AM THIS VILLAGE'S SWORN DRAGONSLAYER! EVERYTHING I DO, I DO TO PROTECT THE PEOPLE OF BARREL-HAVEN!
YOU'RE GOING TOO FAR THIS TIME, PHONEY BONE!
PROTECT US? HOW?! WITH THAT LITTLE FENCE YOU MADE OUT OF TWIGS?! THAT FENCE WOULDN'T STOP A RAT CREATURE, LET ALONE A DRAGON!!
WHAT DO YOU CARE, ANYWAY? ACCORDING TO YOU, DRAGONS DON'T EVEN EXIST!
THEY EXIST, ALL RIGHT, AN' YOU DON'T KNOW ANYTHING ABOUT 'EM!

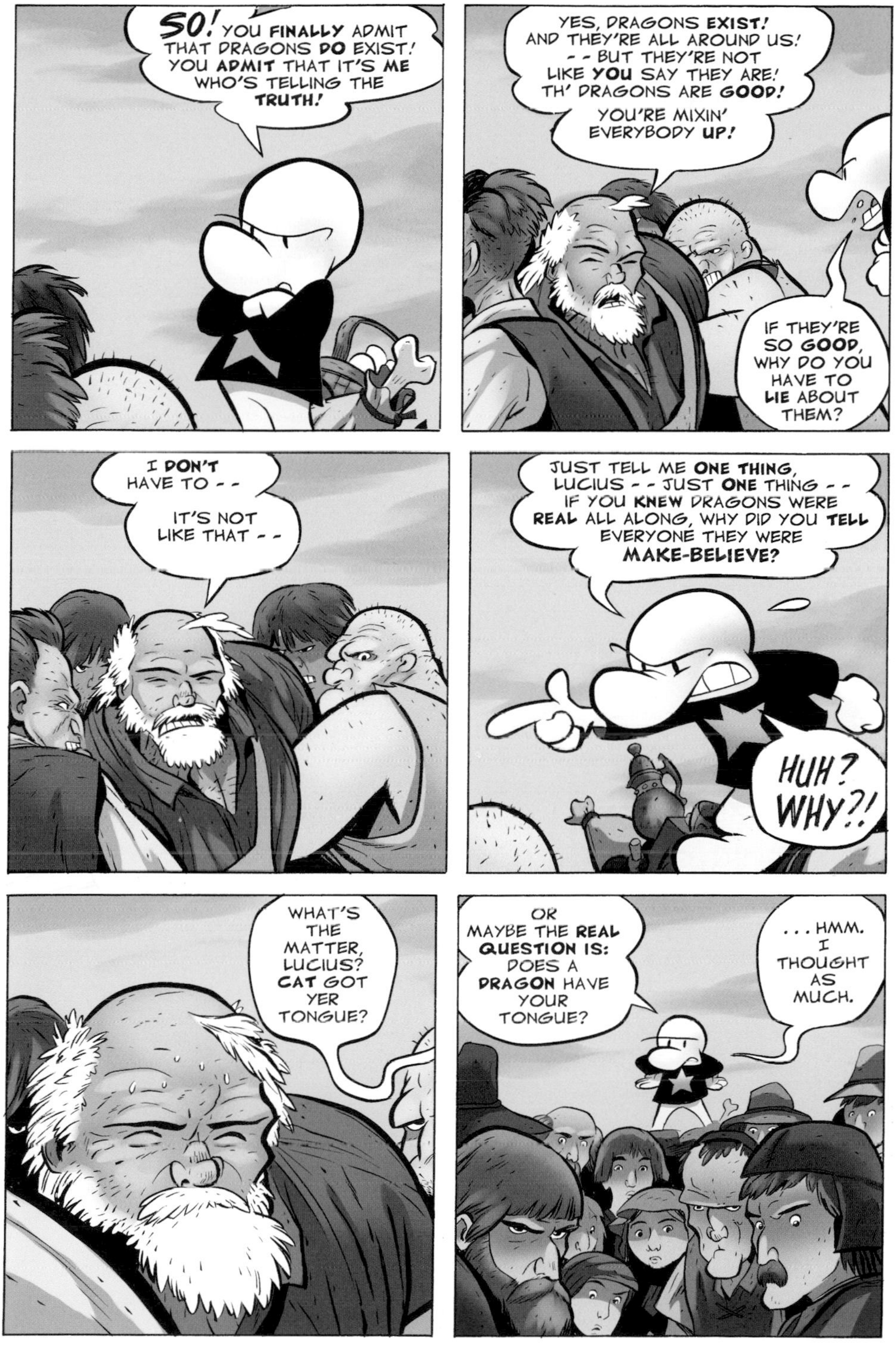
SO! YOU FINALLY ADMIT THAT DRAGONS DO EXIST! YOU ADMIT THAT IT'S ME WHO'S TELLING THE TRUTH!
YES, DRAGONS EXIST! AND THEY'RE ALL AROUND US! - - BUT THEY'RE NOT LIKE YOU SAY THEY ARE! TH' DRAGONS ARE GOOD!
YOU'RE MIXIN' EVERYBODY UP!
IF THEY'RE SO GOOD, WHY DO YOU HAVE TO LIE ABOUT THEM?
I DON'T HAVE TO - -
IT'S NOT LIKE THAT - -
JUST TELL ME ONE THING, LUCIUS - - JUST ONE THING - - IF YOU KNEW DRAGONS WERE REAL ALL ALONG, WHY DID YOU TELL EVERYONE THEY WERE MAKE-BELIEVE?
HUH? WHY?!
WHAT'S THE MATTER, LUCIUS? CAT GOT YER TONGUE?
OR MAYBE THE REAL QUESTION IS: DOES A DRAGON HAVE YOUR TONGUE?
. . . HMM. I THOUGHT AS MUCH.

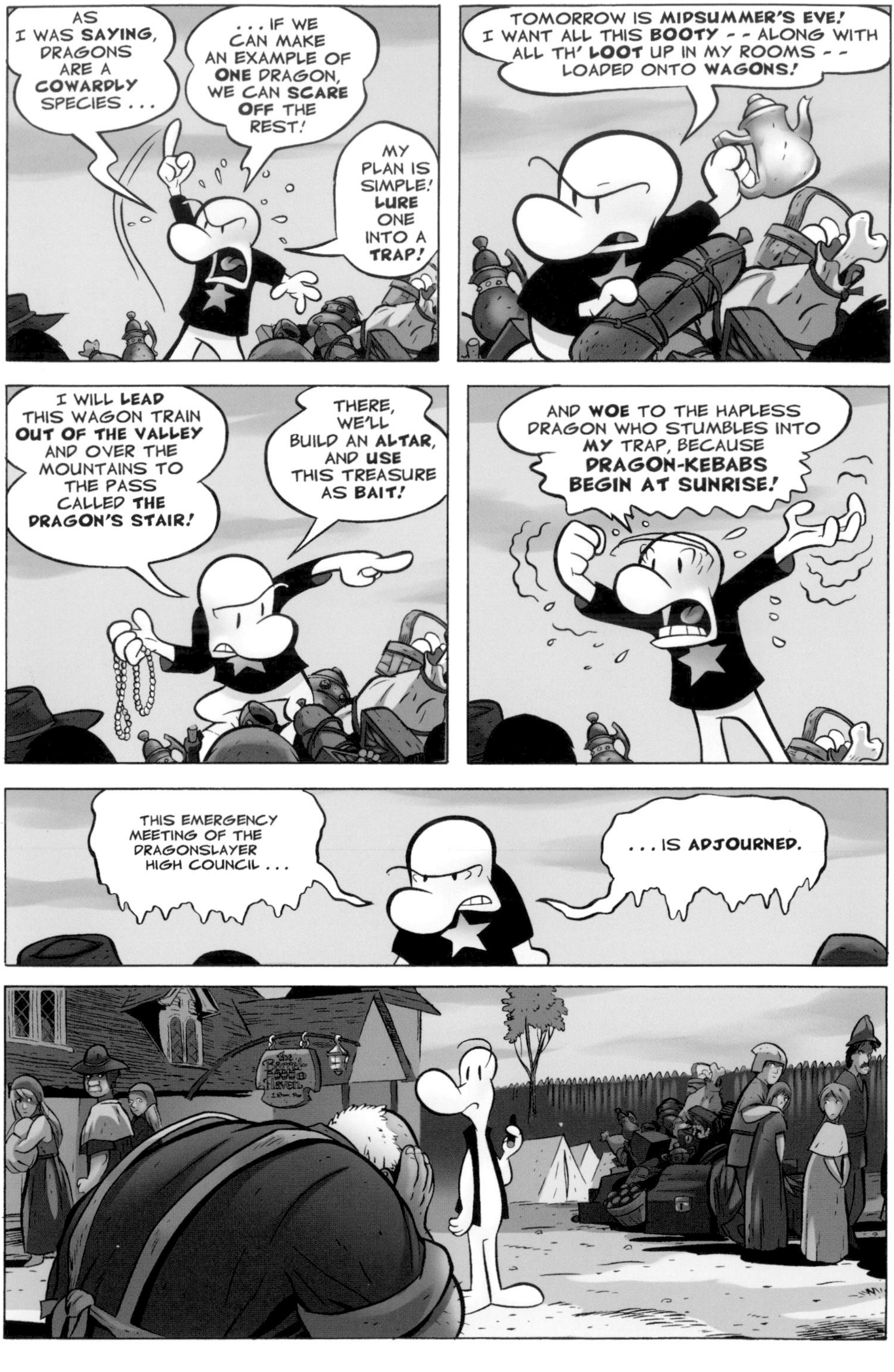
AS I WAS SAYING, DRAGONS ARE A COWARDLY SPECIES . . .
. . . IF WE CAN MAKE AN EXAMPLE OF ONE DRAGON, WE CAN SCARE OFF THE REST!
MY PLAN IS SIMPLE! LURE ONE INTO A TRAP!
TOMORROW IS MIDSUMMER'S EVE! I WANT ALL THIS BOOTY - - ALONG WITH ALL TH' LOOT UP IN MY ROOMS - - LOADED ONTO WAGONS!
I WILL LEAD THIS WAGON TRAIN OUT OF THE VALLEY AND OVER THE MOUNTAINS TO THE PASS CALLED THE DRAGON'S STAIR!
THERE, WE'LL BUILD AN ALTAR, AND USE THIS TREASURE AS BAIT!
AND WOE TO THE HAPLESS DRAGON WHO STUMBLES INTO MY TRAP, BECAUSE DRAGON-KEBABS BEGIN AT SUNRISE!
THIS EMERGENCY MEETING OF THE DRAGONSLAYER HIGH COUNCIL . . .
. . . IS ADJOURNED.

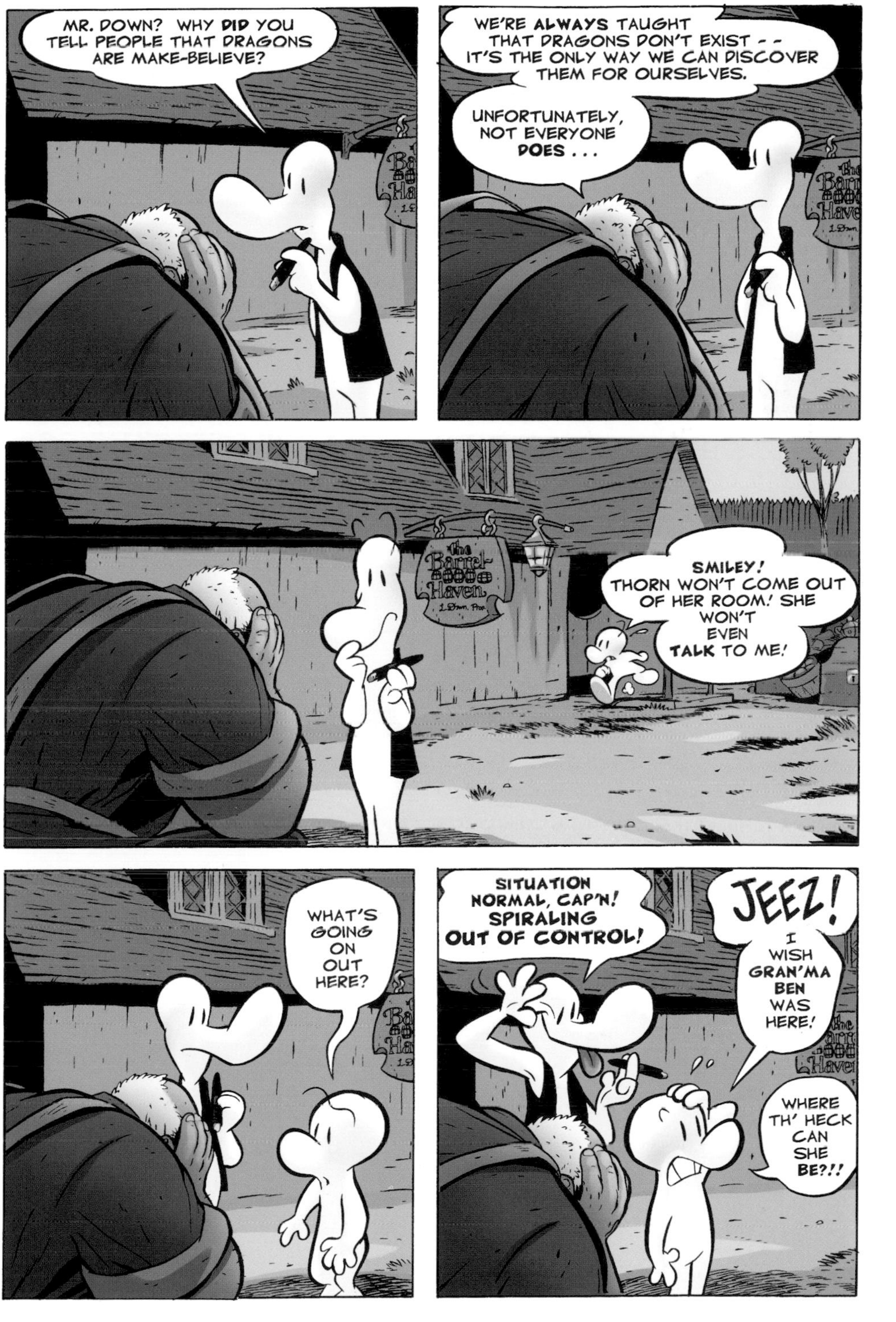
MR. DOWN? WHY DID YOU TELL PEOPLE THAT DRAGONS ARE MAKE-BELIEVE?
WE'RE ALWAYS TAUGHT THAT DRAGONS DON'T EXIST - - IT'S THE ONLY WAY WE CAN DISCOVER THEM FOR OURSELVES.
UNFORTUNATELY, NOT EVERYONE DOES . . .
The Barrel-Haven
SMILEY! THORN WON'T COME OUT OF HER ROOM! SHE WON'T EVEN TALK TO ME!
WHAT'S GOING ON OUT HERE?
SITUATION NORMAL, CAP'N! SPIRALING OUT OF CONTROL!
JEEZ! I WISH GRAN'MA BEN WAS HERE!
WHERE TH' HECK CAN SHE BE?!!

THE DRAGONSLAYER

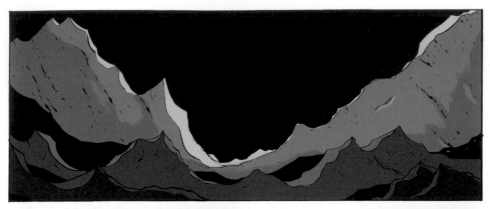

GO!

GO! GO!

DESTROY YOUR ENEMIES!

KINGDOK, I HAVE A **SPECIAL** MISSION FOR YOU . . .

TAKE A PARTY OF YOUR BEST WARRIORS . . . **FIND** THE **PRINCESS** AND THE THREE **BONES!** BRING THEM TO ME . . . . .

. . . **MASTER** ? . . WOULD NOT THE **WAR** BE BETTER SERVED IF I WERE TO ADVANCE **IMMEDIATELY** TO CONFRONT THE **GREAT RED DRAGON?**

YOU WILL DO AS YOU ARE TOLD . . .

THE MIDSUMMER'S DAY PLAN

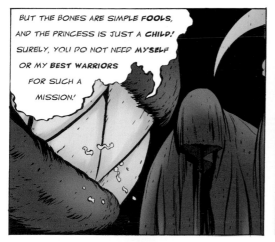

BUT THE BONES ARE SIMPLE *FOOLS*, AND THE PRINCESS IS JUST A *CHILD!* SURELY, YOU DO NOT NEED *MYSELF* OR MY *BEST WARRIORS* FOR SUCH A MISSION!

WHY DO YOU *QUESTION* YOUR *ORDERS?* . . . . THAT *CHILD* AND HER FOOLS *CUT OFF YOUR ARM!* THAT SHOULD BE REASON ENOUGH FOR *YOU* . . . . .

REVENGE IS NEVER FAR FROM MY THOUGHTS, O LORD, BUT THE WAR COMES FIRST . . .

DO THEY POSE A *SERIOUS* THREAT TO OUR *CONQUEST* OF THE VALLEY?

KINGDOK, MY WORTHY COMMANDER . . . TAKING LAND AWAY FROM OUR ENEMIES IS NOT ALL THAT THIS WAR IS ABOUT . . .

. . . . NO . . . . IT IS MUCH *MORE* THAN THAT . . . .

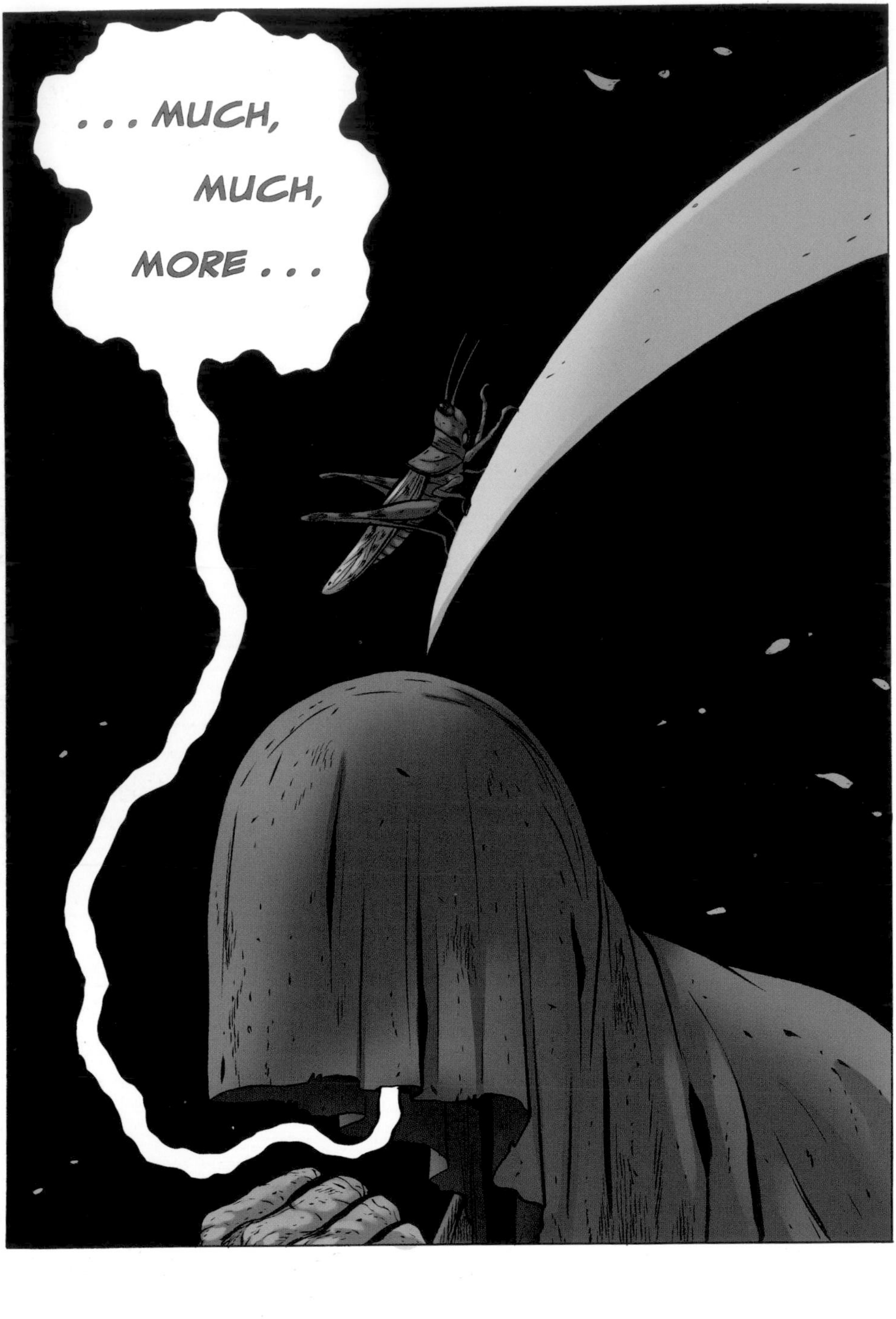
. . . MUCH, MUCH, MORE . . .

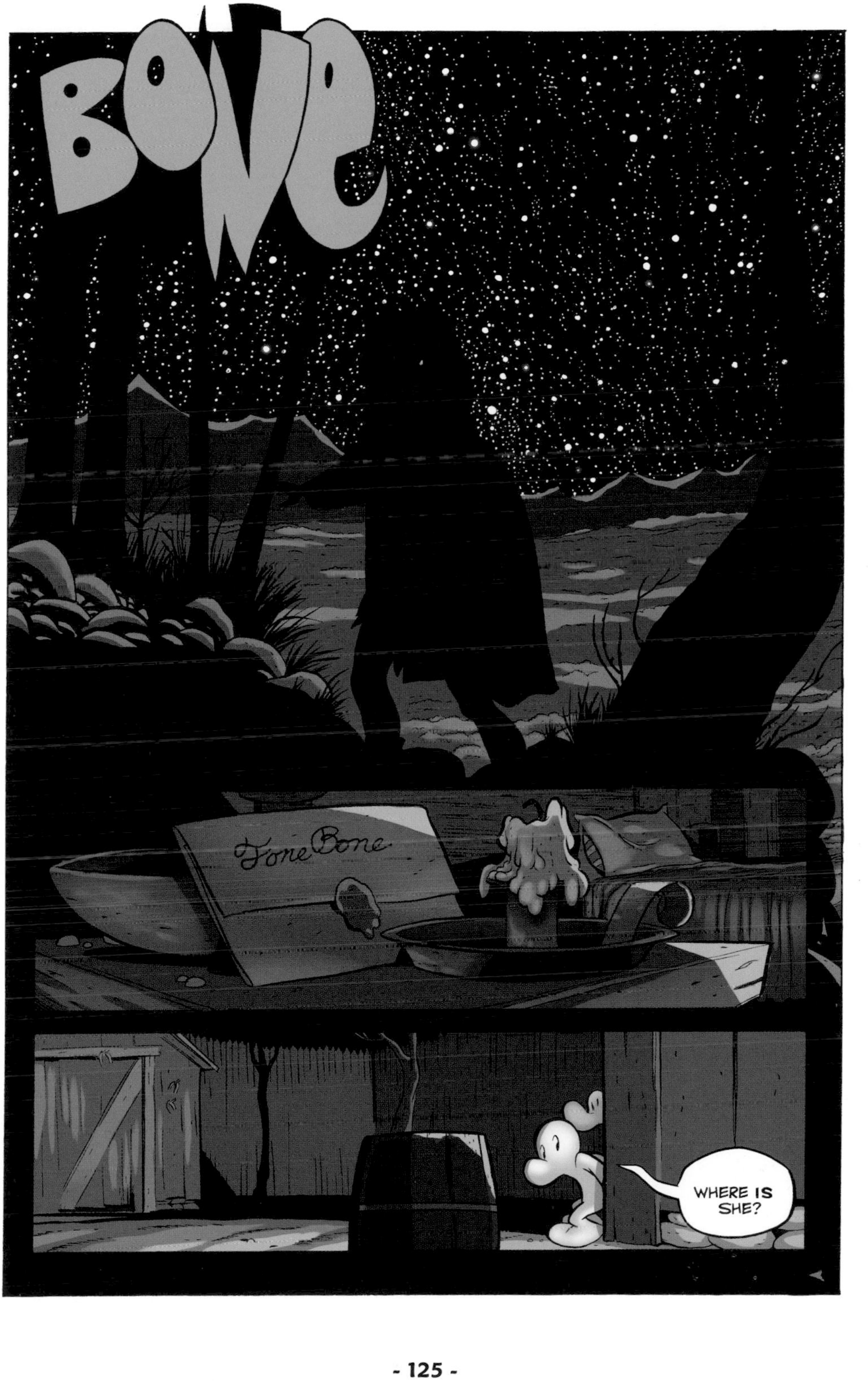
BONE
Fone Bone
WHERE IS SHE?

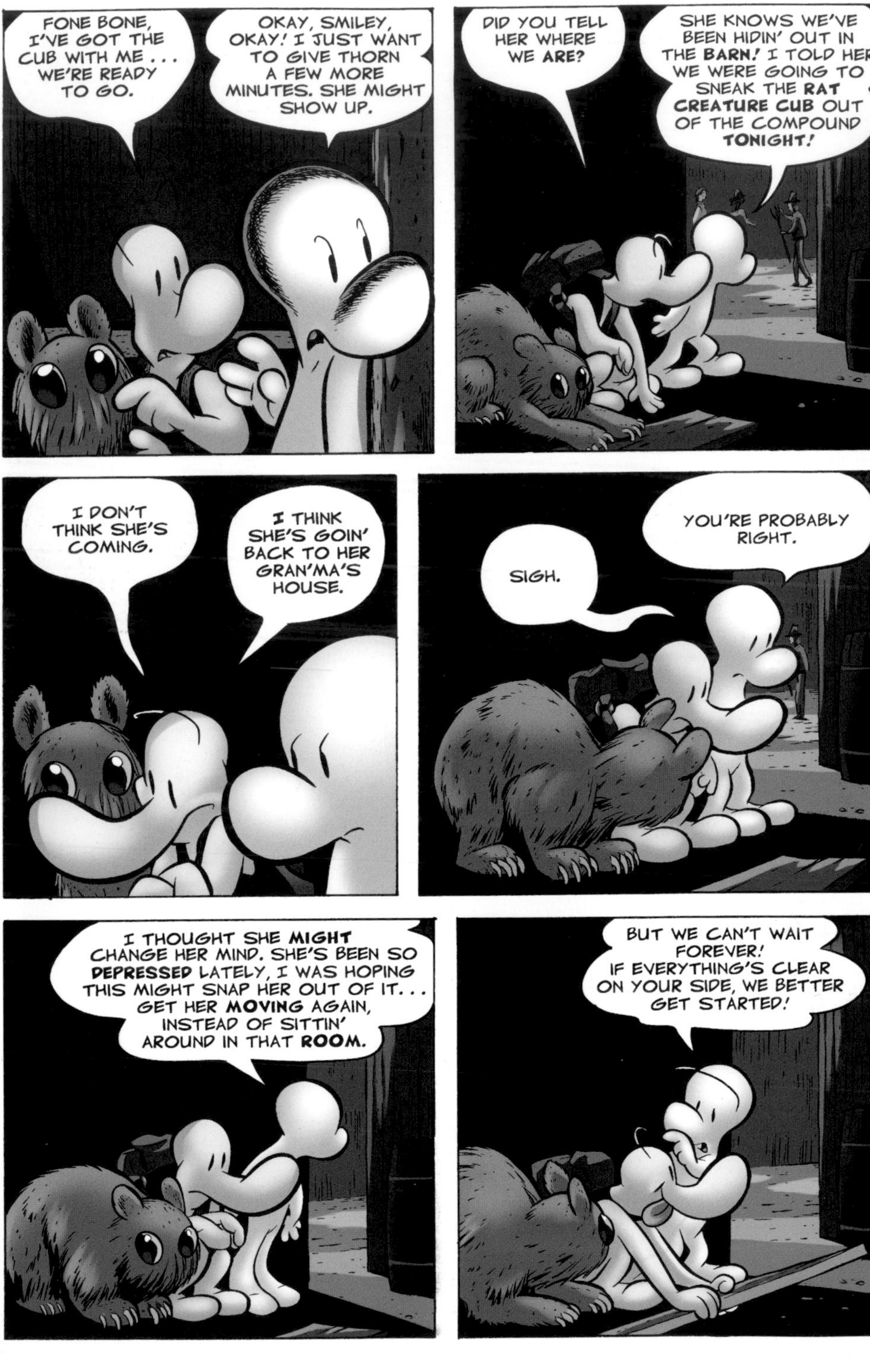
FONE BONE, I'VE GOT THE CUB WITH ME . . . WE'RE READY TO GO.
OKAY, SMILEY, OKAY! I JUST WANT TO GIVE THORN A FEW MORE MINUTES. SHE MIGHT SHOW UP.
DID YOU TELL HER WHERE WE ARE?
SHE KNOWS WE'VE BEEN HIDIN' OUT IN THE BARN! I TOLD HER WE WERE GOING TO SNEAK THE RAT CREATURE CUB OUT OF THE COMPOUND TONIGHT!
I DON'T THINK SHE'S COMING.
I THINK SHE'S GOIN' BACK TO HER GRAN'MA'S HOUSE.
SIGH.
YOU'RE PROBABLY RIGHT.
I THOUGHT SHE MIGHT CHANGE HER MIND. SHE'S BEEN SO DEPRESSED LATELY, I WAS HOPING THIS MIGHT SNAP HER OUT OF IT. . . GET HER MOVING AGAIN, INSTEAD OF SITTIN' AROUND IN THAT ROOM.
BUT WE CAN'T WAIT FOREVER! IF EVERYTHING'S CLEAR ON YOUR SIDE, WE BETTER GET STARTED!

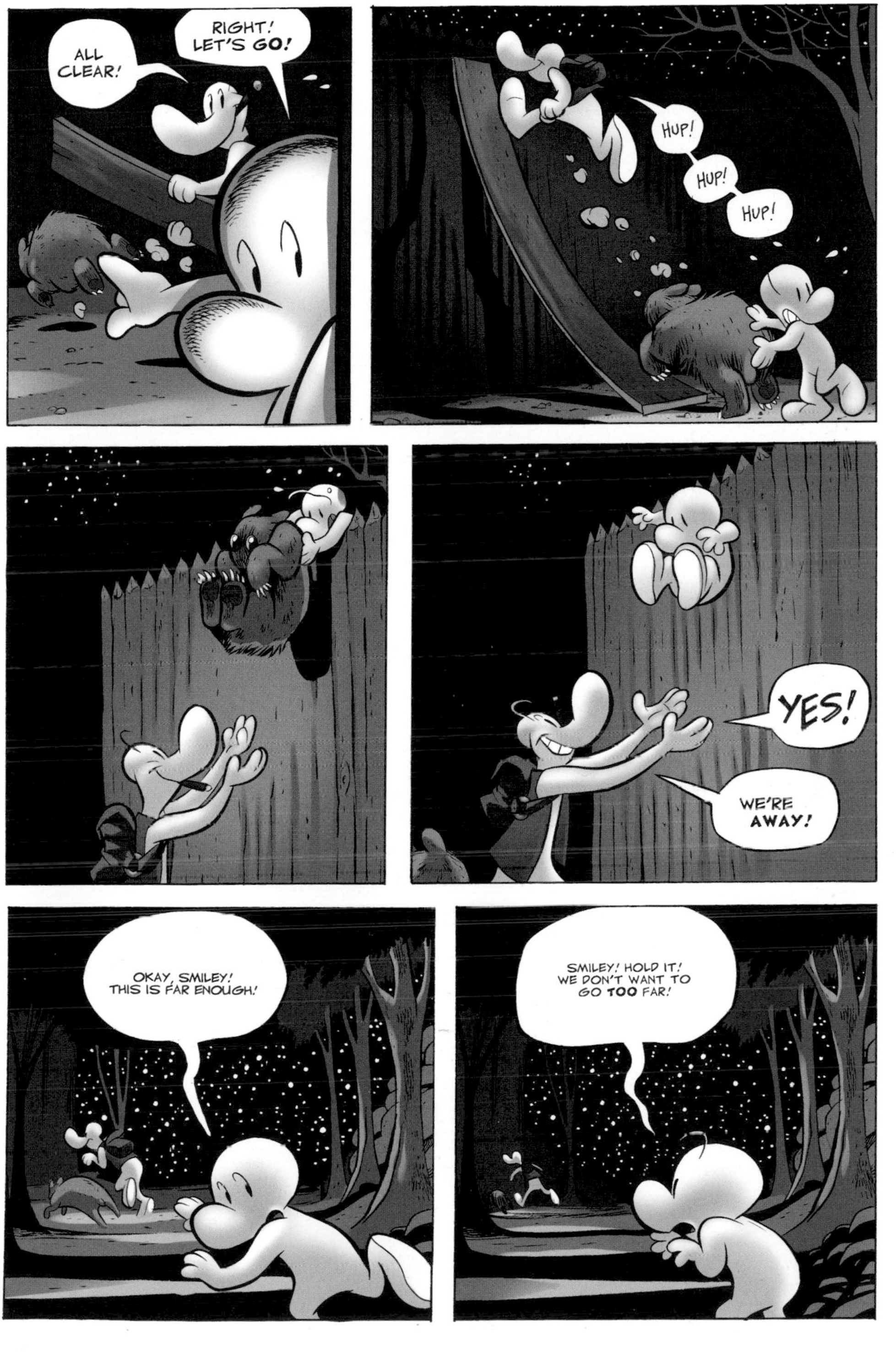
ALL CLEAR!
RIGHT! LET'S GO!
HUP!
HUP!
HUP!
YES!
WE'RE AWAY!
OKAY, SMILEY! THIS IS FAR ENOUGH!
SMILEY! HOLD IT! WE DON'T WANT TO GO TOO FAR!

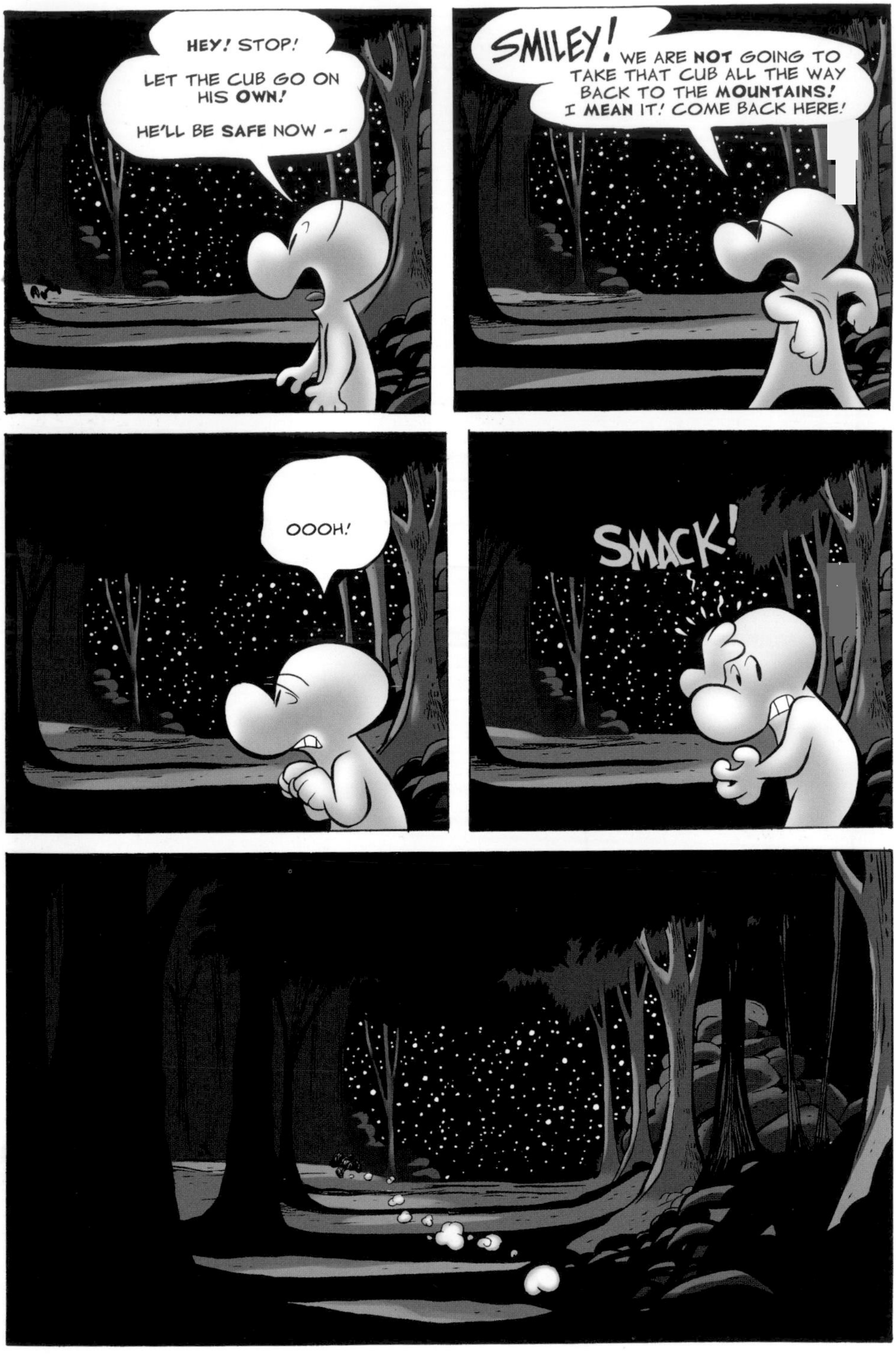
HEY! STOP!
LET THE CUB GO ON HIS OWN!
HE'LL BE SAFE NOW - -
SMILEY! WE ARE NOT GOING TO TAKE THAT CUB ALL THE WAY BACK TO THE MOUNTAINS! I MEAN IT! COME BACK HERE!
OOOH!
SMACK!

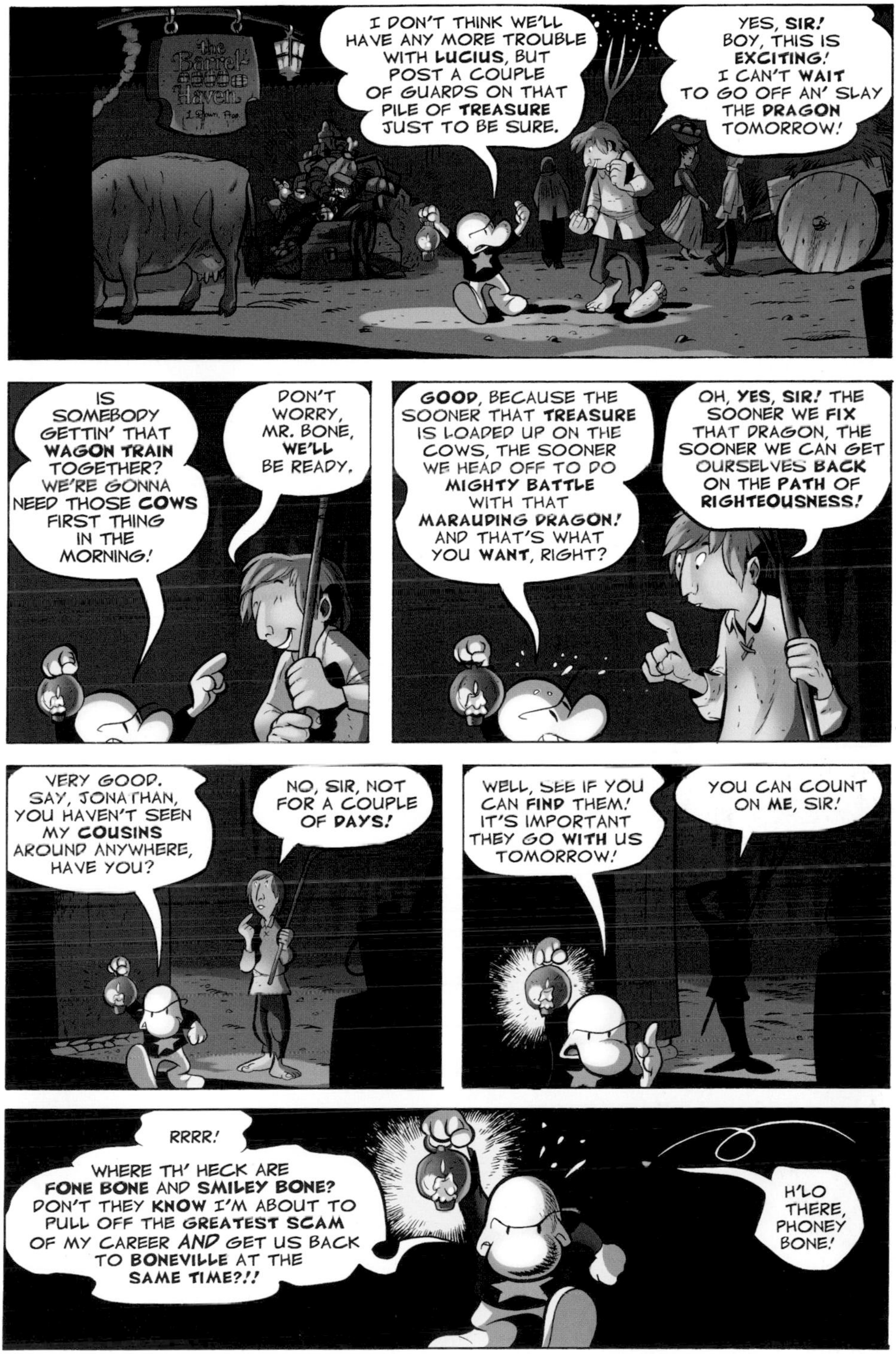

the Barrel Haven
I DON'T THINK WE'LL HAVE ANY MORE TROUBLE WITH LUCIUS, BUT POST A COUPLE OF GUARDS ON THAT PILE OF TREASURE JUST TO BE SURE.
YES, SIR! BOY, THIS IS EXCITING! I CAN'T WAIT TO GO OFF AN' SLAY THE DRAGON TOMORROW!
IS SOMEBODY GETTIN' THAT WAGON TRAIN TOGETHER? WE'RE GONNA NEED THOSE COWS FIRST THING IN THE MORNING!
DON'T WORRY, MR. BONE, WE'LL BE READY.
GOOD, BECAUSE THE SOONER THAT TREASURE IS LOADED UP ON THE COWS, THE SOONER WE HEAD OFF TO DO MIGHTY BATTLE WITH THAT MARAUDING DRAGON! AND THAT'S WHAT YOU WANT, RIGHT?
OH, YES, SIR! THE SOONER WE FIX THAT DRAGON, THE SOONER WE CAN GET OURSELVES BACK ON THE PATH OF RIGHTEOUSNESS!
VERY GOOD. SAY, JONATHAN, YOU HAVEN'T SEEN MY COUSINS AROUND ANYWHERE, HAVE YOU?
NO, SIR, NOT FOR A COUPLE OF DAYS!
WELL, SEE IF YOU CAN FIND THEM! IT'S IMPORTANT THEY GO WITH US TOMORROW!
YOU CAN COUNT ON ME, SIR!
RRRR!
WHERE TH' HECK ARE FONE BONE AND SMILEY BONE? DON'T THEY KNOW I'M ABOUT TO PULL OFF THE GREATEST SCAM OF MY CAREER AND GET US BACK TO BONEVILLE AT THE SAME TIME?!!
H'LO THERE, PHONEY BONE!

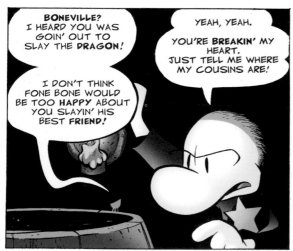

YEAH... WHAT ARE YOU **UP** TO, PHONEY BONE?

WHAT IF I TOLD YOU THERE WASN'T GONNA **BE** ANY SACRIFICE? WOULD YOU TELL ME WHERE FONE BONE IS **THEN**?

WHAT'RE YOU TALKIN' ABOUT?

I'M JUST TRYIN' TO GET THE TOWNSFOLK TO **ESCORT** ME OUT OF THE VALLEY WITH A **WAGON TRAIN** FULL OF **TREASURE**! NO ONE'S GONNA GET HURT! **TRUST ME**!

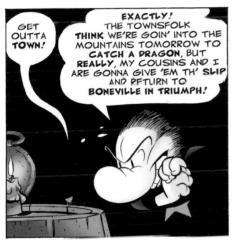

GET OUTTA **TOWN**!

EXACTLY! THE TOWNSFOLK **THINK** WE'RE GOIN' INTO THE MOUNTAINS TOMORROW TO **CATCH A DRAGON**, BUT **REALLY**, MY COUSINS AND I ARE GONNA GIVE 'EM TH' **SLIP** AND RETURN TO **BONEVILLE IN TRIUMPH**!

HOW YOU GONNA GIVE 'EM TH' **SLIP**? AIN'T THEY GONNA **NOTICE** YOU GOT TH' **TREASURE**?

THAT'S THE **BEST PART**! EVERYBODY **KNOWS** DRAGONS LOVE TREASURE, RIGHT? WELL, **THESE** YOKELS THINK WE NEED THE TREASURE FOR **BAIT**-- SO WHEN WE GO TO SET THE **TRAP**, WE CAN JUST **SLIP OFF** INTO TH' **DARKNESS**!

DOES FONE BONE KNOW ABOUT THIS LITTLE SCHEME?

NO! THAT'S THE **PROBLEM**! HE DOESN'T KNOW **ANYTHING** ABOUT IT! IF I CAN'T FIND FONE BONE AND SMILEY **TONIGHT**, THEY'LL **NEVER** GET BACK TO **BONEVILLE**!

WELL... I SEEN 'EM HANGIN' AROUN' THE **BARN** A LOT LATELY. MAYBE YOU SHOULD LOOK **THERE**.

THANKS, BUG!

NOW, REMEMBER! DON'T **TELL** ANYBODY OR YOU'LL RUIN FONE BONE'S CHANCE TO GET HOME!

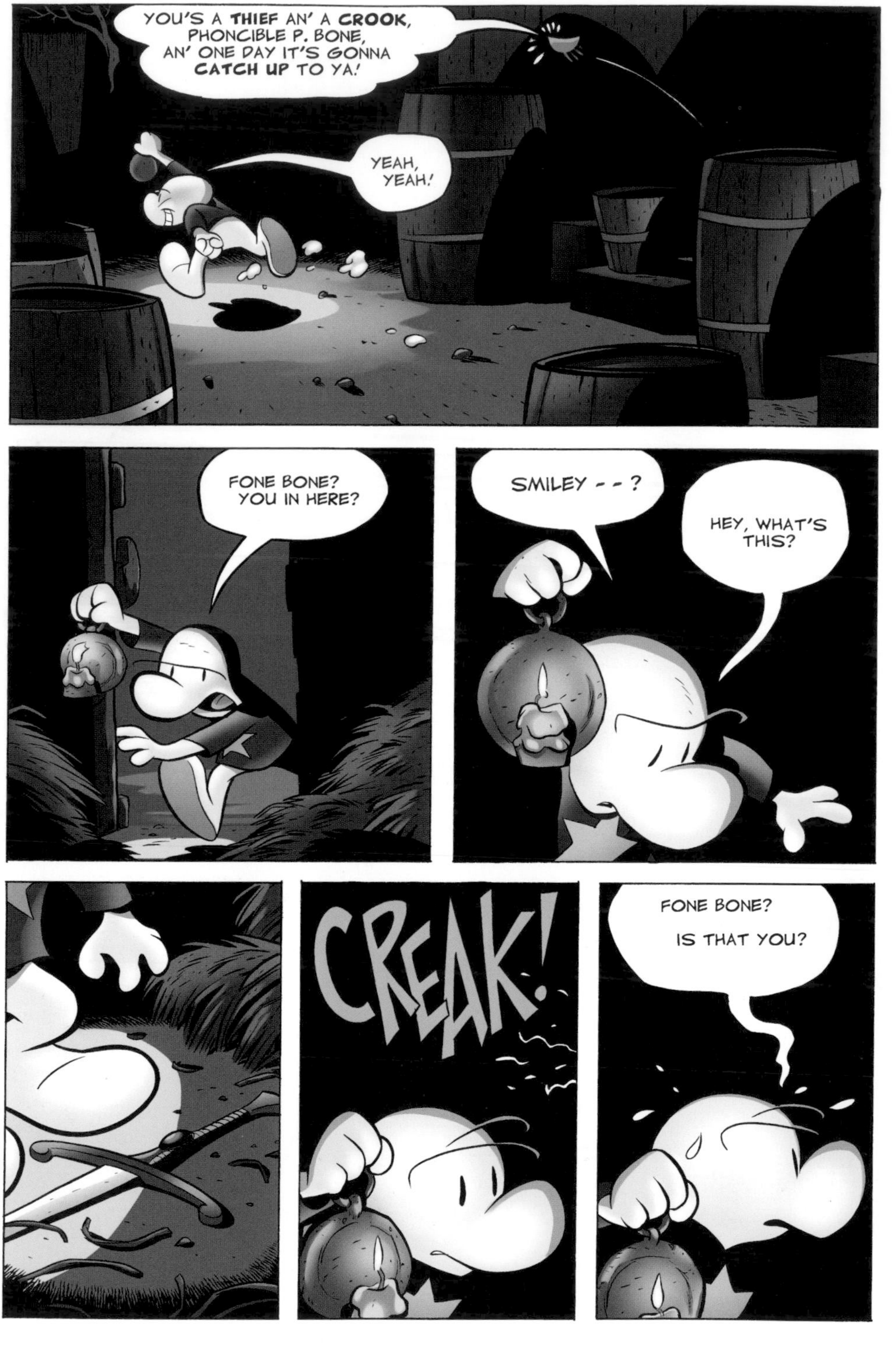
YOU'S A **THIEF** AN' A **CROOK**, PHONCIBLE P. BONE, AN' ONE DAY IT'S GONNA **CATCH UP** TO YA!
YEAH, YEAH!
FONE BONE? YOU IN HERE?
SMILEY - - ?
HEY, WHAT'S THIS?
CREAK!
FONE BONE? IS THAT YOU?

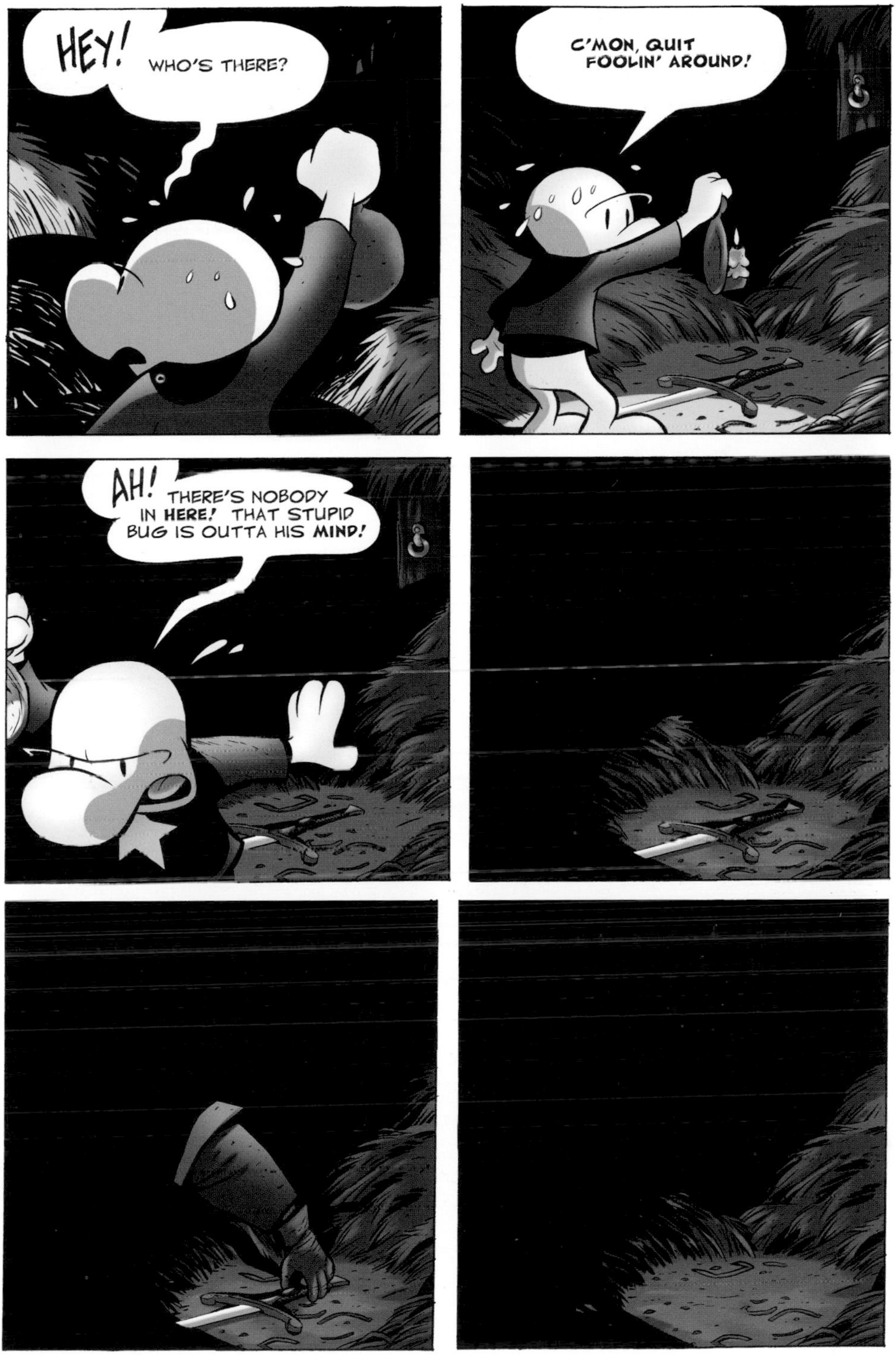
HEY! WHO'S THERE?
C'MON, QUIT FOOLIN' AROUND!
AH! THERE'S NOBODY IN HERE! THAT STUPID BUG IS OUTTA HIS MIND!

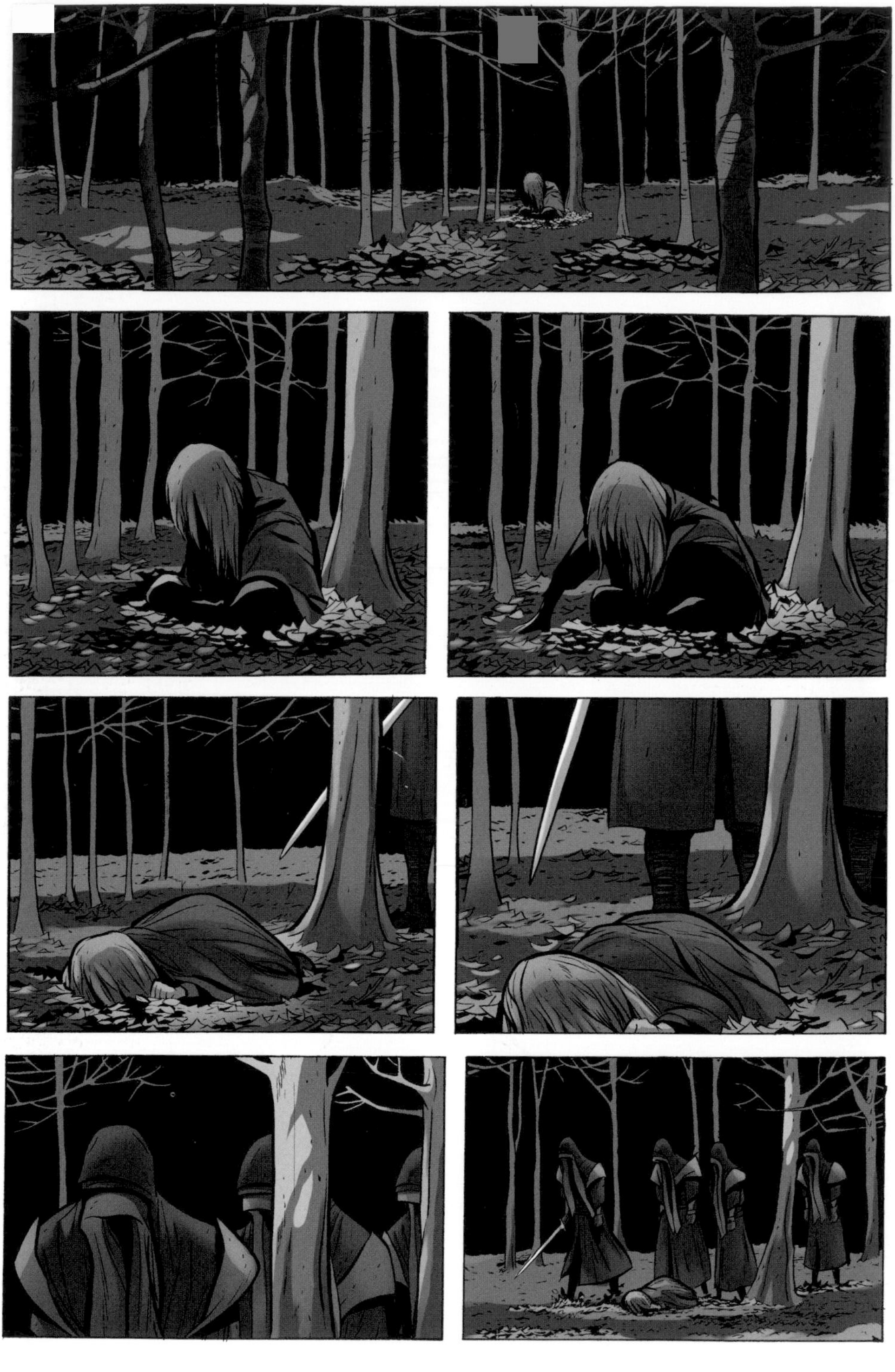

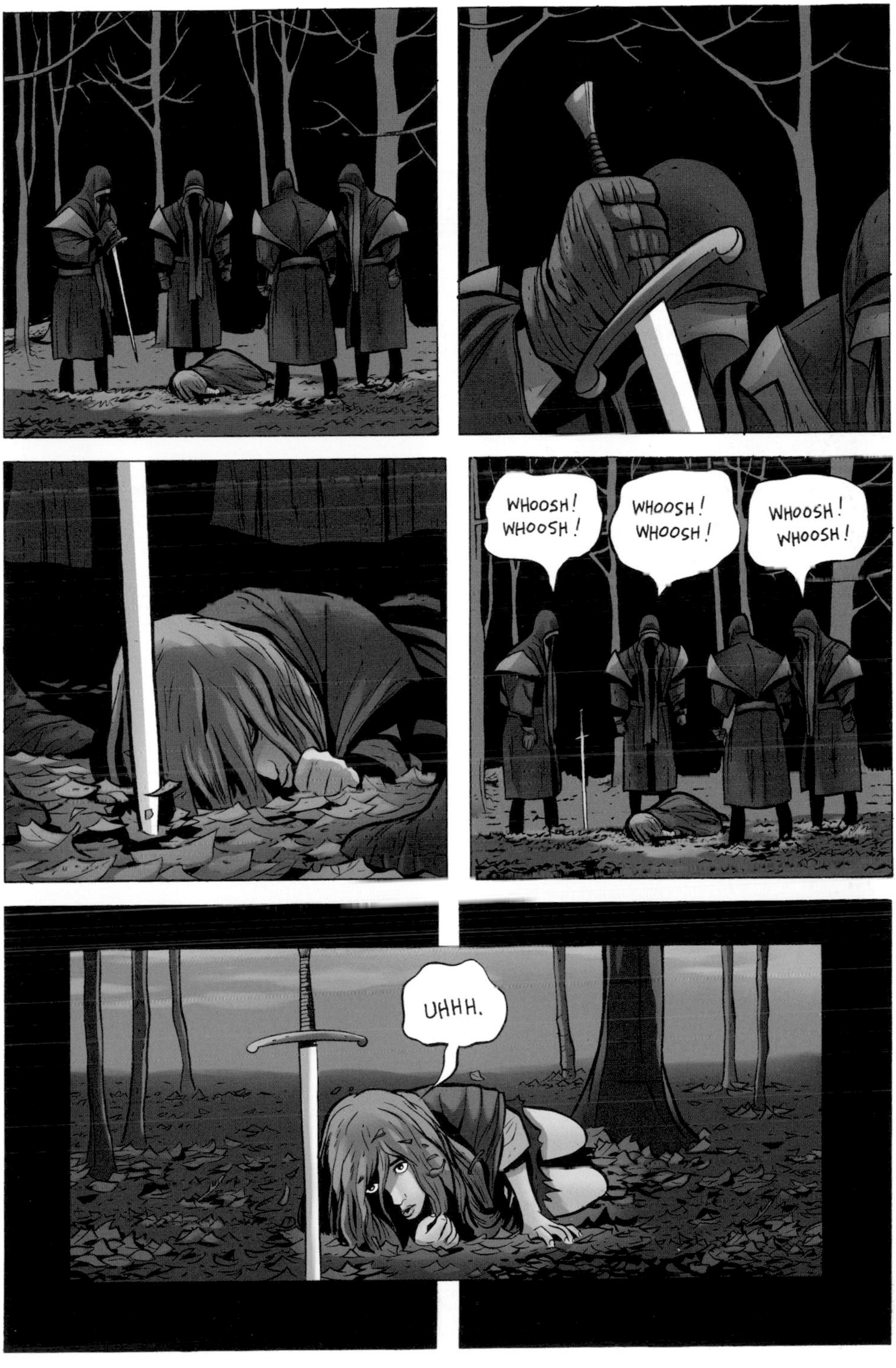
WHOOSH! WHOOSH!
WHOOSH! WHOOSH!
WHOOSH! WHOOSH!
UHHH.

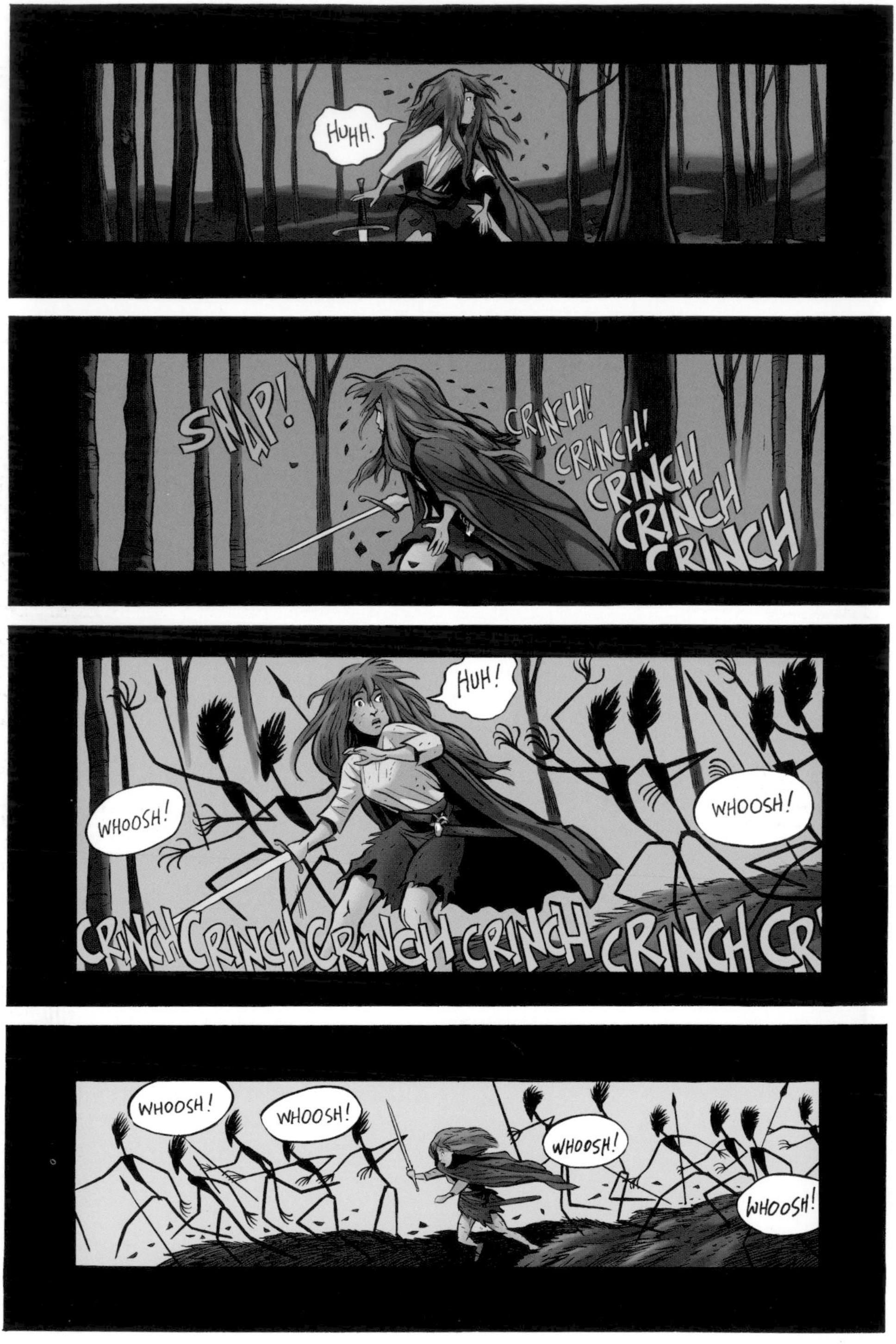
HUHH.
SNAP!
CRINCH!
CRINCH!
CRINCH
CRINCH
CRINCH
HUH!
WHOOSH!
WHOOSH!
CRINCH CRINCH CRINCH CRINCH CRINCH CR
WHOOSH!
WHOOSH!
WHOOSH!
WHOOSH!

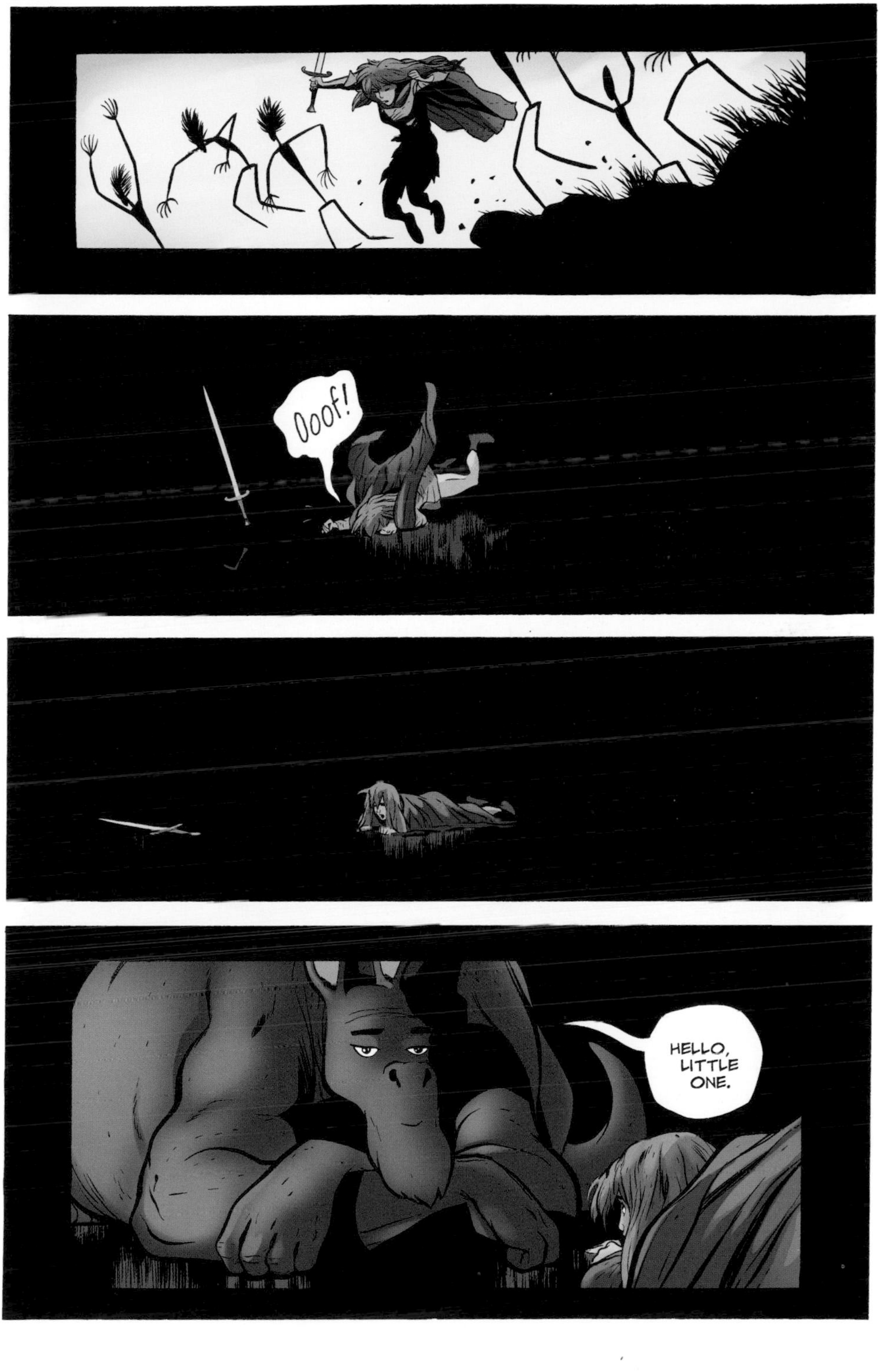
Ooof!
HELLO, LITTLE ONE.

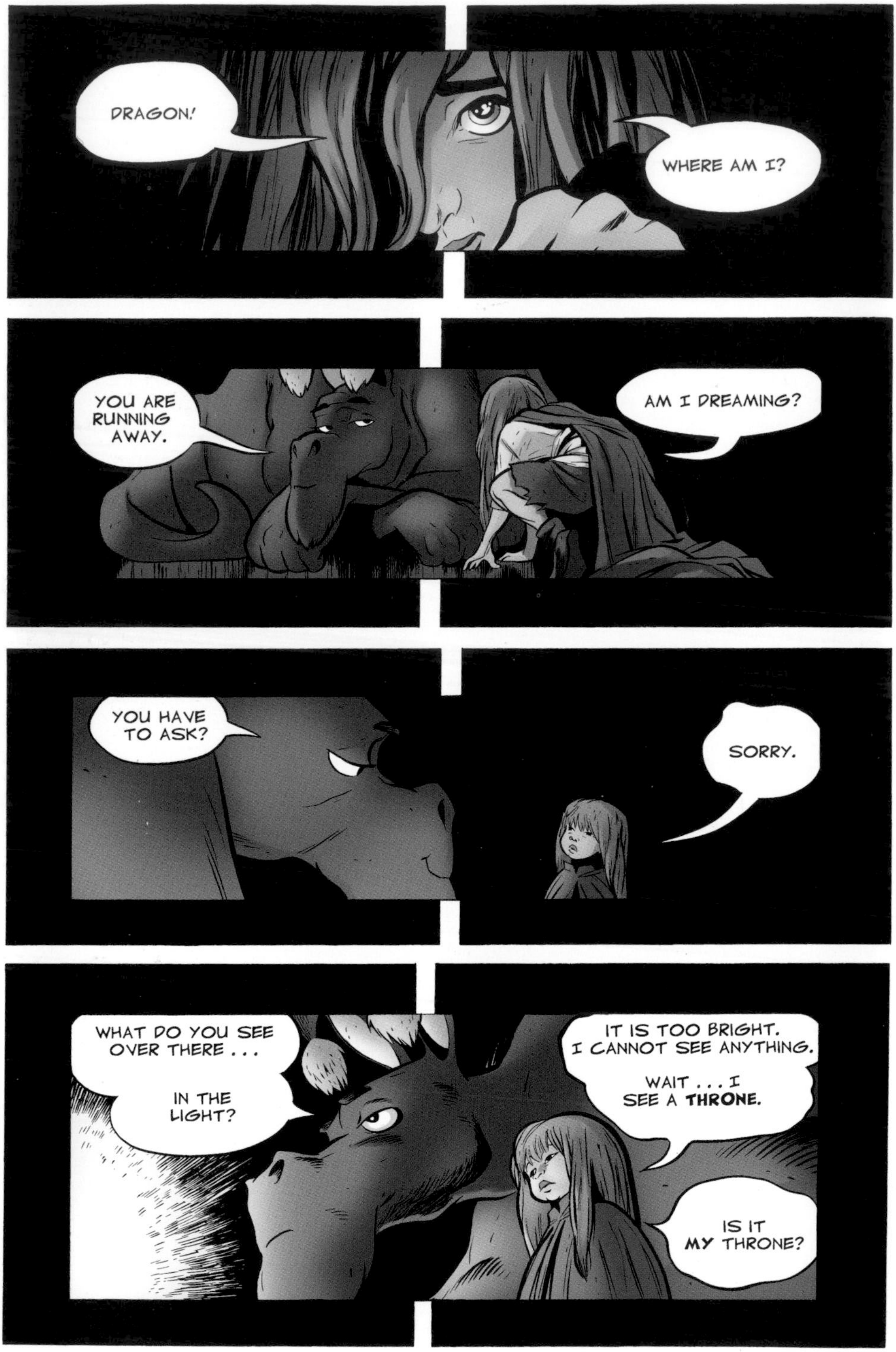
DRAGON!
WHERE AM I?
YOU ARE RUNNING AWAY.
AM I DREAMING?
YOU HAVE TO ASK?
SORRY.
WHAT DO YOU SEE OVER THERE . . .
IN THE LIGHT?
IT IS TOO BRIGHT. I CANNOT SEE ANYTHING.
WAIT . . . I SEE A **THRONE.**
IS IT **MY** THRONE?

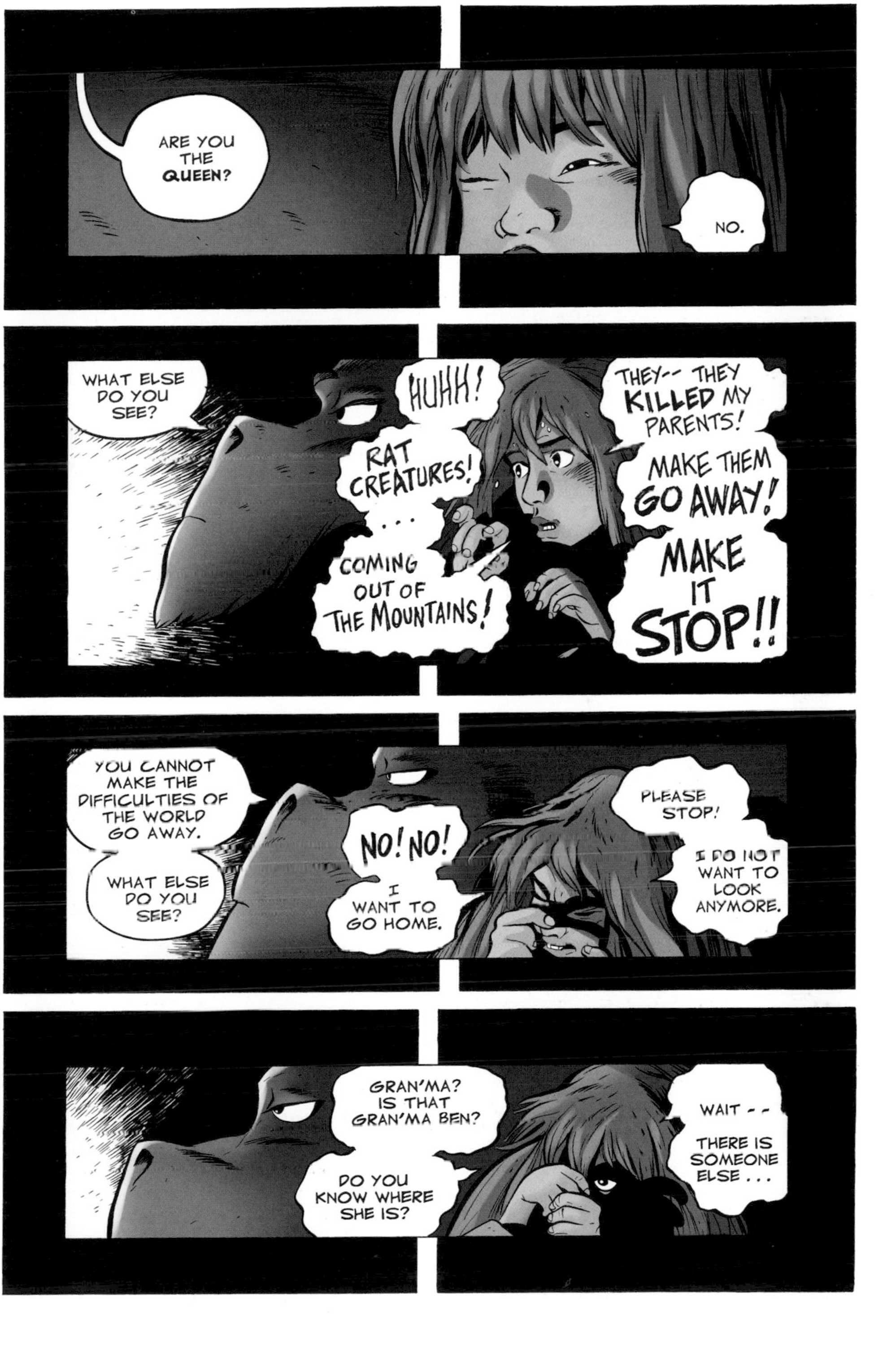
ARE YOU THE QUEEN?
NO.
WHAT ELSE DO YOU SEE?
HUHH!
RAT CREATURES! . . . COMING OUT OF THE MOUNTAINS!
THEY-- THEY KILLED MY PARENTS!
MAKE THEM GO AWAY!
MAKE IT STOP!!
YOU CANNOT MAKE THE DIFFICULTIES OF THE WORLD GO AWAY.
WHAT ELSE DO YOU SEE?
NO! NO!
I WANT TO GO HOME.
PLEASE STOP!
I DO NOT WANT TO LOOK ANYMORE.
GRAN'MA? IS THAT GRAN'MA BEN?
DO YOU KNOW WHERE SHE IS?
WAIT - -
THERE IS SOMEONE ELSE . . .

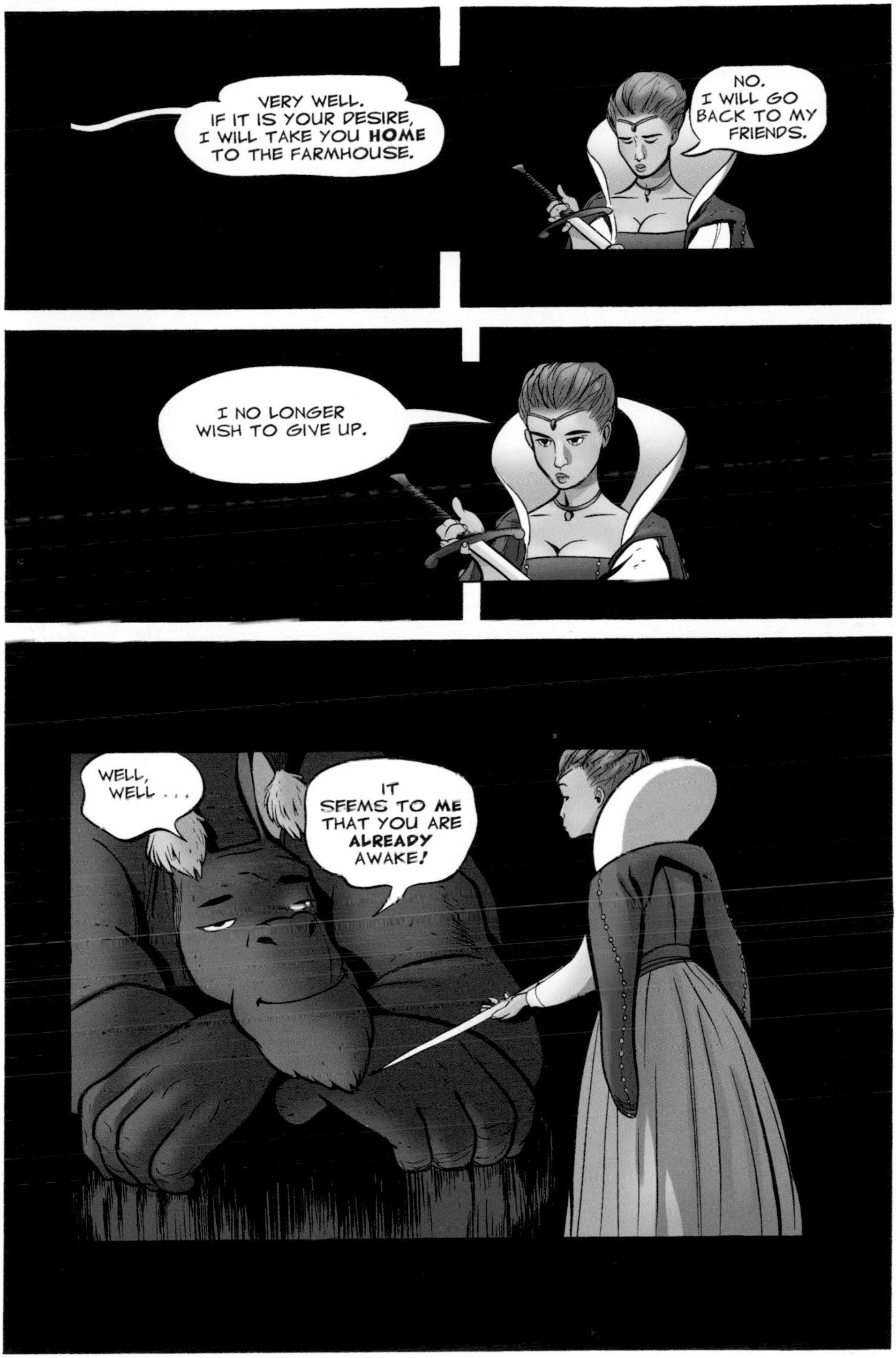
VERY WELL. IF IT IS YOUR DESIRE, I WILL TAKE YOU **HOME** TO THE FARMHOUSE.
NO. I WILL GO BACK TO MY FRIENDS.
I NO LONGER WISH TO GIVE UP.
WELL, WELL . . .
IT SEEMS TO **ME** THAT YOU ARE **ALREADY** AWAKE!

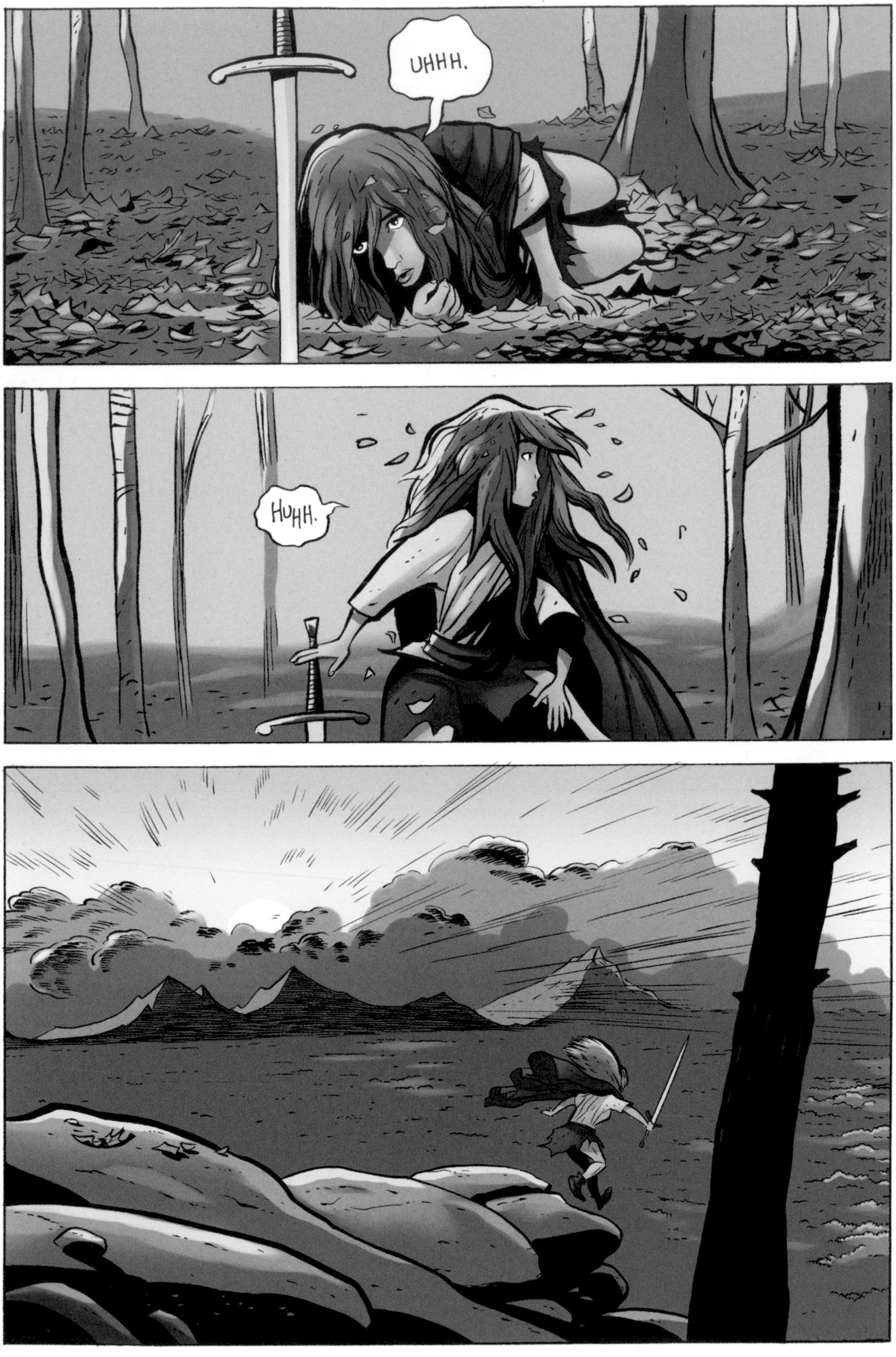
UHHH.
HUHH.

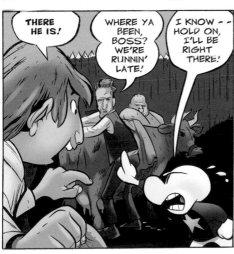

THERE HE IS!

WHERE YA BEEN, BOSS? WE'RE RUNNIN' LATE!

I KNOW -- HOLD ON, I'LL BE RIGHT THERE!

WHAT'S WRONG, MR. BONE?

FONE BONE AND SMILEY BONE DIDN'T COME BACK LAST NIGHT! THEIR BEDS WEREN'T EVEN SLEPT IN!

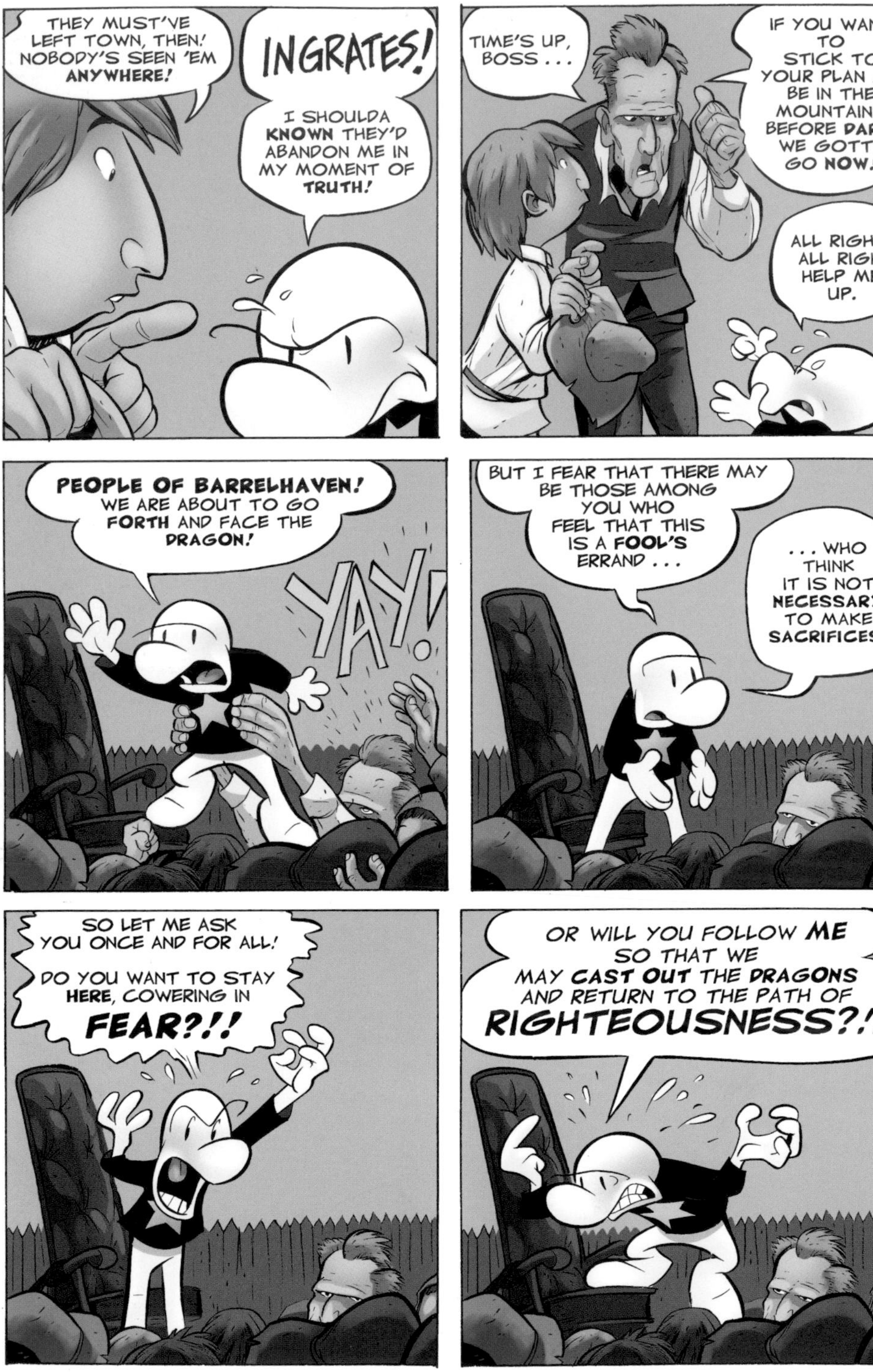
THEY MUST'VE LEFT TOWN, THEN! NOBODY'S SEEN 'EM ANYWHERE!
INGRATES!
I SHOULDA KNOWN THEY'D ABANDON ME IN MY MOMENT OF TRUTH!
TIME'S UP, BOSS . . .
IF YOU WANT TO STICK TO YOUR PLAN AN' BE IN THE MOUNTAINS BEFORE DARK, WE GOTTA GO NOW!
ALL RIGHT, ALL RIGHT. HELP ME UP.
PEOPLE OF BARRELHAVEN! WE ARE ABOUT TO GO FORTH AND FACE THE DRAGON!
YAY!
BUT I FEAR THAT THERE MAY BE THOSE AMONG YOU WHO FEEL THAT THIS IS A FOOL'S ERRAND . . .
. . . WHO THINK IT IS NOT NECESSARY TO MAKE SACRIFICES!
SO LET ME ASK YOU ONCE AND FOR ALL!
DO YOU WANT TO STAY HERE, COWERING IN FEAR?!!
OR WILL YOU FOLLOW ME SO THAT WE MAY CAST OUT THE DRAGONS AND RETURN TO THE PATH OF RIGHTEOUSNESS?!!

THE PEOPLE HAVE SPOKEN! IN CASE YOU DIDN'T **CATCH** THAT, **LUCIUS**, OLD PAL, THEY PICKED ME!

-- NOT YOU --

ME!

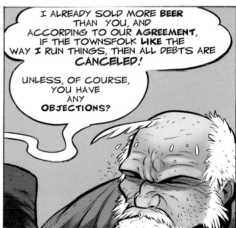

I ALREADY SOLD MORE **BEER** THAN YOU, AND ACCORDING TO OUR **AGREEMENT**, IF THE TOWNSFOLK **LIKE** THE WAY **I** RUN THINGS, THEN ALL DEBTS ARE **CANCELED!**

UNLESS, OF COURSE, YOU HAVE ANY **OBJECTIONS?**

DIDN'T THINK SO.

SEE YA AROUND, LUCIUS!

ALL RIGHT, PEOPLE, **MOVE 'EM OUT!!**

Moo!

Moo!

THREE CHEERS FOR THE DRAGONSLAYER!

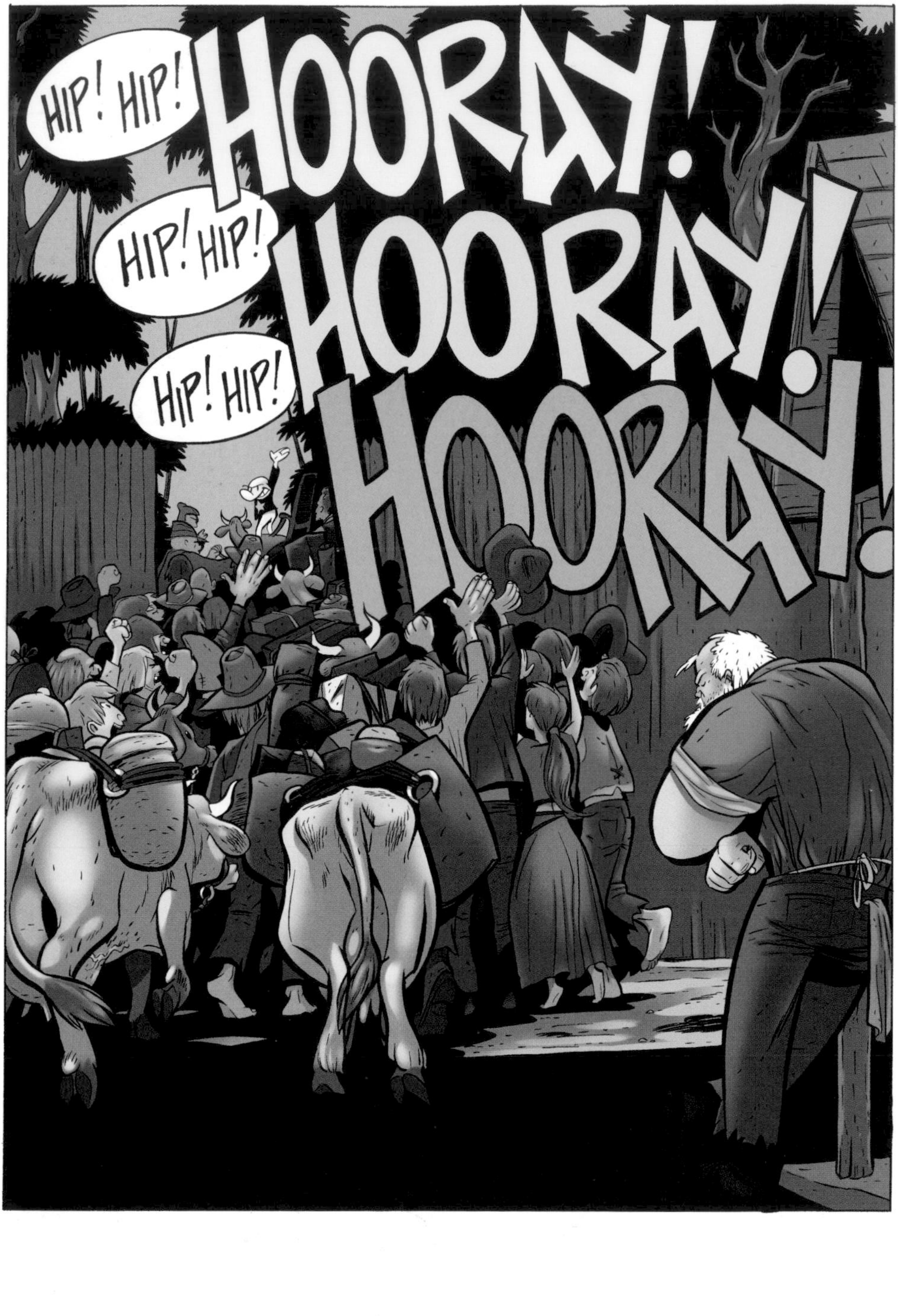
HIP! HIP!
HOORAY!
HIP! HIP!
HOORAY!
HIP! HIP!
HOORAY!

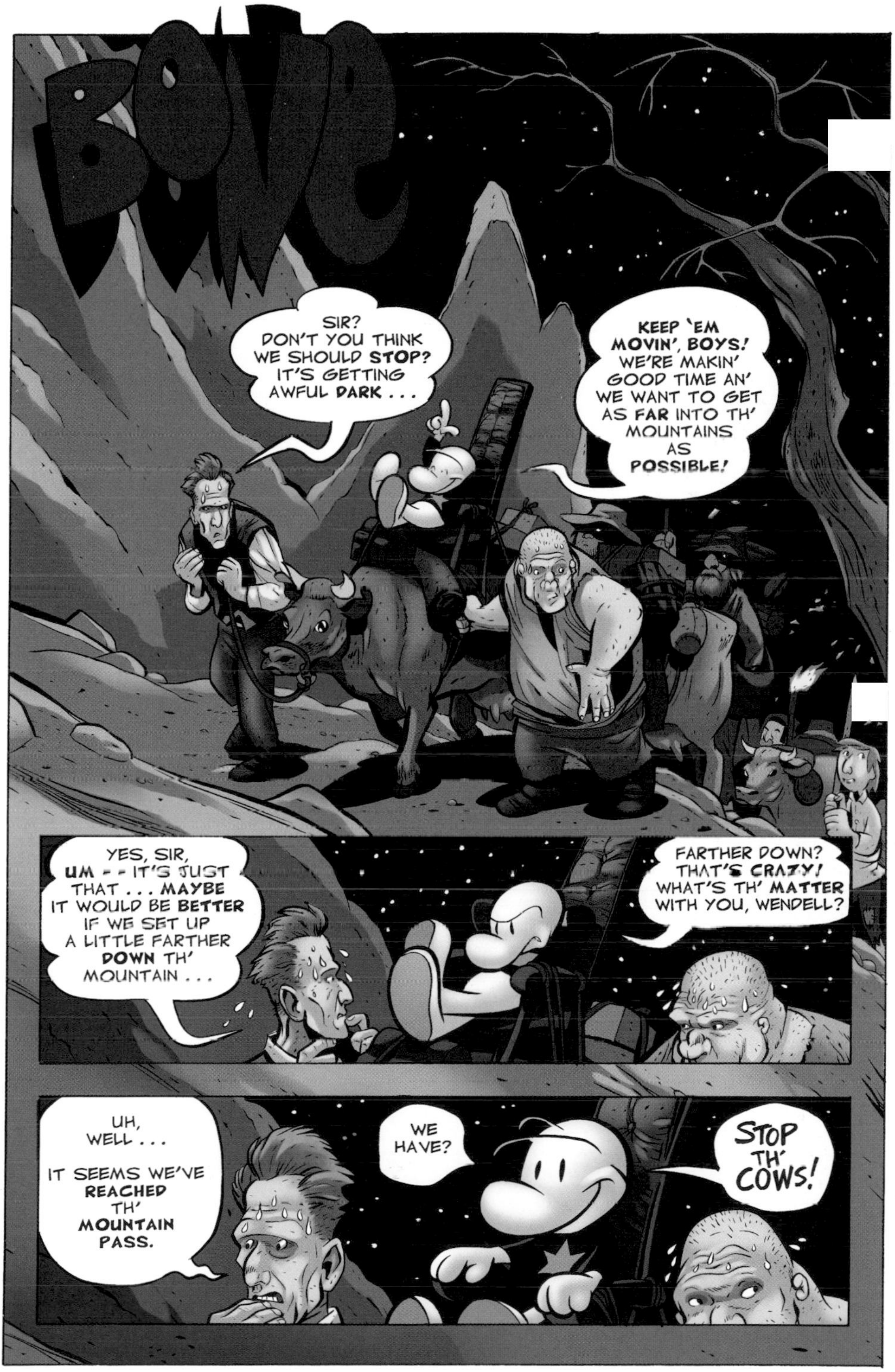
BONE
SIR? DON'T YOU THINK WE SHOULD STOP? IT'S GETTING AWFUL DARK . . .
KEEP 'EM MOVIN', BOYS! WE'RE MAKIN' GOOD TIME AN' WE WANT TO GET AS FAR INTO TH' MOUNTAINS AS POSSIBLE!
YES, SIR, UM - - IT'S JUST THAT . . . MAYBE IT WOULD BE BETTER IF WE SET UP A LITTLE FARTHER DOWN TH' MOUNTAIN . . .
FARTHER DOWN? THAT'S CRAZY! WHAT'S TH' MATTER WITH YOU, WENDELL?
UH, WELL . . .
IT SEEMS WE'VE REACHED TH' MOUNTAIN PASS.
WE HAVE?
STOP TH' COWS!

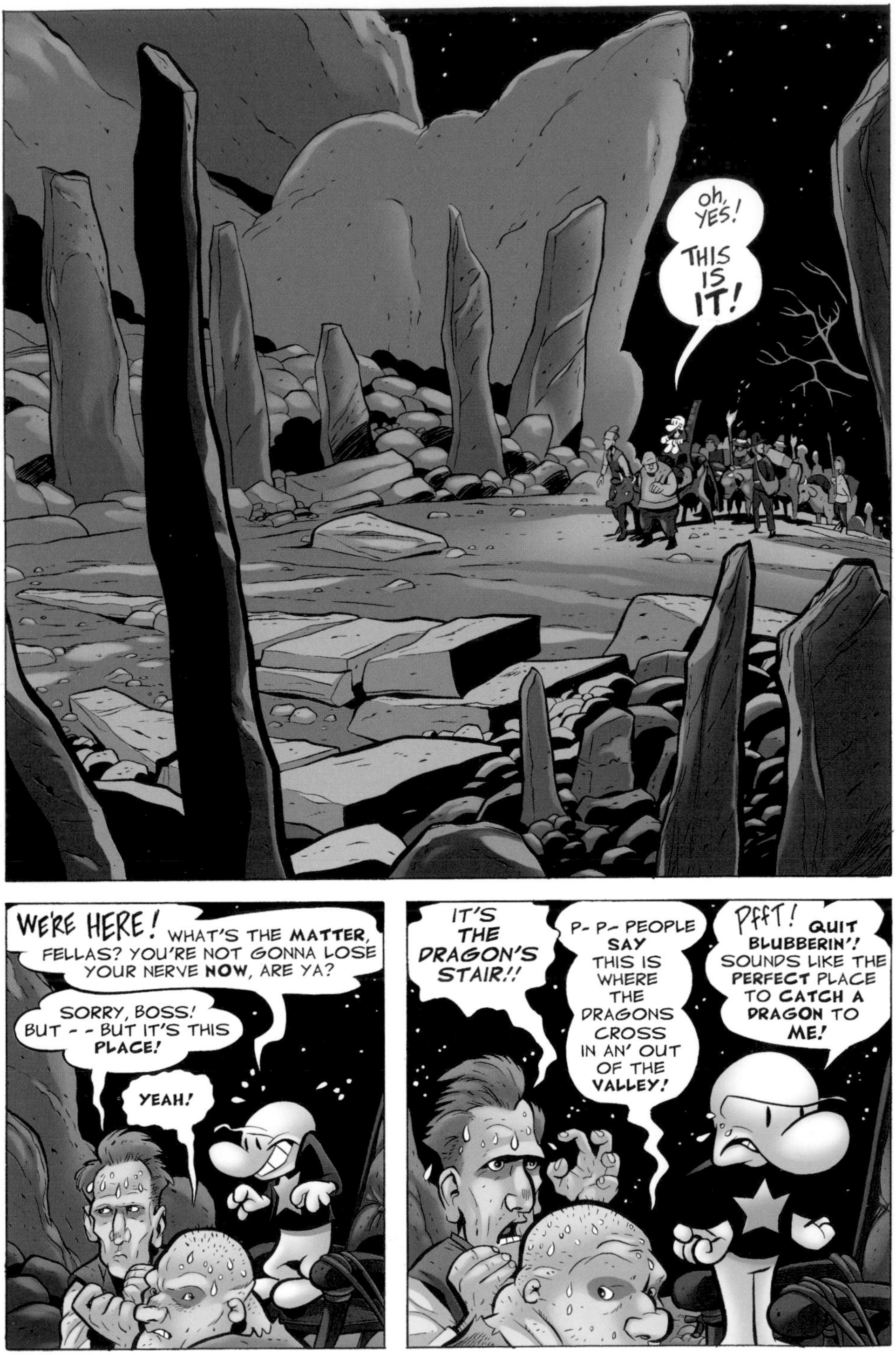
oh, YES!
THIS IS IT!
WE'RE HERE! WHAT'S THE MATTER, FELLAS? YOU'RE NOT GONNA LOSE YOUR NERVE NOW, ARE YA?
SORRY, BOSS! BUT - - BUT IT'S THIS PLACE!
YEAH!
IT'S THE DRAGON'S STAIR!!
P- P- PEOPLE SAY THIS IS WHERE THE DRAGONS CROSS IN AN' OUT OF THE VALLEY!
PFFT! QUIT BLUBBERIN'! SOUNDS LIKE THE PERFECT PLACE TO CATCH A DRAGON TO ME!

BUT WHAT IF A DRAGON COMES **THROUGH** HERE?

THAT'S WHAT WE **WANT**, YOU IDIOTS! NOW, **HURRY UP** AN' BUILD THE **TRAP!**

WE NEED TO SET UP THE **TRIP WIRES** AND GET THE **ROPES** IN PLACE!

WENDELL, GET ALL THE **EQUIPMENT** OFF TH' COWS — **BUT LEAVE THE TREASURE!**

RIGHT! EVERYBODY **UNLOAD!**

REMEMBER! THIS IS A **SUNRISE** CEREMONY, SO WE DON'T HAVE MUCH **TIME** TO GET **READY!**

DON'T WORRY, BOSS! EVERYTHING'LL BE **SET** BY TH' TIME YOU GET BACK!

GOOD! GOOD!

I'LL TAKE THE TREASURE AND START USING IT FOR **BAIT!** I'LL CIRCLE AROUND AN' LEAVE A **TRAIL** THAT'LL LEAD TH' DRAGON **STRAIGHT BACK HERE!**

WE'LL BE **WAITING,** BOSS!

GOOD LUCK, BOSS!

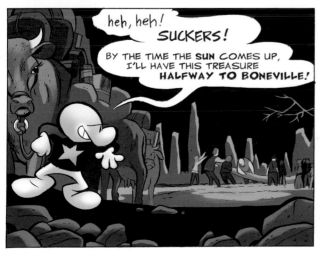

heh, heh! SUCKERS!

BY THE TIME THE **SUN** COMES UP, I'LL HAVE THIS TREASURE **HALFWAY TO BONEVILLE!**

HEY THERE, PHONEY BONE!

AAA!

WHAT'S TH' **MATTER**, PHONEY BONE? AIN'TCHA GLAD TA **SEE** ME? IT'S ME, **TED**!

YOU!

AH, YOU **IS** GLAD!

SAAAY! WHERE'S **FONE BONE** AN' **SMILEY**? YOU'RE NOT SLIPPIN' OFF WITHOUT YER **COUSINS**, ARE YA?

NO, I'M NOT SLIPPIN' OFF WITHOUT MY COUSINS! **THEY** SLIPPED OFF WITHOUT **ME**!

AIN'TCHA GONNA TRY TO **FIND** 'EM?

LISTEN UP, **BUG**! THEY'RE **GONE**! FOR ALL **I** KNOW, THEY'RE BACK IN BONEVILLE **RIGHT NOW**!

WHAT ABOUT TH' **REST** OF YER PLAN? YOU STILL GONNA SACRIFICE A **DRAGON** AT **DAWN**?

I **TOLD** YOU THERE ISN'T GONNA BE ANY SACRIFICE, AN' I **MEANT** IT! NOW **BUZZ OFF** BEFORE YOU **RUIN EVERYTHING**!!

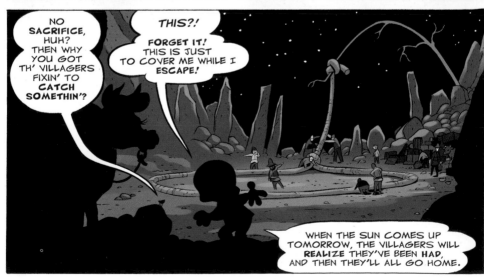

NO **SACRIFICE**, HUH? THEN WHY YOU GOT TH' VILLAGERS FIXIN' TO **CATCH** SOMETHIN'?

THIS?! **FORGET IT!** THIS IS JUST TO COVER ME WHILE I **ESCAPE**!

WHEN THE SUN COMES UP TOMORROW, THE VILLAGERS WILL **REALIZE** THEY'VE BEEN HAD, AND THEN THEY'LL ALL GO HOME.

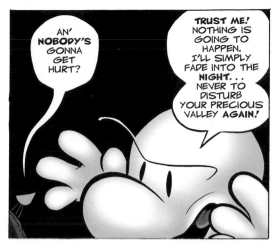

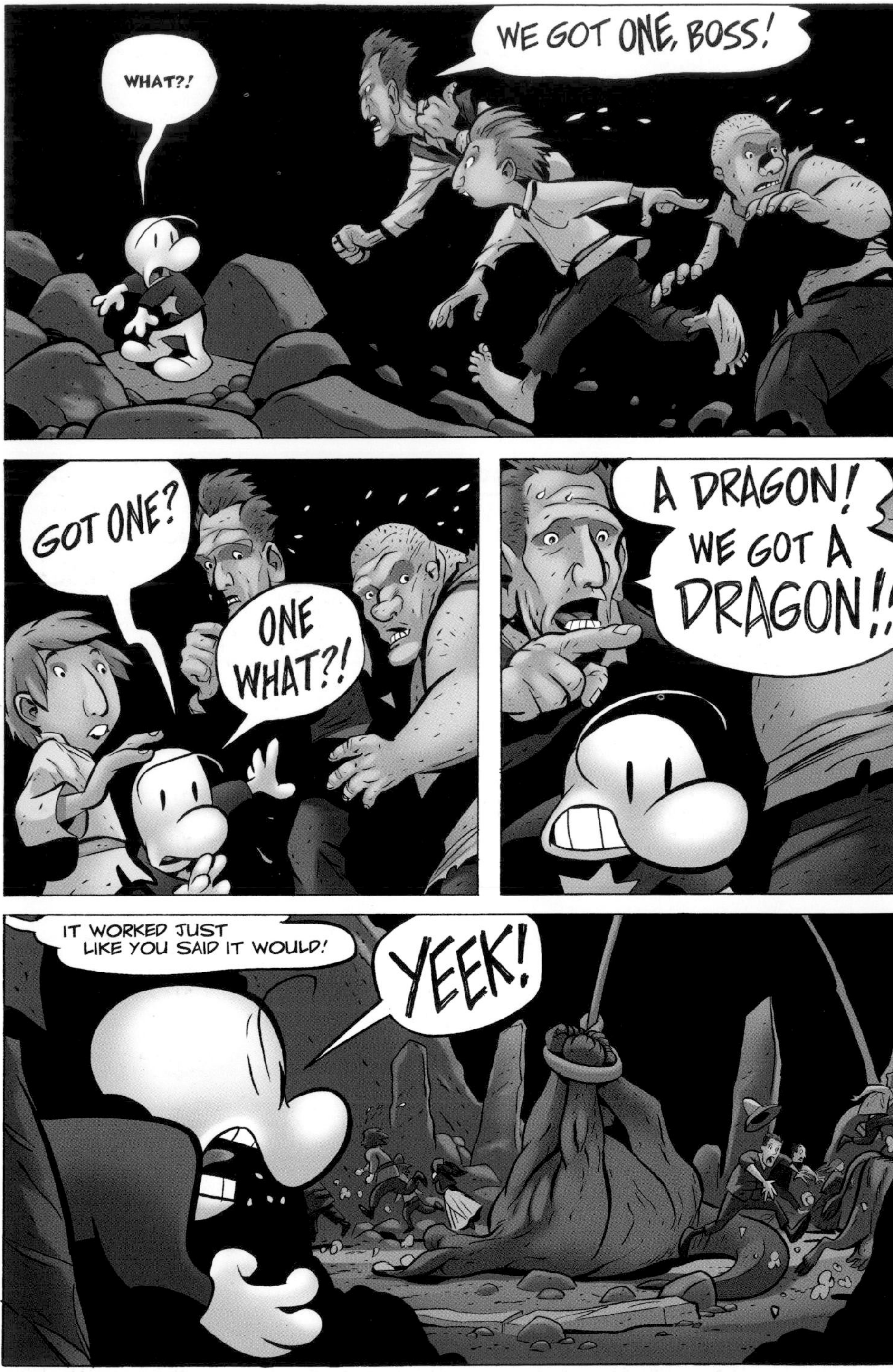
WHAT?!
WE GOT ONE, BOSS!
GOT ONE?
ONE WHAT?!
A DRAGON! WE GOT A DRAGON!!
IT WORKED JUST LIKE YOU SAID IT WOULD!
YEEK!

WHAT DO WE DO NOW?!

JUST STAY CALM! I-- uh---- I'LL HANDLE IT FROM HERE--

ARE YOU SURE THOSE ROPES WILL HOLD HIM?

THEY WERE MADE TO YOUR SPECIFICATIONS!

GULP!

GOL'! LOOK AT TH' SIZE OF HIM!

EVERYBODY! STAY BACK! DON'T BE AFRAID! THE DRAGONSLAYER IS HERE!

IT WON'T BE LONG NOW! SOON WE'LL ALL BE BACK ON THE PATH OF RIGHTEOUSNESS!

OH, BOY.

DRAGON?

H'LO, PHONEY BONE.

!

HELLO?

HELLO?!

WHAT'S WRONG WITH YOU?! THAT TRAP WAS OUT IN PLAIN SIGHT! DIDN'T YOU SEE IT?!

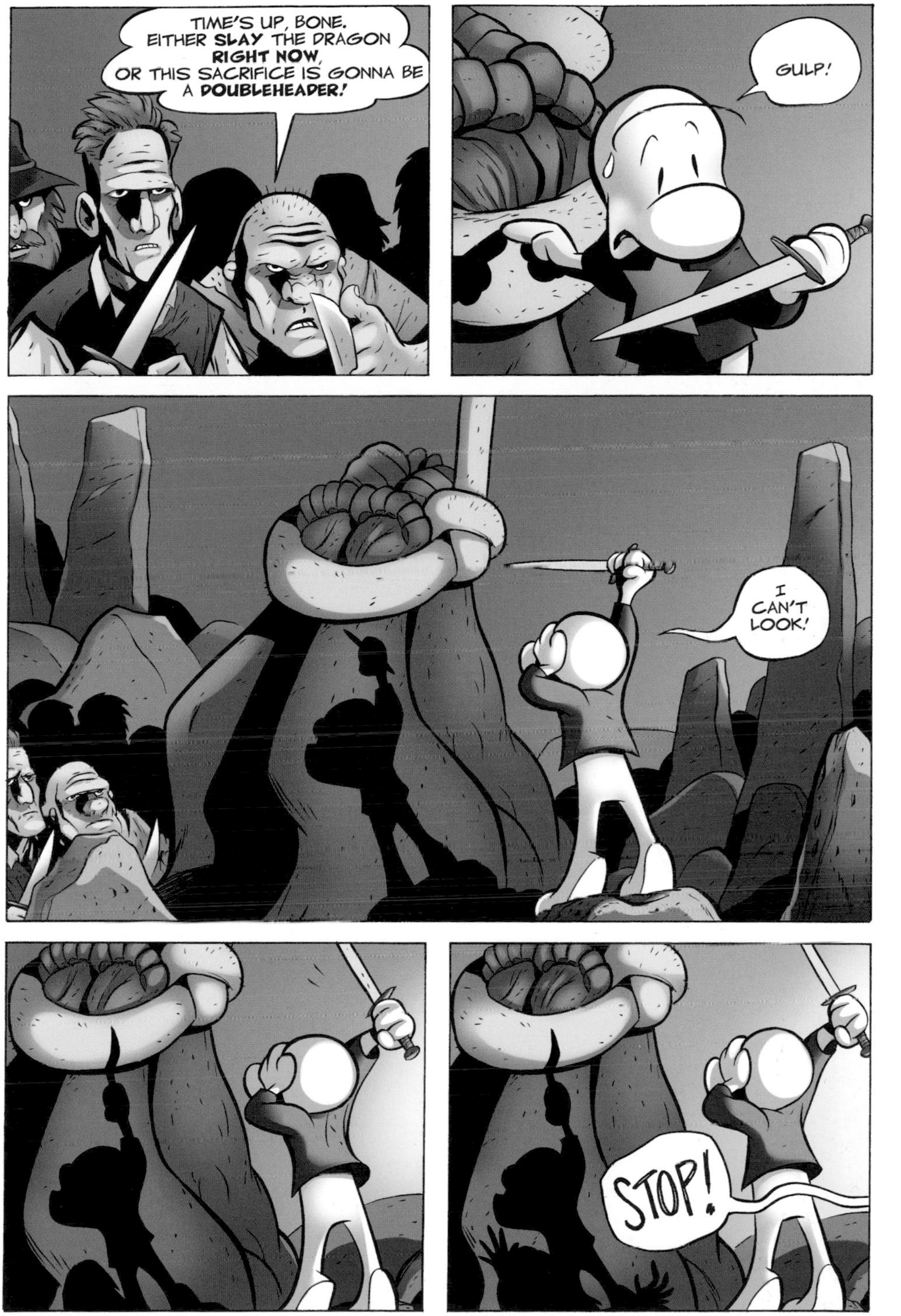
TIME'S UP, BONE. EITHER SLAY THE DRAGON RIGHT NOW, OR THIS SACRIFICE IS GONNA BE A DOUBLEHEADER!
GULP!
I CAN'T LOOK!
STOP!

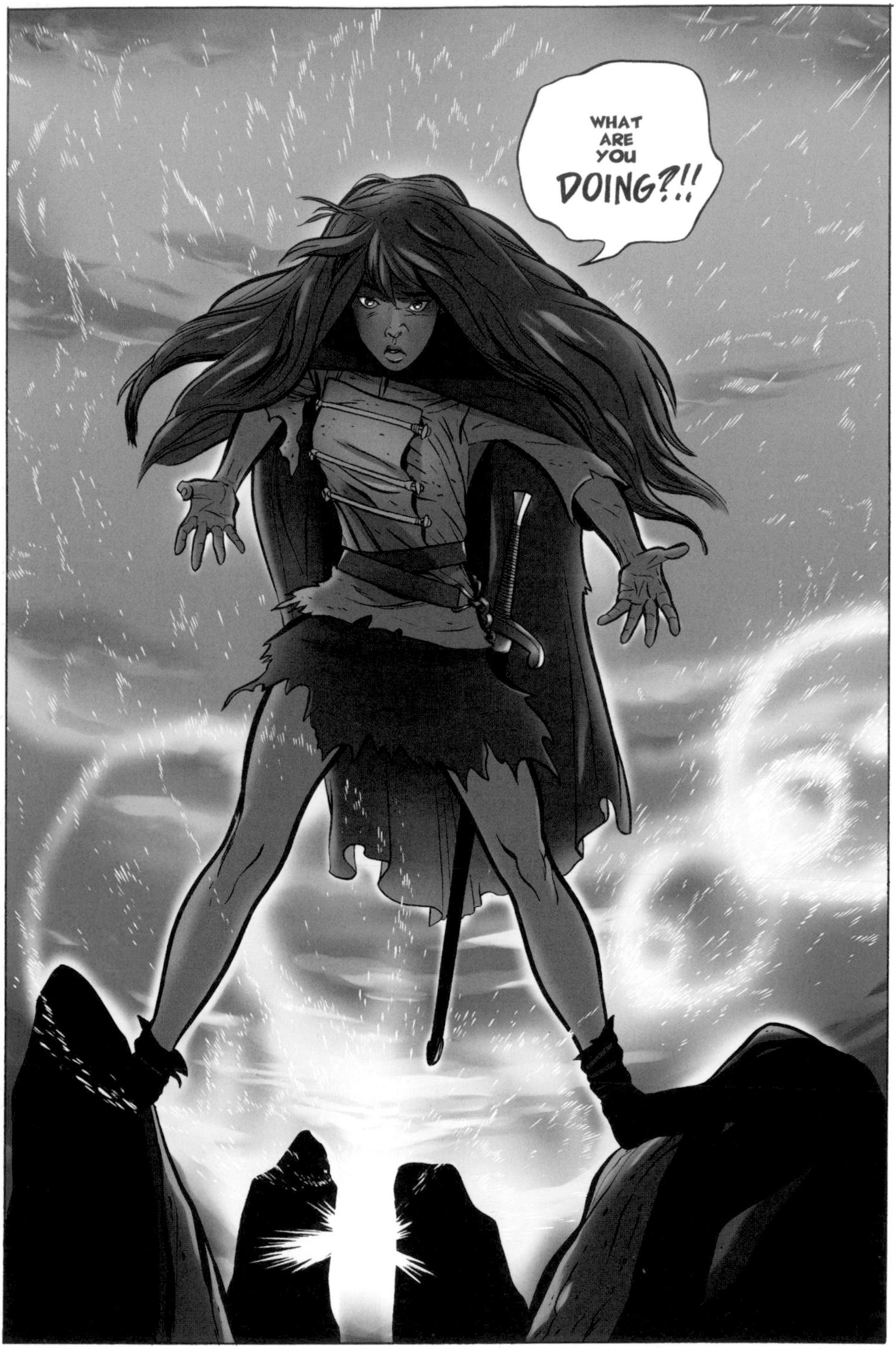
WHAT ARE YOU DOING?!!

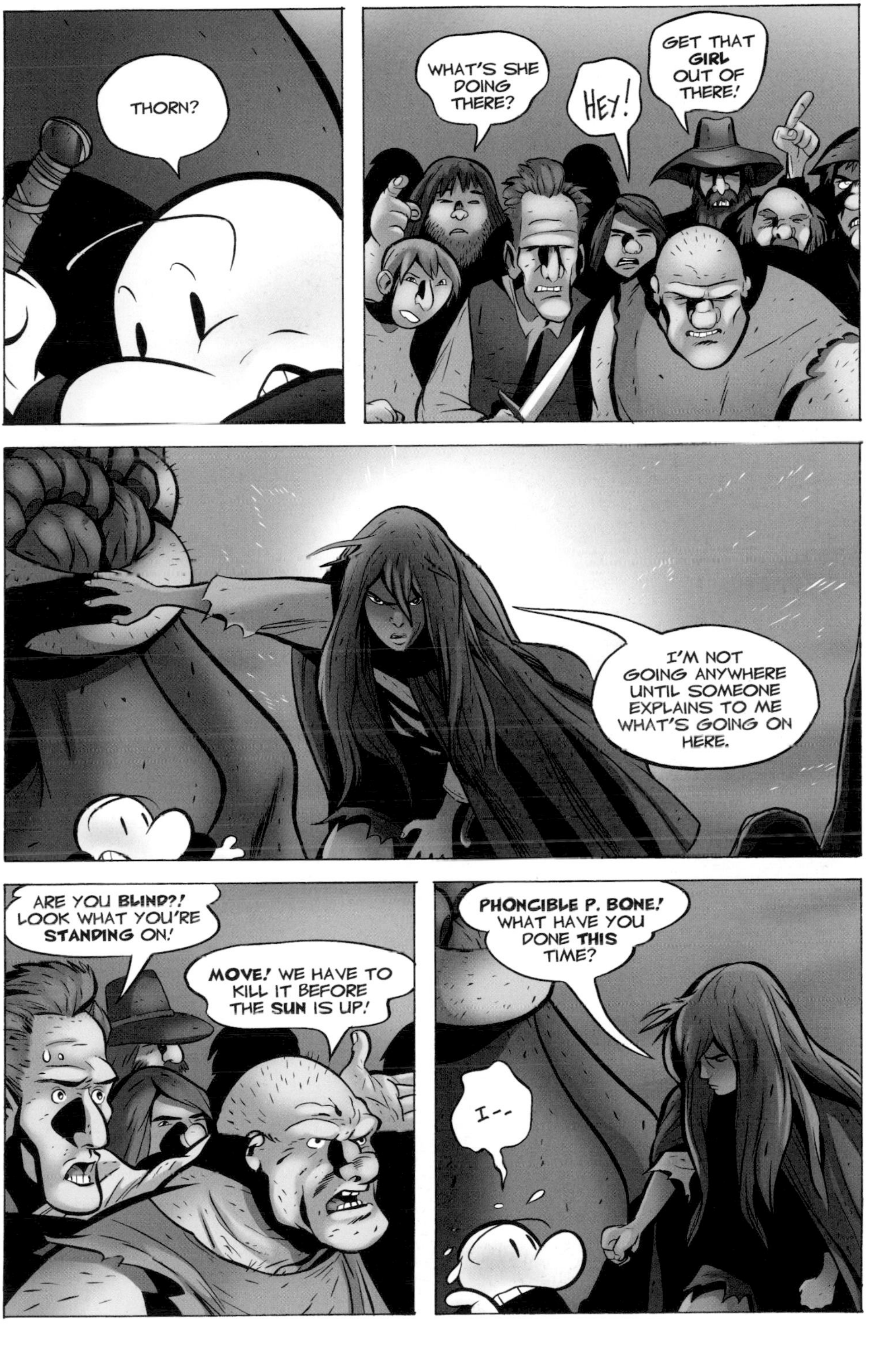
THORN?
WHAT'S SHE DOING THERE?
HEY!
GET THAT GIRL OUT OF THERE!
I'M NOT GOING ANYWHERE UNTIL SOMEONE EXPLAINS TO ME WHAT'S GOING ON HERE.
ARE YOU BLIND?! LOOK WHAT YOU'RE STANDING ON!
MOVE! WE HAVE TO KILL IT BEFORE THE SUN IS UP!
PHONCIBLE P. BONE! WHAT HAVE YOU DONE THIS TIME?
I--

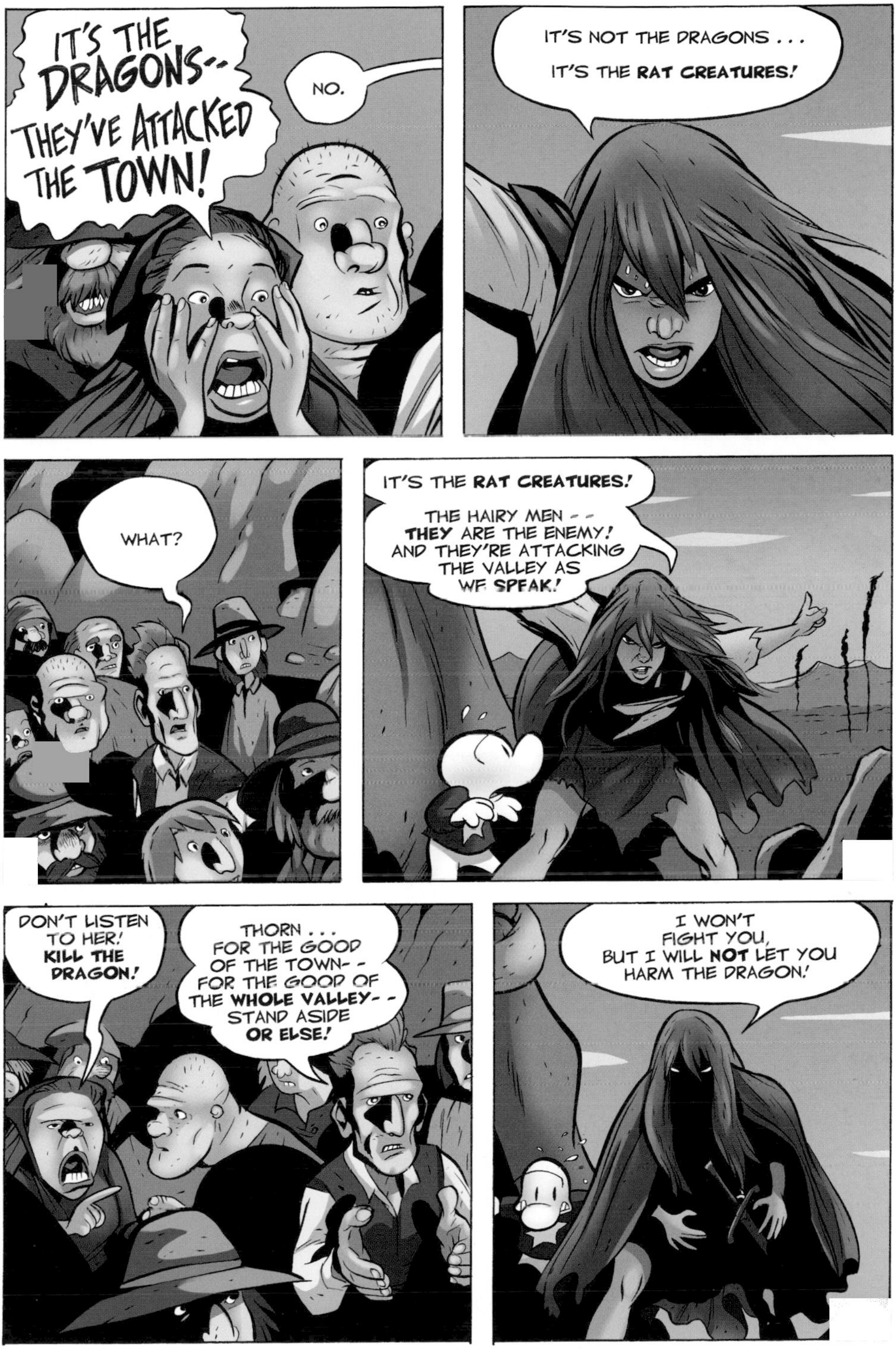
IT'S THE DRAGONS-- THEY'VE ATTACKED THE TOWN!
NO.
IT'S NOT THE DRAGONS . . . IT'S THE RAT CREATURES!
WHAT?
IT'S THE RAT CREATURES!
THE HAIRY MEN - - THEY ARE THE ENEMY! AND THEY'RE ATTACKING THE VALLEY AS WE SPEAK!
DON'T LISTEN TO HER! KILL THE DRAGON!
THORN . . . FOR THE GOOD OF THE TOWN- - FOR THE GOOD OF THE WHOLE VALLEY- - STAND ASIDE OR ELSE!
I WON'T FIGHT YOU, BUT I WILL NOT LET YOU HARM THE DRAGON!

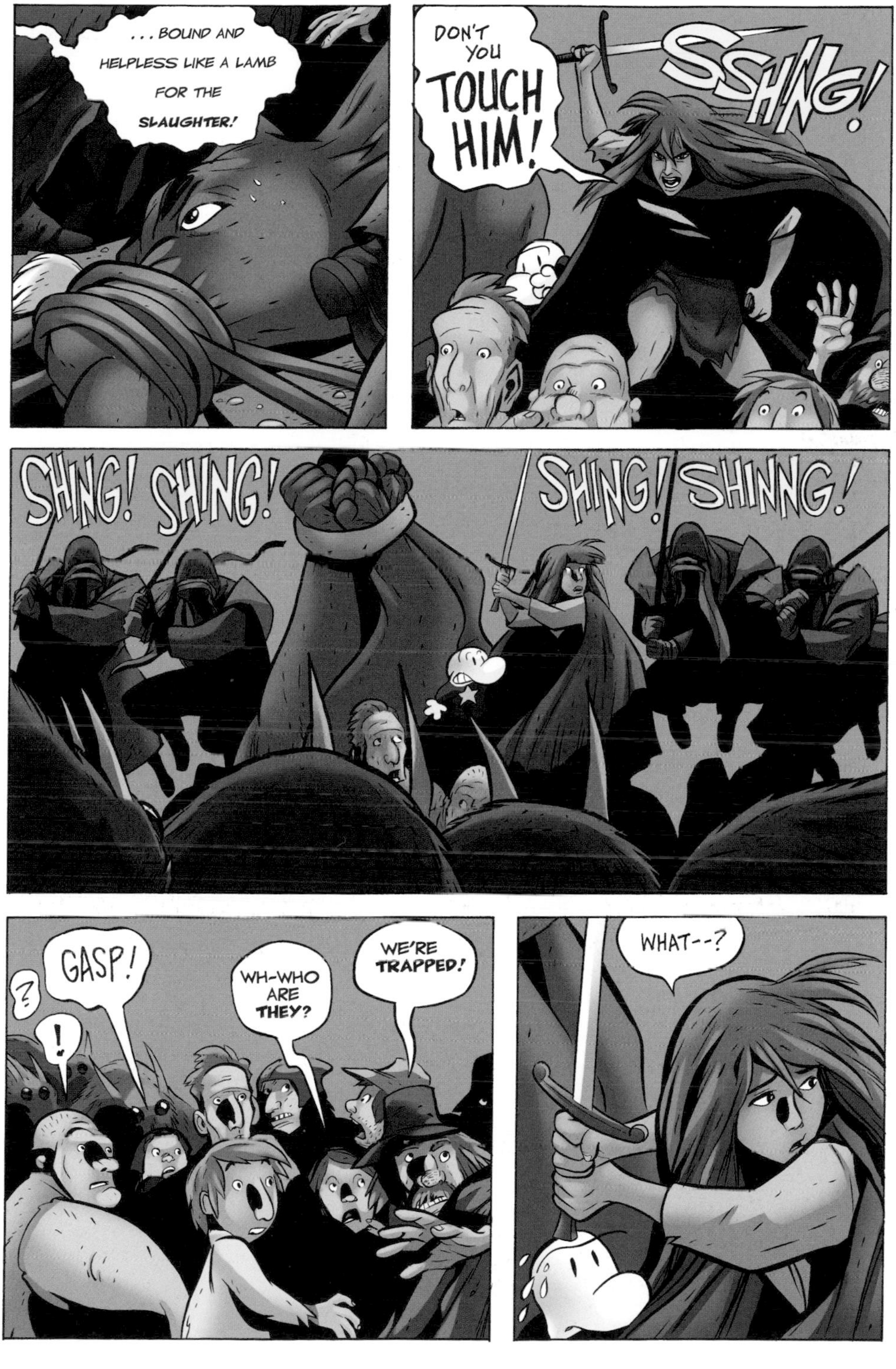
. . . BOUND AND HELPLESS LIKE A LAMB FOR THE SLAUGHTER!
DON'T YOU TOUCH HIM!
SSHNG!
SHNG! SHING!
SHING! SHINNG!
?
!
GASP!
WH-WHO ARE THEY?
WE'RE TRAPPED!
WHAT--?

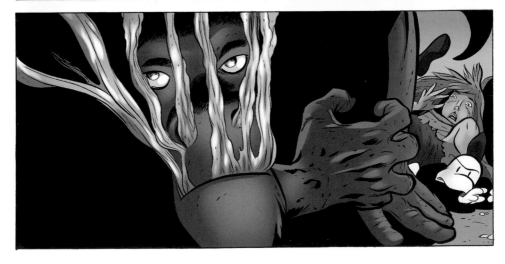

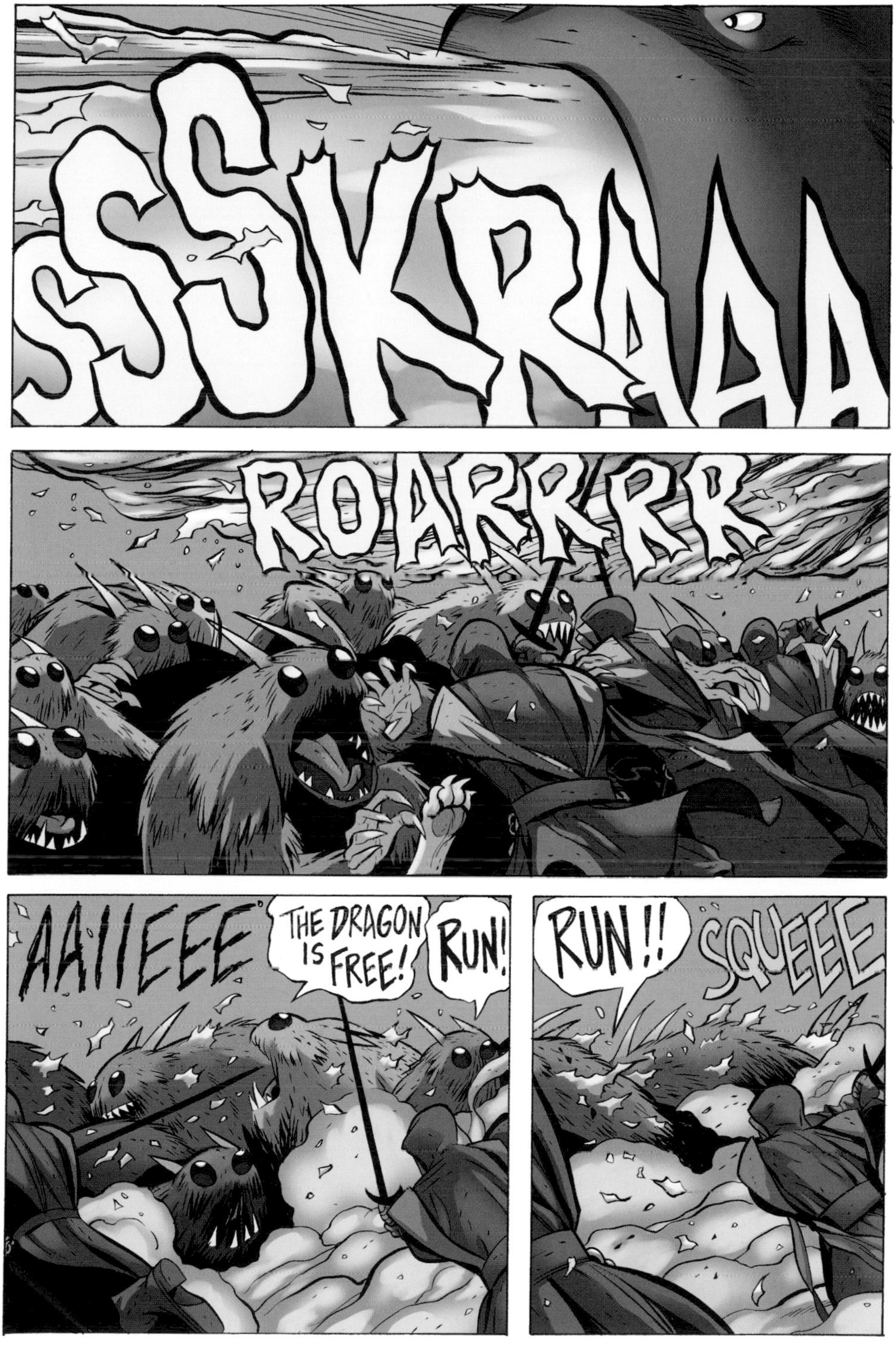
SSSKRAAA
ROARRRR
AAIIEEE
THE DRAGON IS FREE!
RUN!
RUN!!
SQUEEE

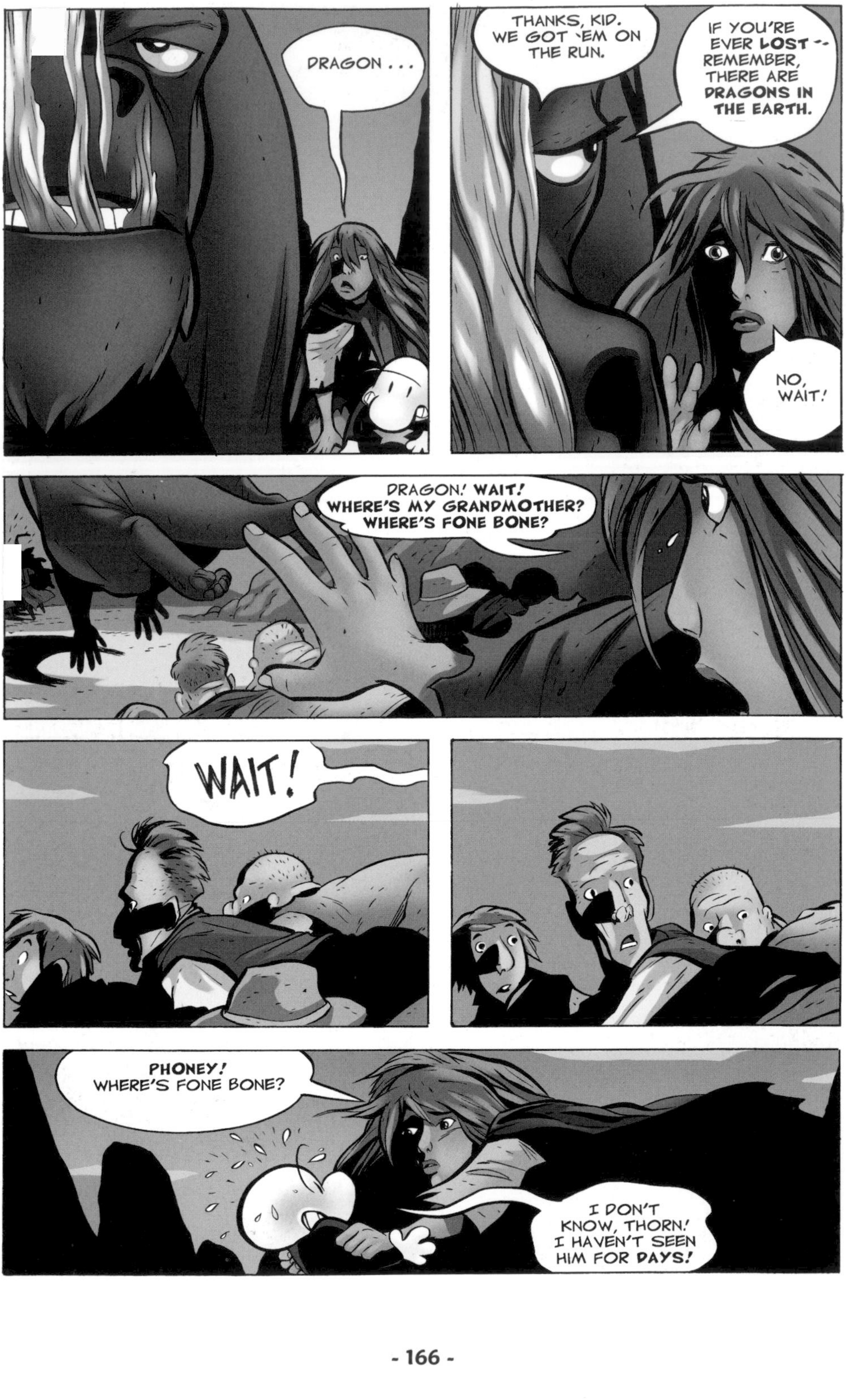
DRAGON . . .
THANKS, KID. WE GOT 'EM ON THE RUN.
IF YOU'RE EVER LOST -- REMEMBER, THERE ARE DRAGONS IN THE EARTH.
NO, WAIT!
DRAGON! WAIT! WHERE'S MY GRANDMOTHER? WHERE'S FONE BONE?
WAIT!
PHONEY! WHERE'S FONE BONE?
I DON'T KNOW, THORN! I HAVEN'T SEEN HIM FOR DAYS!

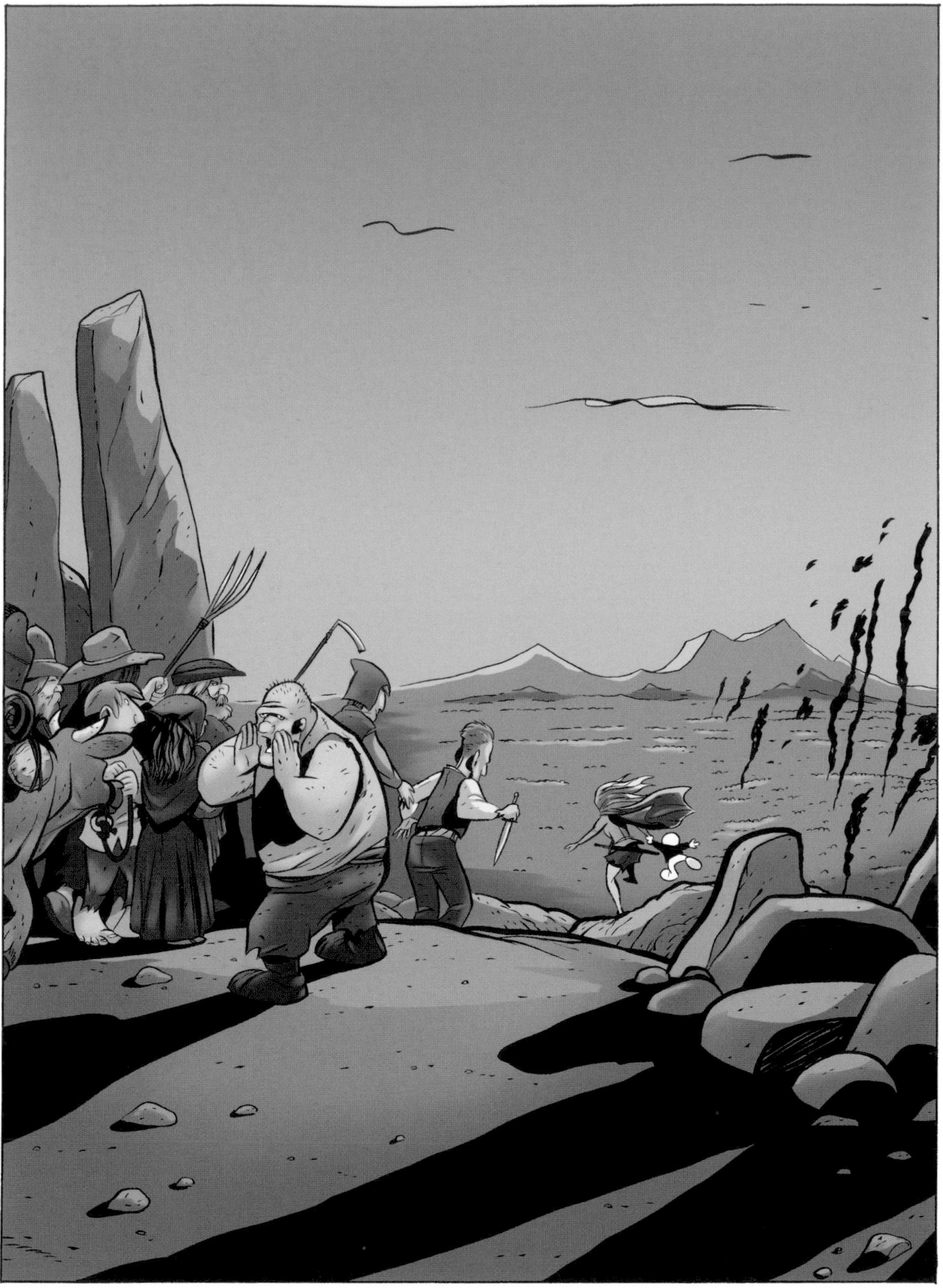

...TO BE CONTINUED.

About JEFF SMITH

JEFF SMITH was born and raised in the American Midwest and learned about cartooning from comic strips, comic books, and watching animated shorts on TV. After four years of drawing comic strips for The Ohio State University's student newspaper and co-founding Character Builders animation studio in 1986, Smith launched the comic book *BONE* in 1991. Between *BONE* and other comics projects, Smith spends much of his time on the international guest circuit promoting comics and the art of graphic novels.

More about *BONE*

An instant classic when it first appeared in the U.S. as an underground comic book in 1991, Bone has since garnered 38 international awards and sold a million copies in 15 languages. Now, Scholastic's GRAPHIX imprint is publishing full-color graphic novel editions of the nine-book *BONE* series. Look for the continuing adventures of the Bone cousins in *Rock Jaw: Master of the Eastern Border*.